TO GIVE YOU PLEASURE

She was alone with him at last, and she wanted to throw caution to the winds ... but did she dare?

"You are exceptionally lovely tonight, Elisabeth," Marco said, leaning closer to her. "And you sang very well."

She knew that he would kiss her, so she moved to stand up, as if to avoid him, though she yearned for his touch. But he grasped her hand, pulling her back down.

"Why do you resist what is natural, *càra?* Have you not felt it? I believe we are meant for each other." His words caressed her, and he gathered her into his arms. He held her gently but firmly and his kiss burned her brow. Her limbs weakened as his kisses trailed down her cheek to her chin.

"Marco, stop," she pleaded, but it was barely a whisper as her body awoke with desire.

"Do not be afraid of me, *mia càra,*" he murmured. "I would never hurt you. My only desire is to give you pleasure. And take it." His last words were hoarse with emotion, and as his hand came up to turn her face to his, and their lips met, he pressed her closer ...

CAPTURE THE GLOW OF
ZEBRA'S *HEARTFIRES!*

CAPTIVE TO HIS KISS (3788, $4.25/$5.50)
by Paige Brantley
Madeleine de Moncelet was determined to avoid an arranged marriage to the Duke of Burgundy. But the tall, stern-looking knight sent to guard her chamber door may thwart her escape plan!

CHEROKEE BRIDE (3761, $4.25/$5.50)
by Patricia Werner
Kit Newcomb found politics to be a dead bore, until she met the proud Indian delegate Red Hawk. Only a lifetime of loving could soothe her desperate desire!

MOONLIGHT REBEL (3707, $4.25/$5.50)
by Marie Ferrarella
Krystyna fled her native Poland only to live in the midst of a revolution in Virginia. Her host may be a spy, but when she looked into his blue eyes she wanted to share her most intimate treasures with him!

PASSION'S CHASE (3862, $4.25/$5.50)
by Ann Lynn
Rose would never heed her Aunt Stephanie's warning about the unscrupulous Mr. Trent Jordan. She knew what she wanted—a long, lingering kiss bound to arouse the passion of a bold and ardent lover!

RENEGADE'S ANGEL (3760, $4.25/$5.50)
by Phoebe Fitzjames
Jenny Templeton had sworn to bring Ace Denton to justice for her father's death, but she hadn't reckoned on the tempting heat of the outlaw's lean, hard frame or her surrendering wantonly to his fiery loving!

TEMPTATION'S FIRE (3786, $4.25/$5.50)
by Millie Criswell
Margaret Parker saw herself as a twenty-six year old spinster. There wasn't much chance for romance in her sleepy town. Nothing could prepare her for the jolt of desire she felt when the new marshal swept her onto the dance floor!

Available wherever paperbacks are sold, or order direct from the Publisher. Send cover price plus 50¢ per copy for mailing and handling to Zebra Books, Dept. 4077, 475 Park Avenue South, New York, N.Y. 10016. Residents of New York and Tennessee must include sales tax. DO NOT SEND CASH. For a free Zebra/Pinnacle catalog please write to the above address.

PATRICIA WERNER

STARLIGHT EMBRACE

ZEBRA BOOKS
KENSINGTON PUBLISHING CORP.

ZEBRA BOOKS

are published by

Kensington Publishing Corp.
475 Park Avenue South
New York, NY 10016

Copyright © 1993 by Patricia Werner

All rights reserved. No part of this book may be reproduced in any form or by any means without the prior written consent of the Publisher, excepting brief quotes used in reviews.

Zebra, the Z logo, Heartfire Romance, and the Heartfire Romance logo are trademarks of Kensington Publishing Corp.

If you purchased this book without a cover you should be aware that this book is stolen property. It was reported as "unsold and destroyed" to the Publisher and neither the Author nor the Publisher has received any payment for this "stripped book."

First Printing: February, 1993

Printed in the United States of America

Chapter One

New York City, 1893

Elisabeth Kendall peered through a tiny slit between the heavy velvet curtains, but it was enough to see the gilded boxes in the Golden Horseshoe. The jeweled and coutured occupants were illuminated in all their splendor by the new rosettes of electric lights ornamenting each level of the opera house.

From her shielded lookout point, Elisabeth could see her erstwhile friend Consuelo Vanderbilt and Consuelo's iron-willed mother in the second row of boxes at stage right. Consuelo's baby blue satin flattered her straight back, narrow shoulders, and hair piled high in curls with a narrow black ribbon tied around her long, slender neck, just like the ones Elisabeth used to wear. Emeralds and diamonds glittered over Mrs. William K. Vanderbilt's satin gown, but the brilliant glitter only seemed to accentuate her determined expression and her ambition to lead New York society.

Elisabeth brushed her fingers across her plain wool skirt. Her small sigh was muffled in the deep blue curtain she held in front of her face, as well as by the noise of the gaily chatting audience, for it was intermission.

In the orchestra seats, men and women in evening dress stood about in the red-carpeted aisle, chatting among themselves, while up above in the gallery, the hardworking citizens were leaning over the ivory and gold balconies to get a better view of the wealthy box holders.

During intermissions the fashionable society members who held the gold-curtained boxes received their guests. Not that the talking would diminish entirely at the start of Act III of *La Traviata*, but the renowned artists on stage would claim only a part of the beau monde's attention.

Elisabeth's gaze drifted back to Mrs. Vanderbilt's first tier box. Gentlemen in their white ties and evening clothes bent over Consuelo's hand, no doubt congratulating her on her upcoming marriage to the Duke of Marlborough.

And there he was, a thin, dark-headed young man in pearl-studded shirt and tail coat, stiffly chatting with a group of older, distinguished men. He had a small aristocratic face with a large nose and intense, prominent blue eyes, visible to Elisabeth even from where she hid behind the curtains at the edge of the stage.

European nobility and New York's new wealth mixed congenially in such a setting.

But Elisabeth's attention was quickly diverted when she saw her father enter the glittering box. She snapped the curtains together and shut her eyes, leaning for support on the stout masonry of the proscenium arch.

Thinking about her father brought shame and confusion. For all she resented the stifling way in which she had been brought up, she ached for a chance to speak to him, as to her old nurse and the other members of the household. But that world and all her former friends were now shut off from her forever.

"Elisabeth, for heaven's sake, what are you doing here?" The voice of the stage manager pierced her thoughts. She turned to see his frizzed hair and anxious eyes in the backstage light as his bony hands mopped a large handkerchief over his glistening forehead. He leaned toward her with urgency.

"Madam Nordica cannot find her white stockings, and her maid is in tears. Surely you can help. Run to her dressing room, quickly!"

Elisabeth felt in her pocket for the key to the star's dressing room, which she kept because of her position of responsibility as wardrobe mistress. The famous divas who sang at the Metropolitan Opera House insisted that their dressing rooms be locked, and they themselves oversaw who was to be trusted with the key. Luckily, Lillian Nordica had taken a liking to the young wardrobe mistress and had begun to rely on her for many small details.

Thoughts of her father in Mrs. Vanderbilt's opera box were banished as Elisabeth hurried around the crowded backstage to help Madam Nordica, who needed the white stockings for her deathbed scene in Act III. She could hardly be expected to collapse on stage with bare legs visible to an audience of three thousand.

As Elisabeth rounded the corner where scenery met the borders in the wings, her foot slipped on the worn wooden stage floor. A pair of muscular legs and a broad torso appeared in front of her. Indeed, she recognized the costume, but it was too late to prevent herself from pitching headlong into the arms of Marco Pietro Giovinco, who sang tonight's leading role opposite Madam Nordica.

Strong arms covered by the muted green frock coat he wore in Act III reached out to catch her. And as she tripped on her hem, she could not help but reach for the arms to steady herself, lest she collapse in a heap at his feet.

A rich, musical laugh emanated from the handsome tenor's throat, and she looked up in embarrassment at the dark, amused face, the teasing, green eyes, that she had seen light up the stage many times.

"Excuse me," she said in embarrassment. "I was going to Madam Nordica."

"Ah, there must be a great need in the dressing room to send the wardrobe mistress spinning about the scenery in such a fashion." His Italian accent rolled from his throat in a disarming manner.

He chuckled, tightened his grip on her arm, and pulled her to his side so that the stage hands could go about their business of setting up props. There was so little room backstage at the opera house that moving scenery about was a major problem, one the architects who had built the place ten years ago had not foreseen.

"Madam Nordica cannot find . . ." and then she choked on her words. She could hardly tell the burly tenor that his leading lady had lost her stockings. It would not be proper.

She swallowed, looked at the handsome face framed by thick, well-brushed, dark hair and felt her heart spin in helpless confusion. She tried to moisten her lips.

Sensing the urgency of her mission, Marco let go of her arm, but he bent his head toward her so that he could be heard above the orchestra, which was now warming up in the pit.

"If Madam Nordica has need of you, then I must not detain you. Your mission must be of some importance, and the act must go on." He gestured theatrically in the direction Elisabeth was headed. "Please, signorina."

"Thank you," she said. Then she paused and glanced back at his arm in concern. "I hope I did not crease your costume."

She raised her hand to smooth the sleeve in an unconscious gesture, but then she drew it back. The costume, to which she had devoted many hours of loving care, was no longer draped on a lifeless mannequin; it now covered the strong, powerful arms of the broad-shouldered and very virile man before her.

He smiled gently, more in understanding than in amusement now. His voice was soft, a stage whisper as he hastened her along. "It's quite all right, my dear. Now hurry. The curtain cannot go up until you help Lillian with whatever it is she cannot complete without you."

He lifted his chin in a salute. Elisabeth blinked and gave him a quick smile. Then she turned, lifted her skirts this time and navigated between the prop men, a group of gypsies who had appeared in Act II, the scenery, and the costume racks behind the stage. Once across the stage, she turned right and ran up a short flight of steps. The first door on the left was emblazoned with a large five-pointed white star. Elisabeth clutched the key in one hand, while with the other she knocked.

The door flew open and a wide-eyed maid stood before her, wringing her hands.

"Thank heavens, miss," said the young maid, who Elisabeth remembered was named Elsie.

"What is it? Have you found them?" asked Madame Nordica frantically.

The diva, normally a rational, handsome woman with a determined chin and broad Maine accent, now stood in bare feet in a dressing room that looked as if it had been vandalized. Her costume for the consumptive courtesan, Violetta, whom she would portray in less than a quarter of an hour, was a flowing white nightdress, and the neck remained unbuttoned. Her brown hair, which had been dressed for the last act, was half unpinned and fell about her shoulders. The whole impression was more of a wraith than a consumptive courtesan, which Elisabeth would have found comical if the situation did not portend disaster should the stockings not be found.

"Elisabeth is here, Madam," said the maid, tossing up her hands as if she could stop worrying.

"I understand you've lost your stockings," Elisabeth said, lifting up a basket of roses that had tipped over in the midst of the crowded dressing room.

"Not lost," said Nordica, frowning. "I fear I've left them at the hotel. There's no time to get them." She pressed her hands together and gave Elisabeth a pleading look. "Can you help?"

Elisabeth met the worried star's apprehensive gaze and settled her own shoulders into a posture of confidence. Such emergencies were not infrequent backstage at the opera house, and Elisabeth had often been called upon to do the impossible at a moment's notice. This, however, was different.

She did not need merely to stitch a seam together or replace one button with another. Now she was expected to produce white stockings out of thin air. She searched her mind to try to remember where she might have seen another pair. The stockings she wore were black, otherwise she would have readily taken them off and lent them to the leading lady.

Providence knocked on the door. Elisabeth turned to answer it. As she opened the door a few inches, she saw that Marco Giovinco stood in the passageway.

"Oh," said Elisabeth, startled to see him again.

His lips curved in a disconcerting smile. Charm radiated from him.

"I was concerned. Madam Nordica is not ill, I hope?"

"No, no," said Elisabeth, rattled both by the fear that Nordica would have to appear in bare feet and by Marco's towering presence in the dimly lit passageway. The seriousness of the situation made her say what she had not said before. "She cannot find her stockings."

"I see," he replied.

Marco glanced over Elisabeth's shoulder, and behind her Nordica called, "Who is it?"

Marco pushed open the dressing room door and moved forward. Nordica jumped up from the stool where she was sitting, her hair, which the maid had been trying to arrange for Act III, flying about her face.

"No stockings, Marco! I have to have stockings!" She glowered at him as if it were his fault.

Marco glanced down at her feet and ankles, visible

from under the costume.

"Hmmm. I see. A serious problem, but one with which I can perhaps assist."

Elisabeth backed into the costume rack, slightly intimidated by being in the small dressing room with the two stars. Marco's presence easily filled the room. On the other side of him, Elsie, the maid was evidently trying to shrink as well, for a rustle and then a crash made them all turn in her direction. A vase had fallen, water spilled out, and two dozen roses scattered across the floor.

Elsie shrieked and backed into the screen around the lavatory. Elisabeth dove between Marco and Nordica, grasping Nordica to move her away from the thorns. She grabbed a towel, tossed it to the maid, and set the broken vase upright. Its base was still intact, only the lip had broken off.

"Don't let the water get to the costumes," Elisabeth ordered the maid.

"Never mind that," said Nordica with an exasperated sigh.

A knock came at the open door.

"Five minutes," called the stage manager.

Elisabeth's heart pounded even faster, for they still had not resolved the problem of the missing stockings. She began to cast about for Nordica's slippers, thinking they would just have to do without the stockings. She sang most of the act from the bed in any case. Perhaps if she were careful as to how she got in and out of the covers . . .

"Wait here," said Marco, as if any of the women were going anywhere in the five remaining minutes until curtain time.

They all looked at him in surprise. He gave Nordica a wink and then turned to Elisabeth, who was on her hands and knees, gathering up the wet roses, and gave her a reassuring smile.

"If it is stockings you need, your search is over. I happen to have a pair in my dressing room."

The three women's eyes widened.

"They were to be a gift," he continued. "For . . . a friend."

He gave a quick nod of his dark head and hurried out, pulling the door shut after him.

The maid blinked.

"Thank heavens," said Nordica as she sat down at the dressing table, raising the costume to expose the dangling elastic suspenders with gilt clips that hung from her garter belt.

Marco's dressing room was next door and in seconds his knock sounded again. Elisabeth struggled to set the roses in the broken vase and stand up. The maid was still on her hands and knees mopping up the water, so Marco did not wait, but entered the room and handed the stockings to Nordica. Neither singer seemed the slightest bit disturbed at Nordica's state of undress; such things were not uncommon in the theater.

Elisabeth reached out a hand in time to catch the stocking Nordica dropped as she lifted her right leg and pulled the other one on. Elisabeth threw the stocking over her shoulder and assisted Nordica in fastening the other one with the four clips.

A rap at the door. "Two minutes," called the stage manager.

Marco's hand removed the stocking from Elisabeth's shoulder. He then deftly arranged the stocking so that

Nordica could plunge her left foot into it. Then she pulled it up and with Elisabeth's assistance, finished fastening it to the clips. Meanwhile the maid had struggled to her feet and, grasping a brush, finished arranging Nordica's hair, so that she would appear to be the poor consumptive Violetta, confined to her bed for weeks.

Elisabeth reached for the slippers, got them onto Nordica's feet, and Marco held out a hand to help the leading lady stand up.

"Curtain," called the stage manager.

Marco opened the door, and Nordica sailed through it. Elisabeth followed. Not that she was needed any longer, but she was caught up in the situation, so that she only started breathing normally when she saw Nordica on stage ensconced in the large bed and Marco standing in the wings, feet slightly spread, preparing for his entrance.

The orchestra began its tranquil prelude, the curtain lifted, and Nordica, now transformed into the noble, dying Violetta, gazed into the eyes of the doctor on stage who assured her she would live.

The new electric lights had lowered in the auditorium, and the chattering of the audience had diminished. Elisabeth stood in the darkened wings a respectful distance behind Marco, who, she imagined, must be concentrating. The near disaster had been averted, and Act III was underway.

Nordica's voice, velvety and luscious, floated above the orchestra. Backstage, Elisabeth moved out of the way of the harried stage manager, rested her arm on the back of the wing chair from Act II, and listened to Nordica's aching rendition of the letter Violetta receives from her erstwhile lover's father. On stage right the doctor and Violetta's maid gravely conferred, for he had lied to the lovely Violetta. In truth she has not long to live. Marco took a deep breath, lifted his head and rushed on-stage. The music swelled as he took Nordica in his arms.

Standing in the wings, Elisabeth raised her hand to her chest, blinking back tears at the intense beauty of the reunion, for now the lover Alfred, portrayed by Marco, asked forgiveness for deserting Violetta earlier. His voice sent a thrill through Elisabeth as she watched his sensual, masculine movements about the stage.

The act continued with Alfred's father entering the scene and likewise asking forgiveness for having misjudged Violetta. The violins played an ethereal, tremulous theme, and the music built to a climax as love was declared just before Violetta's final demise.

Only as the soprano's high notes floated above the orchestra, and Alfred's cry of anguish at his beloved's death penetrated her heart, did Elisabeth realize that she had once again watched the entire final act.

The heavy blue curtain fell, the singers arose and straightened their costumes for their bows, and Elisabeth fled back to the dressing room, remembering now what a state they had left it in.

She found Elsie fluttering about the room, trying to put things to rights. As soon as the girl saw Elisabeth, she launched into a tirade of high-pitched anxiety.

"Madam will be so upset. The lovely vase was from one of her greatest admirers. I cannot mend it. The roses will not stand up properly."

"Never mind that," said Elisabeth, taking the broken

piece of vase from the maid's hand. "The performance went marvelously."

"Is it over?"

"Yes. They're taking their bows now." She bent to pick up a shoe and place it in its shoe bag.

The maid gasped. "Then she'll be here in minutes." And she tossed several scarves off the chair in front of the mirror.

Elisabeth reached out to catch them and hung them over a hook on the back of the door. When she turned, she caught her own reflection in the mirror, framed by electric lights encased in milky glass globes. Alert brown eyes gazed from beneath dark brown eyebrows. her long, dark lashes cast shadows on her high cheekbones in the bright mirror lights.

Unconsciously, she tilted her head slightly, touching the Psyche knot at the back of her head. The dark curls that fell around her forehead were mussed. Her lips were parted slightly as if she had been surprised.

Then she turned quickly, banishing the fantasy that always came when she caught sight of her face in the dressing room mirrors. She ought to get out of Nordica's dressing room. Elsie would help her undress, and Elisabeth would be needed elsewhere. As wardrobe mistress, it was her responsibility to gather all the costumes and hang them on the racks, doing a quick check for any necessary repairs. Tomorrow she would be back to press out wrinkles, mend tears, and make sure all was ready for the next performance.

Carrying the broken vase, she left Nordica's dressing room. The applause and shouts of "bravo" from the audience reached her ears even this far back backstage. She turned away from the stage and headed for the stairs at the far end of the narrow passageway. As she passed Marco's dressing room, she glanced at the white star on the door. Then she hurried down the passage.

As she took the stairs, she heard footsteps in the hall behind her and paused. Marco, followed by a group of admirers, stood with his hand on his dressing room door. He glanced in her direction, and their eyes met. He lifted his chin and smiled in acknowledgment. She nodded quickly and then hastened up the rest of the stairs, turning on the landings until she was in the third floor hallway above.

She then slowed her pace and took a deep breath. She entered a large room and closed the door behind her. The new electric lights lit this room as well. She deposited the ruined vase in a waste can and found a temporary container for the roses. Then she began to make her way along the row of costumes that hung along one wall. Her hands moved quickly over the ball gowns used in the party scenes. With a glance she assessed the state of the garments, straightening the men's shirts, brushing out wrinkles in the evening dresses.

As her hands drifted to Marco's costume for Act I, she ran her hands along it, smoothing the sturdy material. His costume was here only because it needed a slight repair. The image of his twinkling eyes, his merry laugh came into her mind.

She had not fit either of the stars for their costumes. That privilege was given to well-known couturiers and distinguished tailors. But she could not help the warm blush that came to her cheeks as she thought of stretching a tape measure across his torso.

"Stop it," she said to herself. "Just another fantasy."

She hurried through her task. When she was finished, she lifted her cloak from the coat tree, picked up her reticule, turned off the lights and closed the door on the dark room in which the costumes waited for tomorrow's performance.

She took the stairs. On the stage level there was still much activity, but Elisabeth's work was done for now. She gave a satisfied sigh, recalling her small part in averting disaster during this evening's second intermission. Then she recalled where the all too necessary stockings had come from and how easily Marco had helped Nordica's slim legs into them.

She stepped aside allowing a group of chorus members, now in street clothes, to pass. Then she followed them down the narrow stairs that led to the stage door. On Thirty-ninth Street, she paused, breathed in the fresh night air and pulled the hood of her cloak up over her head.

The street was full of cabs, victorias and all manner of shining carriages, high-stepping horses clopping on the granite-block paving. Many of the operagoers had by now repaired to one of the restaurants in one of the elegant hotels along Broadway.

At the curb, a horse stamped and jingled his harness. The footman, attired in a knee-length brass-buttoned coat, high boots, and top hat checked the harness fastenings and then stood at attention by the door of the shiny black brougham. At the sight of the well turned-out rig, Elisabeth's mind drifted back to the sight of her father this evening. Her heart contracted at the thought, and she turned toward Broadway to catch a horsecar downtown.

"Oh!" No sooner did she turn than she nearly collided with a broad chest . . . again!

"Excuse . . ." Marco's words drifted off as he caught her elbow.

She involuntarily backed up a step. "Oh, I'm sorry."

"Again?"

She did not miss the irony in his voice and glanced up at the dark eyebrows arched in amusement.

"Twice in one night must be propitious. Or do you make a habit of bumping into people in the dark?"

Elisabeth's heart turned over in embarrassment. "No of course not. That is, I try not to."

"Then you are admitting to being less than graceful?"

His teasing further confused her. "I'm sorry. My mind was wandering."

"Ah, then that explains it." He had not let go of her elbow and gave her a gentle push toward the black brougham at the curb. The footman opened the door.

"May I offer you a lift? I could not sleep tonight if I imagined that you failed to get home safely because of further accidents."

The idea of getting into the coach with the renowned Marco Giovinco sent her into a panic.

"No thank you. It's quite all right. I always take the horsecar."

He released her arm but still stood near, gazing down at her in curiosity. She was all too aware that people would be watching them. Singers of Marco Giovinco's stature did not go far without being noticed. Normally there was a horde of fans swarming about the stage door, waiting for autographs, or reporters waiting to speak to the star. But it was late, and they had all come and gone.

She looked about helplessly. Surely even on regular

nights during the season Marco traveled with an entourage. What about the woman the stockings had been for? Where was she?

Passersby lingered to stare surreptitiously at Marco, whose presence in top hat and satin-lined black cape could not fail to attract attention. The footman still stood at attention, attempting to be oblivious to his employer's conversation. On the box, the driver sat straight, waiting for the signal to go.

She took a step away from the brougham and its celebrated owner. If she didn't hurry, she would miss the horsecar. But as she opened her mouth to make excuses, her eyes met his. She blinked. He gestured to the waiting coach. Nordica's white coach pulled up behind his. Soon the diva would appear.

"Please allow me to escort you to your destination," said Marco in a most courteous manner. "In appreciation of your assistance during what might have been a calamity for all concerned tonight."

It was silly to refuse, though Elisabeth. He's just being polite. She swallowed and then tried to smile.

"All right," she said. "Thank you."

He assisted her into the coach.

Chapter Two

As Marco followed her into the coach, it swayed slightly. He sat on the seat next to her, a respectful distance away.

"And where am I to instruct the driver to take you?"

"Twenty-sixth Street," she said. "Opposite the square."

Marco gestured to the footman, who had heard the address and shut the door. The footman passed the information to the driver and climbed on behind.

As the coach moved into the street, Elisabeth faced front, risking a glance out of the corner of her eyes. Marco seemed to settle into his seat and then looked out the windows at the street. Carriages and pedestrians on foot were still making their way home from the opera. Here and there, a loiterer stood on a street corner, perhaps looking for illicit excitement.

As the brougham turned down Seventh Avenue, Marco seemed to return to the present. He shifted so he could see Elisabeth's straight profile.

"So Signorina Kendall, have you been at the theater very long?"

"Two years," she said, risking a glance at him. She was surprised he remembered her name. "Not long."

"Hmmm. Long enough to be entrusted with the costumes, no?"

She allowed herself a small smile. "I . . . enjoy the work."

"I see. You like the opera?"

"Of course." Her prim demeanor dropped as she turned fully and faced him, her eyes wide, not trying to hide her enthusiasm. "It is my passion."

Marco lifted his head and gave her a curious look. "That is a strong word. You are either a very fine seamstress or take extraordinary pride in your work."

"That is not what I mean." Then she clamped her mouth shut. Her words were running away with her.

His dark eyes lit with curiosity. "No?"

The desire to tell him of her secret aspirations urged her on, but his presence intimidated her. The image of her father came to her, and she felt herself turn inward. She turned to the window on her side, stifling her words. But it was too late to suppress the inner turmoil. Just as it so often did, resignation came on the heels of dreams, and she stared silently at the brownstone and cast iron buildings along the avenue as the horse's hooves clopped on the paving stones.

But she felt his fingers on her sleeve. "Please," he said. "Tell me."

She turned to look at him again, the lamps from the street casting light and shadows across his face as the carriage moved along. How dare she say it. She tried to make light of it and gave a shrug of one shoulder.

"I've dreamed of singing," she said, following it with an awkward laugh. "But you've probably heard millions of girls say that."

"Ah . . ." He sat back. "I see."

There, she'd said it. Now he could deliver her to her door and forget about her. Not that she was too shy to ask someone like Marco help her attain her goals. But she must prevent embarrassment lest he misconstrue. Marco Giovinco was not only a devastatingly handsome celebrity, he was eligible. His charm could not help but attract women from all classes of society, and some theater hopefuls no doubt would flatter and allow liberties to such a man if they thought he could advance them.

Elisabeth was not like that. Not only did personal integrity insist that she guard her reputation, but she fought constantly with that other burden—the reason for her disappearance from the society in which she had been brought up.

Marco stirred. "Have you a voice?" he asked.

Elisabeth jerked her head. "I . . . I've been told I do. Not by professionals, that is. Only in the drawing room."

"I see. Well, in that case, perhaps we should discuss it. I am interested in a young woman who seems to have so many talents. Perhaps you would like to join me for supper?"

"Supper?" She blanched. "I did not mean to impose. I don't mean to . . ."

Her words tangled, and she frowned, feeling more disconcerted by the moment. She had not intended to throw herself at his feet, no matter how handsome he was, nor how much her heart fluttered when he bent near her. Every woman he spoke to would have the same reaction.

Marco laughed, perceiving her confusion. He rapped on the small window behind him, which slid open.

"Franco," he said to the footman, "Delmonico's."

"Oh no! Not there," said Elisabeth, sitting forward. Her eyes widened. "I can't possibly go there."

Marco lifted a brow. "Why not?"

"I might . . ." she moistened her lips, casting about for a suitable answer. "That is, I'm not dressed."

Marco studied her for a moment. After considering for a long interval, he drew out his words slowly. "I see. Well, I've an appetite, but I won't demand your company. Suit yourself. I favor a modest dining room with a good chef who makes an excellent lobster."

He was offering her a way out, and she didn't know what to say. "You are very kind. Perhaps another . . ."

His hand grasped hers and squeezed it. Amusement mixed with understanding in his face. "I promise not to abduct you. All I seek is a little pleasant company, for I hate to eat alone. I do it far more often than anyone realizes. You seem to be an entertaining person. I thought we might enjoy a pleasant meal."

No matter that her eyes normally drooped at this time of night. For Marco it would be several hours before he relaxed enough to sleep. She took a deep breath and sat back. They were headed down Broadway now. In a moment they would come to Twenty-sixth Street, the location both of Delmonico's and, in the next block, her own boarding house.

"All right," she said, glancing at her lap. "I would be honored."

He released her hand and patted it. Then he rapped

on the little window again.

"Franco," he said to the footman when the window opened. "I've changed my mind. Tell Giovanni I am taking the lady to DeLuci's."

The window shut. The footman relayed the message to the driver. Marco turned back to Elisabeth.

"I hope you like Italian food. DeLuci's is downtown. Little Italy is far from the theater district. Does that suit you?"

She nodded slowly. "Yes, of course."

When he suggested Little Italy, she thought perhaps she would be better off if he took her to one of the brightly lit hotel dining rooms or restaurants on Broadway, but she dared not complain again, lest he think her too waspish.

"You do not need to worry about how you are dressed." There was a touch of irony in these last words. Marco relaxed. "And so, tell me of your singing," he said.

"I have always sung," she said, looking at him again. "At . . . home, that is. Never on the stage."

"But you would like to?"

She felt herself color in embarrassment. The old confusion reared its head.

"It's just that I was raised to believe that all women who go on the stage are immoral. But of course the great divas are respected and admired by everyone."

She did not mention the fact that even Lillian Nordica had changed her name for fear having an opera singer in the family would disgrace her relatives in Maine. Elisabeth pressed her lips together and gazed at him hesitantly. "But of course perhaps that is hard for you to understand."

Marco chuckled. "It does not make it easy to pursue one's dreams and please one's family at the same time. Is that the dilemma? Have you a very strict family?"

Elisabeth's face hardened. "I have no family."

For once Marco's suavity did not carry the conversation. Her comment startled him.

"I see," he said. He did not see, but he could see that this was not a topic to pursue at present. Instead he turned his thoughts to his own cause for celebration.

"I hope you will share a bottle of wine with me at DeLuci's," he said. "I am a fine mood this evening for Mr. Abbey and Mr. Grau have agreed to my terms for next season. After a spring tour down the East coast and the summer in Europe I will return home for a challenging season here. The future is settled."

He said it with evident satisfaction, and Elisabeth's awe of the man was mixed with curiosity. She had assumed that once one was established as a great artist, one had no more worries about engagements or finances. And yet she had heard of bitter arguments between artists and management from time to time. It made her curious and she wanted to know more.

"Congratulations," she said. "How pleasant for you."

"Yes. And so you see I am in a celebratory mood."

She smiled, caught up in his enthusiasm. She longed to tell the dark, handsome man in the coach beside her how many times she had admired his artistry from the wings. She had seen him once too, from one of the plush first tier boxes, but she could hardly explain that. To keep her thoughts from wandering down that path, she cast her mind back to this evening's opera.

"You and Madam Nordica sang very beautifully this evening," she said.

"I am glad you enjoyed it. You listened then, from the wings?"

She nodded. "Oh yes. Nearly every night."

His eyes slid across her face. "A true aficionado."

They pulled up next to a curb, and the footman jumped down to open the door on Elisabeth's side. She gave him her hand and stepped down to find that they were in front of a gaily lit restaurant. Flickering lanterns were visible behind the glass window, and a couple emerged from a painted green door under a scalloped awning. The overhead sign proclaimed "DeLuci's" in large hand-painted letters.

Marco followed her onto the curb and placed his hand under her elbow. With her other hand, she grasped her skirts and climbed the few steps toward the door, which opened as another patron emerged.

Warmth and sound of laughter enveloped them as they stepped into the foyer. Small lamps on every table cast a rosy glow about the room, accentuated by the walls, which were covered in red wallpaper above the chair rails. Elisabeth relaxed in the respectable surroundings, for she could see that the patrons at the round tables covered with white linen tablecloths were bourgeoisie out for an evening of pleasure. Perhaps some of them had been to the theater as well. Some were young men, not much older than her twenty-two years, who looked as if they were enjoying the fruits of their hard work and hoped for prosperous years to come.

She instantly warmed to Marco, for he had chosen to bring her to a place where she would be comfortable. Had he taken her for a floozie, he would no doubt have suggested one of the garish lobster palaces on Broadway favored by the chorus girls. Though she had no doubts that he, himself patronized the Great White Way that was but a few steps from the opera house, her regard for him increased, for he had taken her feelings into consideration.

"Marco! *Il mio amico.*"

A tall man with Italian features came toward them and grasped Marco, embracing him and clapping him on the back. Rapid words were exchanged in Italian, and then Marco turned to Elisabeth.

"Carlos, may I present la signorina Elisabeth Kendall, who has so graciously agreed to dine with me at your establishment this evening."

"I am honored," said the man addressed as Carlos. He was wearing full evening dress and bowed gracefully from the waist, taking Elisabeth's hand and kissing her knuckles. "The finest table for you, my friends," he said when he straightened.

Marco handed their wraps to the coat check girl working behind her half door.

At Carlos' gesture the maître d' approached. Carlos whispered instructions and the maître d' bowed. "This way, please."

He led them down a narrow aisle between tables, while a few heads turned, some with surprised looks of recognition, some with the expression that whoever had entered must be important but they could not think why. Marco greeted several men who rose from their chairs and came over to clasp his hands.

Of course he would be known here, Elisabeth reasoned. For though he was now a celebrity, he was a native of Little Italy. She had read about his difficult road to stardom, and the years of hard study, about how he had worked as a waiter to pay for singing lessons until he made a name for himself in Europe. In fact, it was about those years of study that Elisabeth hoped to hear tonight, if he would speak of them.

At the back of the long, narrow room a short flight of steps led to a raised platform where two tables with snowy white tablecloths were set for more intimate dining, being somewhat protected from the busy floor of the restaurant by potted ferns and replicas of Roman statuary. The maître d' made a flourish and pulled out Elisabeth's chair. Marco seated himself. Even though the two men exchanged words in Italian, there was no mistaking the word for champagne.

Champagne glasses and a silver bucket appeared. Marco approved the label, and Carlos himself poured. Marco raised his glass.

"To Carlos DeLuci, my friend from the old days. May good fortune shine on all your tomorrows."

"Ah, *grazie,*" said Carlos, obviously touched. "I would wish no less for you, my friend. But then fortune has already shone on the great Marco Giovinco."

Then he turned his charm on Elisabeth. "And no doubt this young lady will bring you even more good luck."

She blushed at his flattery. Then she raised her glass and took a sip. She had always loved the taste of champagne, and this bottle sparkled as well as those on Fifth Avenue.

Then she closed her eyes, taking another sip. She had not come here to think about Fifth Avenue. When she opened them she saw that Marco was smiling in

29

amusement. He probably mistook her look of rapture at the taste of the champagne as being a unique experience. His words confirmed it.

"Don't drink it too quickly," he cautioned. "Savor the taste."

She set her glass down and reordered her thoughts. Now that she had the golden-throated tenor to herself, she must make the most of the opportunity. She must think of all the questions she should ask, and since she had determined to study music, perhaps he could recommend a teacher.

The waiter approached, and described in a mixture of English and Italian the specialties of the house. While Elisabeth was not used to eating this late, the dishes did sound tempting. She smiled at Marco.

"The *calamari* sounds delicious," she said.

"Ah yes, very good," replied the waiter. "It is stewed with onion, tomatoes, red wine, tomato paste, garlic, and the most delicate herbs. A good choice."

"I'll have that."

Marco observed her curiously, and she dropped her gaze to her linen napkin. He was probably wondering how often a wardrobe mistress ate stewed squid. He, himself, chose cod cooked in wine, oil, and milk with onion, garlic, anchovies and herbs. Then they agreed on minestrone to start.

When the waiter had taken their order, Elisabeth sipped the champagne and glanced at the surroundings.

"Do you come here often?" she said, trying to make light conversation.

"I grew up a few blocks from here. Carlos and I used to practice our boxing after school."

She smiled. "Fortunately for the music world you traded the boxing ring for the stage."

His grin was infectious. "Besides boxing, we also sang in church. Father Pedroni thought I had a voice."

"And so you began to study."

"Yes, thanks to the generosity of a patron who I later reimbursed, I studied with a very good teacher here. Later I went abroad where I managed to make a name for myself."

Though she knew he must have worked very hard, it sounded like a dream come true.

"If I ever had the opportunity, I would work very hard also," Elisabeth said seriously.

The soup came in wide, shallow bowls, and as Marco lifted his spoon to taste the steaming liquid he glanced at her. "And how long have you wanted to sing professionally?"

"I have always dreamed of it," she said after a swallow of the thick, tasty soup. "The dreams of a young girl are based in fantasy, I know. But then . . ." She faltered and took another spoonful of soup.

"When I began to work at the theater," she gave a little helpless laugh, "the opera . . ."

She still could not express her feelings for the magic that filled the opera house night after night. The rich, powerful voices, the notes that floated from the great singers, the surging power of the orchestra, all enhanced by the spectacle of scenery and lighting. It was a world of fantasy perhaps, but one she loved better than anything else.

Marco's look reflected his understanding. They ate their soup in silence, and the waiter removed the bowls.

Marco placed both elbows on the table and folded

his hands under his chin as he observed her.

"Then you must audition for a good teacher. Would you like to do that?"

She nearly choked on the champagne. "Oh yes. But . . ."

Marco took her look of confusion to mean that even if a teacher accepted her, she could not pay for the lessons.

"You must take first things first. If the teacher likes you, you will at least know you have talent. The rest comes with determination, great determination."

She nodded, saying no more. Strangely, she felt tears moisten her eyes. Marco Giovinco must have taken many young hopefuls to supper and promised them whatever they wanted in exchange for their favors. Was he thinking that he could arrange an audition for her?

He was a charming, sought after artist. And Elisabeth was under no delusions about many of the theater people. Handsome men like Marco would have the opportunity for many women. She must be careful.

She tried to arrange her expression so that he did not get the wrong idea. But the champagne made her relax, and Marco began to speak of incidents at the theater, amusing her with his humor. By the time they were through the main course, she was no longer guarding her reactions, but reveling in the pleasure of his entertaining company.

"Something for after dinner?" The waiter had appeared at her elbow.

Marco ordered coffee and Amaretto liqueur.

The gay evening was coming to a close, and Elisabeth already felt the twinge of regret that it could not last. But immediately, she brought herself up. She still had to make sure she got herself safely home with no untoward advances from the laughing, sensual, generous Marco Giovinco. But the pleasant buzz in her head, together with the excitement of the evening had threatened to push her prim manner aside.

Instead, when Marco helped her up from the table, she swayed unsteadily toward the small flight of stairs and felt his grasp around her waist to keep her from pitching forward. She smiled a little too brightly and held onto the railing with one hand, lifting her skirts with the other to better negotiate the stairs.

Most of the other diners had left, and Carlos came to inquire if everything was to their satisfaction. Marco joked with his friend, each vying with the other to express the largest compliment as she and Marco regained their wraps.

When they finally made it out the door, Franco appeared and opened the door of the brougham. No doubt the footman and coachman had taken the opportunity to entertain themselves in one of the nearby saloons for working men, for Franco's nose appeared ruddier than it had when she had first seen it.

Once settled in the coach, some of the glow began to wear off and reality intruded again. The brougham pulled into the narrow cobbled street, and Elisabeth glanced out at a few passersby staggering homeward to one of the darkened tenement houses. She sobered as she thought of going to her own modest rooms.

Marco instructed his driver, Giovanni, to make for Twenty-sixth Street, and they turned onto Broadway. They said little, and indeed Marco seemed to be lost in his own thoughts. At Madison Square they turned right and she told Marco to have the driver stop in front of one of the row of brownstones with high front stoops. She imagined that even at this late hour, the landlady, Mrs. Runkewich, would peek between her curtains when she heard Elisabeth's key in the door.

Marco got out and assisted Elisabeth onto the sidewalk.

"This one?" asked Marco, pointing to the house directly in front of them.

She nodded. She had wanted Marco to wait on the sidewalk, but he had already grasped her elbow and was walking her to the stone steps. She fished in the reticule for the key, and once she had the door unlocked, Marco reached over her shoulder and pushed it inward. They stepped into the foyer, and Marco shut the door behind them.

Elisabeth heard the creak of Mrs. Runkewich's door to their left. In embarrassed exasperation she called out.

"I'm home, Mrs. Runkewich. A gentleman from the theater has seen me home."

The door, which had opened a crack, pulled shut.

Marco grinned. "A watchful landlady, I see."

"Yes," said Elisabeth. "She is quite vigilant as to the comings and goings of her boarders."

Marco's eyes drifted to the open door of a parlor on the other side of the hall. Even in the shadowy darkness, he could see the fringed lamps and an upright piano at one end of the cluttered room. His gaze then traveled up the narrow staircase with its slightly worn carpet. Elisabeth put out her hand.

"Thank you for a wonderful evening," she said. She didn't know what else to say. She felt now that he was about to leave she wanted to ask more about singing, but it was too late.

Marco grasped her hand and raised it to his lips.

"Of course I won't forget about finding you a teacher. And may I see you again?"

She gave a quick jerk of the chin. "Of course we'll see each other at the opera house."

Marco held her hand firmly in his own. "That's not what I meant." His cheek twitched as he pressed his lips into a line.

Elisabeth tried to still the quick beat of her heart. "I'm afraid that would be impossible. We must leave things as they are."

Marco's dark eyes took on a look of cajolery. "But you have enjoyed this evening, no? We must see about getting you an audition with a teacher. As you can see, I am a gentleman. Will you not consent to dine with me again, lovely lady?"

Her voice rose in desperation as she extracted her hand from his grasp. "I cannot." She swallowed. "It wouldn't be proper."

She glanced away before tears of frustration showed. On the first step she turned back to him, resting her hand on the newel post.

"I'm sorry," she said as calmly as she possibly could. "I did not explain that I am married."

Chapter Three

She fled up the stairs, leaving Marco staring after her, a look of surprise and annoyance on his face. He watched her disappear around the turn at the landing, her skirt flickering above her heels.

Married? He drew in a breath and let it out, at the same time glancing at the tightly shut landlady's door.

"And good night to you too," he said, gesturing to the green painted carved door. He'd no doubt that the scrupulous woman would wait for him to descend the front steps and get into his waiting carriage.

He shook his head, muttering to himself in Italian. Married? And where was the husband? What kind of husband who did not mind if his wife, who had aspirations to perform, no less, stayed out until the wee hours of morning? And she wore no wedding ring.

It confused him. If Elisabeth had been a woman of loose morals, she would have made that plain. On the contrary, though she had evidently enjoyed herself at the restaurant, she had behaved modestly, more modestly than many of the young women about the theater. He felt momentary displeasure at the idea that the girl had wasted his time. Not wasted from her point of view, for he had agreed to arrange an audition with a teacher for her. Ha! He could not even blame her for tricking him, for she had not flirted audaciously as did some of the dancers he had entertained on more than one occasion.

When he took a girl out, he usually let nature take its course. He was as hot-blooded as the next Italian male, and if the lady was willing . . . But often he enjoyed a woman merely for her company. Half the pleasure was in the chase, and he did not mind pursuing a woman if she interested him greatly. Unfortunately, few did.

With irritation he let the front door to the brownstone slam behind him. Then he descended the steps and got into the brougham with a sigh.

"Home, my friends," he said wearily, to which the sleepy footman gave a nod. He glared at the dark, silent house as they pulled away, and just as he expected, he saw the curtain in the front parlor drop. Mrs. Runkewich could rest assured that her charge had not been molested.

On the third floor, Elisabeth opened the door to her cold, drab sitting room. Married. But of course there is no husband to come home to. No one to light a fire for but herself. No husband after all, only a wedding ring she kept in a box and a deep dark secret. She leaned against her door, attempting to stop the twisting feelings from rising and claiming her as they had so many times in the last two years. She had learned to live in the limbo she had created for herself, learned to live with the shame and loss of it all.

She should never have gone out with Marco Giovinco tonight. For as wonderful as the little celebratory supper was, it had caused hope to rise in her breast. And hope was dangerous. Marco would never follow through on his idea to help her obtain a teacher now that he realized she had tricked him.

A pity too, for she found that she liked him, and would have liked to get to know him better. He was a fascinating artist. She had no illusions about the kind of man he probably was when it came to women, but he made her curious. His origins had been humble. Perhaps he had lived in rooms like these at one time. He must know what it was to struggle. For that she respected him. Like many other great artists, he had worked hard and deserved his success.

As she tried to quell her self-pity, she turned on a small gas lamp affixed to the wall. No electricity in this house, but gas jets gave a cozy glow. Light chased away the dark shadows, and from the corner of a well worn sofa, a motley black, brown and orange cat blinked sleep-filled golden brown eyes.

Elisabeth patted the cat's head. "Hello Miranda, sleepy girl. How's my pretty girl?"

The cat licked her paws and purred. Elisabeth patted its head again. "Go back to sleep. I'm going to do the same."

But as Elisabeth passed from the sitting room into the bedroom, she heard the thump of paws on the floor as Miranda jumped down to follow her. The cat leapt gracefully onto the quilt that covered the bed and selected a spot in the middle in which to lie down.

Elisabeth smiled nostalgically to herself. At the

moment Miranda was the only creature that loved her. The cat was a pet that Elisabeth had brought home from the girls school she had attended four years ago. The mixed breed kitty came from a litter of the dean's calico mother cat.

She removed her bonnet and lay her reticule down on the highboy, then she slowly struggled out of her dress and wrapped herself in a dressing gown. Not quite ready for bed after the stimulating evening, she sat in a worn tapestry-covered chair by the window, which looked out the back of the house. Miranda leapt down from the bed and then up into Elisabeth's lap.

A few lamps behind drawn curtains glowed in the windows of the row of houses that backed onto this one. But in her mind's eye Elisabeth saw past the houses to the next street and the next, and on up Fifth Avenue, where she imagined gay theater parties were making their way homeward after supper and parading along Peacock Alley at the Waldorf, where the wealthy went to see and be seen. Images of the past and present swam in her head until her lids finally drooped.

"Let's go to bed, girl," she whispered to the cat, who allowed herself to be lifted back to the bed.

She turned down the light and crawled between the covers.

The autumn sun awoke her just in time for breakfast at Mrs. Runkewich's table. The boarding house served three substantial meals a day, and most of the boarders never missed one. Elisabeth rose, dressed in a practical gabardine dress with ruffled cuffs and high neck. By the time she went downstairs, she had composed her face into a neutral expression to greet her fellow boarders.

Though all eyes turned to her as she entered the half-filled dining room, she smiled sweetly and took her place beside Mr. Barnhill, a young law clerk with fastidious manners who always rose from his chair whenever she joined the others at the table. She nodded to him and said, "Please don't get up," as she did at every meal when she did not beat him to the table.

"No trouble," he replied, helping her with her chair. The ritual had been repeated so many times that neither of them gave any thought to the words anymore. At times Elisabeth feared that should Mr. Barnhill decide to board elsewhere, she would still enter the dining room, nod to the person at the place next to her and say, "Please don't get up," whether or not they made a move.

"Good morning," she said to the others.

Mrs. Runkewich placed a platter of biscuits on the table, which the hungry boarders began to snatch. Two bowls of gravy made the rounds, followed by a plate of bacon, toast, jelly and pears.

Though Elisabeth felt Mrs. Runkewich's narrow-set eyes on her, the slightly bent, dark-haired spinster was too busy at the moment to pry. Mrs. Runkewich never asked personal questions directly, rather she had a way of narrowing her close-set eyes and hunching her shoulders when she had suspicious thoughts.

Sometimes when there was a crisis, she would announce in warbling terms that this was a respectable boarding house, and that her boarders were of the highest morals. Anyone whose morals were in question would immediately get the point. Only once to Elisabeth's knowledge did the landlady have to hound someone so often that he took his leave. But it seemed to work, and the boarding house maintained a very good reputation.

Elisabeth was on the most casual footing with all the others in the boarding house and kept her personal life to herself. She had feared there might be some difficulty when she had come to live here because she had to tell Mrs. Runkewich that she worked in the theater. But her profession as seamstress and wardrobe mistress was deemed respectable enough. Had she been a member of the chorus or a dancer, she might have been refused lodging at this place.

"How was the opera last night?" asked Elisabeth's other neighbor, Margaret Houghteling, a young curly-headed shop girl who had lived at the boarding house for about four months.

"Actually it was very exciting," said Elisabeth, after swallowing a forkful of biscuit and gravy. Silver clattered all around, "Madam Nordica misplaced her stockings for the third act. There was quite some to-do."

"Oh my," said the dark-eyed shop girl. "Whatever did you do?"

"It was all right," replied Elisabeth. "One of ... the other singers had a pair and loaned them just at the last minute."

"Dear me," muttered Miss Selma York, an elderly lady who boarded with her sister, Miss Anne York. "That must have caused quite a fuss."

The two spinster sisters who sat at the end of the table in their lavender tea gowns spoke and gestured alike. One would begin a sentence and the other would finish it, as only two people who had lived together for a lifetime could do.

"Yes," said Elisabeth. "But the stockings were found and Madam Nordica sang beautifully after that."

Selma leaned toward her sister. "We heard her once, you remember Anne."

"Oh yes," said Anne. "A gracious lady she was. And so pretty. I read in the papers that her husband made her retire from the stage after they were married. Only after that, he disappeared over the English Channel in a balloon, so she could sing again."

"Perhaps it's not proper for a married lady to sing on the stage," speculated Selma, cocking her birdlike head and asking the air in front of her.

"Nonsense, sister," said Anne. "Many prima donnas are married ladies. I'm sure I can think of several."

"Nellie Melba had a lover," said Selma, primly reaching for another biscuit. "A royal one at that."

"That doesn't prove anything," said Anne.

Elisabeth smiled in amusement at the opera gossip that found its way even to a humble table like this one. But all New York was fascinated with the opera, and it was true that the prima donnas lived their lives in a fish bowl, thanks to the press.

She had always imagined such publicity to be glamorous, but for the first time she had a glimpse of the disadvantage of such a life. The inclination to keep her supper with Marco Giovinco private made her realize that there were times when one wanted to do things without others' prying eyes.

"And was that handsome tenor, Marco Giovinco singing?" said Margaret, brushing crumbs from her white blouse.

Elisabeth nearly dropped her fork, feeling as if

Margaret had read her mind. "Yes," she managed to answer. "He was."

"I wonder what it's like to have a man like that smile at you."

Elisabeth's heart thumped guiltily. She didn't answer but took a piece of fruit.

Margaret leaned forward, swept away by the idea. "I know what I would do if he ever smiled at me." No one asked her what, so she continued with her fantasy. "I'd swoon right at his feet. And he being charming, would have to pick me up and carry me up the stairs."

"To where?" said Mr. Barnhill, evidently impatient with these silly women. "He would hardly carry you into the opera. And there would be no reason for him to be waiting outside this house for you to swoon at his feet. Ah, but then perhaps he might come into your shop."

Margaret looked miffed, and in spite of the irony of his statements, Elisabeth did not like Mr. Barnhill hurting her friend.

"It was a harmless statement, Mr. Barnhill," said Elisabeth. "She was just having a bit of fun. No need to spoil it."

Mr. Barnhill wiped his lips and placed his napkin on the table. "By all means, do not let me interfere. I have work to attend to in any case. Thank you, Mrs. Runkewich," he said as the landlady came through the door with a china coffee pot.

He got up before she could even offer more coffee. "I'm off," he said.

All the women watched him go. When they heard the front door slam they returned to their breakfasts in silence broken only by the scrape of forks on dishes and the gurgling of coffee being poured into cups.

Margaret shrugged and blotted her lips. As she tucked a curl into place, she lifted her chin and said, "It was a nice idea, that's all. A girl can have ideas." She got up. "Good day, ladies. I must catch the horsecar or I'll be late to the shop."

Elisabeth kept her head bent as she sipped one last cup of coffee. A nice idea to swoon at Marco Giovinco's feet or to have him smile at you? Well, she knew how the latter felt, but she wasn't about to tell anyone.

Later in the day, Elisabeth climbed the stairs to the workroom in the opera house where the costumes were cut, fitted and sewn. Alterations were needed on Madam Nordica's costume for *Faust*, and Elisabeth mustn't keep her waiting. She hurried her steps, her mind only half on the job before her. The feeling of being ill at ease had not left her, and she dreaded encountering Marco.

As she rounded the corner and hurried along the last few steps to the familiar workroom, she again berated herself for having created such a dilemma. In the last two years the opera house had become her home. No one knew her well-kept secrets. Last night was the first time one of them had slipped out. She had the instinctive feeling that Marco was no gossip, but having him know was enough. Whereas before there had been a professional gulf between them, now there would be an added strain. And it was only the beginning of the season. There would be several months of inevitable meetings in the backstage portions of the house.

She opened the door irritably. Inside, several members of the chorus were being fitted by Mrs. DeKoven, head of the costume department and Elisabeth's superior. The box office chief, derby hat in hand, was keeping the women laughing—much to Mrs. DeKoven's admonishments. A cheerful array of colorful material straggled from bolts of cloth thrown helter-skelter on the oversized cutting table. At the far end of the well-lit room, a dancer disappeared behind a curtain to remove a costume she had just tried on.

"Oh, there you are, Elisabeth," said Mrs. DeKoven, her mouth full of pins. "Madam Nordica's maid has been asking for you."

"Goodness, I hope I'm not late," said Elisabeth, removing her straight-brimmed hat and hanging it on a hat rack.

"You'd best run along to the dressing room and see. I had Julius carry the costume down." Julius was the stage manager's son, a tow-headed lad of thirteen who was learning the theater from the ground up.

Elisabeth grabbed a tape measure, flung it around her neck, picked up a cushion of pins and a small basket of chalk, scissors and other accessories, and raced from the room.

She scurried past members of the company congregated in the hall. From the second floor landing she heard laughter and scattered notes on the piano coming from the chorus room. Evidently a rehearsal was about to begin.

Descending the last flight of stairs to stars' dressing rooms, she cast a glance at Marco's dressing room. But the door was shut. He was probably not there.

She knocked on Nordica's door, and Elsie opened it. Madam Nordica looked at her in the mirror where she was examining her face.

"Good morning, Elisabeth. I'm glad to see your sensible face." She turned around in her chair. "Thank you again for your assistance last night."

Elisabeth stepped into the dressing room, which was in considerably better order than it had been the night before.

"I really did nothing," she said, blushing under the crisp gaze of the prima donna.

"Oh, but you did. I have it on authority that you informed Marco of my distress, whereupon he appeared here and produced the solution."

She opened her mouth to say that she had not intentionally told Marco where she was going when she had bumped into him behind the scenery, but she saw instantly that Nordica must have it her way.

Elisabeth shut her mouth and smiled demurely. "Lucky for us he had the solution at hand."

Nordica threw her head back and laughed with great enjoyment at the situation.

When she was finished chuckling she said, "I had Elsie purchase a replacement pair of stockings. Here they are. You may give them to Marco today. I feared his lady friend, for whom the other pair was originally purchased, would be insulted that they had been used. Thus, the new pair. I have sent him a note explaining that I am keeping the original pair, for you never know when I might have need of them again."

She laughed again with great mirth. Elisabeth tried to reflect her humor, but was already worried that the new stockings were being entrusted to her. Why couldn't Elsie return the stockings? She tried to form an argument, but could think of no words. In the theater, one did not argue with prima donnas, especially generally likable ones like Nordica, whose American roots rendered her less temperamental than some of her European counterparts.

Glancing at the thin box that Nordica pointed to, Elisabeth nodded. "I'll see that they're delivered."

With any luck she could slip them into Marco's dressing room and slip out again without being noticed.

She reached for the costume of the peasant girl Nordica would play in *Faust* and held it up. Nordica rose, removed the dressing gown she had been wearing and slung it over the screen.

"Well, let's get on with it."

Between them, Elsie and Elisabeth turned the costume inside out and got it over Nordica's head. But Elisabeth saw the problem immediately. While the simple frock had been faultlessly stitched by Nordica's own seamstress when she had first debuted in the role ten years ago, she had put on weight since then. There was no hope of fastening it, much less allowing the woman room to breathe, an important consideration for one with so big and powerful a voice.

"Most annoying," Nordica said, looking at herself in the mirror. Without the long braided yellow wig that went with the peasant girl's costume, the youthful dress looked ludicrous on the mature performer, especially inside out.

"Well, let me see what can be done," said Elisabeth in a reassuring tone.

She approved the skill with which the sturdy

costume had been put together, and she could see that the original designer had anticipated just such a development in the costume's life. For there was much overlap at the back, and generous allowances had been made at the seams. Her expert eye noted where seams could be let out and where fastenings moved.

With her tape measure, Elisabeth measured the gap to be covered, added two inches for the expansion of the diaphragm needed during the singer's most challenging arias and then made several marks on the material with her piece of chalk.

"I can have this ready by tomorrow for a fitting," said Elisabeth. "Would that be convenient, Madam?"

"Yes, yes. Tomorrow will do. I must come for another rehearsal in the afternoon. We'll fit the awful thing then."

"Very well."

Nordica struggled out of the costume and then donned her dressing gown. She gave Elisabeth one of her no-nonsense looks. Then amusement touched her eyes.

"When I debuted in *Faust* in London, I walked on stage to find a tenor I had never met before, not even in rehearsal. It seemed that the manager had fallen behind in paying salaries. The regular tenor refused to sing the performance because he had not been paid. At the last minute the manager was obliged to use an inexperienced tenor from the chorus."

The story made Elisabeth smile as she hung up the costume. "Whatever did you do?"

"My numbers with him were ruined, of course. But I could still do my arias. And how hard I tried in them. The next day I was known in London."

Elisabeth was still enjoying the story when from down the passageway echoed a familiar tenor voice, gayly singing a line from *Faust*. At the sound of Marco's voice, Elisabeth drew in a breath.

"I must hurry," she said more to herself than to the other two women in the dressing room, and she fled into the corridor.

But she was too late.

"Ah, Miss Kendall. Or rather Mrs. Kendall." He bore down on her, half-frowning. "I hope you are well today."

She swallowed, wishing he would lower his voice, not wanting others to hear their exchange.

"Fine thank you." She gave a forced smile. "I have just finished fitting Madam Nordica."

He took a deep breath and let it out. Then he chuckled good naturedly. "Well that is good. Then she should be dressed for our rehearsal."

And with that he rapped on Nordica's dressing room door. "Lillian," he called out. "It's Marco."

The prima donna opened the door herself and appeared in a pure white blouse with deep lace collar and a narrow dark skirt. Tucked under her arm was the vocal score for *Faust*.

"I know it's you," she said, looking up at the tenor who filled the corridor. "I can hear you coming for miles."

Seeing that she was released from their presence, Elisabeth scurried down the corridor and up the stairs, clutching the costume in her arms.

Upstairs, the workroom was in a flurry. Mrs. DeKoven needed assistance with some of the dancer's costumes. Several chorus members came at once for their fittings during a break in the chorus rehearsal. Julius ran in and out with messages and questions from the managers Mr. Grau and Mr. Abbey. And so it was nearly dinnertime before Elisabeth could get back to the *Faust* costume.

She didn't feel hungry and was relieved to be able to work alone for a while, so she stayed in the workroom after everyone else left for the day. She went downstairs to see that tonight's costumes were all on the proper racks and ready. Then she returned to work on the peasant girl's costume.

A few snips to let out seams, then she basted the costume back together to fit Nordica tomorrow. She removed the cloth buttons and began placing them where she thought they ought to go. She was happily engaged in her work when she heard the distant strains of tonight's opera. She knew that Marco would not be singing in it. Then the next minute she admonished herself for thinking about him. She tried to concentrate on her work, pricked her finger once and wrapped it in a handkerchief so as not to bleed on the costume. She finally got the buttons on and was ready to hang the costume up until tomorrow's fitting.

As she rose, she caught sight of herself in the mirror. Impulsively, she held the costume up in front of herself. The pink, white and gold were flattering to her brown hair and ivory complexion.

She held out the skirt and smiled, allowing herself a bit of imagination. Humming the spinning song from the opera, she began to move back and forth in front of the mirror. So involved was she in her little drama that she did not hear the door open and footsteps enter the room. But she looked up in surprise when Marco's silvery voice softly echoed the phrase she had just sung.

She stopped, staring at him in the mirror as he advanced, still singing the spinning song. She quickly turned around and moved toward the wire mannequin to drape the costume over it. Marco, dressed in gray frock coat and scarf flung about his neck, came around the table as she succeeded in getting the costume on the headless wire form.

"Hmmm," he said. "I believe it would look better on you."

Her face warmed. She could have stammered out some excuse, but instead simply straightened the folds of cloth and said, "It is a very lovely costume and very well-made."

"I see. I was just coming from Mr. Grau's office, and I saw the light on under the door."

"Oh," she said, busying herself by gathering up stray pins and sticking them in the pin cushion. "I did not think you had a fitting now."

His amusement sounded in his voice. "No, I did not. Rather I came to apologize for last night."

She halted her busywork. "No apology is necessary," she said quietly.

"On the contrary," he said, pulling the scarf from around his neck, for it was warm inside. "I did not know you were married. I would not have kept you out at a late supper if I had known. I would like to extend my apologies to your husband. He must think me a cad."

Elisabeth felt herself shrink, and she stared at the space between them, not meeting his eyes.

"That would not be possible."

"Oh?"

She felt awkward, and yet she wanted to tell him the truth. The shell she had so carefully built around herself for two years began to crack. She wanted to tell him the truth, and yet having lived closed-mouthed for so long in order to prevent scandal, it was hard to know where to begin.

She risked a glance at his face, but when she saw the interest and sympathy that lay there, the rest of her defenses began to melt. She sat down in the chair where she had been sewing.

"I have not seen or heard from my husband in two years. It is a long story."

There was a moment of silence, and then Marco let out a breath. "I'm sorry."

She flashed him a look of anger and humiliation and in order to keep a rein on her emotions, she began to move her hands across the work table, arranging tape measure, pinking shears and seam slitters.

But Marco bent over the table and slowly lowered his hand to cover hers. "Would you like to tell me about it? As a friend."

She stared at the hand over hers and tried to look up at him. "I . . . I don't know. I never speak of it. It is too . . ."

He gave her hand a tiny squeeze and stood up. "I do not mean to pry. I am sorry. Of course it is your business."

He turned and began to move away from her. Then he stopped and turned about. "I almost forgot. I spoke to Professor Theodore Schlut today. He asked me to bring you to his studio Friday at eleven in the morning. Would that be convenient?"

Elisabeth forgot all else and stood up staring. An

audition? "He will see me?"

Marco grinned. "Yes. If you sing well, you may have a voice teacher."

"Oh my." Elisabeth clasped a hand to her breast. "I don't know what to say."

Marco came back a few steps. "It is what you wanted is it not?"

"Oh yes, only," she pressed her lips together and met Marco's dark gaze. "What if he doesn't like me?"

Marco chuckled. "You will just have to do your best. Do you have something you can sing for him?"

"Yes, of course. I know many arias." Then she blushed in embarrassment. "As I told you, we used to sing around the piano at home. My mother made sure I was introduced to arias as well as to the popular tunes. I can sing many kinds of music."

Marco smiled in understanding. "Then I am sure you will have no trouble."

They did not discuss the matter of paying for the lessons if the professor did indeed like her, it was enough to think about the first hurdle.

"Well then," said Marco. "We'll leave it at that. Shall I meet you here? We can go together to his studio."

"Thank you," said Elisabeth, wiping sudden tears that appeared at the corners of her eyes. "You are most kind."

In a surge of emotion, Marco moved toward her again, taking her other hand. He did not know what it was about the girl that touched him so. He looked at her tear-stained face and sensed the sturdy character that tried so hard to hide what she was burdened with. Feelings of compassion and a desire to know more of her rent his heart, and he took her hand and kissed it.

"I would have no difficulty laying low the man who has deserted you," he said solemnly. "If you have a cause, I would not hesitate to champion it. Where is this husband of yours? Why does he not return?"

Tears gushed down Elisabeth's face, and she could not hold back the emotions that gripped her. She struggled to turn from Marco's warmth and yet wanted so desperately to be enveloped by it.

"He will never return," she managed to say, gulping for a breath. "I could not allow him to claim me even if he did. I hope to never see him again."

And she suddenly wrenched her hand free of Marco, hurried to the side of the room before she embarrassed herself further, grasped her cloak, hat and reticule and fled, pulling the door shut behind her.

Chapter Four

Marco followed her, muttering to himself in Italian. Since he had met this girl, she had occupied his thoughts in a very strange manner. That she was a mystery was half of it, and now he would not be satisfied until he got to the bottom of it. She behaved prudently, and in that Marco recognized something of character different from many of the struggling artists and hopefuls whose mothers tried to arrange meetings with him. But this girl had somehow gotten under his skin.

He reached the stage door just as it slammed, and outside he had no difficulty catching up with her where she was headed to catch the horsecar.

"Please," he said, grasping her arm and forcing her to stop and face him. Then he lowered his voice so that curious passersby could not overhear.

"You cannot leave it like this. At least let us go somewhere we can talk. I will not rest until I hear your explanation for you have aroused my curiosity."

Elisabeth tried to stifle her sobs by blotting her eyes

with a handkerchief she dug out of her pocket. She had run out of the theater with her hat on but with her cloak still across her arm. Now Marco gently tugged on the wrap until she surrendered it. He draped it across her shoulders and fastened the loop at the neck over the large button.

"Now, what do you say?" he asked as soon as she had better hold on herself.

"I don't see what good it will do for you to know of my humiliation," said Elisabeth, her stomach in a knot. How had she come to this pass?

"I will be the judge of that," he said in his persuasive voice. "If I am to help you, we must be friends, no? Come now. There may be a solution for your dilemma you are not aware of."

She followed him along the sidewalk to Seventh Avenue, where they reached the waiting brougham. Through her blurred eyes, she saw Franco pitch a cigarette into the street, open the door, and after she and Marco climbed in, fasten the door securely.

"Around the park," said Marco through the open window, and then he raised the glass and strapped it shut.

"Now," he said, "we are in utter privacy. You may rest assured your words will reach no ears but these." He tried to lift her spirits, but saw that was going to be a greater task than he was equipped for.

The carriage rolled past scenery stacked against the back of the yellow brick theater building. After a few moments of silence during which they headed toward Central Park, Elisabeth drew deep breaths and tried to gather her thoughts.

"I suppose I owe you the truth," she finally said when

she was calm enough to speak. "Only you will think me an imbecile, either that, or unworthy of your assistance."

He moved to reach for her hand and then withdrew his own. No matter how odd her circumstances, she was by her own words a married lady, and that prevented any thoughts of intimacy, which from the very first night he had begun to entertain.

"I assure you I will not think you unworthy. If misfortune has befallen you, surely it is not of your own doing. If you do not wish to speak of it, I understand." He gazed at the lovely, distraught figure beside him. "But I am curious."

For her part, Elisabeth began to feel better. Just how she had come to be on such friendly terms with the famous singer was beyond her. That he was now offering to be a confidant would have been amusing if her own confused feelings did not prevent her from feeling anything so lighthearted. But it would be a relief to tell the story to someone, for she had kept it within herself these last two years. She began to speak, the words unfolding of themselves as if by finding an outlet at last, they would not be held back any longer.

"To begin with, I should tell you who I really am."

Marco raised a dark brow and crossed one leg over his knee to listen. "That would be interesting."

She tried to smile and blotted her eyes. "Kendall is my married name. My father is Winston Sloane."

"Ahhh..." At the name of the wealthy banker, Marco released a sigh. "I see. That is, I have read of him in the newspaper."

She gave him an ironic glance. "You probably missed reading about his daughter who is abroad studying music. It was a small item in the society columns, but he managed to keep the news brief."

Marco frowned. "I do not understand."

For a moment her old mischievous spirit showed itself. "And neither do those of our friends who travel to Paris, expecting to see me there, but who find that I have gone on to London, or vice versa. I'm sorry, I do not mean to confuse you."

He gestured that he was already confused.

"It was not easy being the heir to a fortune," she said. "I know perfectly well that a lot of men would be attentive to me on that account. After my coming out, I knew I was not wrong. I had many suitors, but none who I could say I truly loved." She shook her head. "I used to dream that I could meet someone who did not know who I was and who loved me for myself."

She paused to glance out the carriage window as they entered the park. Gas lamps shed a glow on the serpentine drive where they passed a few other equipages, lanterns swaying. Once in the park, Giovanni slowed the team to a walk.

"It is quite a long story," she said, "but for your sake, I will try to make it as brief as possible."

"Take your time," Marco murmured. "I have no evening engagements."

"Three years ago I used to walk to the circulating library twice a week. I had to pass by a fashionable boarding house on Madison Avenue when I went." She paused for a moment recalling the scene. "I became aware that I was the object of attention. My vanity was gratified, and I found it exciting to be noticed by young men I didn't know and who did not know me. It was reckless of course, but I assumed nothing would come of it.

"One day when I was returning home, I was overtaken by a thunderstorm. I set off at a run, and just as I reached this boarding house, I slipped and fell. Before I could recover, one of the young gentlemen came to my assistance. I was unhurt, and as I looked into his face . . ."

She hesitated and glanced guiltily at Marco. Surely she need not explain that his face had later won her heart and ruined her life. She cleared her throat.

Marco nodded in understanding. "Go on."

"He took me inside the boarding house where we sat in the cozy parlor waiting out the storm. He offered to walk me home, but I professed I was all right. I was enjoying the sense of daring at being in a strange place, and not allowing anyone to know who I was. I gave him my Christian name but not my surname, and he did not press me.

"He did walk with me to the corner when the storm was over and begged to see me again. Thus began our many walks, some of which extended to the park. I got away from my father's house on the excuse that I was going to the library. Though I was always chaperoned at night, it was not difficult to go out alone during the day. He too seemed to enjoy the mystery surrounding us, for while we spoke of many things, he did not reveal a great deal about himself either. He told me that he was an engraver. I did not press him for more. But I was enchanted, foolishly so."

She broke off and lowered her head, fearing she could not go on.

Marco waited silently, brooding out the window. He

was intrigued by the story, drawn into the drama of it, but at the same time he was aware of the great struggle going on in the girl beside him. Not unfamiliar with life's many storms, he felt a great empathy toward her. And while he did not want her to speak of anything that would upset her, his own curiosity and concern drove him to remain silent and listen. Though what could be gained by it, he was not sure.

Elisabeth finally went on. "I'm afraid I was rather a maverick. I felt too suffocated by my strict upbringing." She gave a little ironic laugh. "My mother used to place a rod down my dress to make me sit up straight while I did my lessons."

She looked at Marco. "My whole life was strict regimentation, even up to the day of my coming out. This was my way of running away." She shook her head.

"It was not long before he declared his love for me. I was girlishly infatuated, and I believed him. He asked to call on me at home, but I told him it was better not to do that because I knew that my father would never allow me to see this man because he was not from my own social class. Moreover, I knew that if I admitted to having gone this far, I would be punished in the extreme.

"I must have been mad, but I wanted to go on seeing him. We became engaged, and finally my fiancé insisted on meeting my father. I warned him the interview would be a stormy one, but he nevertheless was determined to prove his honor by meeting my parent.

"It turned out as I knew it would. I brought the man home and announced rather suddenly that we were engaged to be married. My father threw him out of the house and forbade me to ever see him again. I was more than ever estranged from my father and rebellious at the life he expected me to lead, all the moreso after my mother died. It was almost as if I were to be her replacement."

Elisabeth shook her head. "But I was selfish. We contrived to send messages back and forth, my young man paced up and down in front of my house waiting until I would come out and speak to him, and one night I did sneak out of the house." She lowered her lids, looking into the past.

"I honestly believe I simply wanted to tell him goodbye, for even I was able to see how untenable our situation was. But the minute I was in his presence, his powers of persuasion overcame me. He took my arm and urged me to come with him. So overcome was I at being with him again, that I followed. We went into a house where the lady of the house led me into the parlor. To my surprise a clergyman waited there, prepared to marry us."

Marco lifted his brows, gazing directly at her now, but still he said nothing, wondering where her tale would go.

"My fiancé gazed into my eyes and begged me to marry him on the spot. Without reference to reason, I agreed, for here at last might be a way to escape the bonds I felt imposed upon me by my strict father and by society's rules, which I deplored.

"The clergyman spoke the solemn words and we were made man and wife. The mistress of the house insisted that I remain with her that night, and so I did. To my great surprise, my husband said he had business to attend to and would be away that night, returning in the morning. After kissing me tenderly, he left me alone. I could not face my father, but sent a letter saying that I was married and that he need not worry about me. I would return for my things when we decided where to settle. It was not until late the next morning that my husband returned, saying only that he had been to work all night. Unfortunately, his shift had changed and it would remain so for some time.

"Again the next evening he left before I retired. The next day I sent a note asking my maid to bring me my things. When she appeared she relayed to me the great distress I had caused my father. My euphoria had worn off enough for me to feel guilty, and I wrote him a long letter, entreating him to forgive me. I wanted to see him, but was fearful of his wrath.

"I did return home that day and found my father greatly disturbed. It is hard to describe the emotions that passed between us." She sighed.

Marco shifted toward her, his own feelings wrung by the story she was telling. But he was afraid to break the spell. She continued without his urging.

"Both our hearts were broken, and I knew that my father and I were irreconcilable. What I had done was unforgivable, and I would be banished from the society I did not care two straws for. When my husband came for me the next morning, my father would not even see him. We settled in our own rooms in a pleasant boarding house, and I became used to my nightly desertion.

"But one night I could stand it no longer. I was lonely, living a strange life, and I was determined to discover where my husband went to work and how he passed his nights. I put on my cloak and followed him.

He took no measures to prevent me keeping up with him, indeed he had no suspicion. He turned into one street after another and finally went onto the ferry that crossed the East river to Ward's Island where stands the prison and the hospital.

"You can imagine my extreme agitation as I watched the ferry cross. There could be no mistake, my husband was bound either for the prison or the hospital.

"The next night I contrived to pull a hood about my face and again followed. This time I got onto the ferry, keeping out of my husband's sight. When the passengers disembarked, I managed to follow him right to a side gate of the prison.

"My discovery sent me into an abyss from which I never imagined I could extricate myself. I thought of throwing myself in the river, but I returned on the ferry and wandered wildly about the streets for some time. I believe that night I knew what madness was. But somehow I ended up back at our rooms to await my husband in the morning. There was a slim chance that there was an explanation. Perhaps he worked at the prison. But if that were so, why did he not tell me at the first? Why this secrecy?"

Elisabeth continued in a monotone, looking straight ahead, with no awareness of where the carriage was going, only spinning out her tale to the end.

"The next morning when he returned, I questioned him about his work, but he again refused a satisfactory answer. Shortly thereafter, he did not return. I had no choice but to go home to my father, who was still angry with me. I feared what I had to say would be the death of him, but after several weeks under his roof, I told him the truth. With tears in his eyes to match mine, he told me he would quietly make inquiries.

"Needless to say, our lives were miserable. We let our acquaintances know that we were ill and did not go out. A trusted attorney did make inquiries and brought the news to my father that my husband did not work at the prison, he was in fact a prisoner who had been sentenced as a result of his crimes as a forger. He had bribed the turnkey to let him out to be with me during the day if he promised to return at night. When the jailer was replaced, my husband could no longer go out."

She glanced quickly at Marco, wondering if he too were so shocked he would stop the carriage and let her out, but he merely sat, listening thoughtfully. She hurried to finish the story.

"My father and I were even more shocked. I was so ashamed of what I had done and the strain between my father and me was so great that I left his house once again and took the rooms in the boarding house which you have seen. I am a good seamstress and being drawn to the theater, I found work making costumes. Always before, those who surrounded me thought of the theater as a place where society went on evenings out. But to work in the theater is not something a member of my class does."

She shrugged ironically. "But what I had done already would have gotten me ostracized. In an odd way, moving out of my father's house allowed me to pursue something I had always dreamed about. To see if my illusions remained once I was confronted with the actual life of the theater. And so my life has been for the last two years. My father told our friends that I had gone abroad to study music, and the story has been perpetuated. As to my husband's sentence, I have heard nothing in six months."

Her story had come to an end, and she sat silently as the coach rolled past Cleopatra's needle, the obelisk that had been brought from Egypt. Through the trees beside the monument, the cream-colored building that housed the Metropolitan Museum of Art was visible by the light of the street lamps.

Marco gazed thoughtfully in front of him. Her story had sobered him more than he would have thought possible. He wanted to say something, tell her that his own life had been full of trials and tribulations, that surely there was a happy ending in sight, but he could not find the words. He shifted his weight awkwardly and looked out the window on his side.

They drove slowly past the Great Lawn, and Giovanni turned the carriage onto the transverse road that would take them across the park and down the west drive. As Marco watched single leaves drift to the ground in the lamplight like moths, he reached without looking for Elisabeth's hand. She accepted his grasp for she perceived his meaning before he spoke.

"Thank you for satisfying my curiosity," he said. "One does not confide matters lightly. I can offer only friendship. If I can help you in any way, please do not hesitate to ask."

She said nothing for some moments, conscious of his warm grasp, until the awkwardness of it, made her slowly pull her hand away. He loosened his grip.

"It does me good to reveal the story," she said. "I have spoken to no one about it except Lettice."

"Who?"

"My maid. That is, she was my maid. She begged to

come with me when I left home, but I insisted she find employment elsewhere. I was determined to pay my own way, and I was suddenly in the position of not being able to afford a maid. And I was going to a life she would not be used to. My father arranged for her to assume a position in Boston after that."

"All very well thought out," Marco said. "It would seem that you have a talent for constructing plots as well as aspiring to act them out."

She met his tone of irony with one of her own. "I have been accused of willfulness, recklessness, of saying the wrong thing at the wrong time, and overdramatizing in my own life. My character flaws have been my own undoing."

"In another person they might have been worse," he said seriously. "Thank heaven you did not end by throwing yourself in the river that night."

Her heart missed a beat. He did not know what he was saying. For the first time since the awful debacle, someone was glad she was alive. Her throat constricted.

She had isolated herself to such an extent she had forgotten what it was like to share thoughts and feelings with anyone. The people she knew at the boarding house were nice enough, but she told them only a carefully constructed background and consequently did not reveal her true self to them. Sometimes she thought she would slip up. Of late, her real self was coming close to the surface again in small ways—an opinion, a judgement, thoughts that sprang from the heart. But even in these she must always be careful, lest the truth somehow be revealed by her words or manners.

They proceeded past the lake and the Sheep's

Meadow with no more words spoken. As they approached the Grand Circle at the bottom of the park, Marco rapped on the little window behind them.

"We will take Miss Kendall home now," he instructed.

Then he settled back in his seat again. Being back in the thick of traffic as they drove down Broadway eased Marco's mind back into the world of reality in which he lived, loved and worked.

"We must not forget our appointment next Friday," he said.

"No, of course."

Elisabeth too, was slowly pulling herself from the nightmare her life had been to the present reality, which was tolerable. The willfulness that had led her astray was perhaps keeping her alive now. That and losing herself in music. To contemplate singing for a reputable teacher set her stomach a-twitter. Thank goodness she had a few days to practice.

"I will be ready," she said with emphasis.

Marco was glad to hear the enthusiasm creep back into her voice. His heart warmed to the unusual girl with the very unusual story.

Then again, he mused, as he looked out at the commercial district they passed, perhaps not so unusual in this city where there must be a thousand other stories like it.

Marco dropped Elisabeth off at the corner near her house. This time he remained in the brougham so as not to arouse Mrs. Runkewich's suspicions. As he watched her walk down the street, her head lifted proudly, or perhaps stubbornly, he bade Giovanni turn the coach around and head for the Ansonia Hotel on the Upper West Side where he had rooms.

When she reached the house, Elisabeth let herself in and then entered the parlor. There was no one there, and she seated herself at the upright piano. As she so often did just to find an outlet for her feelings, she ran her fingers across the keys and then rummaged about the sheet music on the piano until she found the pieces she liked to play so well.

Before long the absent phrases her fingers had been picking out turned into a familiar introduction, and she began to sing naturally, sweetly, with a warmth that made those who heard her stop and listen.

Indeed that was what occurred. Across the hall, Mrs. Runkewich opened her door a crack to catch the strains coming from the parlor. Upstairs, Margaret Houghteling was just coming down, and she paused, a smile on her face, to sit on the stairs and listen. Other doors in the boarding house opened one by one. For Elisabeth was singing. And that was something they all loved.

Sometimes she sang only one to two songs and then went about her business, but other times, like this evening, she lost herself in music, and then much to the delight of her fellow boarders, all except for Mr. Barnhill, song after song pealed from the crowded parlor. An operatic aria was followed by "After the Ball Was Over," sung in such heartrending tones that Margaret wiped away a tear. Then came "The Band Played On," "Aura Lee," and other favorites. Then she turned to the Italian melody, "Back to Sorrento," and finally came back to opera again.

Mrs. Hallibrand, a guest in the rooms of the Misses York turned to Anne and inquired, "Who, pray tell is that?"

"Why that's the Kendall girl," said Anne. "She lives on the third floor. Lovely girl, she is. Very proper even if she does work at the theater."

"My goodness, does she sing in the chorus?" asked Mrs. Hallibrand, impressed by the flexibility of the pure, round voice with the glorious high notes.

"Why no," answered Selma. "She is a seamstress. Mistress of the wardrobe, I believe."

"I see," came the reply of Mrs. Hallibrand. "A pity her talent is being wasted. But if she's genteel, it would never occur to her to sing on the stage."

Chapter Five

Even Elisabeth's boardinghouse acquaintances noticed how much more reserved she was that week. She went to the opera house each day, came home and if it were not too late, vocalised and practiced in the parlor. One did not pry into others' affairs in boarding house life. Therein lay the difference from living with a family. While the dinner table offered a chance to chat and gossip, one's personal affairs were one's own business. If one sought out a confidante to exchange personal thoughts, one's own rooms became the scene for such a tête-à-tête.

Then the day before Elisabeth was scheduled to meet Professor Schlut, Mrs. Runkewich hobbled up three flights of stairs and knocked on her door.

When she opened her door, the harried landlady informed her that she had a caller and handed Elisabeth a small white card. Lindsay Whitehurst, attorney-at-law.

"Thank you, Mrs. Runkewich. I'll be right down."

Mrs. Runkewich nodded, huffed and puffed and

headed for the stairs. What a lawyer was doing calling on the girl, she had no idea. She hoped they'd leave the parlor door ajar. If they didn't she might have to resort to eavesdropping from the basement.

She'd left the cover off the old speaking tubes that had been installed in the house when it was built. The speaking tube was hidden by curtains in the parlor, of course, and people usually didn't notice it. All the tubes connected with the servants dining room, or what used to be the servants' dining room. Now Mrs. Runkewich only had two girls who came in to help her, and they only worked days, so the servants' dining room was only used for their lunch and tea.

Elisabeth nervously smoothed her hair and checked her appearance in her striped grosgrain with bands of jet embroidery. Lindsay Whitehurst could only mean one thing—news about her husband.

She entered the parlor and shut the door firmly behind her. Mr. Whitehurst was rocking on his heels and gazing out the front window which looked at the park across the street. He turned when Elisabeth entered. He was dressed in double-breasted frock coat with silk lapels and a broad knotted tie. His hair was parted in the middle, and a monocle hung from a chain attached to his pocket.

"Good morning, Mr. Whitehurst," she said, extending her hand.

He gave it a light grasp and nodded his head. "Miss Sloane, I am glad to find you looking well."

The lawyer always used her maiden name. He had been hired originally by her father and so thought of Elisabeth as a Sloane in spite of the nature of the matter he had been hired to look into.

"Thank you. Please sit down," she said.

They both took seats on the faded crimson upholstered sofa with its thick fringe skirt. Their knees angled so that they nearly faced each other.

Lindsay wasted no time. "I have news of your husband."

Elisabeth glanced away. "Yes?"

"He was to be removed to a federal prison with minimum security, but the ship carrying the prisoners foundered in a storm off the coast of North Carolina. Your husband was not among the survivors who were picked up."

Her head jerked toward him. "Do you mean he has drowned?"

"We cannot be sure. He may have used the opportunity to escape. The search for remains continues of course. But I came to warn you as quickly as possible."

Her heart flew to her breast. "If he is alive, do you mean he might try to find me?"

"It's possible. I thought you should be prepared."

Elisabeth rose and paced across the floral patterned rug. "He doesn't know where I live."

"That's true. But he might trace you here if your previous landlady knew where you were going. He also might contact your father."

Elisabeth turned to face him with an even more horrified stare. "My father would never receive him."

"Then perhaps you are safe. That is, if you do not wish to be discovered."

"I do not."

She turned her back for a moment, clasping her hands together. Then she turned and faced the lawyer, her head erect. However, her trembling lips gave away her emotion when she spoke.

"Thank you for telling me of this complication."

He cocked his head in a professional manner. Lindsay Whitehurst always maintained a neutral expression, never condemning nor approving his clients' comments. It helped him handle many a sticky situation in a businesslike manner.

She took a few paces across the room. "As you know," she said after a moment, "I wanted to be free of my husband. However, I could not further embarrass my father with the publicity divorce proceedings would bring."

"I understand your predicament," the lawyer said soberly.

"You'll keep me informed of any news?" she asked, straining to remain composed.

Lindsay rose. "Of course. And if you should have any word, please notify me at once. I have written my home address on the back of the card you have. Should you need to send a message after business hours, do not hesitate."

"Thank you." Though stunned by the news, she was glad she had heard it from Lindsay and no one else. He was completely circumspect.

She kept her spine straight as she saw him to the door. It occurred to her to tell him of her good luck in getting an audition with a renowned voice teacher, and she did so.

Lindsay looked thoughtful as he listened. Then he nodded. "And this is the endeavor you wish to embark upon?"

"Yes, if he will take me."

"Very good. I wish you good luck with it then."

When she had closed the front door, she hurried up the stairs. In her rooms, she seized her coat and hat and ran back downstairs. She needed to get out of the house for a long walk. She needed to think.

Once on the street she turned west and walked uptown. The residential street was calm, peaceful, unlike the emotions that knotted in Elisabeth's stomach. For several blocks she did not think at all. The rhythmic action of walking along the wide sidewalk beside wrought iron stair rails opening onto steps leading to high stoops, the sunny fall day, and the long stretch of houses, hotels, clubs, and churches helped release her attention. Gradually, she was able to consider the possibilities Lindsay Whitehurst had just placed before her.

She stopped at the corner of Thirty-fourth Street to wait for traffic to pass. The marbled exterior of the four-story Stewart mansion rose at the northwest corner. North of Thirty-fourth Street, a few lettered signs and striped awnings announced the presence of small shops and businesses. Ladies bustled up and down the street on errands, some pushing strollers, while delivery carts rolled past. Life proceeded at its normal pace, for all but Elisabeth.

She turned into a tea shop and took a seat by the window. A waitress served her a steaming cup of tea and a bun. The ritual of sipping tea and nibbling on a bun helped settle Elisabeth's agitation, and staring out at the street helped her arrange her thoughts.

The sins of the past weighed heavily. But she could not forget that tomorrow she was going to actually sing for Professor Schlut. If he accepted her as a student, she wanted more than anything to study music with him. With her husband safely in prison there had been no obstacle between Elisabeth and her chosen work. Of course she realized that if she actually were talented enough to have a career, there would be publicity and her real identity would come out. But she was a long way from that possibility.

She knew it was wrong to hope that her husband had drowned in the storm, and prayed silently for forgiveness for such thoughts. She had long since stopped feeling anything but pity for the man. He had offered excitement, the opportunity to rebel, but she never loved him. She had for so long stuffed the incident of her unfortunate marriage in the back of her mind that it seemed like another lifetime now. She had changed in the two years since then.

"More tea?" The waitress appeared smiling beside Elisabeth.

"Yes, thank you."

The waitress poured more hot liquid and then set the pot on the table in front of Elisabeth so she could help herself.

Elisabeth wrapped her hands around the full cup for warmth. The secrets she had hidden so well from everyone including herself must now be confronted. She needed a way out. She could no longer reside in the limbo she had constructed for herself.

By the time she finished her tea and bun, she knew what she would do. She would go into one of the nearby churches and sit quietly for a while. Then she would try to stop hoping that her husband was dead. She did not want to face hell for such thoughts. And she would pray for the strength to free herself from him if he were found and for a way to do it without dragging her family's name through the newspapers.

For though she was weighted with the burden of the past and unsure what the future would hold, she knew that she had to face it alone. The past must be put to rest somehow.

"Aha," said Professor Theodore Schlut, the kindly looking music teacher, as he came forward to take Elisabeth's hand. "So this is your protégé."

She stood beside Marco in the professor's sunny studio in the two-year-old Carnegie Hall, in which studios like this one offered quarters to musicians who wished to live or work near the beehive of activity of the new concert hall.

Professor Schlut wore a beard and moustache and had a very slight stoop of the shoulders. He examined her through a pair of pince-nez glasses which he then removed and put in the pocket of his drab green jacket. He smiled at Elisabeth and then at Marco, who stood behind and to the right of her and had just made the introductions.

Marco nodded. "We are most grateful for your time."

A large Afghan hound who lay on a plaid blanket in one corner, sat up and eyed the newcomers with his black eyes.

"That is my dog, Governor Worthy. I—er, um—hope you don't mind. He can wait in the sitting room, if you would prefer."

"I don't mind," said Elisabeth, smiling slightly. At least she would have an audience, one with long thick hair, pointed muzzle, and drooping ears.

Governor Worthy seemed to understand that he was going to be allowed to stay, and after turning in a circle several times, lay back down on the plaid blanket, placing his long muzzle between his paws.

Marco had been arranging his words. He did not want to admit to the professor that he had never actually heard Elisabeth sing, for then the debonair older man might think the wrong thing. Indeed, just how he came to be bringing Elisabeth here, Marco was not at all sure. But he had a habit of taking his cues from life and not questioning those things that seemed meant to be. Her story had touched him and aroused his undaunted optimism in the face of having had to overcome many of his own trials. Beyond the fact that he wanted to help the girl he did not question his motives.

"And what have you chosen to sing today?"

Professor Schlut led Elisabeth to the shiny grand piano which filled half the room. She shyly handed him her music, which he looked at through the pince-nez glasses which he replaced on the bridge of his nose again.

"I've brought two of my favorite pieces." She smiled hesitantly. "I've sung these since I was a girl."

"Well, well. Let us see what we have."

He flipped his coattail over the piano bench and took a seat. Elisabeth stood in the crook of the piano, grasping it with one hand for support. She tried to concentrate on what she was about to do, but the butterflies in her stomach sent every thought flying from her mind.

Marco, realizing the importance of the occasion,

gave her a reassuring smile and then started for the door.

"I will wait in the next room," he said.

"No need for that," said Professor Schlut absently as he opened the first page of music.

But Marco softly opened the door and slipped through, understanding Elisabeth's nervousness and feeling that though he himself was curious as to the sound of her voice, it would be better for her to direct her efforts toward pleasing Professor Schlut. As it was, he could still hear through the closed door to the sitting room.

When Professor Schlut began to play, his whole being was transformed into one of feeling and energy. As his hands glided over the keyboard, even his shoulders seemed to throw off their slope.

Elisabeth began "Some Day He'll Come," from *Madame Butterfly* in Italian, and after the first few notes her voice settled into the beautiful and sad melody. Professor Schlut's fingers caressed the ivory keys in accompaniment to Elisabeth's voice, which conveyed all the tenderness, love, and longing that poor Butterfly expressed in the song of lost love. Elisabeth was able to lose herself in Butterfly's longing, and even the dog in the corner gazed sadly as if understanding poor Butterfly's dilemma.

On the other side of the door, Marco smiled as he heard the rapturous tones. For a moment he too was transported. Standing in the studio's cluttered sitting room, listening to the muted tones on the other side of the thick oak door, Marco's heart lifted. He hummed softly in harmony to himself and was hard put to remain in the sitting room as the professor's accompaniment brought the piece to its heartrending close.

"She can sing," Marco breathed to himself, pleased that he could take credit for discovering her. And then he paced back and forth on the worn fringed rug.

"Very nice," said Professor Schlut to Elisabeth on the other side of the door. Beyond that he would not commit, but shuffled the music around so that he could play the introductory chords of another piece. "Your Italian needs a little work, but you have a natural inclination for phrasing."

Elisabeth felt a small surge of encouragement. Surely he would not say anything complimentary at all unless he meant it, she told herself. But it was too soon to hope. She turned her attention to the next piece, the beautiful aria sung by Lauretta in the comic opera *Gianni Schicchi*.

Pouring herself in the heartfelt aria wherein Lauretta begs her father to help her lover's family, Elisabeth's voice easily pealed out the infectious melody. At the aria's end, she glanced at Professor Schlut, who again arranged music.

He nodded and murmured acknowledgement, but said nothing more. Governor Worthy thumped his tail twice on the blanket, and she accepted that as the only praise that was forthcoming.

To finish the audition she had chosen to sing "I'm Called Little Buttercup," from the operetta, *H.M.S. Pinafore*. At the conclusion of the gay tune, Marco could no longer contain himself but burst into the room and stood applauding.

Elisabeth blushed and the professor removed his hands from the keyboard. Marco crossed the room and sang the first few bars of a duet from the same operetta.

Elisabeth could not help but laugh, and Professor Schlut picked up the accompaniment. She could do no less than join in. Not knowing the duet from memory, she hurried around the piano, rescued the music, which Professor Schlut had knocked off in his haste to turn to the right page and found the piece.

The three of them had a gay time and finally got the duet going. Marco strolled about the studio doing his part and Elisabeth could not help but do the same. She quickly fell into the role as the two of them played out the scene. Elisabeth forgot all else, giving herself to the role completely and responding to Marco's actions as a young seaman who plans to elope with his beloved. At the conclusion the professor applauded and Elisabeth laughingly accepted Marco's accolade as he grasped her hands and bowed.

"Excellent choice of music," Marco said, when their laughter had subsided. "I have wanted to sing the role of Ralph for some time now and have not had the opportunity. Ah, but I am sorry for the intrusion. You will have things to discuss with the professor." And he squeezed her hand and offered a wink of encouragement.

"We shan't be long, Marco," said the professor. And he shooed the enthusiastic tenor back out of the room.

Elisabeth smiled to herself. She was having far too much fun. But the nerves she had had at the start had given way to the pure joy of making music. Her heart was dancing with excitement, and she needed to sober herself for what the professor might say.

He crossed the room to shut the door behind Marco, who was banished again to the sitting room. Then the professor returned to the piano and sat on the bench, though he did not place his hands on the keyboard. He adjusted his glasses and cleared his throat.

"You have potential," he said, and Elisabeth allowed herself to breathe. "Luckily Marco brought you to me before some other teacher got ahold of you and ruined you. Your voice has natural flexibility. But we must proceed carefully, only studying roles that are right for your young and as yet undeveloped voice. If you are prepared to work very hard and do exactly what I say, I believe I can help you."

"Oh Professor, thank you." She nearly choked on her words. It was more than she expected to hear. "I do not know what to say."

"No need to say anything," he continued, brushing his palms together. "We must simply make arrangements for your lessons. Luckily I have an opening just now. We can begin next week at this time if that suits you."

"Oh yes, only . . ." the radiance on her face faded as she considered the reality. "I'm afraid my salary from the theater is meager. I have only enough money saved for a few lessons. After that I would have to quit, and perhaps it is better not to start until I can continue and progress as long as need be."

He gave her a benevolent smile. "I understand. However, there is no need for payment." He cleared his throat. "An anonymous party has arranged payment. You have an 'angel' as it is known in the theater. So you see, the fees have already been taken care of."

Elisabeth stared at him open mouthed. "I have an angel?" She was well aware of what that meant. A patron who believed in her potential had offered to pay for the lessons. But her surprise was followed with the realization that the angel could be no one else but Marco. Who else had expressed such interest in helping her?

She shut her mouth and straightened her shoulders. "I am flattered, but I could not possibly accept."

Professor Schlut merely blinked at her. "And may I ask why not?"

"I . . . I could not accept help from an anonymous sponsor without knowing why the help was offered."

"The patron must remain anonymous." The professor shrugged. "If I were you, my dear, I would think it over. The opportunity may not come again."

Her gaze fell. "Yes, I know." She gave a little shake of the head, thinking of Marco. "But it would not be right." She raised her head. "However, if my own circumstances change, may I call on you again? It would mean a great deal to be able to study."

He nodded. "Of course."

He got up from the piano, and Elisabeth knew she must not take up any more of the busy man's time. She extended her hand.

"Thank you, Professor. I cannot express my appreciation enough."

He bowed over her hand. "You are most welcome. Think about the little, er, arrangement. You should not waste your talent. But you must begin work before it is too late. There are other ambitious students who will fill the roles you wish to attain if you wait too long."

She understood his meaning. "Yes, I will give it serious thought. Thank you."

The dog rose as if it understood that the audition was over. Professor Schlut patted the Afghan's head. "Yes, yes, I know Governor. It is time for our walk."

And she turned and walked to the door. Opening it, she found Marco looking at a collection of photographs, humming to himself. He turned and looked at her hopefully. She said nothing, but nodded, and he crossed the room to open the door for her.

They passed down a long hallway, their footsteps echoing on the wood floor, then they waited before the Florentine grillwork that enclosed the lift. Though she knew Marco was curious as to what had passed between the professor and herself, she said nothing until the elevator whined to a stop before them. Marco opened the gate, and they stepped into the lift. It jolted and then moved downward, making several stops to allow others to get on.

It was not until they reached ground level and followed the others into the tiny vestibule and finally out the side door of the hall and onto the sidewalk that Marco spoke.

"Well?" he asked as they took a few steps down the sidewalk, pausing before a large poster advertisement on the side of the building.

Elisabeth lifted her head. "He said I had potential, and that if I were prepared to work very hard, I should study."

Marco clapped his hands together. "That is wonderful!"

"Only I cannot afford more than a few lessons just now. We agreed that it was better not to start until I could continue." She shook her head. "So I cannot start."

She dared not look Marco in the eye, presuming he was the "angel," who had offered to pay for the lessons. She was flattered by his interest, but knew that accepting would only mean one thing. She could not further compromise her reputation by becoming obligated to a man so obviously attractive. She was already dangerously susceptible to his charms. There was only one place accepting such a favor could lead, and she was not about to let that happen.

His reaction to her decision was sober. "I see," was all he said.

They strolled along Seventh Avenue, keeping out of the way of passersby who hurried to appointments or into one of the chop houses that served the nearby theater and business district.

Marco had many questions, but he kept them to himself. He had done what he could.

"Well," he said carefully. "Perhaps there will be a way. May I give you a lift? Franco and Giovanni have no doubt done something with my carriage."

"I believe I'll walk," said Elisabeth.

He lifted his dark brows curiously. "Such a great distance?"

"I am used to long walks. I enjoy the exercise."

He grinned. "Well, then, it is a fine day. If you have your mind made up."

She found it hard to gaze into the handsome face with the teasing eyes. "Thank you for arranging the audition. It was more than I could have hoped for."

Marco waved it away, still glancing around wondering where the carriage had gone. "No trouble. Every aspiring artist deserves at least to be heard."

He took her hand and gave it a light squeeze. "Then I will see you at the theater, perhaps this very day."

She returned the handshake. "Yes, later today."

As they stood chatting, they saw Professor Schlut

emerge from the side door of Carnegie Hall with Governor Worthy on a long leash.

"Ah, there goes the professor," said Marco. "Perhaps I will accompany him on his walk to the park until I can find my conveyance. Alas, perhaps Franco has gone off chasing a skirt and I too, shall have to walk home." He was still chuckling as he gave Elisabeth a wave and left her.

Turning her back on him and joining the flow of traffic down Seventh Avenue, Elisabeth inhaled a deep breath. Well, she had had her audition. But like other dreams, it had come to nothing. There might be a way to pay for the lessons, though, if she thought about it. There might be. To let the opportunity completely slip through her fingers would be madness. She had so little to hang onto in her odd little life at present, there must be a way to make this happen.

The stubborn dreamer in her that had always refused to take no for an answer was already busy hatching a scheme.

Chapter Six

Elisabeth moved down the row of costumes hung on the rolling rack in the wardrobe chamber, ready to be taken downstairs tomorrow. There was no doubt about it, she realized, there was a costume missing.

The door opened and young Julius tumbled in. "There you are, Miss Kendall. Mr. Abbey wants to see you in his office, says to come right away."

Elisabeth felt surprised. She was rarely summoned to the managers' office. When the harried theater managers had things to say to her it was usually in the form of orders called out to her backstage or on the stairwells. As long as the costume department was running smoothly, Henry Abbey and Maurice Grau had little need to interfere. And when they did, they usually discussed matters with Elisabeth's superior, Mrs. DeKoven.

"I'll be right there. Thank you, Julius."

The boy uncrumpled the cap he held in his hands and placed it on his tousled head. His message delivered, he flung open the door and ran back into the hall.

Elisabeth hung up the costume she had been holding in her arms and followed more slowly.

The managers' office was down one floor on the Thirty-ninth Street side. She hurried down the stairs, along the hallway and rounded the corner. Knocking on the newly painted door, she was admitted by Mr. Abbey's associate, Maurice Grau.

"Ah, Miss Kendall. Thank you for being prompt," said Maurice, a soft-spoken man with round face and curly hair. Of the two managers, Maurice Grau was the one who employed the most diplomacy in putting people at their ease.

"Mr. Abbey wants to see me?" said Elisabeth, coming into the anteroom as Maurice closed the door behind her.

"Er, hem, yes. He does. Come with me please." He led the way through a second door.

The office shared by the two managers was brightly lit by large lead-paned glass windows facing downtown. Here the two managers' desks were cluttered with papers, ink wells, and ledgers, and the walls were covered with artists' photographs.

Henry Abbey was a compact, energetic man with well-trimmed beard and moustache. His eyes had a way of penetrating from across the room, and they did so now as Elisabeth took a hesitant step toward his desk.

He looked up from the contract over which he had been frowning. "Ah, yes, Miss Kendall."

Elisabeth never wore a wedding band and had never corrected the impression at the opera that she was unmarried.

"You wanted to see me?"

He transferred his frown from the paper to her. "I'm afraid there is a problem in the costume department that requires our questioning you."

A tremor crawled up her spine, but she beat him to it. "If you mean the missing costume, I just became aware of that while going over the list for tomorrow night."

"Hmmm," growled Abbey. "And have you any idea where it is?"

"No sir," she said. "I was just going to execute a search when you sent for me. Perhaps the chorus member who wears the costume has borrowed it."

"I assure you that is not the case."

Elisabeth could not help but glance at the more sympathetic Mr. Grau, who stood behind his desk with a pained look in his eyes. Slowly Elisabeth realized what they were accusing her of, and her astonishment was so great she merely stared at Mr. Abbey.

"A missing costume is a serious matter, Miss Kendall. Have you no other explanation for it?"

"As I said, it has only now come to my notice. Surely it will turn up. I assure you I will look for it in every conceivable place."

Suddenly tiredness overshadowed Mr. Abbey's glower. "If the costume is not found by the end of today, we will have to replace it. Mrs. DeKoven is already looking into the material. I hope it doesn't come to that. We can't afford this type of loss."

"I understand, Mr. Abbey," she said, standing stiffly. Clearly she was being held responsible as wardrobe mistress. "I will see that it does not happen again."

"I hope so, Miss Kendall," said Abbey. "I hope so. That is all."

She turned quickly and Maurice hastened to hold the door for her. In the anteroom, he tried to give her a comforting word.

"I hope you find the costume, my dear," he said, holding the outer door for her as well. "It does no good to have my colleague so upset. And of course the expense of even one costume . . ."

He let it hang, but she appreciated his concern. "I understand, and I hope you have no more cause for worry. I shall try to ascertain what has happened to the gown right away."

He bid her goodbye and shut the door behind her. In the hallway, Elisabeth let out a deep sigh. A missing costume? The first thing would be to speak to Mrs. DeKoven and see what she thought.

She stopped in the middle of the hallway as the thought struck her that someone might have seen her holding up the *Faust* costume to herself the other night. Now that the chorus costume was missing, perhaps the witness suggested to Mr. Abbey that she had taken it. A long breath escaped her lips. It was ridiculous to suppose that she might steal a costume. For what purpose? And yet she knew that jealousy and backbiting sometimes ran through the company, and someone might have started a rumor to that effect. The best thing to do would be to nip it in the bud.

She remembered that Marco had seen her playing with the costume, but surely he would not say anything to the management about that. She dismissed the thought.

She found Mrs. DeKoven leaning over the work table where she was unrolling a bolt of material for the very costume in question. There was no one else in the workroom when Elisabeth entered. The large windows shed generous light into the room, but Elisabeth did not feel as sunny as the cheerful atmosphere of the workroom.

Elisabeth cleared her throat. "I've just been to see Mr. Abbey. Is that material to replace the missing costume?"

"That it is," nodded the older seamstress. "That is, if we don't find the other one."

Elisabeth threw up her hands. "I cannot imagine what happened to it. I told Mr. Abbey I would instigate a thorough search."

Mrs. DeKoven finished rolling out the shiny material and straightened. Her severe expression held no malice but rather the look of someone who had accepted the fact that she was overworked and spared no time or energy for anyone who did not help in her arena.

"It's not the first time," she said.

"What do you mean?"

"Last spring one of the Egyptian costumes went missing. Fortunately, the size of the chorus had been reduced, and the costume was not needed."

Elisabeth gasped. "Why did no one mention it to me then?"

"Because, as I said, the costume was not needed. You inventoried only the costumes that were actually used."

It was quite clear to Elisabeth that Mrs. DeKoven's words conveyed more than their literal meaning. The fact that two such incidents had taken place under Elisabeth's very nose was disconcerting. A panic threatened to overtake her, and she leaned on the worktable for support. Thinking of no response for the missing Egyptian costume, she swallowed.

"I'll start looking right now. I hope you won't have to sew up another one."

Elisabeth spent the rest of the day combing through the wardrobe chambers above the work room. She hunted through all the costumes, in every closet, under the racks in case it had fallen, and in every nook and cranny, moving crates of masks, feather boas and petticoats. The missing costume was nowhere to be found.

After several hours of concentrated effort, she sank onto a crate and put her head in her hands. Her agitation had not lessened, and by this time, it would be assumed that the costume was not going to turn up. Mrs. DeKoven would be cutting out the new one.

Guilt weighed on Elisabeth, even though she was not the culprit. Still, she felt responsible, and the fact that the earlier missing Egyptian costume had never been found made her even more uneasy. Had Mrs. DeKoven been protecting her and therefore never mentioned it to her? Or had she simply been too busy to bother with a missing costume that wasn't needed anyway.

The hour was late, and she would have to give up her search. Her stomach rumbled, and it would soon be time to go home for dinner at Mrs. Runkewich's table. At least tonight's costumes were in their places and all accounted for. Or were they? She decided to check them before she left.

She turned out the light in the wardrobe chamber and went down to the chorus room. There she counted all the costumes. At the end of the rack she let out a nervous sigh. All seemed to be accounted for. Then she checked the principals' dressing rooms where everything seemed to be in order.

Then she went to the green room where the chorus and dancers would wait for their cues later this evening. She checked under and behind the sofas to see if anything had been left. The room was in order. Just as she was pulling the door shut behind her, she heard Marco's distinctive voice warming up on a melody in his dressing room. She wasn't in the mood to speak to him and so started down the passage the other way.

But as she turned her back, the voice only echoed out into the hall, and the melody broke off. Feeling his glance on her, she could not simply run away. She half-turned and nodded.

"Elisabeth," he said, coming toward her. He was dressed in a great coat with a white scarf flowing around his neck.

"Good evening," she said distractedly.

For a moment they stared awkwardly at each other, and then he took her elbow and guided her down the passage toward the stage door.

"I am glad to see you," he said. "I had wanted to speak to you."

"Oh, I see. I'm afraid I've been busy."

"No doubt." He took a closer look and saw the agitation in her eyes.

"Is something wrong?"

She drew in a breath to answer and then bit her lip.

Giving a quick little nod, she said, "A costume's missing. I'm being blamed."

Marco's face darkened. His lips pressed into a firm line and his brows narrowed into a frown of concern. "Tell me about it," he said evenly.

"A chorus costume," she said quietly. "Mrs. DeKoven's had to make another one for tomorrow night. I looked everywhere, but I can't find it."

"What does it look like? What color was it?" asked Marco.

His question surprised her. "Why, it's a dress for one of the ladies in the chorus. Cream color with yellows and gold. But I don't see . . ."

Marco pulled her into a corner and lowered his voice. "It might be important. Gold, you say?"

"Well, it had gold on it. Gold braid trim."

He dropped her arm and stared straight ahead. Then he shook his head as if clearing cobwebs. He looked down at her.

"I didn't take it," she said, tired and exasperated. "I'm afraid someone started a rumor. Why would I take a costume?"

"Of course you didn't take it," said Marco with more certainty than she might have expected. "I'll speak to Abbey about it."

Her eyes widened at him. "Oh no, you mustn't do that."

She glanced about, embarrassed to be talking to him. It was commonplace to be seen talking to any member of the cast, but her own strange feelings about this man and the growing frequency and intimacy of their talks made her feel like every member of the company would notice and start more rumors.

She turned away from him to go on her way. "Thank you for your concern. But I am sure it will turn up."

Marco watched her go, his eyes narrowing pensively. Then he placed his top hat on his head and left the theater for a small bite of nourishment before warming up for tonight's performance.

Elisabeth climbed the stairs to the workroom and helped Mrs. DeKoven with the new costume. They spoke little and Mrs. DeKoven refrained from looking Elisabeth in the eye, making her feel even more ill at ease. She felt as if the whole thing were her fault, and then silently upbraided herself for feeling that way.

They worked late, constructing the costume to the point where it was ready to be fitted tomorrow. Not until then did Elisabeth feel all right about leaving the theater. By that time the evening's performance was underway. Music drifted through the halls backstage, but Elisabeth did not peer into the wings as she usually did when she found herself still there this late. She had too much on her mind this evening to be able to enjoy the music and the spectacle.

It was dark outside, but she hurried along to catch the horsecar, keeping her eyes well-averted from strange men who stared at her. There were many respectable working girls in the city, but the hour was past that which they usually traveled to their homes.

She sat near the front of the horsecar, and though a few men looked at her, no one spoke to her, and when she got off at Twenty-sixth Street, she hurried along to her own stoop.

Inside, the warmth and cozy lights greeted her, and

the York sisters were just descending the stairs for their game of gin rummy in the parlor. They stopped at the bottom of the stairs.

"Good evening, Elisabeth," said Anne. "Just getting in?"

Elisabeth removed her bonnet and shook out her curls. "Yes. I had to work late at the opera house."

"Well, I hope you were all right traveling home alone this late," said Selma.

"Yes, thank you. Everything was fine." She gave the ladies a reassuring smile.

"Well, we're just going in for our game. Care to join us?"

"Oh, thank you, no. I have some things to attend to in my room. But I hope you have a very good game."

"We will," said Anne, giving Elisabeth a coy wink. "I have to win back the four dollars I lost to my sister last night."

"I see," said Elisbeth, not wanting to take sides. "Well, may the best woman win."

She left the ladies and started for the stairs, but her progress was arrested by Mrs. Runkewich, who opened her door and poked her head through.

"Miss Kendall, that lawyer gentleman was here to see you. He left this."

She held out an envelope, which Elisabeth took.

"Thank you, Mrs. Runkewich."

She turned to take the letter to her room, but behind her Mrs. Runkewich came a little farther into the hallway.

"Not bad news, I hope."

Elisabeth stopped and turned slowly. "Thank you. I

hope not either."

Her business with Lindsay Whitehurst was her own and she wasn't going to give Mrs. Runkewich a clue. She watched Mrs. Runkewich try to form a question, but she did not wait for it. And of course she knew that anyone who came to see her more than once at the boarding house would be the subject of fluttering tongues. She hastened to her room to read the note. It was very short.

"I must see you as soon as possible," it said. "Please telephone, and I will call upon you at once."

She crushed the paper to her breast. It must be news about her husband. She crossed to the mirror, replaced the bonnet on her head and tied the strings under her chin. She would go herself.

Outside, she hailed a hansom cab and gave the driver Lindsay Whitehurst's address. It was only a short distance up Fifth Avenue, and the hansom let her off in front of the brownstone.

The lawyer's housekeeper greeted her and showed her into a study. In a moment she heard footsteps coming along the runner. Lindsay entered the room and closed the solid oak door behind him.

"Why, Elisabeth, I expected a telephone call, and I would have come round."

"I had to work late at the theater, and so I came myself. It saved time." She also did not want to use the boarding house telephone for fear of eavesdroppers.

He nodded and gestured for her to sit down. Then he seated himself on the corner of his polished mahogany desk. His gaze was professional, the right amount of formality and compassion.

"I thought you would want to know. Your husband's death has been confirmed. His body washed up on the beach. There is no doubt. I did not want to trouble you with the identification. The warden identified him."

Elisabeth's head swam, and she raised her hands to her face. Lindsay got down from the desk and came over to touch her shoulder.

"I'm sure this is a shock. Can I get you something. A sip of brandy perhaps?"

She nodded, unable to find her voice. After he poured the amber liquid from a crystal carafe and handed it to her, she leaned back in her chair and took a sip. She closed her eyes and let the liquid soothe her throat. Finally she opened her eyes.

"Then I'm free, at last." She glanced up at Lindsay and then lowered her eyes, tears of relief forming at the corners. "I know I shouldn't feel that way, but I can't help it."

"It's quite all right. I understand. Your marriage, was, shall we say, unfortunate? A mistake of youth. Perhaps it is none of my business, but I have read in your face many times that you did not love your husband. It is easier to bring such news to a widow who does not grieve."

He poured himself a glass from the carafe and raised it as if in a toast to some good fortune.

Elisabeth finished her glass, the effects of the liquid going to her head. Grief welled up in her, but it was not the grief of loss, rather the pent-up emotion that had been suppressed these last years. She began to cry.

Lindsay, took her glass and handed her a linen

handkerchief, waiting for the emotional release to spend itself.

"I'm sorry," said Elisabeth, her tongue feeling a little thick. "It is just such a change. I hardly know what to think."

Lindsay sipped his brandy and sat on the desk again. "I believe I understand what you mean. You are a free woman now. From what your father told me, no one ever knew you were married in the first place. It is like starting over, is it not? You are a lucky lady."

She blotted her eyes and nose. "Yes. I'm sorry for Albert. Truly I am. But I could do nothing to help him. Now he's paid for his crimes, or will do so in the next life. But I . . . I . . ."

She choked on her words again. Lindsay refilled her glass half-full and handed it to her. He had had enough experience with clients in moments of crisis to know that it was best to allow them time to react to whatever news he had to lay at their feet.

Elisabeth took another sip of brandy and wiped her lips with the handkerchief. Suddenly she opened her eyes wider and looked straight ahead.

"My Father. Does he know?"

Lindsay nodded and gave an understanding smile. "Yes. I called on him directly after I left word at your boarding house. He was most relieved."

She raised her eyes to his. "Does he . . . does he want to see me?"

"I am sure he does, Elisabeth."

"But he did not say so."

"Like you, he was so surprised and relieved that I don't think he had time to consider the consequences.

My advice to you is to go see him, my dear."

"Yes, yes, I'll do that." She stood up, somewhat unsteadily, but feeling it was time to leave. "Is there anything else I need do?"

The lawyer shook his head. "No. I'll see that the death certificate is sent to you. He did have a will, which I traced through the warden. There's not much, of course, just a few assets that he left to you. I," he cleared his throat, "will take care of everything."

"Thank you."

Lindsay followed her to the door. "Can I get you a cab?"

"Yes, please. I took a hansom here."

He put on his hat and escorted her to the street. A cab was found, and in moments, Elisabeth was resting on the seat. A free woman.

Marco traveled up Madison Avenue to the brownstone house he had bought for his mother, Rosa. She had not really wanted to move from Little Italy where all her friends lived, but Marco insisted that now that his career was established he could not bear to have her living in a tenement. She would make new friends in the nice church where she could be involved in charity work. She had sacrificed much to enable him to study music in the old days, and he was not going to be deprived of seeing to her comfort now. Another Italian community on the upper East Side was located a little east of the genteel neighborhood where Marco had bought his mother's house. By walking to Third Avenue she would feel at home again where organ grinders played their favorite airs above the clatter of the elevated trains and shouting pushcart vendors.

The brougham pulled up in front of the row of brownstones with heavy stone stoops and balustrades. He dashed up the steps and used his own key. In the entry hall, he tossed his top hat on the coat tree and then removed his greatcoat, tossing it on one of the carved black oak chairs. He did not call out, for it was late, and he might wake someone.

He glanced through the sliding doors that led to the library on the left, but saw no one there. The upright piano in the stair hall waited for someone to touch its ivory keys, and Marco unconsciously walked over to it and closed the lid on the keyboard. The walls of the stair hall were covered with grass cloth and rectangular patterns of oak strips. Three horses reared on a terra cotta plaque, and from a jutting shelf halfway up the stairs, a shelf held several Japanese vases. It was a fine home for his mother.

Marco ran his fingers across the polished wood of the piano and turned to climb the stairs. The light was on under the door to his mother's sitting room on the third floor, and he tapped on the door.

"Mama, it's me," he said softly.

"Marco, come in, my son." The attractive middle-aged woman with salt and pepper hair got up from the love seat where she was doing a cross stitch.

Rosa Giovinco was tall and well-built, not fat, but with strength that came from having to bear a strenuous life. Her complexion, though now accented with lines about the eyes and forehead, was of an even hue that complimented her ash-flecked dark eyes.

Sharp cheekbones made her face look thinner than it really was.

The room was decorated with wallpaper in two tones of blue below a frieze with a bold floral design. Photographs of Marco and his many cousins set about on the mantel, and on the corner tables interspersed with vases of blue cloisonné.

He crossed the oriental carpet to kiss his mother on both cheeks. She smiled up at her son. "You must be hungry, Marco. Come to the kitchen, and I'll find you a nice soup and some bread."

Rosa had let Marco hire her a maid to help with the housework in the big brownstone, but she insisted she could do her own cooking.

He pinched her cheek. "I didn't come to eat, Mama."

"Nonsense, Marco. You sing all night and you look pale. You must eat."

He captured her hands and gave them a squeeze. "Very well, maybe a little. But I must see Lucinda. Is she still awake?"

Rosa nodded. "Yes. She is in her room. She just left me."

Marco kissed his mother's forehead. "Then I will speak to her first. And then I will eat your soup."

As Rosa went downstairs to the kitchen, Marco crossed the hall. The carved oak door was already open a few inches, and Marco stepped in.

"Hello, Lucinda," he said to the dark-haired beauty who bent over a drawing pad at a round table in the center of the room. A kerosene lamp threw a wide pool of light. She was wearing a pink and white muslin blouse with a dark skirt. Her thick, dark hair floated around her face and drifted down her back.

She turned her dark, wide-set eyes to him. "Hello, Marco." Her mouth remained half-parted in surprise.

He stepped into the room and leaned against the door, which he closed softly behind him. His look was stern, but not without love.

"I've come for the dress. The one you took from the opera house today."

Chapter Seven

Lucinda's dark eyes widened even further. She did not answer, and in a moment she returned to the drawing she was making with charcoal pencil.

Marco stepped behind her and looked at the drawing. Lucinda had talent. Anyone could see it in the figures she was drawing on the paper. The faces of two children were alive with expressions of curiosity. But the sadness in the mother's face, and her direct look at the viewer of the page was disturbing. There was something unsettling about Lucinda's art.

"That's very good dear, very good."

He knelt down beside her and slowly and gently, took the drawing pad out of her hands to set it aside. Her eyes followed it, but Marco made her look at him.

"You can finish that in the morning."

She frowned slightly and shook her head.

"Of course you can. But right now I must have the dress. You and Mama were at the opera house this afternoon. Remember, you came to visit me after your shopping spree. We didn't know where you'd gone while we were talking to Mr. Abbey. We thought you were with the nurse in the auditorium. But she thought you were with us. You went upstairs to the wardrobe room again, didn't you? To pick out one of the lovely costumes."

He took her hands and pulled her to her feet. She cocked her head as he spoke, but stared at his cravat. Marco put his finger under her chin.

"I know you like the pretty costumes, Lucinda. But they don't belong to you. You must give me back the dress." His voice became more stern. "If you don't, a nice young girl like you will get in trouble."

Lucinda finally jerked her head up. "You can have it," she said. "I didn't like it after I got it home."

Marco sighed in relief. At least she admitted she had it. Sometimes she would pretend she didn't know what he was talking about when he tried to locate something she had taken. And when he found the article, she would say that it was for the poor women at the Charity Organization Society.

"Where is it?"

She gave him one of her coy, childish looks. Then she suddenly began to sing a little song and turned her attention back to her drawing as if Marco were not there.

But he was used to Lucinda's odd ways. He placed his hands on her shoulders.

"Where is the dress, Lucinda? Is it in the wardrobe?"

She broke off her song for a moment, frowned slightly, and then resumed singing.

Marco walked to the dressing screen, over which a pair of stockings were draped and glanced behind it. Nothing there. He then opened the doors to Lucinda's wardrobe, and saw the costume, hung with her other dresses.

The door opened behind him, and Bridget, the nurse, came in.

"Lucinda, it's time for you to get ready for bed," said the pretty Swedish girl in crisp white uniform. Then glancing at Marco, who was reaching into the closet. "Oh, Mr. Giovinco, I did not realize you were here." Her hand flew to her chest. "I did not mean to interrupt."

"It's all right, Bridget," Marco replied, lifting the decorative costume out of the wardrobe. "I've just come for this."

The nurse immediately understood, and clapped her hand to her mouth in embarrassment. Then her apology rushed forth.

"I'm so sorry about what happened at the theater today. I really thought Lucinda was with you, though it could only have been for a quarter of an hour."

Marco maintained an air of discipline. It would not be good for the nurse to think it was all right to let Lucinda wander off alone. He also knew that the young nurse must have been dazzled by the activity at the opera house and so lost her concentration for a few moments.

"It must not happen again," he said.

Bridget shook her blond head. "No, of course not. It will not." She straightened, looking at Lucinda. "Come along now, Lucinda, let me help you undress."

Marco crossed to the door. "I'll be on my way. Good night ladies."

"Good night, Mr. Giovinco," said Bridget.

Lucinda said nothing, but stared at her drawings.

Marco carried the costume over his arm and descended the two flights of stairs to the first floor. He left the costume in the library and then descended the last flight of stairs to the basement where he knew he would find his mother in the kitchen.

The large kitchen was at the back of the basement. Here, Rosa and the housemaid she had help her had plenty of room for culinary creations. Along one wall china was displayed in several shelves, the cups hanging neatly from brass hooks. Next to the dish racks, an iron sink fitted with drying rack took up the rest of the wall. Across the wooden floor the icebox jutted into the room next to a wide oak hutch. A telephone box was affixed to the wall by the door. Rosa stood in front of the oven range, which was set into a brick alcove at the back, where she stirred a delicious pot of pasta.

"Mama, you do too much for your poor son."

"Don't make nonsense, Marco. What did you talk to Lucinda about?"

He took a seat at the kitchen table and let his mother serve him a steaming plate of her best pasta.

"She took another costume from the opera house. She must have found her way to the wardrobe room while we were talking with Henry. I told Bridget it mustn't happen again."

Rosa took a seat across from him to watch him eat. "So that's where she went. She must have put the costume in with the other things we bought. I'm sorry Marco. Will this get you in trouble?"

He stared grimly at his plate. "It already got someone else in trouble. I will have to find a way to tell Henry."

She reached over and squeezed his arm. "I'm sorry, Marco."

He put down his fork and looked at his mother. "It's all right, Mama. You know I would never allow Lucinda to be put away. We've been able to take care of her here with Bridget's help. Those doctors who want to lock her up would only make her worse. Insane asylums are piteous places, cruel and filthy. Lucinda is not a raving lunatic. She is not quite right here," he said, tapping his temple. "But I still say good food, plenty of fresh air and sun, as long as she is watched, is better than what any of those maniac doctors would do to her if they got their hands on her." He took a breath. "Forgive me, Mama."

He was apt to get carried away on the subject, but Rosa understood.

"You are a generous boy, Marco. Most people in your position, with a career at stake . . ."

"I know," he said brusquely. "Most people who aspire to the status of celebrity would sweep away any blemishes in their own family, lock them up, or dispose of them so that they would not become a public embarrassment."

"And yet you don't do that, Marco."

He took his mother's hand in his across the table. "We are discreet about Lucinda. You know that some days she is completely normal. I would hope that my reputation is built on how well I sing, not whether we harbor a member of the family who is a little touched. So far the newspapers have not got ahold of it. I hope that for a little yet, they do not. But you know I would never put Lucinda away for my own selfish purposes. We keep a little quiet about her. No one who saw her at the theater today thought she was crazy, only a little shy."

Rosa patted her son's hands. "That's my Marco." Her eyes brimmed with pride, and her heart swelled with the love she bore her son.

Marco finished his meal and then got up to leave.

"Marco, dear" said Rosa, walking with him to the stairs. "Don't forget you promised to take Lucinda rowing tomorrow."

"I won't forget, Mama. You can tell her I won't forget. We will go after lunch. I am invited, am I not?"

They had reached the entry hall, and Rosa placed her hands on her hips. "And when is my son not welcome at my table for luncheon whenever he wants it?"

He smiled and kissed her. Then he retrieved the costume from the library, got his coat and hat.

"Buona notte, Mama. Until tomorrow."

"Buona notte, Marco."

"The missing costume has not been returned. Under the circumstances, we unfortunately find it necessary to, er . . . ," Henry Abbey cleared his throat and refolded his handkerchief. "Suspend your employment here," he finished.

Elisabeth stood in crisp white blouse, and navy jacket and skirt in front of the two managers in their office.

"We've had a talk with Mrs. DeKoven, and though she tried to protect you, we ferreted out the fact that this is not the first time this has happened."

Elisabeth was speechless with embarrassment. "I don't know what to say," she said.

"I have instructed Mrs. DeKoven to keep the wardrobe chamber locked. She will be the only one who has a key."

Elisabeth glared angrily at the two men hiding behind their big desks. "Then I am fired."

"Not fired," said Maurice, trying to soften the blow. "Merely suspended. We have to pacify the board of directors. We can't have costumes missing and do nothing about it. However, my dear, it is only a suspension. If the thief can be caught and everything cleared up, why you will again be summoned to your post."

He said it as if he expected everything to turn out rosily, but Elisabeth knew better.

"How do you expect to catch a thief who steals costumes six months apart?"

Henry shrugged. "Perhaps the culprit will try again, and then . . ."

Elisabeth did not wait for his scenario. "Very well. If that is the way you want it. I will get my things and leave immediately."

"Please understand . . ."

Maurice followed her to the door, but she moved too quickly for him to see the tears welling up in her eyes. Fired! And for something she didn't even do. She didn't for a moment believe all the nice talk about being reinstated.

She could hardly think straight, but ran upstairs, brushed past the chorus members coming out of the work room and picked up her things. She didn't look for Mrs. DeKoven to say goodbye. The old biddy probably got her fired purposely, though God knew why. There was certainly enough work for both of them to do. But there was no explaining territorial jealousies.

She fled out of the theater and down the street. Tears blurred her vision, but she rounded the corner and started up Broadway, a street she knew well enough to walk along without even being able to see.

"Look out there, Miss," called a man she nearly ran into.

But she only clamped her bonnet more firmly on her head and didn't turn around. At Forty-second Street, she crossed and caught a horsecar going uptown.

She rode all the way to Fifty-ninth Street and got off. Then entering the park, she walked slowly along the curving sidewalk where the pace was slower. She wiped her eyes with the back of her hand and sat on a bench for a moment just to get ahold of herself.

Her life was changing too fast. A few days ago she was a secretly married working girl living incognito in a modest boarding house. She had been chained to a past that was too painful to look back upon, especially when there seemed to be no getting out of it. Divorce from a prisoner husband would have dragged her name through the newspapers, a difficult thing for a girl raised in "Society" to confront. A few days ago the future meant a routine of going to the opera house, cutting, sewing, fitting costumes, listening to the opera, perhaps dreaming harmless dreams. But all that had changed suddenly.

After a while, she pulled herself to her feet and continued walking, not caring which way she went, for the day was sunny, and her jacket warm. As she followed the other strollers, enjoying this little bit of quiet in the midst of the bustling city, her mind began to sift through what the changes meant. She was no longer married, but rather widowed. And still no one knew it, or almost no one. She no longer had a job. She was free to pursue her dream of music if she wished. Some of the barriers appeared to have come down. And Professor Schlut thought she had talent.

That thought carried her until she had walked as far as the lake, on which canopied gondolas and oar-propelled passenger launches glided across rippling water. On the far side, more boats were tied at the boathouse. Elisabeth stopped to watch the tranquil scene. Central Park was one of New York's blessings. Here one could come when the cobwebs in the mind became too great, or just to escape the harried pace of the city.

Behind her a policeman clopped by on his horse and when she turned, he touched his helmet with his riding crop in a salute to her. She loved the park in all seasons, but the late fall was especially pleasing with the restorative powers of brisk breezes and vibrant leaves swirling around one's feet.

She was gazing at a couple riding across the lake in one of the rowboats, when she recognized Marco. There was no mistaking his dark head, and with his jacket slung in the seat beside him, and his sleeves rolled up, she saw his muscular forearms as he pulled the oars. But it was the lovely young woman in the boat facing him that arrested Elisabeth's attention. She glimpsed a young face, dark hair and thick eyebrows. The girl was smiling and chattering. The sounds of laughter came across the water, but not the words.

Elisabeth turned her face away and pressed her hands to her cheeks. Humiliation flooded her. Marco with a woman, probably the one for whom he had bought the stockings. She walked quickly away from the lake. It was silly to fall apart at the sight of Marco Giovinco with a woman. He must have hundreds of them. Hadn't she told herself so? And yet with everything else shifting in her life, the sight of him laughing and smiling at someone else brought home to her the painful truth that she was nothing to him.

She didn't know exactly what she wanted to be to him, but since their conversations, she had thought they might be friends. It made no logical sense, but her hopes, which perhaps were born the moment Lindsay told her her husband was dead, were crushed. More than that, only now did she admit to herself that she held such hopes.

He might find her pleasant to be with, and he might actually want to help her with her singing, but there was no more to it than that. Or so she had convinced herself. And yet his own words offering friendship echoed in her mind. The complexity of her feelings was suddenly overwhelming, and Elisabeth started to cry. She ran off the sidewalk and through the grass until she was out of breath and flung herself against a sturdy tree. Now the pent up emotions spilled forth in all their fury. Oh, why had Marco had to be with someone? How wonderful it would have been to run into him here in the park and to share with him all her news, everything. To lean on him for support.

She bent over, her sobs escaping and the tears running down her cheeks. She fumbled in her pocket for a handkerchief, then she gulped and sobbed until it all came out. Not only grief, but rather the complex emotions brought about by loss and change, and the frightening prospect of an unknown future.

With relief she finally drew deep breaths of fresh air and wiped her face. Then she started to walk slowly along, kicking the leaves as she went. She must put Marco from her mind. There was enough else to think about.

Finally she left the park. On Broadway, she caught a horsecar for home. A man got on with a bunch of bananas, which he hawked for a nickel, and Elisabeth bought one, realizing she hadn't eaten any lunch. She alighted at Twenty-eighth Street and started toward home, her mind somewhat cleared, but her emotions drained.

She stopped in the middle of the sidewalk, eliciting curses from two businessmen in derby hats who nearly bumped into her.

"Oh, sorry," she muttered and moved toward the store window near which she stood. She blinked in the sunlight, barely seeing the familiar street scene before her. What she must do in light of all the recent developments became clear.

Was it a retreat, she wondered as she slowly began to walk along the sidewalk again, this time out of the mainstream of traffic.

No, not a retreat, she answered herself with determination. It was the right decision. She could not go on living idly at the boarding house now that she didn't have a job anymore. And as a young widow, she was free to start life over. But there were also amends to be made.

It was time she went home. Not to the cozy rooms where gossip was shared by her fellow boarders, each living out their lives in their own way. But home to the mansion on Fifth Avenue, to her other life, and to find out if she had a father who would still claim her.

She turned the corner at Twenty-sixth, and when she came to the corner of Fifth Avenue she stared uptown at that other world she had avoided like the plague since her downfall. What would it be like now? she wondered.

She hurried across the street and marched toward the brownstone stoop and up to the front door. She was going directly upstairs to pack her things and then inform Mrs. Runkewich that she was leaving. It was time to make a new beginning.

Chapter Eight

Marco entered Madison Square park from Twenty-third. The rain had left the park with a newly washed look, and he breathed in its freshness. He had not seen Elisabeth at the theater when he had returned the costume, and when Mrs. DeKoven informed him that she had been let go, guilt wafted through him.

He went directly to the managers and taken responsibility for the missing costume. Though they were shocked by his revelation, they promised discretion. It would not do Marco or the opera company any good to let reporters get ahold of the story.

They asked him if Lucinda had been to the opera house before, and when he answered that she had come several months ago, Abbey and Grau had exchanged looks. They asked Marco if she might also have in her possession an Egyptian costume, for Mrs. DeKoven had told them of that loss as well. Marco promised to look into it, for he had not known of the earlier incident, only that Lucinda had a tendency to take things that didn't belong to her.

Although he had gone to see the two managers with the intent of clearing Elisabeth's name, he found out that they had already suspended her. But now that the matter was cleared up, they agreed they would be only too happy to have her back at her post. Marco offered to take her the word, since he felt it was indirectly his fault in the first place that she had been fired.

Now, after making a slight detour to purchase a half dozen roses from the florist on the other side of the park, he moved briskly down the walk. The roses were an offering with which he would accompany his apology. It was his fault that Elisabeth had lost her position as wardrobe mistress, and he was in a hurry to set things to rights.

As he crossed the park, he visualized Elisabeth as he remembered her. She was not really beautiful, but her wide-eyed direct look and angular features were pleasing. She was not the sort of woman he usually considered a conquest, but he was touched by her checkered past, perhaps because his own had been likewise fraught with obstacles. Marco, too, had been living two lives. In his public one, he was the charming tenor, gay, generous with his colleagues, exacting in his work.

In his private life there had been Lucinda. Friends and neighbors had known of her in Little Italy, and had shown compassion. Many of them had cared for the odd child when both Marco and his mother had to work because Marco's father, a longshoreman had been hurt in an accident at the docks.

Of course they had been too poor to take her to fancy doctors, and some thought she would outgrow her mental and emotional state. And that was probably for the better. Marco had an extreme dislike for doctors who called themselves experts in mental illness, but who tortured and drugged their patients and did experiments on them. Whatever was wrong with Lucinda was a mark that she had to carry this lifetime.

And his theory of a normal household, good food and fresh air had proven best so far. Lucinda had grown no worse. And on many days, she seemed almost normal.

He hurried his steps, the roses wrapped in brown paper swinging at his side. He began to pick out the brownstone on the street in front of him, and then looked up in surprise. An elegant cabriolet stopped in front of the house where Elisabeth lived. Marco at once noticed the well-matched pair of horses with their tails set up a trifle. The large coachman sat on the box, his shiny silk top hat, brass-buttoned livery and white trousers immaculate as were those of the tall, slim footman who got down.

Marco looked up just in time to see Elisabeth come out the front door of the house and descend the steps. The footman opened the carriage door for her.

Marco blinked. He started forward to hail her, and then stopped. Where was she going in such an elegant equipage? Her straight bearing as the footman helped her into the carriage, and the quick nod of her erect head showed a demeanor he had not seen in her before. Something was different.

Rather than making himself know, Marco paused by the iron gate to the park and stood so that he could watch, but not be noticed. Elisabeth settled herself in the carriage, and the footman returned to the box. As Marco watched the carriage leave, a combination of curiosity and jealousy burned in him.

He'd expected to find the girl distraught by the loss of her job, lonely perhaps. But instead, he saw her dressed in elegant clothing he had no idea she could afford and setting out like a lady making a call. He gripped the bunch of roses and glowered suspiciously. He felt he had a right to know the truth. What was going on?

He had hoped to have found her grateful that he had gotten her position restored at the theater. If he confided about Lucinda, she might also have felt drawn to him in his family misfortune as he had been to her in hers. He did not deny his romantic inclinations. He would let matters take their course.

But his surprise interfered with his expectations. He cursed to himself in Italian. Then he walked briskly after the carriage. There was only one thing to do, find out where she was going. On Fifth Avenue he hailed a hansom. Before he got in, he stopped two ladies strolling along the street.

"Please, dear ladies. Take these flowers and put them to good use. They are not going where they were intended." He flashed a smile at the astonished ladies, whose feathers waved from their hats. He didn't wait for thanks, nor did he answer their curious looks.

"Follow that carriage," he told the cab driver, pointing out the distinguished carriage that was rolling up Fifth Avenue. "There is a lady in it. I wish to know where she is going."

"Ah," said the dark-complexioned young driver with Mediterranean looks. "I see." He whipped the team into a trot to catch up to Elisabeth's carriage and then slowed them to a walk a discreet distance behind.

122

Elisabeth would have no reason to suspect she was being followed and would think nothing of the cab.

They continued up Fifth Avenue past the stately brownstones punctuated by costly mansions. At Forty-second Street they passed the holding reservoir, ivy climbing up its sloping walls. From the top, couples and families strolled around its railed perimeter to view their fellow New Yorkers as they passed below. Still, the carriage rolled on.

Marco could not still his suspicions as the cab continued up Fifth Avenue. Besides the lofty spires of St. Patrick's Cathedral, St. Thomas Episcopal Church, and Fifth Avenue Presbyterian, the mansions of the wealthy dominated the street here. In a race to outdo each other, Vanderbilt relations had commissioned magnificent houses along this stretch as evidenced by twin Italianate palazzos set on the block next to William K. Vanderbilt's ornate white stone mansion in the French Renaissance style at Fifty-second Street.

Marco himself had been invited to dine and to sing in many of their salons, and he had gotten used to mixing with the wealthy. But the fact that the poor little wardrobe mistress was venturing into this high real estate district bothered him. He did not stop to wonder if she were traveling here to perform the duties of a seamstress. A seamstress did not dress in flowered silk and lace when she was going out. His naturally excitable mind caused him to leap to the most obvious conclusion.

Before the cab reached the southern boundary of Central Park, Marco was fuming with certainty that Elisabeth had lied to him about her circumstances. When her carriage stopped in front of the stately carriage gates to a large Renaissance style brick mansion lavishly frosted with marble, he narrowed his eyes.

"Stop here," he told the cabby.

He got down in time to watch the iron gates open and the carriage roll into a drive beside the house. It stopped under the porte-cochère, and the footman got down. Marco was inclined to ring the bell on the gates himself, determined to ask what she was doing here, but he restrained himself.

Realizing it would be better not to be seen, he crossed the street to the edge of the park. Here nurses in stiff muslin caps pushed their charges into the park. Ladies in large hats with spotted veils strolled along holding their skirts, which swept the ground.

Marco walked along the sidewalk, finally taking a position where he could get a better look at the elegant mansion. The front entrance jutted out from the house on the Fifth Avenue side. The four-story house was surrounded by formal gardens, the flower beds now barren, but yew trees and hedges were neatly trimmed. French doors on the second floor led to a small balcony with white marble railing. Elegant indeed all the way to the red-tiled roof.

It did not for a moment worry Marco that he was spying on his protégé. His interest was piqued. It was his business to know.

To his surprise, a moment later, the French doors on the second floor opened and Elisabeth herself appeared. She walked to the railing, grasped it with her hands and looked at the view. Marco turned and strode into the park, stopping next to a gas lamp on a thick iron pole. Somewhat camouflaged by nearby bushes, he again risked a glance at the mansion. Now someone else emerged. A tall, distinguished-looking man. From this distance he appeared to be somewhat older than Elisabeth.

She turned to face him, leaning back with one hand braced against the railing. The man spoke to her, and for a moment, the two exchanged words. Finally the man held out a hand, and Elisabeth rushed to him. To Marco's astonishment, the man clasped her to him, and they embraced.

Marco swore. The scene was full of emotion. Perhaps they had not seen each other for some time. It was obvious to him that Elisabeth was a woman of many wiles. It was not hard for Marco to fit the pieces together. She had lost her position at the theater. Being thrown on her own, she had fallen back on a former means of assistance. She must have been this man's mistress at one time and was now being reconciled to him.

Being unable to stand watching any longer, he turned his back and walked farther into the park. But the bright November sun, the rhythmic sound of horses' hooves on the dirt trails, and the laughter of children did nothing to lift his black mood. He swore aloud, not noticing the shocked expressions of ladies he passed very near. What was Elisabeth Kendall to him? He had thought she had a refreshing innocence, a unique story, was a damsel in distress, but he saw that he was mistaken. Let this tycoon, whoever he was, help her with her so-called singing career. Marco was done with her.

*   *   *

It had taken all of Elisabeth's courage to actually step into the carriage her father had sent. She had labored the day before with her note to him. It had been simple and businesslike, informing him that she had heard from Lindsay Whitehurst, as she knew her father most likely had as well, and that she was now a widow. She also mentioned that she was not at present working at the theater. She dared not use the telephone box at the bottom of the stairs at the boarding house. There was no privacy there, and everyone would crack their doors to listen.

Her father's reply had been immediate, coming back by messenger the same day.

"I will send the carriage for you at four," it had said.

She had not known what to expect, and she felt dizzy riding up Fifth Avenue in the carriage. The servants, while reserved, had shown pleasure at seeing her, welcoming her home, and she knew the moment she stepped into the house that it had been worth it to look her best for this meeting with her father. Apparently her father had succeeded in making them all believe that she had been in Europe for the intervening two years since they had last seen her.

Gunther, the butler who had been with the family ever since Elisabeth could remember, bent his tall, thin frame, as he opened the door for her and she entered the marble-floored entry hall.

"Hello, Gunther," she said.

"Welcome home, Miss Sloane. Your father is expecting you."

The balding, elderly gray-haired butler showed no emotion other than polite respect, but gestured that she should enter.

But for Elisabeth, it was difficult to keep her own emotions from running away with her. How she had both hated and loved this house over the years. She stood in the center of the hall, the grand staircase sweeping upward, the heavy chandelier catching some of the sunlight that came in through the high windows. Large hunting scenes and portraits in muted colors expressed the taste with which her mother had decorated the house when it had been built, and since her death, no one had changed a thing.

Gunther gave her time to compose herself and then started toward the staircase.

"Mr. Sloane asked me to show you to the Gainsborough room." They called it the Gainsborough room because of the four large eighteenth-century landscape paintings done by the English painter that adorned the walls.

How different her life had been these last two years, Elisabeth thought, as she ran her hand along the polished, curving wood railing as she followed Gunther upward. She would have felt like a little girl again as she climbed the carpeted stairs behind the well-trained butler, but the butterflies in her stomach and her clammy hands made her feel like she didn't really belong here.

On the second floor landing she nodded to Gunther as he crossed the foyer and opened the white carved doors with gilt trim to the room where she would wait for her father. He closed the doors after her, and she was left alone.

The large blue and white drawing room faced the Fifth Avenue side of the house, with French doors that led to a square balcony above the front entrance. The off-white color of the walls and curtains in the room was repeated in the Aubusson rug with its rose and blue flowers. An Adam mirror with carved gilt frame hung on one wall, and the huge Gainsborough landscapes were set into the other two walls. A low marble-slab coffee table sat in front of a French sofa covered in dark blue striped satin and plush, and French chairs and tables formed groupings around the room.

The past seemed to come back to her as Elisabeth crossed the room, approached the French doors and opened them. She crossed the tiled balcony and gazed at the treetops of Central Park across Fifth Avenue, then she walked to the balcony and leaned on it, gazing up and down the street at the well turned out carriages. Clicking hooves came from high-steppers pulling ladies' victorias, while young men drove roadsters on their way to Harlem Lane where they could race. The spirited thoroughbreds pranced along in contrast to the tired, bony horseflesh that pulled horsecars along the curbstone.

Feelings tumbled over one another inside her. On the one hand were the many memories of growing up in this big house. Of games with friends, of crouching behind the balustrade of the musician's gallery to watch the formal dinners her parents held in the dining room below.

But later came the disillusioning life in the society she was reared to, of feeling stifled by the regimentation. She had wanted to explore new ideas, discuss philosophy and see the newest in art. Instead, she had been expected to attend endless social gatherings attended by the same people, for the most part with their minds set on two things—a good marriage for girls her age, and continued rise up the social ladder.

After a trip to Paris where she had tasted the intellectual and artistic influences on society there, a rebellious spirit had taken root inside her. In Europe, poets, artists, and gay young scholars were always in attendance at elegant soirées. But that was not true in New York's monied class.

It was an ironic fact that many of the boxholders at the Metropolitan opera did not even like music. They supported the opera because it traditionally began the social season. Mrs. Astor never appeared in her box until nine o'clock and always left after the second intermission. The opera was someplace to go after dinner before a late night party. But not so for Elisabeth.

And so the old conflicts stirred again as she absorbed this familiar scene. But she had no more time to sort out her thoughts. She heard a step on the tile and turned to look at her father.

Winston Sloane was a distinguished man of nearly fifty. He strode forward onto the balcony as Elisabeth turned around, then he stopped without speaking.

Her lip trembled as she gazed at his slightly craggy face. His hair was touched with gray at the temples as well as on the sideburns that framed his face. His dark eyes gazed at her somberly. Her first thought was one she used to have as a girl, that Winston Sloane had the righteous look of a fire-and-brimstone preacher. A person meeting him for the first time might never guess that behind that sanctimonious exterior lay the meticulous mind of a successful banker. She felt small before him and held her head higher to make up for it.

"Hello, Father," she said.

He took another step forward, and she saw his own jaw quiver as he slowly raised his chin.

"It's good to see you Elisabeth."

"You too, Father."

Then he slowly raised a hand. She ran to him. His one small gesture was enough, and as he clasped her to him, she felt her tears start. How often when she was a child had she run to him to be comforted on his strong shoulder. For Winston Sloane had been a stern, serious father, but he had also offered her comfort when she had skinned a knee, or when her older cousins and their friends had teased her too hard.

He released her and handed her a lawn handkerchief to dry her eyes as they walked back into the drawing room.

"You look well, Father. It's good to see you. Oh," she broke off and had to swallow another sob. Then she stepped into the center of the room.

Winston motioned awkwardly toward the sofa. "Sit down, my dear."

She took a seat and angled her knees to face him where he sat at the other end.

"Lindsay called on me," said Winston. "It's all over, isn't it?"

"Yes," she gulped.

She could not help but feel the relief that swept through her again as she contemplated what had happened. She stared at the hues in the floral patterned carpet at her feet as she crumpled the handkerchief.

"I was a fool. I know that now." She breathed deeply.

Winston moved a hand as if to pat her knee but then hesitated.

"I believe it is for the best. You were not . . . happy in that marriage. I know that."

"No," she said, shaking her head and letting her watery gaze roam around the room. "I was a rebellious soul." She gave a little anguished laugh. "Perhaps I am still, but I hope I have learned something from my mistakes."

Winston could not keep the emotion out of his own voice, which shook as he spoke. "Then it has been a worthwhile lesson. Many people make mistakes, not everyone learns from them. And not everyone has the chance to start over."

She nodded and smiled through her tears.

After a moment he spoke again. "Do you wish to return home?"

She darted a glance at his face. "You would have me back, after what I've done?"

He stared at the room before them. "You are still my daughter."

"Oh Father, I did not dare hope to hear you say those words."

Then she leaned toward him and he pulled her into his arms again for another embrace, leaning his head against her soft curls. She felt the moisture from his eyes on her temple.

When she straightened up again, she had more control of herself. "There is more to tell," she said.

"When you are ready," said Winston. "But perhaps you would like some refreshment first. We will have plenty of time to talk."

She shook her head. "No, I would prefer to talk first."

"As you wish."

He settled against the sofa to listen. His grave expression was one he had cultivated in his business dealings, but now it was touched with a compassion he could not stem. A man did not show emotions, and Winston Sloane had learned to steel his away. His wife had died. And when his daughter had run away from home it had been more than he could bear, but bear it he must, for he was from a stoic breed. But in two years his armor of defense and the trappings of his lifestyle had worn thin. Seeing Elisabeth sitting in this drawing room again brought emotions to his heart he dared not yet inspect.

"I am no longer working at the opera," she said.

He moved his head slightly. "Oh?"

She was embarrassed to have to explain it, but she went ahead. "There was a misunderstanding. Two costumes were taken. The managers thought it was my responsibility. Oh, I don't think Maurice Grau would have let me go, but Mr. Abbey probably thought that no matter who took them I should have known. After all, it was my responsibility to see that all the costumes were ready for the performances. As it was, Mrs. DeKoven and I had to make a new one."

"And so they fired you?"

"They only suspended me. I think if the costumes ever turn up, they'll apologize. However, I've made a decision." She glanced at her father. "I don't want to go back, as wardrobe mistress anyway."

The tense muscles in Winston's face began to relax. "Well, I am glad about that." He got up and pressed the button on the call box at the side of the room. "I think we should have some tea to celebrate. It looks as if you are making a new start entirely."

132

Something like a smile relaxed his lips, and his dark eyes began to reflect a little light. "We must plan what we will say to everyone about your return."

Elisabeth lowered her head again. "I'm not sure I'm ready to return as you say. I have changed, Father."

"Of course you have, my dear. But you have grown the wiser. We will move slowly."

She looked up at him. "Are you sure you really want me here?"

Winston rocked on his heels, his hands clasped behind him. He did not quite look at her as he said, "This house has been quite empty. I've done little entertaining except for a few dinners with business associates. It would be . . . good for us both."

"I would hope so," she said slowly, still hesitant to commit herself. "But there would be a difference. There is something I want to do."

"What is that?"

She moved forward on the sofa a little. "I had an audition with Professor Theodore Schlut. He is one of the finest vocal teachers in New York. He thinks I have talent, and he has encouraged me to study."

There was a rap at the door, and then the double doors opened and Opal Turnbull, the housekeeper, entered with a tea tray. Elisabeth and her father broke off their conversation as Opal bustled in.

"Hello Opal, how are you?"

"Well, Miss Elisabeth. How good it is to see you," said the plump, middle-aged woman in crisp black grosgrain and starched apron. Her frilly cap covered graying hair, and her wan face lit in a smile.

She came to stand before Elisabeth, who rose to kiss her cheek.

"It's good to see you too."

"I hope you're going to stay this time," said Opal, whose efficient demeanor became touched with emotion. She wiped a hand across her cheek and made a hasty retreat to the tea tray to pour from the silver tea service.

She served the tea and then left father and daughter to their tête-à-tête. After they drank their tea and indulged in some sandwiches Elisabeth resumed her conversation about Professor Schlut, keeping her eyes on her food.

"He said I should study. He could take me as a student."

Winston gave a dry chuckle. "Rather fits in with our story, at least. Supposedly you've been in Europe studying for two years. It would not seem odd for you to continue here. There's no harm in a woman being accomplished in music. People always liked to hear you play and sing."

She set her cup into its saucer. "I know. It's just that now I have something more in mind than just after-dinner entertainments."

"What do you mean?"

She lifted her chin. "I'd like to see if I have what it takes to perform."

Winston coughed on his sandwich and set down his tea cup. "You don't mean professionally."

"I'm afraid I do." She rushed on. "Oh, I know it's a dream, and nothing may come of it. But if you honestly want me to live here, I wanted your approval to pursue this. If you would advance me the money for the lessons, I would pay it back if I did have a career."

Winston brushed a crumb from his lap. "I can't

believe my ears. Have you learned nothing from the debacle you've made of your life? By sheer luck and a bit of discretion no one knows where you've been, but it hasn't been easy. I thought when I heard from you yesterday that you had come to your senses. You're out of that dreadful job. And yet now this foolishness."

He stood and paced across the room. "Your mother and I tried to raise you to be a lady," he remonstrated. "We failed somewhere, God knows. Why can't you be satisfied with marriage and a family like other women? God I wish your mother were here to help me."

He moved to a mahogany cabinet, from which he extracted a carafe. He lifted the stopper and poured amber liquid into a glass, then tossed it back. "I'm sorry, Elisabeth. Perhaps I heard wrong."

A dull anger crept through her, and she knew it was not just the present argument heating her blood. How many other earlier arguments had she had with her parents about any unconventional thing she had wanted to do. It had been this divergence of goals that had driven her from home once. She had hoped that time and maturity might help her as well as her father overcome their differences. But his flaring temper at the mere mention of a singing career was evidence that he hadn't changed.

"You didn't hear me wrong Father. What I meant was that I might be good enough to go on the stage."

"And ruin your reputation for good?"

"Surely I've already done enough to ruin it," she said, unable to prevent her voice from rising. "I see I was wrong to come here. I don't mean to place myself under this roof if you do not approve of my actions."

She prepared to get up, but her father crossed the room toward her.

"Wait," he commanded.

She sat back down. They blinked at each other. She could see that he was making an effort to control himself, and she tried to do likewise. Already she chided herself for letting things come to a head so fast. She hadn't meant to start an argument.

She took a deep breath. "I'm sorry, Father. I didn't mean to be difficult."

He ran his hand through his hair. "You don't know what I've been through on your account, Elisabeth."

She lowered her head. "I know, and I'm sorry. I never meant to hurt you."

Her own emotions were running rampant, and she did not think she could carry on a rational conversation anymore. "Perhaps I should go. I'll come back. We can talk about it another time," she said futilely.

"No don't go." He almost barked it, but she could tell that he too was straining not to let their reunion end in a disaster. "Please . . . stay, Elisabeth. Opal will have prepared your room. You'll want to rest and refresh yourself." He let his shoulders drop. "I would be pleased if you would dine with me this evening."

She pressed her lips together. "All right, I accept, if you're sure."

"Of course I'm sure. You're my daughter!"

Again the anger and exasperation in his voice. Elisabeth rose unsteadily. "I know it might not have been right to come home," she said. "Things have changed."

"This is your home, Elisabeth. You are always welcome here."

There was a time when I wasn't welcome here, she wanted to remind him, but she didn't. "Thank you," was all she said.

Their conversation about her music studies was not over, and she knew that if she stayed under this roof there would be other battles to fight. But she was tired, drained of emotion, and all she wanted was a nice long bath in her luxurious bathroom. Then a nap on her soft bed. And perhaps after a meal, she could make her father see how badly she still wanted to do something her own way with her life. He would make the old arguments. Get married, raise a family.

But get married to whom? she wondered. The world of motherhood and the conventional life still gave a sour taste in her mouth. There were yearnings in her that cried out to be satisfied. And she hardly knew where to turn.

Marco's image came into her mind, and with a little pang of regret she banished it. He represented everything she knew she wanted, for herself. Talent, and a chance to use it. Devotion to an art. Variety in the people one met and worked with. That was the life she longed for.

If Marco Giovinco aroused other thoughts, she pushed them far, far to the back of her mind. She had seen clearly enough that romance with a man like that would be dangerous. Like all men with money and good looks, Marco would never be tied to love. She herself had been burned by infatuation once, and was not about to let it happen again.

Chapter Nine

Elisabeth knew that her return would set the household servants gossiping. She and her father would have to stick to their story about her two years abroad even in their own house except when they were certain they were alone. She hoped they could carry it off successfully.

Her mixed feelings about returning stayed with her as she climbed the stairs to the floor above. Gwendolyn, the upstairs maid was coming down and stopped to greet her. She was a pretty girl with light brown curls stuffed under a mob cap.

"Miss Sloane, I heard you were home. Mrs. Turnbull did up your room herself."

She tried to curtsy and demonstrate respect, but the girl's innate curiosity came through in her rounded eyes and fluttering eyelids. She had been a new hire when Elisabeth had gone abroad some two years ago and had settled into the household nicely, her only complaint being that the big house was quiet as a tomb most times. She herself longed for some excitement and now that the young mistress was back, maybe she would at least have some callers to gossip about.

"Thank you, Gwendolyn. I'm . . . glad to be home. I hope, um, things have been running smoothly."

Gwendolyn shrugged one shoulder. "Not much to do since you left. Very little entertaining goes on. It's been rather dull."

Elisabeth could not help a trace of amusement at the outspoken girl. Even the servants got more out of life when their master led an exciting life. She could imagine they were short on gossip. She must be doubly careful not to supply them with any of her own. For what her own household servants learned would quickly spread to other households and a maid would tell a mistress. The wealthy class was bad enough when it came to gossiping, but to that fuel the servants added their own fire.

Elisabeth continued to the landing and then down the long hall to her own room. She opened the white door with its gilt molding and stared at the sunny pastel room. The wall was painted a delicate blue with a darker blue on the molding. The drapes and valances were peach, and white dimity curtains covered the windows.

She stepped onto the thick carpet, remembering how she had always loved the feel of it barefoot. Dropping her hat on a chair, she crossed the room and sat down on a satin upholstered bench in front of the dressing table. She looked at herself in the mirror and then glanced at her lavish surroundings.

"Quite a change from Twenty-sixth Street," she said to herself.

There was a rap on the door and Opal came in. "I've

run you a bath, Miss. I hope it's not going to be too hot for you."

She crossed to the tall painted oak built-in wardrobe and opened it, extracting a dressing gown for Elisabeth to put on.

"I'm sure it will be fine."

She let Opal help her out of her dress. "My, um, things will be coming later," said Elisabeth, realizing that she had ostensibly arrived home from a European sojourn without a stick of luggage.

"No matter. You didn't take much when you went on your trip. Most of your dresses will be ready to wear, though I'll see that they are aired out. I imagine you found some time for shopping abroad even though you were busy. You would look wonderful in the latest Paris fashions."

Elisabeth swallowed. "I'm afraid my mind wasn't on shopping."

She dismissed the housekeeper and went into a small dressing room, which in turn opened on to her private bathroom. It was annoying to contemplate the details that must be considered in her trumped up story about where she'd been. New clothes, of all things. Well, if she were to carry out this charade, she would have to have a new gown or two made.

As she stepped into the white carpeted bathroom, she paused. She had forgotten how elegant it was. Indeed, she had shared a bathroom with three other people on her floor at the boarding house, and she hesitated a little, staring at the huge carved gilt mirror that hung over the mahogany-framed copper tub. Cabbage rose wallpaper covered the walls. She felt momentarily guilty that no one had used the bathroom for so long.

She tested the water, which was warm, but not too hot, and shed her dressing gown to get in. The warmth seeped into her, and as she slid down in the water, she gave way to the enjoyment of it. The Misses York and Margaret Houghteling would never enjoy such luxury, she thought with a pang. Life certainly wasn't fair.

But she couldn't help but enjoy the long, quiet bath. She soaped her skin, used the long-handled scrubber and pampered herself longer than she had planned to.

She had just returned to the bedroom and was contemplating a nap when Opal rapped on her door again.

"I'm sorry to disturb you, Miss, but you have a visitor."

"A visitor? So soon?"

"Miss Madelaine Lord is waiting downstairs in the French parlor. I told her I would see if you were here."

"Oh my." Elisabeth sank onto her dressing table bench. "I suppose I'll have to see her." Then she glanced up again. "I mean, I'm so tired. But I won't deny her a few minutes. Tell her to wait while I dress, and I'll be right down."

"I'll send Gwendolyn to help you dress. Mr. Sloane informed me that your French maid remained behind in Europe. I hope Gwendolyn will do for now."

"Yes. Thank you. Send Gwendolyn."

Opal nodded and closed the door. Elisabeth leaned on her hand, her elbow on the dressing table. She had hoped to have a day or so to get oriented to life at the mansion. Still feeing unsure about her decision to stay here, she had not wanted to plunge back into society so soon. But it seemed she would not be allowed time to readjust. Drat. How could Madelaine know she was back already?

There being no time to contemplate, she went to the closet to select a dress. Gwendolyn came in, a look of eagerness on her face at getting to help the mistress dress.

Elisabeth selected a frilly tea gown of dotted swiss with lace yoke. Gwendolyn flitted about, doing up the buttons and then seeing to Elisabeth's hair. Elisabeth had to force her hands to stay on the dressing table, so used to doing her own hair had she become. But Gwendolyn did a credible job, and even Elisabeth was forced to admire her own appearance when they got done.

Then, taking a deep breath and preparing to play her part, she descended to meet Madelaine.

The French parlor was on the main floor. To get to it Elisabeth passed through the checkerboard tiled corridors and anterooms, past the painted blue Louis XVI bookcases along one wall, the yellow and brown taffeta curtains, the gleaming brass candlesticks and polished statuary in curved niches. There was a feeling of stiffness about the place, however, as if this part of the house was not being lived in.

The high-ceilinged French parlor looked out onto the patio and gardens behind the house. Madelaine was standing by the French doors looking at the garden. When she heard Elisabeth enter, she turned and shrieked a greeting.

"Elisabeth, I can't believe it's really you. Why didn't you let anyone know you were coming home?"

The bubbly blond girl darted around the sofa in the center of the room and crushed Elisabeth in a hug.

Then she held her away.

"My, my, I don't think you've changed. Well maybe just a little. How have you been?"

Elisabeth smiled at her friend, feeling disoriented and yet swept along by Madelaine's zest.

"I'm fine. That is, I'm quite tired at the moment. My return was rather sudden."

"Do tell me everything. I want to hear it all. Two years, in Europe. Did any of my letters reach you? Your father said that as you were touring much of the time, you might not get your mail. But he promised to forward the letters I gave to him."

Elisabeth followed Madelaine around the sofa so they could sit down, facing the gardens. There was nothing to look at in the flower beds, but the trees still offered some fall colors.

"Well, I'm not sure where to begin. It's true, I did move around alot." She tried not to look Madelaine in the eye. "I um, did get your letters in a package from Father. I'm sorry I never wrote back. I've always been a terrible correspondent. And I, uh, didn't expect to be gone so long."

"Oh well, I suppose you were busy. But tell me about your music. That's why you went, isn't it? Your father said only that you were studying privately."

"Oh, yes. Well, I suppose it went all right. I hope to continue studying here," she said with somewhat more resolution.

"You were missed at all the parties you know."

"Was I?"

Madelaine gave a knowing look, her blue eyes full of secrets. Then she launched into a spate of gossip about all their mutual friends. Many were engaged, some had broken off. Consuelo Vanderbilt had agreed to marry the Duke of Marlboro.

"I don't think she wants to marry the Duke. Everyone knows Winthrop Rutherford's in love with her and she with him. Lord knows what will happen."

All in all, it sounded like two years of the gay life with which Elisabeth had been acquainted before her disappearance.

"And what about your social life?" Madelaine said, coming abruptly to a halt in her recital.

"Mine?" Elisabeth looked away quickly again. "There wasn't much. I mean, I was so involved in the more cultural aspects of Europe. I . . . saw a lot of opera."

"Oh?"

Madelaine considered her friend for a moment. When she spoke again it was with a different tone.

"Elisabeth. I do believe you met someone over there. Perhaps that was why you stayed so long." She leaned forward. "Is that it? Did you have a love affair?"

Elisabeth hesitated. "Well . . ."

Madelaine pressed her hand on Elisabeth's. "Oh, I don't mean to invade your privacy. From the looks of you, it couldn't have been a very happy experience. Oh my, now I've stuck my foot in it. Of course. I understand. You had a romance, but you broke off with him. That's why you're back."

Warmth crept up Elisabeth's face. "Well, as a matter of fact. There was something like that. Yes," she looked up. "I thought it was better to end it and to come home."

Her friend leaned back, flinging an arm over the floral upholstered sofa back. "How dramatic. To put an ocean between you."

Elisabeth winced.

"Was he a cad?" asked Madelaine. "Oh, you don't have to answer that if you don't want to. Only I am dying to know. Was he rich?"

Elisabeth shook her head quickly. "No, not rich."

"Ahhh. A fortune hunter then. In that case you're better off rid of him. There are plenty of eligible men in our social class still, in spite of all the latest engagements. I can see you've not yet recovered from your unfortunate experience. But perhaps a round of parties and outings will put you out of mind to it. Alexander Rochat has been asking about you."

"Alexander?" Elisabeth had not thought about the insincere playboy for a very long time. She knew him quite well and had flirted with him several years ago. But she always knew that Alexander Rochat was fickle. He had charm and he loved a good time. But he would not remember the next day what he had said the night before.

"Alex will fall head over heels in love a dozen times this year," Elisabeth said good-humoredly, "but woe to the girl who takes him seriously."

Madelaine creased her brow. "I'm not sure. I think he's changed. He's been working for his father's firm since he graduated Princeton."

The Rochat Brokerage firm was in Wall Street. Winston Sloane did much business with Alex's father.

Shaking off the speculative mood a moment later, Madelaine raised a gloved hand. "I've been tiring you. I can see that. Rude of me to come the very day you returned. But I simply could not stay away."

"How did you know I had arrived?"

"Why I saw you. Mother and I were driving down the avenue, and we saw you turn in. I nearly leapt out of the carriage on the spot. But we were on our way to Lord and Taylor."

"I see."

They both got up. "I'll let you rest now if you promise to come shopping with me day after tomorrow. I need a new gown for Mrs. Astor's party. Did I tell you? We've been invited."

"Well, I don't know. I haven't really made any plans."

"Then you'll be free. I'll come for you at one o'clock."

Elisabeth felt too tired to refuse. "All right. I suppose I can be ready then."

Madelaine's face lit with the simple pleasure of a plan well-laid. She squeezed her friend's hand and kissed her cheek.

"Then you must start to tell me everything you saw and did in Europe. I can't believe you spent all your time on your music. You must have attended concerts, seen the latest masterpieces in the galleries and looked at great architecture. You can describe it all to me when we stop for tea."

Elisabeth could not help but be amused at the girl's simplistic approach. Since she seemed to carry on most of the conversation anyway, it might not be hard to create a few minor details to satisfy Madelaine's questions.

They passed through the corridors to the side entrance where Madelaine had a victoria waiting. She turned to bid her hostess goodbye as they stood on the porch.

"Oh, now that you're back. Perhaps mother can get you an invitation to Mrs. Astor's ball." She laughed. "It seems her ballroom can now accommodate more than four hundred."

Like Winston Sloane, Madelaine Lord's family had made their money in the last two generations, and so were considered new rich. "Society" was ruled by Mrs. Astor and her deputy, Ward McAllister. No individual was accepted into their circle unless backed by four generations of gentlemen. Word was that Mrs. Astor's ballroom only accommodated four hundred, therefore society was limited to that number. But the new rich were not to be denied, and in the last few years Mrs. Astor had accepted invitations from some families whose names did not necessarily date back to the revolution. Times were changing.

"Frankly, I've heard Mrs. Astor's parties are terribly dull," Madelaine went on. "Dinner from eight to eleven o'clock, all with the proper decorum and boring conversation." Madelaine made a little face. "But there's dancing afterward."

At least Madelaine concentrated on getting fun out of life. She had been raised to be a lady, but there was enough of the maverick in her to make her an enjoyable companion. She could be entertaining, as long as Elisabeth could block out the last two years of her life. Madelaine would probably even understand Elisabeth's desire to sing professionally, for it would seem exciting and daring.

Madelaine hopped into her open carriage, a glowing ray of sunshine on a gray November day. She waved a hand.

"Remember, day after tomorrow. I'll ask Consuelo

to join us. Poor girl, she doesn't get out much without that witch of a mother of hers."

Elisabeth stepped back and waved. Then she turned and went back into the house, wondering how she was going to deal with her new life.

The next day Elisabeth returned to the boarding house to fetch her cat, get her things and settle up with Mrs. Runkewich. She gave Lindsay Whitehurst's address in case there were any mail or messages to be forwarded. She felt too embarrassed to tell her friends at the boarding house the truth. They would never understand. So she simply said that through her lawyer she had located a relative who had invited her to come live in his house.

The Misses York twittered their good luck, and Margaret seemed genuinely happy for her. She promised to visit when she could.

She was surprised to find a note from Henry Abbey and Maurice Grau, asking her to call on them at her convenience. The note was so solicitous that she suspected something had happened to make them change their view of her. She decided to pay them the courtesy of calling on them, and stopped there on her way up town, sending the cab she had hired with her belongings and her cat on to her father's house.

She did not use the household servants a second time, fearing they would not believe her story about visiting a sick friend when she had first arrived from the "steamer." If any of the servants saw her carrying luggage from a boarding house, they would immediately gossip. Thus, the anonymity of making this trip in a hansom, which would deliver the luggage and the cat with no questions asked, and the driver had been paid in advance.

By the time she was ushered into the crowded office of the two opera company managers, she was very curious.

"Miss Kendall, how nice to see you," said the ever-courteous Maurice. He showed her to a chair.

Even Henry Abbey seemed meek as he got up from his desk until she sat.

"Good morning, Miss Kendall," he said. "Good of you to come."

"Good morning, Mr. Abbey. I trust your note has something to do with my former position."

Abbey cleared his throat, and Maurice stepped to the window, clasping his hands behind his back.

"We have made an error and wish to rectify it," Abbey said. "I'm afraid I reacted a little too quickly about the missing costume, which I believed to be your responsibility."

"Oh? Has it turned up?"

Abbey looked at his desk, a perplexed frown on his face as if he did not want to explain the circumstances. "It has."

"Who—?"

She looked from one man to the other, but neither would meet her gaze. Obviously the culprit had been caught but was being protected by the management. It made her bristle slightly, but she tried to keep her temper. After all, they were apologizing to her.

"Were both costumes returned?"

Abbey and Grau briefly exchanged glances and then looked away from each other. Abbey raised his head to look at Elisabeth, sitting in front of his desk.

"They have."

"Well, I am glad."

He made a gesture indicating that all was solved. "So you see. You are welcome to resume your duties as wardrobe mistress, if you so desire."

Elisabeth sat very straight. "Thank you. But I have decided not to return to work."

Abbey glowered at her, but Maurice turned around quickly. "We had in fact decided to increase your salary. You've worked two years without an increase."

Her expression softened as she addressed the more genuinely concerned of the pair. She also realized that it would not do to leave behind enemies. If she were to pursue her foolish dream, she would need all the friends in the music world she could get.

"It's not that I don't enjoy the work. On the contrary, the opera has become my life. But my circumstances have changed recently. I have . . . ," she glanced down at her gloved hands, folded in her lap.

But she forced herself to raise her head and assume a composed expression. "I have decided to take up singing myself. I've auditioned for Professor Schlut, and he agreed to take me as a student."

Maurice lifted his brows and Abbey blinked at her.

"Indeed," said Maurice. "Professor Schlut does not waste his time on pupils who have no talent. Consider yourself fortunate, my dear."

"I do. I . . . that is, the arrangements have not been finalized. But I would truly like to study."

Maurice came around the desk rubbing his hands, his innate enthusiasm beaming in his eyes.

"Then you have the, er means?"

"I believe so. As I said, my circumstances have changed. And if I am to embark on such an undertaking, it is best I do it now, while I am young enough for the necessary vocal development."

"Yes, yes, of course," said Maurice, momentarily forgetting that they were permanently losing their wardrobe mistress. "You are right. It takes years of work, as you no doubt know from meeting the artists who sing here. Do you think you have the stamina and the drive?"

She could not help but respond to his honest inquisitiveness. "I don't know, but that is what I wish to find out."

He seized her hand. "Then I wish you the very best of luck. That is, Abbey and I both do."

"I'm sure," said Abbey from behind his desk.

He looked as if he remained unconvinced. But Elisabeth knew she would see that look of disbelief on many people's faces. She glanced away, but when she did, her eye fell on the many autographed photographs of stars that hung about the room. It only took a little such inspiration and the encouragement of someone who could understand her dream to make her spine tingle.

Yes, she decided at that moment, she would find a way to take the voice lessons. It was important enough to make her want to save money by living in her father's house and borrow the money from him for the lessons.

She suddenly smiled radiantly and stood up. "Well then, you see how it is. But I am glad that you recovered the costumes so that there are no hard feelings."

Abbey got up. "Yes, yes, that has been taken care of."

She approached the big desk and extended her hand, which he took.

"I want to thank you for everything. Working for the Metropolitan Opera has meant a great deal to me."

Her ingenuity seemed to penetrate Abbey's gruff reserve and he thawed a little.

"We've enjoyed having you here, my dear. And if the, er, singing does not work out, you would always be welcome back here," he said beneficently.

She thanked them again for the thoughtfulness and Maurice saw her to the outer door. Before she left, he lowered his voice and whispered.

"Good luck, my girl. Who knows? We may be seeing you in quite different circumstances in a few years. I for one, would be delighted."

A little thrill tingled in her spine and she laughed modestly. It would be indeed a number of years before she would be ready to contemplate such a thing, and she was as yet an untried quantity. It was hard to keep the fluff of dreams at bay. For if such a thing as singing on the stage could come to pass, there would be nothing she would wish for more.

Chapter Ten

Marco was crossing the stage with long strides, singing softly to himself, when he saw Elisabeth in the wings and stopped abruptly. The planes of his face turned into a scowl, and he muttered an Italian oath to himself. But he pasted an expression of polite indifference on his dark features and continued toward the wings. In a booming voice, he greeted Madame Nordica, with whom Elisabeth was exchanging words.

"Good morning, Lillian. You're here early."

"Good day to you, Marco," said the no-nonsense soprano. "And it is afternoon, in case you hadn't noticed."

Marco sent her an imperious look. Then he turned his gaze on Elisabeth.

On first seeing him she was filled with the embarrassing self-consciousness that seemed to plague her in his presence, and his haughty glance almost made her step backwards.

"Good morning, Miss Kendall," he said, leaning on the *Miss*.

His sense of irritation surprised her, but it all the more quickly brought back the memory of seeing him with another woman in the boat the day she'd had so much to share with him. Her own temper flared and her resentment tumbled with the tinge of disappointment she'd had since that day. It was as if she had once reached out to him as an understanding friend and gotten her hand slapped. She drew herself up as haughtily as possible, even though she felt like a mouse beside the two great stars.

"Good morning," she replied.

Lillian Nordica carried on as if unaware of the tension between the other two.

"Elisabeth has just told me that she won't be with us anymore. That misunderstanding between the wardrobe department and the management has been straightened out, but our dear girl has decided to move on to other endeavors. Our loss, but we must wish her well, Marco."

Marco still stood rooted to the floor, a grumpy look on his face. "I can see that," he said, indicating her fine appearance in Venetian striped silk dress, gray suede gloves and sweeping bonnet with ostrich tips. "Obviously she has come into good fortune."

Elisabeth began to sense the cynicism in his tone and it surprised her. Her own complex emotions in regard to this man were topped by her complete bewilderment as to his present mood. Italian, she thought. That must explain it. Well, she was not going to let it bring her down, now that she was set on her own course.

"My circumstances have changed, it is true," she said, lifting her chin. Once she would have liked to tell him how drastically her life had changed. But obviously her moment of sharing with him had passed. He was no more than another incident in an already checkered life. She would give him a simple explanation, and then get on with it.

"I have decided to leave the employment of the opera company," she said. "Mr. Abbey and Mr. Grau were kind enough to apologize to me about the missing costumes. Evidently they have been returned and the managers offered to reinstate me in my position. However, I have no need of it at present. I . . . ," she hesitated, her expression muted. She did not really want to get into a personal discussion with so many listeners. "I have had a change of fortune," was all she said. "Through a relative." There, if he wanted to know more, he would ask.

But he did not ask. Instead he glowered. "I can see that. May I congratulate you?"

"I must run, my dears," said Nordica, who waved a hand and called out to the conductor, Maestro Antonio Gatti, as she lit out after him.

Marco touched Elisabeth's arm and started walking with her toward the door. He would give vent to his thoughts outside, not where others could hear them.

They reached the street and stepped out of the earshot of passersby. She could not understand his attitude, and it miffed her that he had previously seemed so interested in her career. Why now did he seem so filled with resentment?

"I suppose I should be happy for you," he said as they proceeded down the sidewalk as if they had a common destination.

"I don't see why not."

"Only that I was surprised to learn of your secret

life," he said in a mocking tone. "The boarding house had me fooled. I will admit that I happened to see you enter the house on Fifth Avenue where your benefactor no doubt lives."

So, he had seen her. "Well, what if he does live there? I have taken up residence there as well."

"I can only guess the reason for the secrecy. Otherwise you would have mentioned it to me before."

His comments annoyed her. She knew that Italian men could be domineering. Marco was obviously no exception, with his inflated ego. They had reached the corner of Thirty-ninth and Broadway and stopped to cross. An organ grinder smiled and nodded to them, but Marco glared at the monkey, who spread its lips and grimaced back.

Elisabeth stepped into the street behind a passing cabby, and Marco plunged after her. They navigated the traffic to get to the other side, and she continued onward. Not turning to look at him, she gave out a reply. If he were going to behave in so insulting a manner, then so could she.

"Apparently I am not the only one with secrets," she said. "I happened to see you the other day as well, in Central Park, as a matter of fact."

His long strides easily kept pace with her hurried steps. "Oh? What of it? I often walk there."

She slowed down and then stopped and turned to face him. "You were not walking. And you don't own me, Marco Giovinco. I thought I owed you some thanks for listening to me and encouraging me. I probably mistook your interest in me. I suppose I thought a friendship had formed." She bit her lip and looked down. She had not meant to say all this.

Suddenly Marco remembered being in the park with his sister. He narrowed his eyes as he studied her.

"Tell me, was I with someone in the park?"

Her head snapped up as she remembered the pain she had felt seeing him with the woman.

"Yes, a woman in fact. You were rowing her in a boat." And she turned and strode purposefully along the sidewalk.

Marco watched her for a moment, and then caught up to her again. He was not about to tell Elisabeth about his unfortunate sister while standing on a street corner.

"It is not my whereabouts we were discussing, signorina, but yours. You were not incorrect to have understood that I offered you my friendship. But then I did not know you were lying about your so-called husband. Or was there some truth to it? A husband in prison, and a gentleman who keeps you? Is that how it is? Tell me now if you are indeed the mistress of the gentleman in the big mansion. I usually like to know with whom a woman I take to supper is sleeping."

Elisabeth stopped dead and turned to stare at him in horror. Her ears rang with the insult. It took a moment for her to understand how he had misconstrued what he had seen at her father's house. She started to defend herself and then stopped. Marco himself was the philanderer. She would not waste words on him. Her rising temper and disappointment made her want to do nothing more than to extricate herself from the conversation quickly.

She turned and continued across Sixth Avenue. Once on the other side, she walked on, but at a slower pace. Marco stayed up with her, determined to be satisfied.

"Tell me, signorina. Did you make up the story about your 'husband' as well? Or was that a blind?"

"What business of it is yours?" said Elisabeth, feeling less and less able to deal with the conversation. "Or do you pry into the personal lives of all your female companions? I appreciate your help with my dreams of singing, sir, but I must make it clear that you cannot expect me to repay that kindness in the fashion you seem to construe. In case you had not understood before, I do not accept gifts of stockings from gentlemen friends."

Marco blinked. Her non sequitur comment left him nonplussed. What stockings?

They had reached the corner of Fifth Avenue, and Elisabeth turned and walked uptown. Marco paused at the corner by a stone railing. The rattle of traffic was quieter here, and he watched Elisabeth negotiate around a mother with a baby stroller and large parasol. A gentleman in a bowler hat accidently bumped Marco and begged his pardon.

Finally Marco realized what Elisabeth meant about the stockings. The ones he had lent Nordica had been intended for his sister, and Elisabeth had misconstrued their meaning. He would have laughed had it not irked him that Elisabeth had turned the tables on him. She still had not explained her visit to the Fifth Avenue mansion, where she was no doubt now headed.

He was hesitant to tell anyone connected to the opera about his sister for fear of the publicity that might ensue, and it annoyed him that Elisabeth might force his hand. How exasperating. Nor did he like it that she had gained the upper hand in the conversation.

Not noticing the interested stares of ladies and gentlemen he passed as he hurried determinedly to catch up to Elisabeth, Marco formed the Italian oaths that spun in his mind into a question to put to her. Touching her elbow in a manner that was a degree possessive, he bent his head toward her.

"Just tell me the truth, is it your husband who lives on upper Fifth Avenue? If so, then you have my apologies and we will cease this senseless conversation."

Again Elisabeth paused and turned her face toward him. She definitely did not understand his mad accusations.

"No," she said impatiently. "It is not my husband."

Marco's face darkened. He did not blame a man for wanting to take her as a mistress. But what he couldn't stand was her innocent, untouched look. She was more accomplished that he would have guessed.

He dropped her elbow and gave a mock bow with his head. "Then I can only assume the worst. I did not know you were someone else's property," he said, not bothering to cover the fact that he himself had begun to imagine her in those same terms. "I am sure you will do very well for yourself."

Elisabeth blanched at being called a courtesan to her face. Anger and vexation swam through her so that she could not bring herself to speak. How dare he call her such names? Just like a man to blame the woman he suspected of easy virtue, when it was perfectly all right for him to squire as many women as he pleased. Words could not express her fury.

She turned and marched away as quickly as she

could, not wanting to give in to the exasperation and disappointment that threatened her armada of angry emotions. While at the same time she saw that her ability to judge a man's character was growing poorer by the day. Why was she so lacking in that ability? She would be better off in a convent. But at least she had found out about Marco Giovinco in the early stages of her growing infatuation with the man. Perhaps she had learned her lessons the hard way. He was not to be trusted, and she could not afford to make that mistake again. Her life had been saved from ruin by some stroke of providence. She would not be so lucky a second time.

Marco watched her go with vexation. He had the impotent feeling that he had not said what he had wanted to say at all. Nor could he help the regret that pervaded his heart. In spite of his male pride, he knew he had not handled the situation well.

He turned and started back toward Broadway. A walk would do him good. He would walk home to his apartment in the Ansonia uptown. He would most likely not have occasion to speak to Elisabeth Sloane Kendall about anything personal again. The doubt about not revealing Lucinda's identity unsettled him. But why should he have to tell anyone? It was none of Elisabeth's business. Ha! The very words she had thrown back at him. And he didn't like the twisted feeling in his heart. He needed a woman. And yet at the moment bedding one of the show girls or women of easy virtue whose favors he had occasionally paid for in the past did not appeal to him.

* * *

Feeling the need to do something other than return to her father's house and fume, Elisabeth went to Professor Schlut's studio. He was just seeing a student out the door and invited her into the sitting room.

"Ah, it's good to see you, my dear. I hope you've come back to tell me you are ready to start studying." He motioned her onto the worn brown sofa.

"I would like to study," she said after they had both sat down. "But I wanted to tell you that I will make arrangements. I assume my, um . . . that is the person who offered to pay for the lessons is no longer interested in so doing. In fact, I would prefer to pay for the lessons myself. I believe I have found a way."

Professor Schlut raised a hand. "There is no need for concern, my dear. I can assure you that the funds are in no danger of being discontinued."

Elisabeth blinked in puzzlement. Perhaps Marco had not had time to tell Professor Schlut that he would not be paying for her lessons. But surely he would do so before long.

She smiled at the professor. "I really would prefer to pay for the lessons myself. When can we begin?"

The professor consulted an appointment book on his cluttered writing desk.

"I believe Thursdays at eleven in the morning would suit. Could you be here this Thursday?"

She got up. "Most certainly. I will look forward to it."

A scratch sounded on the other side of the door leading to the music room.

"Oh, yes, it's time for Governor Worthy's walk. Would you like to join us? We are going to the park."

She looked at the droopy-eyed Afghan that Professor Schlut let into the room. A walk through the park might be nice. "Thank you, I can walk home that way."

The three of them took the elevator and walked the two blocks to the park. Elisabeth began to feel hopeful, a feeling that was new to her.

She didn't work at the opera house anymore, and so she would not have to run into Marco. Thoughts of him disturbed her, but it was better to forget him. Odd how he had come into her life just at the time he did. It was almost as if he were a sort of bridge between the life she had been living for the last two years and the life on which she was now going to embark.

Elisabeth breathed in the fresh November air. It was almost Thanksgiving. She had been to a degree reunited with her father. The holiday season was not a time to be alone if possible. With her old acquaintances, her music studies and the festivities that would no doubt take place at the brick and white stone mansion this month and next, she had much to look forward to.

Opal helped her get settled in her room. Miranda seemed to take to the new surroundings. The housekeeper was glad to help take care of the cat and made a bed for it in the kitchen. Elisabeth insisted on allowing Miranda to sleep in her room, but promised to bring her down to the kitchen during the day so that the puss would not have an opportunity to dig her claws into fine furniture.

Dinners with Winston became less strained, almost pleasant as they avoided dangerous subjects and made plans for the holiday season and agreed on a date for her "welcome home" party. Elisabeth knew she would find that event artificial since she would have to be on her guard every moment about what she said.

Luckily she had actually been to Europe many years ago and could remember enough about what she had seen to be able to carry off conversations, she hoped. It would no doubt be tricky. Someone might catch her out, but there was no other solution. In any case, most of the guests would be more interested in talking about themselves than in caring about what she had done in Europe.

As she and Winston took coffee in the French parlor, she brought up the matter of the music lessons in such a way as to not arouse her father's suspicions about wanting a career.

"Of course I don't object to your lessons," he said. "I'll write a bank draft for the amount as long as you plan to develop your talent for purely domestic purposes."

"Thank you, Father," she said, making a mental note to keep track of the amount he spent so that she could pay him back if she did make a career. The matter settled, she retired to bed with more ease. She had escaped an unfortunate past. Opportunity beckoned. If she were careful, perhaps her life would amount to something after all.

She climbed between the sheets and Miranda sat down on the coverlet, curling her tail around her. She blinked large golden brown eyes at Elisabeth and then stretched out as if her feline world had gotten settled too, and she could have a long nap. Elisabeth stroked her soft fur.

"You don't care if we live in a palace or a boarding house, do you, little one?" she said. "As long as there's food in your bowl."

Miranda licked her fingers and purred.

The next morning Gwendolyn helped Elisabeth into a walking out costume with tight, high collar and ruffled wrists. The velvet jacket with braid trim was fastened at the waist and matched the flared velvet skirt. On her head was a large hat and tight veil fixed with large steel pins.

Madelaine was waiting for her when she came downstairs. "How marvelous you look," exclaimed Madelaine. "Oh, we shall have such a fun day."

Elisabeth could not help but return Madelaine's sunny smile. The day was sunny too, and as they climbed into the open victoria, they chattered about where they would shop. Elisabeth shook her head to herself in amusement. She had not had a shopping spree since she could remember.

Their first stop was at a well-known couturier they had both used in the past. They took seats in the elegant salon, and the models paraded and turned before the girls. Elisabeth found herself examining the workmanship of the gowns with a more appraising eye than she did the styles themselves. She was examining the depth of a hem when she felt Madelaine's eyes on her, and she slowly straightened and dropped the hem.

"Very nice . . . material," she said, trying not to display her guilt.

"Yes it is," said Madelaine, but her eyes retained a look of curiosity.

It might have meant nothing, but Elisabeth felt the flood of uneasiness that accompanied the fear of being found out. For the rest of the showing she sat back in her chair and forced herself to admire the gowns, not wondering how they were constructed. She nodded and mumbled assent whenever Madelaine insisted that this or that gown would be perfect for her. The colors and materials began to blur, and she was relieved when it was over.

Their selections made, the girls stood to have their measurements taken. Afterward, they returned to the street and went on to the dry goods palaces. They were just entering Stewart's large iron-fronted store on Broadway when a voice rang out behind them.

"Madelaine, halloo."

Elisabeth turned and the tall, slender young man hurrying after them came to a halt, his fair countenance lit with surprise.

"I can't believe my eyes. But it is Elisabeth Sloane, isn't it?"

Elisabeth glanced sidelong at Madelaine. There was something a bit rehearsed about Alex Rochat's greeting, and she wondered if Madelaine had dropped a word to him that they would be shopping here.

"It is I, Alex. How are you?" She smiled and extended her gloved hand.

Her old friend and sometimes suitor clasped her hand warmly and raised it to his lips. When he raised his head, his warm blue eyes settled on her. The old charisma emanated from his expressive face. The white scarf that was loosely thrown about his neck and drifting down his double-breasted top coat and his sandy blond hair, ruffled by the crisp breeze when he removed his tall hat gave him a devil-may-care look. His lips curved under the blond moustache, slightly twisted at the ends.

"You look wonderful, Elisabeth. I admit Madelaine told me you were in town. I was actually planning to call on you right away. How fortunate to run into you like this."

She lifted an eyebrow. Although she could see right through Alex's charm, he could be a pleasant companion, and she was not unhappy to see him. In a way, he represented happy times from the past when she had frolicked with her friends at parties and in the country when they could escape their chaperones.

"I'm glad to see you too, Alex. Were you, um, planning on shopping today?"

He did not at all mind her teasing tone and delivered a cavalier reply. "I get lost in these large stores. I no sooner enter the floor than I forget what gift or trifle I came for. If one of the clerks approaches me, I break out in a cold sweat, feeling inept in foreign territory and end up by beating a hasty retreat. Christmas and birthdays are all the same, I have to send my valet to negotiate the aisle and procure what's on my list."

The two girls laughed, winking at each other, and taking each of his arms pulled him farther into the main floor.

"Well now, Alex, since you're here, perhaps Elisabeth and I can help you," teased Madelaine. "What did you have in mind? A pin cushion for your mother? Some French yard goods? A new cravat for yourself? Surely you will need stocking stuffers for the servants. I assure you, you are in good hands, isn't he, Elisabeth? We will make your Christmas shopping a pleasure."

"Indeed," agreed Elisabeth.

With Alex protesting, they dragged him along the aisle, pausing to admire accessories on the first floor. Then they climbed the wide staircase to the second floor where they examined men's hats, more for the amusement of trying them on Alex than in any serious attempt to make a purchase.

At the end of half an hour, Alex insisted he had no more stamina for this and claimed he would drop if they did not proceed at once uptown to the Waldorf for a pot of tea and some cakes. Elisabeth was relieved that they did not spend more time at the store. Her world of late had been so consumed by operatic costumes and her mode of living had been so simple that it would take some adjustment to become aware of the latest fashions again. Instead, she allowed herself to be swept along with her two friends.

The Waldorf-Astoria Hotel fourteen blocks uptown was a monument to elegance and fine cuisine. As Elisabeth stepped into the German Renaissance building, with its gabled and tiled roofs, the memories all came back to her. Here society and those who wished to be accepted by society paraded along the public corridors to see and be seen. The pale green satin hangings, frescoes and marble pillars set off the wealthy patrons to great advantage.

The three passed along Peacock Alley to the main dining room, and both Madelaine and Alex nodded to acquaintances along the way. Elisabeth set a smile on her face in case she was expected to exchange pleasantries with someone she should know.

At the door to the main dining room, Alex greeted Oscar, the maitre d'hôtel, who welcomed them warmly.

Oscar exchanged greetings with them with a practiced aplomb, welcoming them all by name.

"You will remember Miss Sloane," said Alex. "She's just returned to us from abroad."

Oscar bowed. "Of course. It has been some time since you have graced the Palm Garden with your presence."

"Thank you," said Elisabeth. "I am glad to be back."

After the maitre d' ushered them to a table in the center of the elegant room, an army of waiters sailed around them, draping linen napkins over laps and filling water glasses.

The Palm Garden was much like a fish bowl with its glass walls and wide open doors. Far from an intimate chat with friends Elisabeth felt like they were on display, which indeed they were. Those who dined in the Palm Garden were always flushed with the excitement of watching interesting people around them and of being watched. A glass wall separated the dining room from the Men's Cafe, and floor-to-ceiling mirrors offered the diners an uninterrupted view of themselves and others.

"Thank heaven we're here," said Alex. "I think that after all I must leave shopping to those more qualified to do it. Now, what shall we have?"

They studied the menu which offered sandwiches and delicacies to go with their tea, and after dispensing with their orders they launched into an animated conversation.

"Alex is working for his father's firm now that he's graduated from Yale," said Madelaine. "He must work very hard for we don't see him at nearly so many social functions anymore, much to our loss."

Alex waved a hand. He had seated himself beside her at the square table where he could face the glass wall that gave onto the Men's Cafe, a place where men of business affairs gathered to exchange stock tips, financial advice, drink and keep an eye on business all within view of the main social dining room of the entire nation.

"I suppose it's true. I must say I've learned more on the floor of the stock exchange than in my years at college. Of course I'm lucky. My father and grandfather made our fortune. All I've got to do is manage it."

The waiters brought the tea and sandwiches and they dived into the repast.

"But how was your trip, my dear Elisabeth?" asked Alex after his stomach had been satisfied at least to some degree. "We pined away for news and got so little."

Elisabeth managed to maintain the right expression as she set down her teacup. "I am sorry about that. I am a terrible correspondent in any case. And I was so intent on studying music, moving every so often so that I could meet different teachers."

"And did you find your pursuit satisfactory?"

"Quite." Elisabeth gave him a direct look. "I intend to pursue it here, as well. I, . . . that is, a few of my teachers were encouraging enough to say that I should not give up my studies."

Alex reached across the table and squeezed her hand. "I remember that you had a good voice. I can't wait to hear you sing for us again."

Elisabeth blushed.

"Why yes," chimed in Madelaine. "You did say you

171

were going to have a party. You can entertain us then."

"Well, I don't know if I'm ready. My teacher told me I must proceed cautiously," she managed to get out.

"Well in two years you must have learned a song or two. You are just being modest. It becomes you."

She did not miss his flattery and tried frantically to turn the conversation away from herself.

"But tell me more about yourself, Alex. I cannot believe that work has kept you away from all your social pursuits."

"Oh I do manage to go the opera. I'm actually quite a fan of it."

Elisabeth swallowed, suddenly remembering peeking out from behind the curtain not so long ago and feeling as if Alex might have actually seen her do so, though the idea was preposterous.

"Yes," she said with a croaking voice. "I look forward to attending again."

"You must have seen many fine performances in Europe," said Madelaine. "Did you go to Bayreuth to hear Wagner? Wagner was all the rage here last year, you know. But the box owners got tired of such serious music and now we're having the gay Italian opera back. I for one am glad." She leaned closer to Elisabeth. "And that wonderful tenor, Marco Giovinco. Really, you must see him. I think he was only appearing in minor roles when you left. But now he is everyone's favorite."

"I . . . um . . . knew about the happenings at the Metropolitan." She searched for something to say. "I'm glad the Italian opera is back." She smiled wanly.

"We must all go. You must come sit in our box, Elisabeth," said Alex. "Unless of course you invite me to call on you in yours."

She stared at him blankly. Of course she would now have the opportunity to see as much opera as she wished since her father was a box holder. It would be interesting to see it from the auditorium instead of from the wings. A twinge passed through her. She was not sure which she preferred.

Alex entertained them with anecdotes that kept them laughing as the waiters brought fresh pots of tea. Elisabeth began to feel her stays squeezing after eating and drinking so much, and it seemed the gay afternoon was coming to a close. Then she glanced up at the mirror a few tables away, and to her horror she saw Marco rise from a table with a group of people. She glanced down, her face flushed, hoping he would not notice them. But Alex foiled her plan to remain anonymous.

"Say, I do believe that is the famous tenor we were just speaking of."

Chapter Eleven

Madelaine twisted in her chair, leaned out and gawked. She gave an audible gasp. "My heavens, it is him."

She turned back in her chair, all atwitter at seeing the handsome star. But Alex was already out of his chair. He had met Marco at a salon, and if he passed this way, he was prepared to shake his hand.

Marco followed the group of matronly ladies and a gentleman in a ministerial collar. His gaze swept over Elisabeth, who was trying to melt into her upholstered chair. Simultaneously Alex stepped into the aisle.

"Mr. Giovinco, excuse me. We met at Madame Lyndhurst's soirée last spring. But of course I do not expect you to remember. I am Alexander Rochat."

Marco halted and blinked, taking the proffered hand. "Of course, of course," he said.

"It was a May evening, as I recall," Alex continued. "You sang grandly for us as Madame's daughter accompanied. Then we all drank punch on the flagstone patio."

"Yes, you're quite right," said Marco. His gaze was beginning to drift over Alex's companions. Apparently his party did not miss him, for the minister and the ladies had continued out of the dining room, no doubt to wait for him in Peacock Alley.

There was no place to run and Elisabeth knew that the game was up. There was no chance to beg Marco not to give her away even if he would have abided by her wishes, which was doubtful.

"May I present my companions, Miss Madelaine Lord and Miss Elisabeth Sloane." Alex gestured to each young lady in turn.

Marco bowed to Madelaine who was thrilled to meet the famous idol.

"How marvelously you sang the other night in *La Traviata,*" exclaimed Madelaine.

Elisabeth knew she must be beet red and gazed with fright at Marco. When his eyes met hers, they registered her panic.

There was a moment's hesitation and then he said, "Miss Sloane and I know each other already," and he bowed to her in turn.

She couldn't speak but sat as if stone dead.

"Oh, you must have met in Paris," said Madelaine. "Elisabeth, why didn't you tell us you knew Marco Giovinco? But of course you moved in operatic circles there. How rude of us not to give you a chance to tell us."

Marco raised an eyebrow, but he read the look of panic on Elisabeth's lovely face. He also sensed her desperation. Something was amiss here that he would have to sort out later. It seemed his lovely protégé never tired of charades. However, prudence and his good manners kept him from exposing her game now. He was not insensitive to her look of distress.

His mocking look turned to something more understanding and with his next words her heart began to beat again. He gave her a look filled with the polite charm he used for flattering strangers.

"Of course, Paris. You will excuse me if I forget exactly where we first met." He made a gesture with his hand that indicated forgetfulness. "You would be so kind if you would refresh my memory."

Elisabeth gulped a breath. "Yes. Of course. Wasn't it Professor . . ." She cast about for a likely French name.

"Giroux?" said Marco, getting into the spirit of their little lie. He saw clearly now that she needed a story to fool her friends. What harm was there in helping her? He was an actor, was he not?

"Maxamillian Giroux, of course, of course," Marco went on, giving Elisabeth time to concoct a story. "I forget if you were one of his students or a friend. Eh?"

"Yes, yes, a student," stammered Elisabeth. "He . . . he introduced me to many of the people in his circle."

"Ah yes."

Marco was beginning to enjoy the scene. Alex and Madelaine swung their gazes from where Elisabeth sat to where Marco stood opposite her. Obviously they were engrossed in watching the conversation, and having an audience only served to stimulate Marco. He placed an index finger on the side of his chin and searched his imaginary memory.

"I remember seeing you at an evening soirée at the professor's. Perhaps that was the first time."

Elisabeth allowed herself to relax a trace and tried to lean more casually against the back of her chair. To her surprise, Marco was not going to give her away.

"Uh, yes, the soirée. You were so kind to come."

Marco brightened. "It was a little evening of song, and Maxamillian's students sang. I remember being very impressed with you that evening. You sang 'Someday He'll Come,' and then something from that operetta, one of Gilbert and Sullivan's." He cleverly mentioned the pieces he had indeed heard her sing at her audition with Professor Schlut. "Delightful indeed."

This time her smile was genuine. With Marco playing along she took in Alex's and Madelaine's reactions out of the corner of her eye. They were believing it, and she allowed herself a small victory.

"It was in the summer, of course," Marco explained to the others. "I have summer engagements with the Paris Opera."

"Of course," said Alex.

"And then there was the little group that dined at the Cafe Rémy. How could I forget that night? Our table by the fountain, the strolling violin players."

Elisabeth caught the glint in his eye. He was having fun with their little drama. In spite of the knot in her stomach, she was determined to play along and laughed lightly.

"How right you are. I so enjoyed the after opera suppers. My friend Madame Blanche..."

"Of course," Marco snapped his fingers. "Madame Blanche. She always brought her protégés to the cafe after the performances. Those were memorable evenings."

He held her gaze and for a moment what they described seemed almost true.

"It is nice to see you again," faltered Elisabeth, thinking they had said enough.

"I assure you the pleasure is mine. I fear that I must leave this enchanting group. I must catch up with Father Petrillo. I have agreed to sing at St. Michael's parish on Christmas eve."

"How wonderful for the congregation," said Madelaine.

Marco nodded humbly. "It is a tradition I observe every year. I grew up in that parish."

Alex shook hands with him. "It was good of you to stop and say hello. We did not mean to detain you."

"My pleasure," said Marco. Then he nodded to Madelaine and to Elisabeth.

As they watched him walk away, Elisabeth exhaled a sigh of relief.

Madelaine's eyes were round with excitement. "How marvelous, and we didn't even know you knew him. I think he is just as handsome in person as he is on the stage. Tell us, did you see him very often in Paris?"

"Well . . ."

Alex was frowning. "Come now, Madelaine. Elisabeth doesn't know him that well. You could see that they could barely remember meeting each other."

Elisabeth felt relieved that the little scene had gone well, but she didn't want to perpetuate the lie. To her chagrin, she found it was not so easy to extricate herself.

"I have an idea," said Madelaine. "Since you know Marco Giovinco, why not invite him to your soirée?"

Elisabeth looked horrified, but Madelaine continued on a tear. "Surely he'd not refuse you."

"Oh come now," interjected Alex. "You can't impose on the man's schedule like that. He must have social engagements from now 'til doomsday. The party is for Elisabeth. We don't need an opera star. Elisabeth will shine as the center of attention."

Elisabeth blinked wide eyes at him. From his look of irritation, she might guess that he was actually jealous.

"On the contrary," said Madelaine. "It would be a feather in her cap to have such an illustrious guest. Oh do ask him, Elisabeth. It would be such fun. In fact," she said, turning to Alex. "We can invite him to our box after the opera. Didn't you say we would all go together, Alex? Just imagine what everyone will think when they see one of the stars in our box."

Elisabeth twisted her gloves in her lap. "Well, I don't know. I'll have to see."

"Oh just send him a note at intermission," said Madelaine. "We'll go on Monday night."

Elisabeth felt swept away by the plans and resolved to think her way out of the dilemma later. Alex signed the bill to his account, and they went on their way.

Apparently their shopping spree was over, for outside they strolled along the avenue, looking in the shop windows. Alex bid them goodbye and headed for the elevated train to take him all the way downtown to his office on Wall Street. He kissed Elisabeth's hand warmly and then scurried off.

"Alex is a dear, isn't he?" said Madelaine as the girls left the busy avenue for a quieter side street. "I think he has settled down."

Shaking her head, Elisabeth smiled. "Knowing Alex I'm not sure that's possible."

When they got tired of walking, they hailed a hansom and rode uptown. After bidding Madelaine goodbye, Elisabeth gratefully retreated to her father's house and climbed the stairs to her room.

Miranda rose from her position in the middle of the embroidered silk coverlet on the bed when Elisabeth entered the room.

"Meeeow." The cat stretched and then hopped down to trot across the rug and greet her mistress. Elisabeth bent down and picked the kitty up, cuddling her against her neck and rubbing her cheek on the soft, comforting fur.

"Hello, girl. You're supposed to be in the kitchen, hmmm?"

She carried the cat to her wing chair by the window and sank into it. Miranda curled in her arms and licked her face. Outside the bare branches moved with sudden gusts of wind. Marco was most likely getting ready for the opera house. She sighed, shaking her head at the rapid events that had chased her these last weeks. What she needed was a long hot bath and a toddy before dinner.

Acting on the idea, she shooed the cat off her lap, pulled the bell rope for Opal to ask for a bath and a hot toddy. How easy it was to fall back on the habit of being waited on. The idea made her feel slightly guilty.

Then she changed to a dressing gown and spent the rest of the afternoon relaxing. She tried to sift through the social events to which it seemed she was going to be obligated and tried to think about her coming voice lesson. At least she could throw herself into her singing, for that would give her an anchor. Everything else would have to take second place.

The thought steadied her. Friends and social events, even embarrassing confrontations might come and go. But now she had a purpose.

The next morning she and her father discussed the party that they would be obligated to give now that she had returned to society. The date was set and they went over a guest list. Elisabeth began to write out invitations. As she wrote the names on the gilt-edged envelopes and sealed them with wax, the images of the old acquaintances came to mind.

She paused over the invitation to Consuelo Vanderbilt, remembering seeing her in the box the night she had gazed out from behind the curtains in the opera house. She wanted to see Consuelo. They had been close friends as girls, and she had the feeling her friend's life was not going well. Her mother was too domineering. And now she was being courted by the Duke of Marlboro. What had happened to Winthrop Rutherford?

In spite of Consuelo's extreme wealth and her family's social position, Elisabeth guessed that the girl was lonely. She decided to call on her soon. For though their lives had been different in the extreme of late, she felt a kindred spirit with the Vanderbilt heiress.

Later in the morning, she left her invitations and dressed to go out. For today she would actually begin her singing lessons. The day was gray and nippy, but bells jingled on harnesses and passersby wished each other Thanksgiving greetings reminding Elisabeth that soon she would need to do some serious Christmas shopping. Thanksgiving was two days away, and no sooner was that over than the household would begin to prepare for Christmas. She mentally ticked off a list of gifts for the servants and pondered what to get her father. She also decided she would take a hand in the Christmas dinner. Such thoughts lightened her steps. She would like to send gifts to her friends at the boarding house, but that presented a problem for they would want to know where she had gone.

Alighting from the carriage at Fifty-seventh Street, she went in the side door of Carnegie Hall and took the lift to Professor Schlut's floor.

He answered her knock and ushered her in with enthusiasm. She automatically greeted Governor Worthy who was curled up in his spot by the andirons. The dog's ears perked up as the professor ran his finger over the Steinway's keys and led Elisabeth in a series of vocal exercises to warm up her voice and to enable him to become familiar with her range.

But she soon forgot the dog, forgot her domestic worries and everything else as she began to experience the joy of singing. Her voice lifted her spirits and Professor Schlut gently showed her how to open her top notes without straining.

"The voice must be exercised gently every day," he said. "Do not strain. Using your voice in the right way will make it stronger. It is in some ways like chopping wood in the woodshed. You must go to the woodshed everyday. You have a natural gift, and we mustn't force it. Now let us take up a piece from the Italian repertoire and begin to work on phrasing and style."

After she sang a piece for him, he commented that her Italian was a little flat and showed her how to pronounce the vowels correctly. Elisabeth found it a great deal of fun and threw her whole body into the pronunciations as he guided her. At the end, he praised her efforts.

Governor Worthy, used to the routines by now, had gone to sleep by the time twelve o'clock struck on the grandfather clock by the wall. Elisabeth reached for her reticule.

"My father has sent a bank draft for several months of lessons," she began, but the professor cut her off.

"As I said before, the fee has been taken care of, my dear. Your father may keep his money."

Elisabeth blinked. "But that is impossible. Surely . . ." She was about to make a comment on the fact that Marco could surely have no reason to sponsor her lessons now. She frowned, but the professor rose from the piano bench and gestured toward the door. He gazed at her over his pince-nez glasses, his look signaling that there was no need to discuss it.

"I assure you, the matter is arranged. You need to trouble yourself no more."

Bewildered, she put the bank draft back into the reticule. "In that case, perhaps I can repay my benefactor someday."

Professor Schlut's eyes reflected a perplexing expression. "That would be difficult, but if it makes you feel better. . . ." he let it drift off.

He saw her to the door of the sitting room, took her hand and expressed his admonishments for her to practice.

"We have a fine piano in our music room," she said smiling. "I am sure the servants will not mind listening to me sing for several hours every day."

She had already decided to practice her music while

her father was at the bank so as not to aggravate his concerns that she might be too serious about her pursuit. She bid the professor goodbye and left, feeling invigorated after the lesson but perplexed about her benefactor.

As she descended in the lift she decided there was only one way to handle it. She must speak to Marco. The idea of seeing him filled her with dread. She had still not gotten over the hurt he had caused her with his accusations. But their strained relationship could not go on. She had to seek him out and explain everything in order to avoid complications in the future. She held out no hope that he would sing at her party, but if she told him what had transpired after he had left their table at the Waldorf, at least she could tell Madelaine that she had asked him.

The opera house was a beehive of activity, and Maurice Grau was the first to spy her as she came through the stage door and up the stairs. He hurried over to grasp her hands.

"Elisabeth, my dear, what a pleasant surprise."

He cleared his throat in embarrassment. She smiled. He had never addressed her by her Christian name before, but her comfortable manner seemed to put him at ease.

"It's good to see you, too, Maurice." Now that she didn't work for him, she saw no reason to maintain the formality of using his surname.

He seemed reluctant to let her hand go. "I would like to think you have returned to the fold," he continued. "But from your look of prosperity, my hopes are dashed. Do not keep me wondering. Tell me at once if the nature of your visit is business or, dare I hope even more, social?"

She laughed good-naturedly but warded off his warm insinuations. She suspected that Maurice Grau's hovering concern for her in the past meant more than professional courtesy, and she had the feeling that if she let him, he would pursue her in another arena.

"You're right. I'm not presently in need of work. I'm afraid I've come to speak to someone."

"And the singing? Are you practicing?"

"Yes. I just had my first lesson today. I feel I am going to enjoy it."

"Then that is good."

Just then there arose the sound of a squabble coming from the main stage, and she recognized Marco's voice issuing a string of Italian interjections. She did not recognize the female who shrieked back at him, but Maurice's face at once paled. The stage manager came running in their direction and grasped Maurice's arm.

"Come, Maurice. The maestro is getting nowhere with Madame Melba and Giovinco. They hated each other on sight and it is getting no better."

Maurice turned to Elisabeth. "Excuse me, my dear."

She nodded. "Of course."

She followed more slowly. From the wings she could see that a piano had been rolled to the center of the main stage, and that Maestro Gatti was standing beside it arguing and gesticulating with a small man in a bowler hat, who in turn was pleading with a short, pretty, dark-haired woman, who stood with her hands on her hips. Elisabeth at once recognized the famous Australian diva, Nellie Melba.

But her eyes were drawn to Marco who was now

engaged in conversation with the stage manager and with Maurice, both of whom were doing their utmost to make the peace.

Elisabeth's lips drew up in amusement. She knew better than to interrupt now, but decided to make her way into the auditorium and watch the rehearsal for a while. When they took a break, she could approach Marco and settle with him what must be settled.

She slipped down the steps into the auditorium and walked back along a side aisle to take a seat in the shadows where she could see the stage very well.

The group on stage were dressed in street clothes against the half built set. Marco leaned his back against the head of a large dragon, his arms crossed and his dark brows knotted in a frown. He looked as if he had just slayed the wrong dragon.

The maestro returned to his chair near the edge of the stage where he had a score open on a music desk in front of him. As if he were conducting an orchestra and not just two singers and a piano, he lifted his baton and began.

Elisabeth sat engrossed as the scene progressed, and found herself moved by Marco's poignant singing. Even sitting in a chair and pretending to be asleep, which the scene demanded, Nellie Melba was straight as a rod and domineering even in the simple white lace blouse and dark skirt that came to her toes. But when she opened her mouth the stage was transformed into the home of the gods. Her pure and silvery singing was spectacular in its brilliance, but she had none of Marco's warmth.

As Elisabeth watched the scene, her heart beat fortissimo, and she could not help the sensations

Marco's movements aroused in her. She sank deeper into the plush seat, embarrassed by her warm cheeks and her grasp of the chair arms. Marco's passion and his voice soared over her into the depths of the opera house, and the piano accompaniment expanded to a full orchestra in her ears. When he grasped Melba, Elisabeth felt as if his hands were closing around her own shoulders and she felt her breath catch.

Gradually Melba's iciness on stage melted as did Elisabeth's defenses watching from the auditorium, and when Marco sang his love and the lovers embraced on stage, Elisabeth had to shut her eyes. The exultant duet throbbed with high ecstasy, filling her with rapture as it would fill a real audience with rapture at the performance.

She was grateful that she was sitting down, and when she opened her eyes again, she swallowed. Her breasts ached with desire as she imagined Marco's lips on them, and she flushed in shame. How could she speak to this man who had such an unpredictable effect on her? She could not face him. She must escape quickly to the fresh air outside.

She sprang up and tried to slide into the aisle, but it was too late. She heard her name repeated from the stage and then Marco turned on his heel and crossed to the edge of the stage.

"Well, Miss Kendall is it? Or Miss Sloane? Which? I did not know that I had an additional critic in the audience for today's rehearsal."

She stiffened her back at his cynical tone as he came down the steps. She took several deep breaths and tried to even her physical reactions as he took the remaining steps toward her.

"Good afternoon," she finally managed as he reached her.

His dark eyes bore into hers even in the dim auditorium where only the light from the stage penetrated the inky shadows.

"Good afternoon to you," he said.

For a moment they stood facing each other, and she was intensely aware of his breathing and hers. But she had to say something.

"I wanted to speak to you," she said stiffly, trying to keep her knees from quaking. She could never admit how his singing had affected her.

He seemed about to make a rejoiner and then some doubt made him change his mind. "I see," he said.

She took a deep breath and plunged in, resisting the impulse to flee. "I wish to straighten out a misunderstanding you have about me and to apologize for placing you in an awkward position at tea yesterday."

He gazed at her for a long moment as if assessing her. When he spoke his voice was less angry and it was full of that caressing quality that so unnerved her.

"Well then, speak."

"I am not . . . ," she swallowed before going on. "I am not the mistress of the gentleman who lives in the mansion you saw me enter the other week. Winston Sloane is my father."

Marco blinked. Then he frowned. Finally he took her elbow and ushered her a few steps farther into the back of the auditorium where no one would bother them.

"Your father?" he finally asked. "Then why were you living at the boarding house, if I may ask?" But the edge had gone out of his words. Even as he spoke them he could well imagine what had happened and anticipated her answer.

"What I told you about my former marriage was true," she said in a hush. "My father disowned me at the time. Then when my husband went to prison I had to have a way to support myself. I was a good seamstress and found work here. That is the truth."

He stopped and faced her, catching the moisture reflecting from her eyes even in the dim light. He resisted an impulse to raise his fingers to brush her cheek.

"I see," he said more gruffly than he felt in order to hide his own feelings.

Elisabeth rushed on. "I received word that my husband is dead. I am free again. And my first wish was to be reconciled with my father. I returned home and he welcomed me. It seemed an opportune time to make a clean break with . . . with everything."

She turned her face to the side, finding it hard to meet Marco's intent gaze. She felt Marco move beside her.

"I see," he said. It seemed a long moment before he said in a low voice, "Then I was mistaken. I jumped to conclusions. I'm sorry."

She laughed with relief and nervousness at the same time. "I can't expect anyone to understand. I've made rather a mess of things."

Now Marco did not resist taking her hand and raising it slowly to his lips. As he did so the warmth flooded through her again, and this time she could not stop the tingling of her flesh at his touch.

"You must not suffer for it," he said, his voice a whisper close to her ear. "I am truly sorry for the faulty accusations. I was foolishly jealous."

She closed her eyes and leaned against him as he reached around her and closed his hand on her shoulder as she imagined he might do. He pulled her against his chest and brushed her ear with his lips.

"I am sorry for the man who lost you," he said. "It is not good to speak ill of the dead. But I hope you do not waste your grief."

"No, no," she said, unable to resist from languishing in his arms. "It was a mistake from the beginning. I am only grateful that I have been freed. His soul must find its way to the next life on its own."

She heard the pleasure, the relief, and the enticement in Marco's voice as he whispered in sensuous tones, "Yes, you are free at last."

Now you can get Heartfire Romances right at home and save

Get 4 Free Heartfire Novels. A $17.00 Value!

Home Subscription Members can enjoy Heartfire Romances and Save $$$$$ each month.

ENJOY ALL THE PASSION AND ROMANCE OF...

Heartfire

ROMANCES from ZEBRA

After you have read HEARTFIRE ROMANCES, we're sure you'll agree that HEARTFIRE sets new standards of excellence for historical romantic fiction. Each Zebra HEARTFIRE novel is the ultimate blend of intimate romance and grand adventure and each takes place in the kinds of historical settings you want most...the American Revolution, the Old West, Civil War and more.

SUBSCRIBERS $AVE, $AVE, $AVE!!!

As a HEARTFIRE Home Subscriber, you'll save with your HEARTFIRE Subscription. You'll receive 4 brand new Heartfire Romances to preview Free for 10 days each month. If you decide to keep them you'll pay only $3.50 each; a total of $14.00 and you'll save $3.00 each month off the cover price.

Plus, we'll send you these novels as soon as they are published each month. There is never any shipping, handling or other hidden charges; home delivery is always FREE! And there is no obligation to buy even a single book. You may return any of the books within 10 days for full credit and you can cancel your subscription at any time. No questions asked.

Zebra's HEARTFIRE ROMANCES Are The Ultimate
In Historical Romantic Fiction.
Start Enjoying Romance As You Have Never Enjoyed It Before...
With 4 FREE Books From HEARTFIRE

TO GET YOUR 4 FREE BOOKS MAIL THE COUPON BELOW.

FREE BOOK CERTIFICATE

Heartfire Romance

GET 4 FREE BOOKS

Yes! I want to subscribe to Zebra's HEARTFIRE HOME SUBSCRIPTION SERVICE. Please send me my 4 FREE books. Then each month I'll receive the four newest Heartfire Romances as soon as they are published Free to preview for ten days. If I decide to keep them I'll pay the special discounted price of just $3.50 each; a total of $14.00. This is a savings of $3.00 off the regular publishers price. There are no shipping, handling or other hidden charges. There is no minimum number of books to buy and I may cancel this subscription at any time. In any case the 4 FREE Books are mine to keep regardless.

NAME _____

ADDRESS _____

CITY _____ STATE _____ ZIP _____

TELEPHONE _____

SIGNATURE _____

(If under 18 parent or guardian must sign)
Terms and prices subject to change.
Orders subject to acceptance.

HF 110

Heartfire Romance

GET 4 FREE BOOKS

HEARTFIRE HOME SUBSCRIPTION SERVICE
P.O. BOX 5214
120 BRIGHTON ROAD
CLIFTON, NEW JERSEY 07015

AFFIX STAMP HERE

Chapter Twelve

For an instant, Elisabeth felt suspended in the sweetness that encompassed her. Marco's breath fanned her forehead, and his arm clasped her waist.

Marco breathed in her enticing feminine scent, and the desire that sprang up in him was undeniable. He had been drawn to her before, disappointed when the barrier of her marriage had stopped him from pursuing her, poignantly touched by her situation when she had told him her story, and then he had tried to subdue his male instincts and help her as a protégé. But now that her ties were undone, his urge to possess her roared through his veins, throbbing in his ears. He gripped her lovely frame, but he disciplined his hands.

They were in a public place, and while most people at the opera would turn their eyes away from a flirtation that might occur backstage or in some nook of the opera house, he had his reputation to think of. It was bad enough already, he supposed, because of his naturally romantic Italian inclinations. But he considered himself a decent man. And his desire for

Elisabeth was deeper than a release of male passion. He wanted to get to know the flower leaning against him. He wanted to savor her, to reveal her to himself slowly. And he would seek the right time and place.

She shifted nervously, and he released her. She batted her eyelashes, her face tinged with a flush.

"We should go back."

Although there was no one waiting for them, Marco did not argue. He touched her waist to guide her toward the light spilling from the stage.

When they had reached the steps leading to the main stage, he spoke. "I'm glad you told me of your situation. I certainly hope you'll accept my apologies."

"It was my fault too," said Elisabeth moistening her lips. Then she paused and looked at him before turning toward the stair. "There is another matter."

"Oh?"

Elisabeth was not sure how to ask, especially in light of what had just occurred. She needed to get away from Marco. It was embarrassing to stand and speak to him now. No telling what he thought about the way she had swooned against him. If she had her wits about her she would be angry at him for affecting her so, but her head still swam, and it took all her self-possession just to stand there and speak. She would rather have fled from the opera house, now that she had made her explanation, but she had to speak to him about the party, if only so that she could tell Madelaine and Alex she had. She cleared her throat.

"My friends, the ones you met the other day." She paused, unsure how to proceed, while at the same time she was uncomfortably aware of the way Marco's long-lashed eyes dwelled on her face. "They wanted me to ask you to a party my father is planning. When they learned we were acquainted, naturally they thought I might impose on you. Of course I would do no such thing. I realize you lead a busy life. But since we created such a false impression the other day, I was left no choice but to tell them I would speak to you about attending. But please don't feel obligated. I will explain . . ."

Marco's eyes had been drifting over her face, and finally he seemed to come alert. "Of course," he interrupted her. "I would be honored. I would not want to miss it."

She was so unprepared for him to say yes, she did not know how to respond.

He looked at her with a question and then repeated what he had said. "Your party, I would be delighted. When is it?"

She pressed her hand to her breast and cleared her throat. "Oh, I would not want to trouble you."

He seemed amused. "Signorina, you have just invited me to a party. A social invitation is not usually thought to be an imposition."

"I thought this one would be," she said. "Perhaps I did not explain. You will be expected to perform."

"No trouble, I assure you. Do you have any special requests as to repertoire?"

She could not believe he actually wanted to attend. "No, no, you be the judge. I'm sure whatever you choose will be appropriate."

She blushed, the notion striking her that she was becoming more and more obligated to Marco, and the thought disturbed her.

"We have set the date for December twenty-second.

I'm afraid it will be a 'welcome home' party. It cannot be avoided."

"Why, surely it cannot be that bad," he said.

She lowered her voice. "But you see, everyone is under the impression that I was in Europe these past two years. My father has perpetuated the story, and in order not to embarrass him, I have . . ." Her expression went rigid. "I am living the lie," she finished.

Marco's expression was sympathetic, and he took her hand. "Then I must help you."

"I'm sorry," she said feeling humiliated. "I would not ask you to do such a thing."

He chuckled. "Why not? I do not believe such a white lie is a mortal sin. I am an actor, am I not? Surely together we will fool them all."

In spite of her resistance, her heart warmed at his willingness to help. "I do not know how to thank you." She looked away, but she felt his gaze on her face.

"No thanks are necessary, I assure you," he said. But his tone of voice said otherwise. "I will help you with your little charade." He studied her. "Now, is there anything else I should know? If I am to help you, it is best that I know everything, yes?"

She shook her head quickly. "That is all. Just that I studied in Europe, in Paris, and that we met there."

"And that you were never married," he added.

"No. Of course not."

He patted her hand. "Good, then I think I understand the role I am to play."

She retrieved her hand. Her mind flashed to the woman in the boat, but she said nothing. Just because he knew everything about her was no reason to expect him to tell her everything about himself. He was helping her out of a desperate situation. She had no other claims on him.

She reminded him of the date and time, adding that she would send an invitation to him here. He escorted her backstage and she bid a few of her erstwhile colleagues farewell. Maurice appeared to say goodbye, but he seemed stiff and formal in Marco's presence.

With one hurdle overcome, Elisabeth returned home, preoccupied all the way with the next one, the night of the upcoming party. She ground her teeth as she contemplated what she must now confront. For one dizzying moment she clutched her reticule in a fierce grip, ruing the fact that because of her own foolish actions she was now paying for them. But she knew that self-pity would get her nowhere. She must bear up. If her life must be a continual charade, she had one thing that meant something, and one arena where she could be herself; in her music she could pour out her heart. Even if she never performed on a stage, it was enough for now to hold onto the dream, to have something in which to pitch her efforts. In that way, she might keep from going mad from the constant social pressures she felt.

Her mind drifted back to Marco. Why did he have to be so devastatingly attractive? She felt like a plaything in his hands whenever he was near her. And the way he had breathed her name . . . a shiver of desire passed through her, which she instantly squelched.

Her disastrous first marriage had left her even more certain that where men were concerned she was playing with fire. She must remain distant from Marco, seeing him only when she had to and then in crowded rooms. She had been burned once, she would not be burned again. One more reason for throwing herself into her music. It would keep her mind off more dangerous matters.

After returning home, she found that her father was out. She went into the music room where the Steinway piano sat at one end of the pale yellow room with blue drapes. Two Ionic columns formed a sort of stage with potted palms behind. In this room they had held many soirées when her mother had been alive. Opal must have kept the piano keys dusted, for when she opened the lid on the keyboard, the ivories gleamed.

True to her word, she did the vocal exercises Professor Schlut had assigned to her. Then she took one of the pieces of music they had worked on and began to sing. It was a romantic love song, and as she warmed up, the passion of the music and her own heated emotions swept her away.

Her voice hung on the high notes with a poignancy born of sweet innocence. Alone in the music room she gave vent to her emotions. But the face that came into her mind as she sang of her longing was Marco's. The final notes drifted off, her fingers caressing the keys. But when she finished, she shut her eyes and gave a little sob. She clenched her fists together and slammed them down on the keys, making a sudden harsh sound.

She rose and crossed the parqueted floor so swiftly that when she flung open the double doors, she caught sight of Gunther tottering along the hall, as well as a flash of skirt around the corner at the far end of the corridor.

The sight of the servants taking flight from obvious eavesdropping made Elisabeth pause. In spite of the temper tantrum she was about to have, humor touched the corners of her mouth. She shook her head and smiled to herself. Then she slowly turned and reentered the music room, shutting the doors behind her and leaning on them, feeling a little more calm.

Marco, Marco, always thoughts of Marco. She must unchain her thoughts from him. He was a fascination, thrown into the vortex of her life. But he was not for her. He was a playboy, momentarily attracted to her. But it was such theater romances that often led to scandal. The very thought of her name being associated with his in the gossip columns brought goose flesh to her arms. Her father would have her hide, and she could not expect forgiveness twice.

Stiffening her resolve, she marched back to the piano and sounded middle C. On "Ah" she sang the octave. Then on "Eee," then on all the other vowels. She spent the rest of the time in the music room working on technical exercises. Then she sat on the piano bench and stared at the words to the song Professor Schlut had used to coach her in Italian. She spoke the soft, sensual words, practicing the rolling accent. Standing up, she walked about the room pronouncing them, articulating, trying the proper accent again and again.

At the end of an hour she felt jubilant. Her work was well done, and she felt a sense of accomplishment. And she had forced Marco Giovinco from her mind.

The next morning Elisabeth and Opal consulted on the details of the party. Gunther brought in fresh boughs of fir, and all the maids assisted Elisabeth in making wreaths, intertwining holly and red ribbons. The house began to take on a festive look, and when Winston came home that evening for dinner, he congratulated them all on their efforts.

"I see you are enjoying yourself, my dear," he said, kissing his daughter on the cheek.

"It is a pleasure to make the house look so gay," she said.

He looked at her warmly, and for a moment she could forget the strain of their old arguments.

They ate a cozy dinner in her father's sitting room, for when it was just the two of them, the formal dining room seemed too big and cold. A table was laid in the smaller room where they were surrounded by her father's heavy upholstered furniture. Dark oil paintings hung on walls painted forest green above the chair rail. The chandelier above her head had been converted to electricity for Winston was an electric company subscriber, and tiny bulbs brightly glimmered. In addition, two colored glass Tiffany lamps glowed warmly. They had just sat down in the lady's and gentleman's chairs for coffee when Gunther knocked on the door.

"Mr. Alexander Rochat has come to call," he announced.

Elisabeth frowned. She had been about to lose herself in a novel, but then she turned the thought over in her mind. Alex might provide some diversion. As long as he didn't press her, he might be just the thing to help her keep her mind off Marco. For Alex posed no threat to her equilibrium as long as she was careful about what she said. And even there, all she needed to do was keep Alex talking about himself and his interests.

He appeared in dark gray frock coat with a gardenia in his buttonhole. His moustache was curled, his hair brushed into place, and his complexion ruddy from the chilly air outside.

"I was out walking," he announced. "The air is bracing, and I felt the need for exercise. Somehow my feet brought me here. I hope you don't mind."

He shook hands with Winston, who roused himself out of his favorite chair. Then he moved to where Elisabeth sat.

"How are you my dear?" he asked, tickling her hand with his moustache as he gave it a light kiss. "Recovered from our shopping spree together?"

She laughed good-naturedly. "Alex, that was hardly a spree. At least after you joined us, we never bought a thing."

He made pleasant conversation with both father and daughter for a half hour, during which Gunther served tea and coffee with little cakes. Then Winston, suppressing a yawn, picked up his book and excused himself. Elisabeth lifted an eyebrow. Her father never went to bed this early. Obviously he wanted to leave the young people alone.

Gunther came to inquire if they would like anything more, but Elisabeth dismissed him, saying they might take something more off the tray and to leave it. At last with the door shut, she was left alone with Alex.

"I have an idea, my dear. Why don't you sing for me?"

"Now, at this hour?" she asked.

"It is only eight thirty," he said. "You will be singing later than that at your party. Shouldn't you rehearse? I assure you I can be the best audience."

"Well, all right," she said.

She didn't mind singing for Alex. He would not be

able to tell whether she had been studying for two years or one day. He attended the opera, but he was not himself a musician. They proceeded to the music room, their footsteps echoing on the tiled floors.

In the music room, Elisabeth turned on the electric lights that gave a muted glow from decorative flower-shaped fixtures on the walls. Then she took a seat and arranged her skirt. Alex seated himself on a loveseat to one side where he could see her face and hands as she bent over the keyboard.

Ruffling through the music, she chose the Italian song she had practiced that afternoon. It was a good bet because she had indeed worked out all the difficult passages and had rehearsed the dynamics. Her fingers danced over the introduction, and her voice lilted through the room.

Alex watched enraptured. Music always moved him, and to have such a lovely creature perform solely for his pleasure satisfied his deepest needs. He and Elisabeth had always been friends. He could remember when she was in pigtails and her mother placed a steel rod down her back to make her sit straight. Now here she was a lovely young woman, her girlish curves matured into tantalizing lushness. He had suspected his feelings for her had changed when Madelaine had sent word that she had returned. He had agreed to meet the two girls at the department store that day just so he could see for himself. He was glad he had done so. Elisabeth was a peach.

Marriage would make sense. Their families were well-acquainted, though Winston had kept to himself since his wife had died. But the man knew Alex's financial position, and Alex himself had vowed to be a good manager of the fortune his father and grandfather had accumulated.

He sighed as Elisabeth's voice soared passionately. Her face portrayed the emotion of the young girl in love and Alex was touched. As with every time he had fallen in love, his heart was immediately hers. He was her prisoner. He must tell her so immediately.

He clapped his hands together when she finished. "Such a gift. That was marvelous. You will have your audience in raptures. I know you've captured my heart." He looked at her seriously, and Elisabeth lowered her eyes.

"Alex, you are a flirt. But I thank you for the praise."

Indeed it was nice to have her efforts applauded. It gave her confidence for what was ahead. Alex was such a willing audience she decided to try another. It was indeed easy to perform for someone who would be easy on her and not criticize too harshly. She sang "I'm Called Little Buttercup," and Alex's eyes danced when she flung the saucy words in his direction.

When it was over, he rose and came to the piano, sitting down beside her on the bench and capturing her hands in his.

"Elisabeth, my dear, you are too beautiful. Don't sing anymore. My poor heart can hardly stand the ecstasy as it is."

His serious look surprised her. Alex had always been free with compliments. But she sensed the seriousness of his ardor and it made her nervous. She tried to tease him out of it.

"Oh, Alex. I am glad you like my music. It means a great deal to me, more than you can imagine."

He leveled his blue eyes at her. "It is more than your

music, my dear. It is you." He gave a lovelorn sigh. "You've gone and done it, made a prisoner of my heart."

Now she had to hide a smile. His dramatic declaration was more in keeping with the old Alex she knew.

"Only temporarily, I'll wager," she said.

She got up and circled to the center of the room. "The next thing you know you'll tell me you're in love with me, and I know better."

He jumped up and followed her. "But it's true. I am afraid the worse has happened. I have fallen in love at last, and with the very child I grew up with. Then again perhaps we were fated for this and never knew it. Only your prolonged absence has made me see it. Something was missing from my heart, a corner torn off, and now it is restored. You must believe me."

She gave him a bewildered look. "Alex, don't be silly. We've always been friends, and I am happy to see you again, too, but I know only too well how easily you lose your heart, only to regain it again the moment another pretty face crosses your path."

His hurt look surprised her. She expected some quip, some further declaration of love. Instead, he raised his thumb and forefinger to his moustache to smooth it out and studied her intently as if realizing the truth of her words, only knowing himself that this time it was different.

"Come sit down," she said, leading the way to a loveseat.

He sat down stiffly, facing forward. Then he sighed, leaned back and crossed one leg over the other.

"I can understand your concern, Elisabeth. You

have known me too well." He turned to face her. "I have learned much about life these last two years. I have taken on much responsibility at my father's firm. I plan to be a good provider the day I marry."

She patted his knee in a sisterly fashion. "I am sure that is all to the good. Only you can't think that you will marry me. You mistake what you feel for friendship. You'll see, in time you will agree."

He grasped her hand desperately. "I know what you think. I have been a gadabout, I'll admit. But I am ready to change all that, change it for you. I can wait until you, yourself, have seen my change in character and believe that it is indeed a new Alexander Rochat whose only wish is to be your servant."

She tried another tack.

"I don't want any suitors, Alex. I have determined to devote my life to music."

He looked at her aghast. "What, no love? How can you say that, Elisabeth. You are a, ... a beautiful woman. How can you live without love?"

His words sent a barb through her heart, but she answered that she really intended to have a music career. Surely if it sank into his mind that she planned to go on the stage if she were good enough, he would reconsider his offer of marriage. But he only looked at her like a misunderstood, lovesick calf.

"I am studying opera, Alex. I will be an actress if any company will take me. Don't you realize what I am saying? Actresses are not considered respectable wives." She said it with an air of sarcasm, but she wanted to jar him out of his silly yearning.

The door creaked open where it had been left ajar, and her father entered.

"Sorry, to disturb you," he said. "I was looking for my pipe and was going to the study. I thought I heard voices in here."

Alex sat up straighter. "Quite all right, Mr. Sloane. What we were discussing involves your approval. Please join us."

Winston raised and lowered his brows. He was now attired in burgundy smoking jacket over white shirt and trousers. He came into the room and Alex rose.

"I have proposed marriage to your daughter, Mr. Sloane. I should have asked your permission first, but my passion ran away with me. I hoped that because of our families' acquaintance you would give us your blessing."

Winston nodded. "I have no problem with that," he said. "I respect your father, Alexander, and I would feel free to give my daughter's hand in marriage to you after certain, er, um," he coughed into his hand, "matters were laid out. It was my daughter's reply that startled me. I'm sorry, I overheard."

Elisabeth knew what was coming.

He gazed sternly at her. "I thought we had discussed this matter of your music studies, Elisabeth. Surely they do not stand in the way of marriage."

"We did discuss it," she said.

"And did I just hear you utter the words that you planned to go on the stage?"

She did not quite meet his eyes. "You did."

He cleared his throat and straightened his shoulders. "I had believed you wanted to continue your music studies for your own sense of accomplishment and to perform for our friends in intimate surroundings. But surely you cannot think. . . . That is after. . . . After being away all this time surely you have learned . . ."

His words drifted off in a fit of exasperation, and she knew what he was trying to say. But because of Alex's presence he could not say it. She did not help him out of his dilemma. Winston tried another tack, drawing himself up like a preacher. For all her joy at having been reunited with her father it was this manner in him that had estranged her from him before. He had the near-sightedness of many of their class, an adherence to a strict behavior pattern that had made her rebel in the first place, and she entrenched herself into a stubborn position for battle.

"A daughter from a respectable family does not go on the stage," Winston continued. "No professional artist can be a good wife and mother, surely you can see that."

Elisabeth flared, looking at both men. "There are many great and respected singers of our day who are accepted into the finest homes."

Alex nodded in agreement.

Winston frowned. "But from the scandal mongers surely you realize that some of them are immoral and have exposed their children to the worst upbringing imaginable. Need I name names?"

She was well aware of some of the actresses and singers who had earned a reputation for themselves, the most notable being Nellie Melba, who had had an affair with the Duke of Orléans, Bourbon Pretender to the French throne. And of course Mrs. Langtry, who was rumored to be the Prince of Wales' mistress when she had already had a child by another lover. There were other stories of singers having torrid affairs with their managers, but Elisabeth was neither interested in following their example nor in defending them. She was already committed to circumspect behavior, having learned her lesson the hard way.

Winston continued, his voice a trace softer. "What I want for you, my dear, is a happy life with a respectable and established husband."

At these words, Alex puffed his chest, though he did not interrupt the discussion. Elisabeth sent him a cold glance. Alex was evidently easily swayed to whichever side was winning.

"Besides," boomed Winston, "your voice is meant for the drawing room, nothing more." He turned to Alex. "Perhaps you can talk some sense into her, son."

With that he left the room, forgetting what he had come for.

Chapter Thirteen

Her father's words cut to the quick, and she stared glassily after him. Her voice, which her teacher found good enough to recommend for serious study, and on which Marco Giovinco had complimented her, was only good for the drawing room!

Tears welled up in her eyes, and she stared dumbly at Alex, who had to repeat what he said.

"Your father has given his permission for me to call on you, Elisabeth dear. I only hope you agree."

His words penetrated her pain, but she had to repeat them in her mind to digest the meaning.

"Oh, I see."

It was neither acceptance nor rejection. But at the moment all she wanted was to be left alone. She stood up and crossed to the piano, tears threatening.

Alex followed her. "You don't seemed pleased. But I am patient. You have known the worst of me." He coughed against the back of his hand. "I only hope I can persuade you that there is another side."

He turned her by the shoulders, but then raised his

eyebrows at the distress he saw in her eyes. She shook her head.

"It's not that, Alex. Let's not talk about that. It's what my father said—," she broke off into a sob.

Alex rummaged in his inner pocket for a fresh handkerchief to hand her.

"You mean about your plans for a career. Why my dear, if you truly decide to have a career rather than marriage, I can understand it. Please don't think that lessens my ardor for you in the least. No," he said as he seemed to shift his viewpoint to this new idea.

"No. Why I can think of nothing more exciting than squiring you about town. What do I care if you go on the stage? As long as you will receive me and I may worship at your feet. If you will not accept me as husband, there are, er . . . other ways."

"Alex!" she said. "You sound as though you are asking me to become your mistress. Is that what this notion of going on the stage means to you too? I would have thought you had better sense."

"Oh." He looked befuddled.

She flung his handkerchief at him and stormed across the room. At the doors she paused and turned around. He remained where she had left him, his expression nonplussed.

"Good night, Alex."

No one understood her, she thought, as she climbed the stairs. She shut her bedroom door hard and scooped Miranda up off the bed where the cat had been taking a nap. The cat blinked sleepily as Elisabeth squeezed her tightly.

"Mrrrow."

"I'll just have to show them," she said, her grief

giving way to frustrated anger. "I'll just have to show them all."

After a determined practice session in the music room the following day, Elisabeth went out for a walk. Her spirits still felt leaden after the unpleasant experience of the night before, and she thought a walk in the brisk, fresh air would revive her.

When she passed the brownstone house on East Sixty-eighth, she could not have known that she was walking right past the house in which Marco Giovinco had ensconced his family. But Marco was standing in the bay window of the library where he had been conversing with Rosa. She sat at a mahogany writing desk where she was going over some accounts with her son. Rosa Giovinco had never been a business woman, leaving such matters to her husband until he had died. Now she managed the household accounts, but she sought Marco's advice when she could.

Marco saw the familiar figure pass on the sidewalk opposite the house and squinted after her. The sight of the trim figure marching resolutely along a sidewalk that was just dusted with a light snowfall awakened recognition and he peered closer. Surely he had seen that fur hat before.

"Marco, you're not listening," his mother said.

He turned, blinking. "I'm sorry, Mother. I'll be right back. I just saw someone I know."

He strode out of the room and grasped his greatcoat from the coat tree in the hall. Then he was out the door and down the steps.

Elisabeth was startled by Marco's voice behind her.

She pivoted on her heel, then dropped her jaw when she saw him. For a moment she could say nothing.

He started to speak but took a moment to take in the vision of frosty beauty standing before him. Her breath was visible in the cold, and roses danced on her cheeks. A fur collar framed her face and her hands were buried in a muff.

"Signorina," he said taking the steps that closed the gap between them. "You look frozen."

Her long-lashed eyes blinked twice at him. "What are you doing here?" she asked.

He smiled and pointed to the brownstone across the street and some distance behind them. "That is my mother's home."

She looked at the house and then back at him. "Oh."

Then for some unexplainable reason, tears welled up in her eyes and confused emotions coursed through her. She glanced at Marco once more and then turned and walked swiftly in the other direction.

"Ma che cosa, what's wrong now?"

She walked faster, but he kept up. The angry tears flowed down her face and she bit her lip.

Seeing her agitated state, Marco tucked his hand under her arm. When they reached the corner where there was a coffee house, he steered her toward it.

"You are in need of something bracing," he said, not taking no for an answer. "I will buy you a cup of coffee laced with brandy."

She did not resist, but when they found seats in the corner, she burst into tears, clasping the linen napkin to her face. Then to both her surprise and Marco's the words came pouring out.

"No one understands me," she cried. "My father says

my voice is fit only for the drawing room. He forbids my going on the stage."

Marco listened in wonder as she rattled on about her father, about Alex, condemning herself for her previous entanglement. He did not even make sense out of much of what she said, but saw before him a woman distraught with her life. She even hurled accusations at him for trying to lead her down the primrose path, accusations at which he might have taken offense except that he saw clearly that at present she was not in her right mind.

And it touched him that she was speaking to him thus. She needed someone to talk to and he had miraculously crossed her path. It strengthened his belief that their lives were fated to meet, and it tugged at his heart to be needed, for he surprised himself by realizing he wanted more than anything to offer her solace.

And she was beautiful in her distressed state. Her eyes were red-rimmed and tears smudged her cheeks, but she glowed with life. The anger that made her strike out at her surroundings kindled him with desire, for he knew that she was a woman of passion to be reacting thus. As her breast heaved with emotion, he felt his loins ache. He wanted to reach across the small table and gather her to him. He even found himself not listening to her words anymore only responding on an instinctive level to the need she was expressing and to the fire in her soul.

The waiter placed the porcelain mugs of steaming coffee before them, and Elisabeth took a sip. Her pause brought Marco back from his imaginings and he drank some of his coffee as well.

"Good, no?"

She nodded and set the cup down. Now that she had spilled her troubles, she felt a little foolish. She took another swallow. The brandy-laced coffee did something to steady her.

"I'm sorry," she said. "I should not have said all that. I am wasting your time."

He reached across the table and grasped her hand, which she had removed from her glove. "Your hands are cold in spite of the glove and that muff," he chided.

She pulled her hand out of his. Marco took the hint. She was not in a state to be wooed, it was just that seeing her like this touched his heartstrings. And Marco Giovinco had never shied away from acting from the heart.

Elisabeth studied Marco seriously. "What did your family say when you told them you wanted to sing?" she asked.

Marco thought for a moment and then gave her a wide smile. He leaned back in the creaking wooden chair and folded his hands in his lap.

"That was different, you see." The picture of his hard working family came to mind. "My beautiful mother had to scrape out a living for us after my father, who was a longshoreman, was injured and confined to a wheelchair."

"Oh, I didn't know."

Marco's eyes narrowed as he recalled scenes from his own not uncolorful past in lower Manhattan. "He hated being idle. Checker games and drinking with his friends was not enough for Giovanni Giovinco. He had been a strong man. The roof in the neighborhood cafe caved in one day, pinning him beneath the beams. He was killed."

Elisabeth gasped. "Oh, how awful."

Marco took a swig of the coffee, wishing for something stronger. "Perhaps it was for the best. He himself did not think he was living if he could not work and support his family."

"Is . . . is that when you started to sing?" she asked tentatively, caught up in the tragedy he had just described.

"I always sang in church. Everyone knew I had a voice. When I started to sing professionally it was a blessing. Then I could take on the role of family supporter."

"I see."

Elisabeth lowered her gaze. She had been so caught up in her own problems, she had not stopped to think that someone like Marco had also had his struggles. He seemed so confident. She would never have guessed. She sighed and looked up at his dark eyes again.

For a moment her heart was caught. She could not help but warm to the way he looked at her. For a moment she wished there were no other women in his life. That she was his. But it was a foolish thought, and she looked away, through the letters painted on the glass window at children running past, and at a man carrying a heavy load of parcels up his front steps. It would be Christmas soon, but first she had another great encounter to face, the socialites who wanted to welcome her home.

She had escaped most of the calls from erstwhile friends except for Madelaine and Alex and had written polite notes on all the invitations. Better to get the horrid evening over with so she could go on. But go on to what? At the moment she felt low, almost as low as she had ever been. She was still thinking about what her father had said about her voice. For the drawing room only. She turned her head back and gazed at Marco inquisitively.

"What is it, my dove?" he said softly.

"Do you really think I have a good voice?" she blurted out.

He blinked. "Of course. Didn't Professor Schlut say so?"

Her mouth was turned down in an angry line. "My father said it was good only for the drawing room."

Marco muttered in Italian, then in English. "What would he know?"

She shrugged. "I just thought he might be right."

Marco leaned closer. "Don't listen to him. You must only listen to professionals."

Her lip quivered a little. "Do you really think so?"

He nodded solemnly. "I know so."

Marco sat back and drew out a pocket watch. "Now, my dear. I must go. My mother will wonder what has become of me." He smiled disarmingly. "And I must be at the opera house in one hour."

He threw coins on the table to pay for their coffees then offered her his arm. They walked along companionably in silence. Then before they reached the brownstone where he had to turn in, he stopped.

"Will you have dinner with me this evening after my rehearsal? I am not singing until tomorrow night. Besides, I would like to meet your father."

She wanted to say yes, but she hesitated. Marco perceived her hesitation and continued to persuade.

"After all, perhaps I should meet the man at whose home I am to perform next week? He might have some matters of repertoire to discuss with me, no?"

For all she had warned herself about spending time with Marco, at the moment he was the only one who understood her. She tried to ignore the signals passing between them and told herself it was only a matter of kindred spirits. And right now she needed the comfort of that kind of friendship desperately. She needed someone to believe in her, and Marco did. She took a deep breath and said yes.

She dressed that evening in a gown of turquoise satin accented with pearls. As Gwendolyn dressed her hair, Elisabeth could not help but feel elegant. She tried to feel guilty about her return to the lap of luxury, but as she looked at herself in the mirror over the dressing table, she also felt that she deserved some pleasures. Her life was still not smooth, and beautiful clothing of rich materials did something to help her self-esteem. She had always thought herself rather ordinary looking, but as Gwendolyn wrapped her tresses into curls and fixed them with pins, leaving teasing tendrils about her temples and dropping below her ears, she felt that she looked attractive.

Would Marco think so? She chided herself for the natural feminine desire of wanting to please the man she was dining with and considered changing into something more severe and less revealing of her curves. But it was too late. Opal knocked on the door to inform her that Marco Giovinco was downstairs in the Gainsborough room with her father.

She descended the stairs carrying her plush cloak with fur trimming. She heard both Marco's and her father's voices in conversation before Gunther opened the docrs for her. The two men were so engrossed in conversation that it was a moment before they broke off.

Marco turned when he saw Winston glance at the door. His eyes took in the vision of beauty standing there and he responded with a slow smile. Then he bowed formally.

"Good evening," he said when he straightened.

He took a few steps toward her and lifted her hand, all the while gazing into her eyes. Elisabeth warmed. His back was turned to her father or else surely the older man would disapprove of what was being conveyed. Then Marco lowered his lips to her hand, on which she had not yet put her glove and kissed it with ardor.

Her father waited patiently behind them, and Marco turned, still holding her hand aloft and led her into the room as if he were presenting her at a grand reception.

"Good evening, Father," she said.

He nodded. "You look lovely, my dear."

"Thank you."

Marco made the smooth transition back to the conversation he had been carrying on with Winston.

"Your father and I were discussing repertoire." He smiled sidelong at Elisabeth. "You did not tell me he was a Wagner fan."

She had dreaded this meeting, but she began to relax as she saw clearly that Marco had her father awestruck and eating out of his hand.

"Why yes. He introduced me to Wagner's music as a little girl."

"Then I will include some of the heavier numbers on my program for your soirée. Of course, not too many. The audience bores easily with too heavy a fare. I will sing some of the old favorites as well, and perhaps end with something from *Pirates of Penzance*."

It was amusing to hear him pronounce the name of the British operetta in his heavy Italian accent. But she could well imagine his playful, flirtatious manner in singing the rollicking songs.

"And then of course you will want Elisabeth to sing."

She raised her eyebrow waiting for her father's reply.

He cleared his throat. "Of course. That would be appropriate," he said, glancing from one to the other.

Marco continued. "When I heard her sing in Paris, I was entranced. Surely you will want your guests to appreciate the great progress she has made in her studies."

Elisabeth turned away to hide her amused smile. Winston's eyes bulged. He blustered an answer, obviously embarrassed at having Marco play a part in the conspiracy.

"If that is what you wish to say," Winston finally answered.

"But of course. It is our little joke, is it not?"

Winston chuckled tentatively. "I almost believed you at first." Then his look of respect returned and he clapped his hands together. "But you are a great actor. I will double your fee for the evening since you must be 'on stage' not only when you sing but also when you circulate with the guests."

Marco waved a hand. "There is no fee. I do this for a friend."

Winston's eyes settled on his daughter, and she immediately read the meaning. He was wondering just how well she knew Marco and what the circumstances were in which they'd met at the opera house. But she wore a demure expression and the old rebellious devil in her was not about to satisfy him. She was rather enjoying the expressions that were passing over her father's normally stern face. His eyes had widened more than usual, and he was obviously impressed with Marco Giovinco's presence in his house. At the same time there was the fear and helplessness he had for his daughter. Fatherly love made him want to protect her, even though he had failed to do so in the past.

Her heart was touched by the mixed emotions she read in him, and she was moved to take his arm and kiss him on the cheek.

"I shan't be late, Father," she said. "I must get my rest. But don't wait up for me."

Winston seemed moved to a new emotion, a look that said he wanted to trust this man with his daughter while at the same time he was worried about her.

Once in the carriage, Elisabeth laughed at the predicament they had put her father in. Marco joined her in her humor.

"Your father is pleased that I will sing for his little affair, is he not? Surely this is good for you too? He will see that great things await you if you can make a grand singing career."

"I don't think he'll see it that way," she answered, appreciating Marco's encouragement and his vision nonetheless. "And besides, no one yet knows if I will make a career."

Marco closed his hand over hers. "We will see, we will see. But it is a good beginning, is it not? Perhaps it is time for good things for you, my little one, no? A little romance as well, perhaps."

He had bent his head closer and Elisabeth pulled away.

"Not romance," she said stiffly. "Never that."

He drew his brows down in surprise. Already he felt drunk with her presence and they hadn't even had any wine yet.

"Why not?" he asked.

She jutted her head forward. "I do not intend to have romance—with anyone. People who live for the stage oughtn't to have hearts. Surely you know that."

Her resistance irritated him, but he made himself speak prudently. "If you mean that the life of the stage is difficult, yes that is true. We who live on the other side of the footlights do not live normal lives. Up late at night, sleep late in the morning, eat lightly before a performance and then heavily afterward, for you cannot sleep. You must travel a lot, for if the world is to hear of you, you cannot remain at home. No, you are right it would be difficult for one who does not understand to have a liaison with one who does live that life. But surely, for two people who do understand . . ." His tone of voice was suggestive.

But she shrank further to her side of the coach. She did not like his allusion to a liaison. The barb stung her, but at the same time it helped bring her back to reality. Marco would enjoy a sexual liaison with her or with any woman who attracted him, not worrying about her reputation. For he himself had just said that theater people were different.

Marriage to someone like him would be even worse. To be consumed with the trivial details of housekeeping while one's famous spouse went out in the evenings to be worshipped and fawned over by everyone would leave her a mousy nobody waiting at home alone with babies and nursemaids for company. If she ever married, she wanted a companion for a spouse, not a celebrity who was married to the world.

The thought filled her with renewed self-doubt. She wanted the life of the theater for herself, but she had been brought up with strict morals. She had erred once, but now she intended to keep her reputation intact. Not all the great actresses and singers were courtesans, though some were. Could she withstand the temptations that would be inherent in associating with these heady, talented, charming people while she struggled to see if she would be good enough for her own career in the music world?

The way her heart pitched and rolled in her chest as Marco leaned casually toward her made her wonder.

Chapter Fourteen

They reached Rector's, one of the new lobster palaces on Broadway above Forty-second Street, and Marco escorted her into the opulent interior where the maître d' greeted them both by name. Marco was hailed by several men Elisabeth recognized as figures from the theater world. Unlike the Waldorf, which catered mostly to elite society and their guests, the gilded lobster palaces were thronged with the theatrical crowd.

The aura of celebration permeated Elisabeth, and a little tingle raced through her as men openly stared at her, though their looks said they would not step beyond open admiration, for Marco's claim on her for the evening was not to be questioned.

They moved through the crowd of revelers. Here and there a champagne cork popped. Laughter filled the air. Her own eyes widened as she spied a large man adorned with jewelry on his fingers, lapels, and belt buckle. She recognized Diamond Jim Brady and his consort, the lovely actress Lillian Russell, wearing a skintight glittering gown and the largest white feather boa Elisabeth had ever seen. And when Marco steered her to their table, she didn't know what she would do.

"Marco, darling," said the blond actress.

He uttered Italian compliments and kissed her hand. Then he seized Jim Brady by the shoulders as the man stood and embraced him.

"May I present Miss Elisabeth Sloane," Marco said. "I have discovered her talent and will be presenting her to the stage within a year," Marco said grandly.

Elisabeth swallowed and tried to speak.

"If her abilities on the stage match her looks, I'd say you picked a winner," said Brady.

Lillian Russell smiled easily at her. Elisabeth answered their questions with small talk until Marco steered her to their own table farther back in the restaurant, where she began to enjoy the heady atmosphere.

Marco sent for a bottle of champagne, and soon a tuxedo-clad waiter was filling up her champagne glass. They clinked glasses, and as Marco met her eyes, she felt a shiver run up her spine.

Marco's dark-lashed eyes closed as he sipped the bubbly liquid. Then he opened them to gaze at Elisabeth sitting opposite him. His own heart doubled its beat, and suddenly Marco knew with a certainty that surprised him that that was where he always wanted to be—with her sitting opposite him where he could gaze at her.

Marco was not afraid of losing his heart, and he was experienced in the sensual side of life. But he had never before grown close to a woman. He had had his family problems to deal with at the same time he had been launching a career. Now his name as a performer was the talk of the town. But he knew from past heartbreak how fickle audiences could be. He could not afford to squander his newfound fame or relax in taking care of himself and of his voice. He would still have to please audiences and managers time and again. But perhaps there was time now to allow himself a few pleasures in life; pleasure he knew he could find in Elisabeth Sloane if she would let him. But suddenly, gazing at her calm unassuming loveliness in the midst of the noisy restaurant, he asked himself the question, *could it be more than just pleasure he saw in her?*

The large menus were handed to them and interrupted his reverie. They discussed the entrees and agreed on the specialty of the house: seafood with cream sauce. The din around them faded into the background as they conversed until it seemed that they were all alone. Marco took up the conversation they had begun in the carriage.

"Do you still think that people in the theater should not have hearts?" he asked her after they both had finished their first glass of champagne and the waiter refilled them.

"Yes," she said.

For all she was enjoying the gay evening, even enjoying the looks of those who noticed who Marco Giovinco was dining with, she was not swayed from her belief that to allow her heart to be lost would be disaster. A gay nightlife was the reward for long arduous hours of work in the studio, at rehearsals and giving one's all on the stage. But it did not fool her.

"But what about romance?" Marco asked. He tried to make it sound flippant, but it came out with more weight than he had intended. Perhaps because he feared her answer.

"A lovely fantasy," she tossed back.

The waiter brought an appetizer dish of fried prawns. Elisabeth ate them with delight, realizing also that she ought to get some food in her stomach quickly, for the champagne buzz was making her feel dizzy.

With a bit of food in her stomach and more champagne, she felt bold, ready to meet Marco's challenge about a life of love mixed with that of the stage.

"You, for example," she said, pointing a prawn at him before she put it into her mouth. "You can afford to squire whoever you please whenever you please, no doubt. Very pleasant. Surely you realize that is not the sort of relationship a respectable woman can afford, actress or not."

She clamped her mouth shut over the prawn and chewed slowly, her eyes challenging his. Now was the time, she thought to herself. Now was the time to find out about the woman in the boat.

Marco blinked in surprise. Of course he had squired women about town when he could afford the time for entertainment, but something in her words and look hinted at jealousy and he did not know how to take it, from her resistance he did not even think she cared a whit for him. Of whom could she possibly be jealous? He had not been seeing anyone for many months.

"I do not know what to say," he finally said.

She had him now, and she knew it. He could not fool her, and he was about to find out.

"Who was the woman in the rowboat?" she asked. She tried to make it sound matter-of-fact.

"What rowboat?" He tried to dodge the question but somehow felt she was not going to let him get away with it.

In spite of her resolve, she began to feel sickeningly agitated thinking of it. She was further irritated that he was playing innocent.

"In Central Park. Two weeks ago, or so. I was passing by, and I saw you."

The memory formed clearly in Marco's mind. "Two weeks ago?"

"Yes." Now she was inexplicably angry. Probably too much champagne. It made no sense, but she wanted to raise her voice. "You can't actually expect me to believe you don't remember. Is that how much your liaisons mean?"

Tears threatened and she pressed her lips together. If he forgot an outing with a lady that easily, she herself meant less to him than even she had begun to imagine.

Marco knit his brows. He would have to tell her. "That was my sister."

"Of course. A likely explanation. I suppose they're all your sisters."

A sob escaped, and Elisabeth flushed with embarrassment. Having suppressed all emotion having to do with the incident, it now came pouring out. She held the linen napkin to her lips to stop them from quivering. Marco stared at her in amazement. Then he reached across the table for her other hand and took it firmly in his own. When he spoke it was with serious intention, gentle but insistent.

"It was an afternoon outing with my sister, Lucinda. You happened to see us. I'm sorry I didn't see you, otherwise I would have spoken to you."

"I was on shore," she managed to get out. She still believed he was lying. She simply did not trust Marco Giovinco.

The waiter brought the main courses, and Elisabeth concentrated on her food, not looking at Marco. When she finally did glance up, he was frowning at his plate as well. Surely anyone watching them must realize they were not having a good time. Aware that surely they must be being watched, for who wasn't in such a public place, she forced her head up and, though strained, arranged a more agreeable expression on her face.

Marco caught her glance and did the same. Still, his cheeks appeared sallow, and his mouth had lost its gaiety. He did not know what to make of this young woman who had so recently gotten under his skin. She rebuffed his advances and yet fell apart over the idea that he had been with another woman. Though he felt reluctant to speak about Lucinda and her problem, having kept it secret from his public life, he saw that Elisabeth must be told.

He was forced to open his soul. It was difficult to talk about Lucinda, for the only person he had discussed her with since taking her out of the hands of the doctors was his mother. He felt the struggle in his breast, but when they finished the main course, he forced himself to speak.

"Lucinda is truly my sister," he said. "You must believe me."

Elisabeth had surreptitiously blotted her eyes with the napkin and jutted her chin out. She downed another swallow of champagne.

"Then I would like to meet her. If she is your sister you might take me to meet her after dinner."

Even as she said it she knew it made no sense. But she had a right to change her mind about what she wanted to do, didn't she? She had no claims on Marco. He was a mentor. But if he were a friend and he had a sister, then why not meet her? She did not admit to herself that she was challenging him.

Marco glanced away distractedly. The silence he had kept about Lucinda strained. He panicked at the thought of telling anyone in the theater world the truth, especially Elisabeth. Ignorant people still believed that the stain of insanity was inherited. Telling Elisabeth that he had a crazy sister would only drive her away, wouldn't it?

He grew more and more nervous and poured the last dregs of the champagne into his glass to gain time. But across from him, Elisabeth's intense brown eyes were challenging him. There was nowhere to turn. He could not lie, she would see through it. Feeling as if he were exposing his soul, he faced her.

"My . . . my sister is not well."

Elisabeth raised an eyebrow. "What is wrong with her?"

Marco lifted his chin. "I would rather not discuss it here. I will tell you outside."

This made Elisabeth curious, but she accepted his answer. They ordered coffee and dessert and said little else. As they left the restaurant they put on smiles and spoke to Marco's acquaintances.

She should not have been surprised to see Maurice Grau come into the restaurant. He spied Marco and Elisabeth and started over to greet them. But as soon as he perceived that they were together, his eyes took on a hangdog look.

Elisabeth greeted him sweetly. She liked Maurice, for he had helped her when she had been in difficulty at the opera company. But his glance from Marco to herself said more than words. She felt embarrassed, and a sudden fear struck her. Rumors would start about Marco and herself. The thought filled her with shame and she hurried on to the vestibule where Marco helped her with her wrap. The doorman sent for the carriage, and then they went out to the street.

As they settled themselves in the carriage, Marco felt troubled. He instructed the driver to go through the park. Elisabeth had trapped him. He knew now that he wanted her badly, but not in the way he usually wanted women. Glancing sidelong at her he knew that nothing but the truth would do. And why should he fear it? She was not the sort to spread rumors. She herself had too many things to hide. Why then could he not trust her with his secret?

He exhaled a long sigh and faced front. His voice was low, but clear. He said, "I said that Lucinda is not well."

"Yes?" said Elisabeth. She was half ashamed of having pressed the point and nearly asked Marco to have the driver take her home. But they were headed to the upper east side anyway. If Marco wanted to tell her about this Lucinda, then she would listen.

"It is not the normal sort of illness," he hedged.

She waited.

"That is to say, sometimes she has good days, and sometimes bad ones."

Elisabeth began to perceive what he was talking about, and felt a tightness in her chest. From his voice and attitude what he was saying must be difficult for him. She glanced toward him, watching the shadows from street lamps slip over his face as they rolled past.

"What do you mean, exactly?" she said softly.

The haze from the champagne had been dulled by the food, and now it was she who felt like taking Marco's hand and comforting him. Her reaction was visceral, and his words began to penetrate her brain, moving her to an empathy for which she was not prepared.

"I mean," he said with a trace of strain in his voice, "that my sister is insane."

She drew in her breath. Neither spoke. There was no sound except the clop of the horses' hooves outside and the chiming of church bells from somewhere in the city.

She leaned back in her seat. "Oh, I'm so sorry, I didn't know."

The thought was sobering, and she was instantly ashamed. Marco said nothing, but sat beside her, his hands folded in his lap where he slouched in the seat. Her mind tumbled over possible explanations, but none seemed to fit. Such family matters were no business of hers, but it was too late now to apologize.

Of course, he could be lying, she considered, puckering her brows into a frown in the dark. He was still an actor. How did she know he wasn't making it all up?

The carriage came out of the park and Franco rapped on the window to ask where to go. Marco glanced at Elisabeth and then gave his mother's address. Elisabeth realized where they were going and felt terrified. But if he were determined to introduce her to Lucinda, then she must be gracious about it now that she had created the situation. Something else occurred

231

to her. Marco must care enough to prove to her he was not lying. She tried not to consider the deeper meaning as they passed down the blocks leading to Marco's mother's house.

Now she recognized the street. It was where she had been walking the day she had been so upset and had run into Marco. So he had been at his family's house that day.

They halted and Marco assisted her to the street. He dismissed his servants, telling them to enjoy the rest of the night, and then he led Elisabeth up the steps of a wide stoop. The tall bay windows on the first floor were dark but lights shone from windows on the second floor. Using his key, Marco ushered Elisabeth into the entry hall. Her eyes took in the piano, the carved black oak chairs, the Japanese vases and terra cotta horses.

"I hope it's not too late," Elisabeth said hesitantly. Except for the entry hall, there were no other lights downstairs. However, a gas lamp softly illuminated the floral print wallpaper on the stairs.

"My mother and Lucinda should still be up," he said, unconcerned. "It's not that late."

And he escorted her up the stairs. On the second floor they saw lights coming from under the door, and Marco tapped softly. From inside the room came a woman's voice.

"Marco, is that you?"

As he pushed the door inward, a warm glow greeted them. A younger woman and an older one sat in wing chairs in a pleasantly decorated parlor. The older woman had a sewing basket at her feet and set it aside when they came into the room. The younger one had a sketch pad on her knees and glanced up from it. Pieces of paper with half-finished sketches on them littered the floor beside her.

Elisabeth was at once struck with the younger woman's beauty. Her hair was long and dark and it cascaded about her shoulders. Her eyes were dark and set a little narrower than Marco's, but there were features about her face that at once marked her as his sibling. Elisabeth's heart filled with embarrassment. She recognized the woman that had been in the rowboat with Marco weeks ago, and her own cheeks flushed with the knowledge that she had been secretly accusing him of seeing another woman all this time, when in fact it had been his own sister. She needed no more proof.

The young woman stared at them intensely. Marco crossed to greet his mother and then bent to kiss his sister, who seemed not to notice her brother but stared intently at Elisabeth, whose light brown hair and fair complexion were a marked contrast to the dark, handsome looks of the three Giovincos.

"Mama, may I present Signorina Elisabeth Sloane."

Rosa smiled gently and extended a hand, which Elisabeth took.

"A pleasure to meet you my dear." She smiled warmly at Elisabeth, who was at once disarmed by the ambiance of the comfortable family setting.

Marco touched his sister's shoulder. "Lucinda, this is Elisabeth. Elisabeth, my sister, Lucinda."

"How do you do?" said Elisabeth.

Lucinda said nothing for a moment, and then she got up, the sketch pad sliding off her knees. She walked closer to Elisabeth and stared at her face. Then she slowly took her hand in her own.

The girl's manner was a little odd, but Elisabeth had tried to prepare herself for that. She squeezed the girl's hand and met her scrutiny.

"It's nice to meet you," Elisabeth said.

Marco felt relief as he watched the scene. He could hardly believe the terror he had felt at bringing Elisabeth here, but the moment he saw her with his family he knew it would be all right. His mother cast him a glance that said she knew this was a momentous occasion, but she could wait for an explanation from her son at a later date. She got up from her chair and joined the girls.

"Perhaps you would like some refreshment, Elisabeth. I have just baked some cookies. A pot of tea will take the chill off. We let the help go in the evenings, but if you would like to follow me to the kitchen, we will help ourselves."

Elisabeth warmed instantly to Rosa and smiled. "I would like that. I am rather used to serving myself."

Mirth bubbled up in Marco, and suddenly he was uttering a stream of words—half Italian, half English—as he told his mother how he had met Elisabeth. He left out the intimate details of her personal life, of course, but told how she had worked in the opera house and had recently been reconciled to her father who lived in a millionaire's mansion where both Marco and Elisabeth were going to sing next week.

"How wonderful," said Rosa as they clattered down the stairs to the kitchen.

She turned up the gas lights and set an oil lamp on a red-checkered covered table at one end of the kitchen to which four chairs had been pulled. She waved away Elisabeth's offer of help and soon had a tea kettle humming on the iron cook stove. A tray of cookies was set before them, and Elisabeth, who had lost her appetite at the restaurant and so had not ordered a dessert, bit into crisp, flaky cookies that made her mouth water.

Soon she and Marco were telling Rosa about the incident at the opera when Lillian Nordica had needed stockings. Marco convulsed with laughter as he described getting the stockings he had bought for Lucinda's birthday and lending them to the frantic soprano. Elisabeth had to lower her eyes as she realized now how she had built a case for Marco's gallivanting out of those stockings. She was swept up in the cheerful conversation and the closeness she sensed between Marco and his family.

No one made mention of Lucinda's illness, but Elisabeth remembered that Marco said sometimes she had good days and sometimes bad ones. She took that to mean that on a good day, they did not have to be concerned about her, that she could live almost normally. She found herself hoping that the girl would have more good days than bad ones. Surely such a loving family as this deserved that much.

Chapter Fifteen

Elisabeth stood at the top of the main staircase next to her father greeting the guests as they arrived. The balustrades were strung with wreaths of fir, spruce, and huge red velvet bows. She accepted the handshakes and embraces of old acquaintances, some of whom she found she was genuinely glad to see.

"Elisabeth, my dear, that color is lovely on you," gushed Mrs. Henry Clews. "Europe must have been good for you. You have color on your cheeks."

"Thank you," she replied to the woman and turned to the next guest.

She had chosen to wear the blue tulle and gauze over silk because the color flattered her and thus gave her confidence. It was one of the gowns she and Madelaine had picked out, and when Madelaine came up the stairs in pale green satin looped up with bows and water lilies, she exclaimed at seeing the dress on her friend for the first time.

"It is wonderful," said Madelaine admiring the effect of the stiff bodice extending to a point in the front and to an even deeper one in back. But it was the avalanche of draperies adorning the back, accented with silk flowers that gave the dress its elaborate look. And Elisabeth had made sure that she still had room to breathe in it.

"I'm glad you like it," she said.

Just behind Madelaine came Consuelo Vanderbilt following her mother and father, and Elisabeth's attention turned to them. She remembered her pledge to call on Consuelo and felt guilty that she had forgotten to do so.

Mrs. Alva Vanderbilt came first, spine straight, diamonds covering her brocaded satin with its point lace flounces. She extended a gloved hand, her shoulders squared.

"Welcome home, Elisabeth. I hope you found Europe charming. We were there twice, but failed to locate you both times even though your father told us you were staying in Paris. My goodness you must not have socialized a whit. My friend Lady Paget had never heard of you."

Elisabeth smiled innocently, for she had expected such challenging barbs all evening long.

"I'm afraid I did not socialize much. I went to study and to see the great art. And so much traveling made it difficult to get to know people who would invite me to parties. I was not in one place long enough. I'm afraid I was rather antisocial."

Mrs. Vanderbilt smirked condescendingly. Then she seemed to remember Consuelo, trailing behind her.

"I'm afraid it was rather the other way with us. Consuelo and I got so many invitations it was difficult to return all the calls. But perhaps you have not heard the news, Consuelo is engaged to the Duke of Marlboro."

"Hello, Consuelo," said Elisabeth reaching out to grasp her old friend.

Consuelo Vanderbilt was a tall, slender young woman with dark hair and fine, even features. Her fluid grace helped her rise to the occasion, but Elisabeth could see that the wan smile she gave was more one of resignation than of joy. Elisabeth shut her eyes as Consuelo kissed her cheek, remembering having covertly stared at her from the opera stage.

"Elisabeth, it's really good to see you," Consuelo said. "I've been visiting an aunt in Boston the last two weeks or I would have come to see you. How long have you been home?"

"Not long," Elisabeth said as they faced each other. "I'm glad to know you were gone. I felt guilty not calling on you sooner. I'd meant to do so."

"Don't give it a thought, dear. But you must come to see me now that we're both in town. I'm so lonely." It was a statement of fact more than a complaint.

"Of course. I promise."

"Perhaps we'll see you at the opera next Monday night?" asked Consuelo.

Elisabeth hesitated. She could see that the girl was not happy and needed her friends, though Elisabeth could not abide Alva Vanderbilt and didn't quite understand the hold the older woman had over Consuelo.

"I hope so," she finally said.

Consuelo gave her a gentle smile and followed her mother and father into the reception room.

The guests came on and on. Alex appeared with his

friend James Burden, whose moustache curved gracefully upward and ended in a saucy twirl. Alex kissed her hand, but he seemed intent on showing James, who seemed a bit down at the mouth, a good time and so rushed him into the room that was growing lively with guests and waiters circulating with long-stemmed wine glasses.

"I think we can join our guests now, my dear," said Winston when the last of the stragglers had left their wraps with Gunther and Opal downstairs and climbed the wide staircase to join the party.

The doors between reception rooms had been left open so that guests could mingle. Then after an hour's socializing they would all gather in the music room for the performance. Elisabeth's nerves began to tingle, but whether it was from the excitement of singing before such a large group, or anxiousness about seeing Marco here, she did not know. He had not yet arrived, but that was as planned. As the guest of honor, he would arrive last, and she would circulate, introducing him. She turned toward the door expectantly and, as if her thoughts were his cue, there he appeared, devastatingly handsome in tail coat and red cummerbund at the waist.

He caught her eye, and as she moved toward him through the crowd, her skirt rustling about her, the din of voices began to fade away. Marco beamed a smile upon her and bowed over her hand. *"Bellissime,"* he said, complimenting her appearance.

She smiled nervously, and as she took his arm to introduce him to the guests, she nearly tripped over Madelaine who had been standing directly behind her.

"Oh, you remember Madelaine Lord," she said to

Marco who greeted her.

"I do indeed. How are you this evening, Miss Lord?"

Madelaine smiled coyly. "I am very well, thank you. You know it was at my prompting that Elisabeth asked you to sing tonight. I thought you would not refuse, seeing as how you knew each other so well."

Marco laughed, used to the gawks from the ladies surrounding him. "How could I refuse the opportunity to mix with such lovely company?"

They made their way onward, and Elisabeth introduced him to everyone they came to. She was frightened that she would forget someone's name, for she was seeing many of the guests for the first time in two years. But she had studied the guest list diligently and did not make a mistake. When they came to Alva Vanderbilt, Elisabeth did not miss the suspicious look in the woman's eye.

After the woman was introduced to Marco, she turned a burning eye on Elisabeth. "I see you did some socializing in Europe after all," she said.

Elisabeth flushed. It was not the type of remark she felt obligated to answer. They moved on, and when her father saw that she was tiring, he took over the introductions so that Elisabeth might excuse herself to get ready for her performance.

She fled to her room and shut the door, glad for a brief respite in order to gather her thoughts. She wasn't worried about the music, for she had rehearsed it for many hours and she was only singing three numbers. Marco would do the rest, but she also had to accompany him. They had practiced three times in the last two weeks so that she could get a sense of the pacing and dynamics he wanted. Being an accomplished pianist, that part came easily to her.

She thought back to their rehearsal yesterday at Professor Schlut's. There had been an unmistakable sense of camaraderie between them, and she suspected that it was built on their secret knowledge of each other's lives. She had tried to keep the rehearsal session professional, but every time Marco glanced at her, she felt a response in her soul that was difficult to ignore.

But now was no time to ponder it. Too much hung on how well they carried off the performance at the soirée. As she sat down now in front of the dressing table and drank a glass of water, she composed her rattled thoughts.

"So far, no mishaps," she whispered to herself. Miranda appeared out of nowhere and jumped up on the dressing table. Elisabeth stroked the kitty, then shooed her away, fearing the sharp claws might tear her gown or that cat hairs would make her sneeze.

She checked her appearance, and then picked up the music she planned to sing, going over in her mind all the phrase markings and emphases she wished to make. She had sung at parties all her life, and so this one should not present a problem, except for the fact that she had supposedly been studying for two years instead of for a few lessons with Professor Schlut.

But only Marco would know. It was perhaps lucky that New York society was more interested in money and social standing than in the arts. The opera was a place to go to visit with one's friends. She knew this was not so in Europe where, had she actually gone there and been invited to the parties Mrs. Vanderbilt thought she should have, she would have rubbed shoulders with highly cultured people who could hear nuances in music to a greater degree and who would speak about the music with more intelligence. But New York's Society's use of the arts as a symbol of their wealth was to her advantage this evening.

She stood and took a deep breath. Feeling ready, she descended to an anteroom where Marco was humming scales to himself and had evidently been likewise preparing. He broke off and smiled as she came in.

"Well," he said. "Are we ready to entertain your friends?"

She took his meaning. For they were presenting more than a musical entertainment. Their pretense of her whereabouts for the last two years drew them together. It was also perhaps good for her to see how a star of his caliber was fawned over by all the women and watch the way he charmed them. Her own jealousy reaffirmed her determination to keep her distance from the attraction he seemed to encircle her with every time they were together.

"I owe you a debt of gratitude for appearing here this evening," she said.

His expression was full of amused understanding. "It is a pleasure, I assure you."

Winston came to inform them that the guests were seated. Everything was ready. Elisabeth took her father's arm and entered the music room, taking a position in front of the gleaming Steinway grand piano.

"It is my pleasure," she said to the expectant audience, "to offer you a treat this evening. Marco Giovinco has graciously agreed to entertain us with a few selections."

Polite applause followed, and she turned to wait for

Marco to make his entrance. As he did so, the applause swelled. He came to where she was standing and bowed deeply to the audience. She moved to the piano bench and arranged the music, concentrating on the first piece.

Marco gave her a nod that he was ready, and she began the introduction to the "Flower Song," from *Carmen*. His voice began the romantic aria, which was a favorite of the opera-going crowd. For even if New York's opera lovers were not as well-versed as a European opera-going audience, they knew what they liked. All the pieces on this evening's program had been chosen with that in mind.

But Elisabeth soon forgot the audience as she was carried along by the impassioned music, Marco's voice caressing each note and his naturally flawless musicianship lending an even greater sensuality. She leaned into the keyboard and together the phrases swelled and soared. Her own emotion responded to his, and she was delightedly transported.

From the response of the listeners, the effect was as she had expected. She did not break the spell for moments, but when she finally turned to smile at the guests she saw the rapture on their faces as they began their applause. Marco bowed and bowed again and then gestured to her. She nodded from the piano bench and then turned to concentrate on the next piece.

Each piece built to a romantic crescendo until Elisabeth's soul lifted to the stars. Her hands conveyed her emotion to the keys and the music she and Marco made filled the room with beauty and pleasure. When they were finished, she took a moment, soul aloft, her head bowed over the keys.

Then Marco reached for her hand, and she was off the piano bench bowing with him. Then he graciously escorted her to the anteroom. The applause echoed behind them as they closed the door. Marco reached for the pitcher of water left for them on a side table.

"I think they liked us," he beamed.

She could see that the music had elevated his spirits as it had hers, and she felt at one with him on a new level that surpassed anything she had known.

"After your arias, mine will be paltry, I'm afraid," she said.

Marco shook his head. "Not at all, my dear. I have merely warmed them up for you."

He bent to kiss her cheek. "You will do marvelously."

The door opened and Madelaine, who was to accompany her, rushed in.

"That was marvelous," she gushed to Marco. "Everyone loved it." Then she turned to Elisabeth and winked slyly.

"Now it is our turn."

Elisabeth appreciated her friend's confidence. Girls in their social class were raised to play piano and accompany one another, and even following Marco Giovinco did not seem to daunt the sprightly Madelaine. She smiled. "I'm ready when you are," she said.

Elisabeth took several deep breaths and followed Madelaine into the music room. Madelaine took the piano bench and opened the music to "They Call me Mimi," from *La Bohême*.

Elisabeth nodded, and Madelaine began the introduction. The piece was a simple but charming aria and one that allowed Elisabeth to demonstrate her voice and emotion without the difficult vocal gymnastics that would come in later selections. Well into the piece, she saw the faces of the guests and knew suddenly that she would be a success.

Alex beamed thoughtfully beside James Burden, whose black mood seemed to have lifted slightly. Consuelo Vanderbilt smiled as if the music made her forget her shackles. Beside her, Alva Vanderbilt studied Elisabeth curiously, but the woman was no expert on music and her expression of curiosity did not bother Elisabeth.

She turned to sing to the other side of the room and caught her father's upraised brows. Pride shone in his eyes, and made her heart lift with gladness. She brought the aria to a delicate close and the notes drifted off.

The guests applauded warmly, smiling at each other as if they had known all along that Elisabeth Sloane had talent. She bowed and waited for them to also acknowledge Madelaine, who sat down quickly and brought out the next piece.

The piece from *Carmen* was more of a challenge, but Elisabeth felt warmed up and ready for it. Her voice, while youthful and fresh, catapulted saucily through the difficult passages with ease, and she felt she impressed everyone listening. The piece was a resounding success.

Her third offering was the rollicking "I'm Called Little Buttercup," from the Gilbert and Sullivan operetta and the guests beamed with pleasure. Marco, watching from the anteroom, warmed with delight at the way she carried it off.

She is a natural born actress, he thought to himself,

and when it was time to join her, he clasped her hands warmly, greeting her as he would any accomplished colleague with whom he was privileged to perform.

The final number on the program was the love duet from *Lucia di Lammermoor,* and the combination of voices thrilled the audience. The women were again swept away by Marco's thrilling voice and sex appeal, and the gentlemen gazed with stunned appreciation at the young woman who threw herself into the part.

As involved as she was with the music and the role she was acting out with Marco, Elisabeth was aware of the curiosity and appreciation that blanketed the audience. By the time they were finished, and Marco was holding her hand in a warm clasp, she thrilled at the waves of applause that came their way. The guests began to stand in an ovation. Alex leapt to his feet, shouting "bravo," and "brava," followed by others.

Elisabeth thought her heart would burst. It had been a complete success. The guests swarmed toward them to offer congratulations. Mrs. Van Rensselaer cooed over Elisabeth's singing and then engaged Marco in a conversation. The two singers were surrounded and congratulated. Elisabeth knew that the only explanation for her singing being so much better than when she last performed in the music room was that her voice had inevitably matured with age. She had not strained it when she had practiced at the boardinghouse. And tonight's inspiration had come from singing with Marco. He had been responsible for her achieving new heights. But she did not have time to consider that, for she was being ushered into the refreshment room with the crowd, her friends buzzing about her.

She saw Madelaine and Consuelo not far behind,

deep in discussion. Alex took charge of Elisabeth and would not let go of her elbow, handing her a glass of wine.

Mrs. Van Rensselaer pounced briefly. "Wherever did you learn to sing like that, my dear?" she asked. But rather than waiting for an answer she went on to exclaim how Elisabeth's voice was reminiscent of the great Adelina Patti, who was now retired, but who still gave "farewell" performances upon occasion.

The party was exhausting, and every so often she would get a glimpse of Marco, either listening intently to the comments of some matron, or with his head thrown back with pleasure at some joke uttered by a debutante. He was clearly charming everyone.

She passed near him once and heard him say, "Of course, it was in Paris, I believe. Or was it in Rome? You will forgive me if I forget exactly where we met. There were several occasions. She has talent, don't you think?" No one pressed him for details.

The wine and the gay spirit of the evening infected everyone. Eventually a group gathered around the piano and with Madelaine playing they all sang loud versions of "I'll Take You Home Again Kathleen," "Love's Old Sweet Song," and other favorites.

While all the guests were amusing themselves Elisabeth snuck off for a respite, away from the enforced gregariousness. She made her way along a painting gallery and followed the moonlight that shone into a long corridor. Tall potted ferns drew sunlight during the daytime from the large windows on the east side of the house, looking onto the garden. Elisabeth touched the ferns, letting them tickle her hands as she wandered along the corridor. Her mother had decorated this part of the house, and as she moved quietly, she could almost feel her mother's presence.

"I wish you could have heard me tonight, Mother," she whispered. It had always been hard to please her mother. She wondered if she would have done so tonight had her mother been here.

Thinking again of the pieces she had sung and how her voice had lain so beautifully on the high notes, she acknowledged the musicality that had come partly from being exposed to music as a child, for which she was grateful.

She heard the scrape of a heel on the marble floor behind her and turned. Moonlight reflected from Marco's dark eyes and she drew in a breath, releasing a fern as she moved away from its feathery protection.

"I'm sorry if I startled you," he said.

"That's all right. I was just taking a rest from in there."

"I had hoped for the same thing."

"Are you not enjoying it?" she asked, thinking of the way he had entertained the guests as much in conversation, as he had in singing.

"It is a very nice affair," he answered coming down the corridor to where she stood. "But these things can be tedious, can they not?"

When he moved closer she could see better the strain in his face. His shoulders looked stiff, and he seemed almost as if he longed to be away from the glitter.

Curious, she asked, "Do you like privacy very much?"

"I do, very much."

They strolled down the corridor together until they came to a recess where a wrought iron seating arrangement faced French doors leading out to a patio with steps down to the garden beyond. Outside a hoarfrost covered the dormant garden. When she sat down she realized how good it felt to get off her feet.

"You're in the public eye so much," she said. "I would think you loved the admiration, the adoration."

He sighed. "I do. It is hard to explain. I love being acknowledged for a job well done. But after a time the flattery is wearing. Then I want to retreat to my own rooms, take a walk in the country, enjoy a lazy afternoon on the boardwalk." He laughed softly. "In short, I long to do all the things most people do when they're not working. Is it not the same for you? Or do you crave the limelight?"

"Me? Oh, I hadn't thought about it, I suppose."

"Come now," he admonished. "Surely one who believes she is destined for the stage has considered the increased attention she will inevitably acquire."

"I don't know," she said, leaning back into the cushions that protected them from the hard metal loveseat where they sat.

She smiled. "You must admit that while these people think I have been studying for some time, in reality there is much work to be done before I have the problem of being noticed. Perhaps by that time I will be ready to handle it."

"Hmmm. Who can tell? Some artists are stimulated by the constant adulation. For me, I like something else . . . more quiet . . . like this."

The way he said it was full of meaning and she tensed. She halfheartedly remembered her resolve to keep her distance from him, and formulated words to use in defense in case he made another advance to her.

But he neither moved nor suggested intimacy, rather he went on talking about things he liked as if finding refuge in her understanding. When she was alone with him like this and he opened himself up to her, she wanted to throw caution to the wind. This was the side of Marco Giovinco to which she was growing closer and closer. A warm, yearning sensation engulfed her and she followed his train of thought with comments of her own. With every image he conjured she had a similar one, until it seemed they had yearned for the very same things, desired the same things all their very different lives.

"You are exceptionally lovely tonight, Elisabeth," Marco said after they had conversed for a while.

"Thank you."

"And you sang very well."

"Do you truly think so?"

"I do."

He turned to gaze at her, and she knew in the next moment he would kiss her, so she moved to stand up. But he grasped her hand, pulling her back down.

"Why do you resist what seems natural, Elisabeth? Have you not felt it? I believe we are meant for each other."

A tingling rushed through her as his words caressed her and he gathered her into his arms. But she pushed against his shoulders.

"No."

"But why? Why not yes, yes, yes?"

He held her gently but firmly and his kiss burned her brow. She fought with herself against the warmth of his thrilling embrace. Her limbs weakened as his kisses trailed down her cheek to her chin.

"Marco, stop," she pleaded, but it was barely a whisper as already her body awoke with the desire that he kindled in her.

"Do not be so afraid of me, *mia cabQra*," Marco said. "I would never hurt you. My only desire is to give you pleasure. And take it." His last words were hoarse with emotion, and as his hand came up to turn her face to his, and their lips met, he pressed her closer.

Elisabeth warmed. Her resistance turned to an embrace. Her mind whirled as the emotion from the evening and the intimacy they had created turned to passion as they found each other. Before she knew what she was doing her arms were entwined about his neck. His mouth was devouring hers and his hands held her against him.

For a long thrilling moment he kissed her and then as the embrace grew tighter and tighter his hand moved along her torso pressing her breast and then moved down along her skirts, searching for her hip and thigh. She was lost. His strong masculine frame was a comfort and the object of intense desire. Here was pleasure of the highest order and she was tired of fighting it. She could not stop him any longer, her poor rattled mind told her. Perhaps he was right. Perhaps she was fated to be his, however he wanted her.

Their passion mounted as Marco felt her resistance give way and his movements and explorations grew more urgent and excited. His tongue probed against her teeth, and she arched backward as he kissed her throat, her shoulders, her round bosom.

"Elisabeth, my beauty. You thrill me so much. I want you badly," he said in a low voice that moved her to wave upon wave of pleasure.

She nestled her head under his chin as her own hands found their way under his coat to embrace a strong, muscular torso. Her gown had slipped low on her shoulders as his large, firm hands caressed her smooth skin, cupping her breasts with a gasp of pleasure.

He took her mouth again, his hand inside the material of her bodice and the fire in her body kindled to a fever pitch. Now she knew the difference. This was far more than the girlish infatuation that had led her to rebel against her upbringing before and seek marriage to a man who was no match for her. Then she had known nothing of matrimonial bliss. Now Marco was introducing her to secret pleasures of which she had never dreamed. And yet some tiny whisper in the back of her mind told her it was wrong . . . wrong.

He guided her hand to his thigh, and with her chin on his chest she tried to utter words of her fear and confusion.

"Marco, I can't. Please . . ."

Marco himself had unleashed the passion he had felt building within him for some time, but the desperation in her tiny plea made him stop. He ached for her. In another moment he would have had their clothing undone, throwing caution to the wind, and he would have taken her here in the gallery, on the love seat, anywhere, so great was his need. But he wanted her to want it too. He knew that his pleasure would be complete only when hers was. Her words undid him.

He raised his hands to her face, cupping her face and kissing her warmly again. He felt her surrender, but also her pain, and he cradled her against him.

"Do not worry, my pet. I said I wouldn't hurt you,

and I meant it." With torture, he suppressed the ache in his groin.

She heard the emotion in his voice, and it brought tears to her eyes.

"I want you to be mine, Elisabeth," he said. "I want you now, but only when you want me."

How could she explain that she wanted him badly, that she was almost ready to lose herself in him, but that she could not.

"Marry me, Elisabeth. Our life could be happy together. Can't you see that?"

She moved her head slightly. Marriage? Was he actually proposing marriage? Was it only because his body yearned for hers? He surely did not want to be tied down by marriage any more than she did. She clenched a fist against his chest. If only she weren't tied to her morals so. Why hadn't she been born into another world? Then passion could be had without any strings attached. But try as she might to accept that idea, it would not come.

"No," she said, tears running down her cheeks. "I cannot."

He lifted his fingers to her chin and made her look at him.

"Why not?"

But she shook off his fingers and her gaze escaped him. "You forget, I was married."

"Oh that. Forget that. This is different, Elisabeth. Surely you can see that."

Indeed he had nearly forgotten her former marriage. When her erstwhile husband had been lost in the river the entire incident had been erased from his mind, but evidently not from hers. He frowned. That was what was wrong. She had made a mistake once, and she was afraid. He exhaled a breath through his lips. In that case he would have to be patient with her. He would have to wait for her, slowly show her how he loved her.

Saying it to himself surprised even Marco. Yes, he did love her. It had crept up on him, but now there was no doubt. He loved her humility and the determination underneath it. He loved the way she glowed when she sang and the way she looked to him for approval. He admired her spirit and he craved to make love to her.

Could he wait for what he wanted? His passion did not want to be reined in. Perhaps soon he could show her, soon he could love her. Soon. It would have to be soon or he would go mad himself with dreaming of her. His body would not let him wait forever. He must awaken her to the passion they could share before too long.

Chapter Sixteen

The mood broken, they rose and walked slowly back to the party. Elisabeth was glad they had wandered so far away, for it allowed her a chance to gather her wits and to blot moistness from her face with a handkerchief Marco gave her before meeting the gay crowd again. By the time they entered the reception rooms, she had pasted a smile on her face. Her flush could be explained by the excitement of the evening.

As soon as she rejoined the crowd, Alex broke off his conversation and came to her. "Where have you been, my dear? You've been neglecting your guests."

"I had to get some air," she replied as sweetly as she could.

Alex frowned over her shoulder at Marco, who entered the room a few seconds after her, and tightened his grip on Elisabeth's elbow.

"I do hope you're not taken in by that Romeo, the way all these other silly women are," he said in her ear.

"Taken in? Oh, of course not." She could not meet his gaze.

Some of the guests began to drift by and thank Elisabeth, again welcoming her home. She bid them all goodnight. Marco came to formally bow over her hand. She felt self-conscious as she looked him in the eye to say goodnight. Then Marco turned to bid Winston good evening, and the older man saw him to the door.

It was with relief that she watched Marco go. Her feelings about him were growing more and more confused, and she needed time to think. Alex and Madelaine were among the last to leave, and Elisabeth was so tired that she hardly knew what she was saying to them, agreeing to future outings, anything to see them out the door.

Finally she and her father were left alone. Elisabeth uttered an enormous sigh, her hand on the balustrade near the bottom of the stairs for support.

"Well," said Winston, brushing his hands together. "A successful evening, if I do say so."

"Yes," Elisabeth agreed. At least it was over.

They climbed the stairs and said good night, Gunther gliding behind them and turning off the lights as they went. Gwendolyn had been dozing in a wing chair and stood up sleepily when Elisabeth entered the room, and as soon as she had the fastenings of Elisabeths dress undone, she sent the maid along to bed.

"I can finish by myself, Gwendolyn. Go and get some rest."

"Yes, Miss."

Once out of her clothes and into a dressing gown, Elisabeth collapsed onto a wing chair. Miranda, who had been awakened by the rustling of gown and petticoat, padded slowly over and hopped up into Elisabeth's lap. She petted the cat tiredly.

One hurdle was behind her. Tomorrow was another day, and she would see Professor Schlut and tell him how well she had sung. And then what? It was hard to know.

The next morning Elisabeth slept in, then asked for a breakfast tray. It was quite late in the morning by the time she was dressed and ready to go out. Opal told her that her father was in his study, reading the paper, so she went in to see him.

"Good morning, Father," she said sunnily when she entered the room. A night's rest and a hearty breakfast had renewed her vigor to face whatever the day might bring.

He put down his paper on the desk in front of him. "Good morning, my dear. I hope you slept well."

"Yes, I did, and you?"

"Quite well, thank you. I see you're going out."

"Yes." She hesitated to say where she was going.

As if reading her thoughts he said, "You sang well last night, Elisabeth. I was . . ." he glanced away as if embarrassed to say it. "I was proud of you."

Her throat tightened in sudden gratitude. "Thank you, Father. It means a lot to hear you say that."

"However," he said, returning to his usually stern demeanor. "I hope this does not encourage you in that foolish notion to have a career. Surely you can see that entertaining our friends is good enough. You give pleasure and people appreciate you. I hope you've given that some thought."

She took a seat gingerly on the chair near which she was standing.

"I did enjoy last night, and I am glad our friends enjoyed it." She pressed her lips together trying to phrase what she would say next. "Marco Giovinco was quite encouraging."

"Hmmmm." Winston pulled at his beard. "That is another thing. I hope you are not planning on seeing him again."

His comment surprised her. "Why ever not? I thought you liked him."

"Of course I was favorably impressed. He handled himself well. He is a great artist." He cleared his throat. "Anyone can see that for themselves. But as company for my daughter, he's not the, er, sort of person you should be associating with, especially now."

She took his meaning and understood the indirect reference to her unfortunate past. But in spite of her own confused thoughts on the matter, anger flared in defense of Marco.

"Is that why you don't want me to sing in public? We have salvaged my reputation, and it must be protected at all costs," she said cynically.

"Well, don't you agree that it must? Artists are all very well and good on the stage, but they must keep their place in society."

"How can you say that?" Exasperation and anger got the better of her. "I'm not so sure. I'm not sure if I want to spend the rest of my life among people who have a nodding acquaintance with the arts but who flee from mixing with artists. Surely you can see that this is only stuffy prejudice."

Tears stung. She did not mean to start the old

arguments again. Wasn't this why she had flown from this house three years ago and landed an outcast? Well, maybe she didn't care if it happened again. It was all very well to enjoy the comforts of a private bath and satin sheets, but if the price she had to pay for it was giving up her own goals, never!

"I'm sorry, Father," she managed to say before she stood, turned and ran out of the room.

She nearly collided with the housekeeper as she brushed her hand across her cheek before bursting out the front door and down the walk to the gate. Opal held her feather duster in her hands as she clucked her tongue.

"Whatever is wrong with the girl, now?" the housekeeper muttered to herself sadly. She had begun to think there might be some cheer back in this house what with all the girl's music and the gay party they had given last night. But from the thunderous look Mr. Sloane gave her as he emerged from the study, she could tell that father and daughter's conversation had not bode well. She hurriedly bent over a piece of statuary to check it for dust specks.

When Professor Schlut opened the door to Elisabeth, he saw that she was troubled.

"Ah, come in, my dear, sit down."

She halted in the center of the sitting room as he took a seat in his large leather chair. Normally they proceeded through to the music room for the lesson.

"Go on," he gestured, "sit down."

She did as he said. The Afghan came over to sniff her hand. She scratched his ears absently, then the dog ambled over and took a seat regally beside the professor. Both professor and dog looked at her from across the room.

"Is something wrong?" she asked. She had the momentary fear that he had decided not to teach her anymore.

"Well now, why don't you tell me," he said gently. "I would say that you are not in the best frame of mind to sing this morning. Am I wrong about that?"

She eased her back against the sofa, dropping her portfolio of music beside her. "You are not wrong, I'm afraid," she said.

He pressed his fingertips together, elbows on the arms of the chair. "Aha. Did something go wrong at your little soirée? It was last night, was it not?"

"It was last night, and it was a great success. Marco sang wonderfully, and I . . . did justice to your coaching."

He smiled humbly. "Come, come now, my dear. We have had only a few lessons. If you sang well it was your own doing. I merely made a few pointers to help you here and there. But your guests, they were pleased?"

"Very pleased."

"Then, why such a long face today?"

Instead of answering his question, she gave him a thoughtful look.

"Professor Schlut, you must give me your honest opinion. Do you think it possible that I can have a career? I must know now, you see. For if I commit myself to doing this, then everything else . . . everything else will be ignored. My father wants me to marry, but I've seen what marriage does to people in my social set. One becomes stifled by rounds of social obligations. I feel that is not for me. But it is a matter of commitment. If I have no other options then I would have to settle either for keeping house for my father and becoming an old maid or perhaps accepting the hand of a husband who would support me. I do not think I am an unreasonable person. If that were all that was left for me, then I suppose I would have to accept it."

Professor Schlut nodded. "I cannot see the future. I do not have a crystal ball."

She sighed. "I am not being fair, of course. I am asking you to help me make a personal decision."

He smiled in understanding and Governor Worthy thumped his tail. "I know what you are going through. You are not the first one to have had such a dilemma. Tell me, do you have a suitor who is pressing for your hand in marriage? Or is it just your father who is pushing you in the matrimonial direction?"

She thought of Alex. "I do not take the suit seriously. As soon as the novelty of marriage wore off, he would leave me with the little ones and go in search of excitement. But it is also my Father."

She rubbed her palms along her skirt in a nervous gesture. "For reasons I cannot discuss, he is anxious to see me settled in a respectable marriage. He is very much against my going on the stage."

Professor Schlut shook his head. "An unfortunate prejudice among many of your class. I do not know what to tell you, my dear. As you can see, I am not a marriage advisor."

She had a fleeting thought of Marco, but pushed it out of her mind.

"If I try, and if I fail . . ." She could not even envision

such a disaster. If she alienated her father again, there would be no turning back a second time. If she could not make her way on her own, there would always be the life of the boardinghouse, but the thought of ending her days there like the spinsters she had made friends with somehow depressed her. She could not get over the belief that she was meant for a joyous life, even though so far the joy had been sporadic.

Professor Schlut attempted to put her out of her misery. "You have the voice, my dear, if that is any help. And you have the heart. With guidance you will learn how to treat your voice so that it will grow. But there are many other things that make a success. Only you know if you have the determination. You must want to sing above all else. And even then you'll need a competent manager. You must have the right exposure when the times comes." He shook his head. "I'm afraid there is simply no guarantee, not the kind you seem to need."

She nodded. "I know that. I did not expect you to make a guarantee." But the things he had said began to lift her heart. "You said I had the voice and heart. I know I have the determination, Professor Schlut. Thank you. Perhaps you have helped me, after all."

He smiled at her. A little conversation often went a long way toward unburdening the heart. He saw the dedication return to her eyes. Ah yes, he thought. Now we can begin. He rose from his seat and gestured toward the inner door.

"Then," he said, "we should waste no more time."

She smiled, stood, picked up her music portfolio, and entered the studio.

An hour later, as she rode down in the lift, still

humming one of the melodies she had sung for the professor, her goals were back in place. She had set her sights on where she wanted to go, and she felt the distractions fall away. Marco intruded on her thoughts, and those thoughts filled her with confusion. He symbolized what she wanted more than anything—the life of the stage, success, filling halls with glorious music, joining with other artists to create something intangible and magical.

She remembered her father's words about not wanting her to see Marco anymore. In working toward her goal, it would be hard to avoid him. Not that she would see him immediately, for her work was cut out for her between the professor's studio and her own music room at home. But Marco would undoubtedly cross her path somewhere, sometime. And when she thought about him in that context, she wanted him to be there for her. He was a mentor. He himself encouraged her artistry. He would undoubtedly share in her victories if and when they came.

But when she thought about the other side of their relationship, her hands got clammy, her heart tightened in her chest. When she was with him, she felt herself falling in love with him. He wanted her, he had made that plain. They had a certain empathy. But what was growing between them was dangerous. Being alone with him was like putting a match to a flame. She fought the titillating pleasure that mere thoughts of his nearness brought her. Marco himself could too easily make her forget everything, including her goals. He could ruin her in a night, and she could not let that happen.

She swallowed, her throat dry, as she stepped off the

lift and exited Carnegie Hall, turning her face uptown. The clip-clop of horse traffic and the hurried pace of pedestrians on the sidewalk helped her set her mind on business. Clutching her music tighter under her arm, she thought of her plan. It was simple, really. Her father was out of the house for several hours each day attending to business. She would use those hours to practice.

When he was home, she could still play the piano, but it would be the lighter tunes, made to sound like she was playing for her own enjoyment. Even if in truth she would be memorizing songs and arias, practicing the pronunciations and phrasing she had learned at the professor's.

Yes, it would not be hard to fill her time in this way. And there would still be time to satisfy her friends with a few outings so that they wouldn't think her a complete recluse.

As she marched along Seventh Avenue, she felt pleased with herself and with her plans.

Chapter Seventeen

The wind blustered throughout New York the rest of December and into January. Snow drifted down in February, covering the city and nearly paralyzing traffic. March brought cold drizzles that chilled everyone's bones.

But in the marble and brick mansion, steam heat warmed the rooms. Elisabeth kept pleasant relations with her father. Everyday when he left the house she repaired to the music room to hammer out her lessons. She would have been pleased if she had known how the servants spent an inordinate amount of time in that wing of the house. The brass gleamed from excessive polishings as Opal and the housemaids used the excuse of working there to listen to the music that came from behind the music room doors.

Even Gunther stopped in his duties to listen. When Hildie the downstairs maid washed the floor, the tiles in the passages to the music room seemed to gleam more than the rest of the house.

And when Gwendolyn started singing along to herself, Opal started to reprimand her. But with her finger in midair, the housekeeper stopped. Wasn't that the tune she herself had been singing the other day?

Opal stuffed her hand into her apron pocket. There was no one about to hear them humming. If music helped the staff get their work done what was the harm in it after all?

Just as she was thinking it she turned a corner and practically collided with Gunther who was humming the piece Elisabeth was playing at the moment. He broke off and blinked his watery eyes.

"Mrs. Turnbull. I did not see you."

Her normally wan cheeks took on a tinge of color. "Too busy singing to know where you were going, I'd say."

He glowered at her and continued on his way, his bowed back and gliding step reminiscent of one of the wraiths in the opera *Faust,* from which he had been humming the ballet music for the demons' dance.

When Marco left for a tour of several eastern cities, Elisabeth told herself she was glad. But the hollow in her heart could not be attributed to the blustery early spring.

She visited with Madelaine and Consuelo as she had promised herself, seeing in Consuelo a ghost of a young woman who was about to plunge into a marriage she did not want.

On an unusually fine day in the beginning of April, she and Consuelo strolled along the quarter-mile esplanade at the lower end of the park, flanked by a double row of elms and statues of literary and musical heroes. The mall led to the stone-carved terrace, where the two girls leaned against the carved stone railing and watched others strolling beside the placid lake below, while little boys played ball on the lawn to their left.

Both girls wore large bonnets trimmed with ribbons, Consuelo's even had a stuffed bird amidst the trimmings. Her sharp features took in their surroundings with an air of resignation.

"How is your music coming, Elisabeth?" asked Consuelo.

"Very well."

Today Elisabeth had been able to put music aside and revel in the enticing spring weather. A cloudless sky spread above the trees, the color blue that was never quite captured on either satin or china.

She brought her eyes from the sky to look at her friend and turned to lean her back against the railing over which they had been looking. She felt incredibly lazy, a feeling she had not indulged in since she could remember.

"Soon you will be married," she said to Consuelo. "Are you happy about that?"

Consuelo lifted one thin shoulder. "I shall be, I suppose. It doesn't seem that I've been offered the choice of happiness this lifetime."

Elisabeth wrinkled a brow. "I'm worried about you, Consuelo."

Her friend looked at her sharply. "Me? Why should you worry about me? I have everything don't I?" She did not try to disguise the irony in her voice and immediately looked apologetic. "I'm sorry. I know I can't fool you, Elisabeth. I seem to have everything except the man I want."

Elisabeth's heart turned in her chest. "Winthrop Rutherford?"

Consuelo gave a little jerk of the chin. "It's too late for that."

Elisabeth shook her head. "But surely he tried to see you."

"Yes. I finally learned from my maid that my mother ordered all my correspondence confiscated. He did try to write to me."

"Then why do you not confront your mother on the matter?"

"I have, of course. But I believe she really means it when she says she'll shoot Winthrop if he tries to see me."

"Surely she cannot mean that."

"You do not know my mother."

Elisabeth thought about the ambitious, determined woman and agreed that perhaps she did mean what she said. But Elisabeth hated to see her friend being pushed into plans that weren't necessarily hers.

"You mustn't worry about me," Consuelo insisted. "The matter is decided."

Elisabeth gave her a sidelong glance, blushing as she said, "But you do not love Marlboro."

Consuelo set her lips in a firm line. "He is not very lovable. But we shall get along."

Elisabeth saw that Consuelo was as determined to forge ahead this arranged marriage as she herself was not to marry at all. A sudden surge of grief and nostalgia pressed her heart, and she turned to look at the budding trees, and the trailing ribbons of little girls chasing a gray squirrel along the mall.

Why did love have to be so difficult, she wondered. why did it always go awry for some people? Even in the operas she was singing love nearly always ended in a tragedy.

She forced the little feeling of yearning aside and turned to walk back with Consuelo. There would be other consolations, she told herself. Voicing her thoughts, she said, "Do you want children?"

"Of course," said Consuelo. "I shall enjoy that."

"Then there is something."

"Yes." After a moment Consuelo turned the conversation. "And you? Have you any offers of marriage?"

"I don't want any."

Consuelo turned an arched brow on her. "Never?"

Elisabeth shook her head, blotting out the past. "No."

"Why not? You can't become a spinster. You have too much to offer."

"I want to sing."

"But you do sing. That doesn't prevent you from marrying."

"I mean professionally, on the stage."

Consuelo stared at her. "Really? Have you told your father?"

"Oh yes. He does not approve."

"Well my dear, I can see why. It's not the sort of thing a lady from our class does." She studied her friend. "I knew you studied music in Europe, but I had no idea this was so serious. Have you any prospects?"

"My teacher thinks I have talent, but it is I who must have the determination."

"Are you sure you want to do this?" Consuelo sounded doubtful.

"I am sure."

"Well then," Consuelo said thoughtfully. "That does put marriage out of the question. Even Alex . . ."

"What about Alex?"

"Oh nothing. I mean, everyone knows you and Alex have been seeing each other."

"He does come round from time to time, but I've told him where things stand between us. You know Alex, he's a playboy. He'll find someone else."

"I'm not sure. He seems to have settled down quite a lot since he finished college. He is rather eligible, Elisabeth. But he would not. . . ."

"Yes?"

Consuelo stumbled over her words. "Well, I know he sees ladies of the theater from time to time, but you . . . Well, he would hardly put you in that class."

Elisabeth bristled at the recurrent prejudice separating people of the arts from the rest of upper class society.

"I would rather he did not."

The girls walked on in silence, each involved in her own thoughts, realizing that while they cared for each other, they did not quite understand each other.

Elisabeth was coming in the front door when she heard the familiar resilient, booming laugh that made her heart stop. She paused in the foyer. *Marco.* What was he doing here? And who was he talking to?

She crept up the stairs to the second floor landing

272

and turned in the direction of her father's study. As she neared, she could hear voices, muted by the carved door. Perhaps she had been wrong. Perhaps she was hearing things, but the quickness of her heartbeat gave away the fact that she hoped she was not wrong.

She knocked tentatively at the door and her father answered, "Come in."

She opened the door, and there he was.

"Marco," she said on a breath of surprise and a rush of joy that she could not stop.

He was dressed in morning coat, gray striped trousers and broad knotted silk tie. When he turned his smile on her his face took on an expression of excitement that matched her own. He crossed the room to take her hands. She saw his spontaneous movement to take her in his arms, and then he restrained himself and bowed over her hands instead. But his kiss was warm and lingered on the back of her wrist, and when he raised his head, his eyes drank in hers.

"How good to see you, Elisabeth. I was just talking to your father."

Her eyes were wide, her cheeks flushed with excitement, her mouth parted in delight. She wished more than anything that her father were not in the room. She had so much to tell Marco.

"I did not know you were back," she said, seeking a compromise between her own anxiousness to revel in conversation with him for the next few hours and the knowledge that they were at the moment being watched by her parent.

And it wasn't the chaperonage of her actions that she resented so much, she simply had so much to share with

Marco that her father simply wouldn't understand. At that moment it was more than ever real to her that she and Marco shared a world apart from everyone else she knew. And she had been missing it desperately.

Marco squeezed her hand and led her to a seat where the three of them could continue to visit. "I have just been telling your father of my experiences up and down the coast. An exhausting tour it was. I'm glad to be home."

She was curious as to why Marco was bothering Winston with these details. From her father's polite but wary expression, she could see that while her father was impressed by Marco's stardom, he was not quite comfortable with it. As she watched Marco deftly handle the conversation she became aware of something else. Marco was not entertaining Winston for his own pleasure. He was doing it for her. He must have known he wasn't welcome in this house, but using his status as a star, he'd gained entrance as a social caller. It amused her that he seemed determined to win Winston over. And her father, while remaining stuffy in his viewpoints, couldn't resist Marco's easygoing charisma and his status in the world of opera.

" . . . the people in the hinterlands are better versed in music than one would expect," Marco was going on when Elisabeth finally began to listen. "Though of course every concert is rounded out with popular favorites."

As he continued to make small talk with her father Elisabeth gathered her wits. Finally, Marco turned his attention to her.

"And I hope you've been practicing your music

lessons, my dear." His head was turned so that Winston couldn't see him wink.

She knew they were acting out a little drama for her father's benefit, and she played along, acting the part of a good socialite daughter who had done her lessons well.

"I've been studying *Madame Butterfly*. It's a very sad story, do you not agree? I am nearly moved to tears when I sing it."

Marco nodded thoughtfully and then launched into a conversation about the composer, Puccini, and his other operas. Soon Winston began to yawn, and Marco quickly apologized for monopolizing the conversation.

"Quite all right," said Winston, still trying to maintain decorum even though he still did not seem certain whether to be honored or offended by Marco's continued presence.

"Well," he said, rising from the chair. "It's late, the servants have already gone to bed. I'm afraid I must retire."

Marco did not appear to take the hint, and Elisabeth kept her neutral expression. She went to kiss her father on the cheek.

"Good night, Father. I shall be up before long."

"Good night, Sir," said Marco. "It was a pleasure to see you and to thank you for the charming affair in December. I can only hope it will be repeated."

Winston shook his hand and bid them both good night, not without a suspicious look. But when he closed the door and they heard his footsteps leading in the direction of the stairs, Marco turned to Elisabeth with a grin, and she put her hand to her mouth, covering a smile.

Then Marco opened his arms and she went to him. Her soft laughter tinkled in his ear as he embraced her in an affectionate hug.

"We fooled him, I'm afraid," said Marco.

She stood back and gazed at Marco's face, which showed signs of strain from his tour, but also a light of devilment at getting his way.

"I've flattered him into thinking himself an expert on opera. Who knows? Perhaps I have done a favor to the arts?"

They laughed in shared amusement, and Elisabeth couldn't stop her heart from racing, so glad she was to see him. For the moment she didn't question it, but simply beamed her delight. Then she took his hand and led him to the sofa.

"How was your tour?" she asked. "I want to hear all about it."

He sat down by her, throwing one arm over the back of the sofa.

"But of course you want to know the details of the music I sang and how I was received."

"Of course."

"And of the hardship of railroad travel, of the irregularity of schedule and the unpredictability of the food one must eat on such a journey. And then of the endless calls one receives after performances when all one wants to do is eat and relax."

"But don't tell me it was such hard work," she chided. "Don't tell me you didn't enjoy it."

"Aha," he said, capturing her hand. "I can see that

your concern is all for the artist and nothing for the man, poor me."

"Well..."

He was teasing her, luring her on. But she played cat and mouse with him, pulling her hand away and folding her hands primly as she sat, straight-backed beside him. "Of course I must know. You must tell me everything. After all, someday, even I..."

"Even you will make such tours."

She blushed. "If I'm so fortunate."

Marco slid down a trace in the corner of the sofa, resting more easily as if he needed the comfort of being himself and not having to present his professional self everywhere he went.

"You will be, I think," he said. "That is, if Theodore Schlut has anything to say about it."

She perked up. "You've seen him?"

"I did stop by his studio today."

"Oh? What did he say?"

"Nothing more than what he has said to you himself, I'm sure."

She leaned forward, needing the reassurance. "Oh please tell me, Marco, don't be mean."

He grasped her hand again, pulling her even farther toward him. "How badly do you want to know?"

She remonstrated against his suggestive tone. "Marco, you are teasing me."

He gave up and released her hand. "Very well. He told me you have talent and that you are working very hard. It seems you have already learned two entire roles. The real test of course is how you'll be received by those who hear you and by your own determination."

His glance turned more serious. "Are you sure, darling, that this is what you want to do?"

She frowned and stood up, her energy too much to keep her in her seat.

"Everyone asks me that," she said in exasperation. "It's not a question. I've already decided."

Marco propped his elbow on the arm of the sofa and rested his head on his hand.

"Then you're as determined as before."

She felt his gaze on her and saw the many emotions he held within himself. She believed he was sincerely interested in her music, but she also saw that the powerful yearning between them hadn't changed. If anything Marco looked more inviting, more needy, and more sensual. Perhaps because he was so drained after such a long trip, he needed her. He was a man, and he needed a woman.

All this she observed in an instant, and she couldn't look at him. The situation was impossible. How could she go to him for advice, for sustenance in her chosen field without being entangled by the warp of emotions he aroused in her? How could she protect her heart from making more mistakes in the matter of love? Why did she have to respond to him so undeniably?

Marco saw her conflict, but he saw much more. He saw her supple beauty, and yearned for release in her, yearned to be filled up with a woman's love that could renew him. He was on his feet and gathered her into his arms.

She didn't resist as he came to her but yielded to his strong embrace. Her senses came alive at the remembered masculine scent, and her body tingled as he pulled her against him in spite of the warning thoughts. His lips brushed her hair, her cheek and found her mouth. She met his kiss with desire of her own that had been suppressed these many months. Sensations flowed between them as each revelled in pleasures long put aside.

"Marco," she whispered as he released her mouth and led her to the sofa. He handed her into a seat and then crossed the room to turn off the light that was glaring from tulip shaped wall fixtures. Only the soft glow from a single fringed lamp left the room in dreamy dimness.

This time when he returned to sit beside her, she did not fight him but melted against him as he held her and delighted in her soft body.

"I came to you as soon as I could," he said in a low, emotion-filled voice. "You can't know how often I thought of you. How I wanted you with me."

"That could never be," she said haltingly as he passed his hands over the curve of her breasts and along her waist to her back and hips.

He kissed her and kissed her, tasting her mouth, her cheeks, her eyelids, her chin.

"We must talk about us," he said between kisses. "I can't take no for an answer very much longer."

The need and desire in his voice moved her, and her own emotions matched his. But though her body and soul cried out for him, her mind hadn't changed.

"I can't," she mumbled, even as his fingers found the buttons on her collar and undid them.

"Why?" He lowered his mouth to the base of her throat and teased her skin.

She leaned back as his hands and mouth did their magic. How she wanted to hold his strong body to hers. She even let her hands drift along his chest and down his thigh where his leg had trapped hers.

"Marco, I can't. It's wrong."

"Hmmm," he said, only half listening.

His hands were more insistent now and his desire was expressing itself as he pressed himself as close to her as he could. Her bodice came undone and he drew in a breath at the sight of the delicate skin of her rising bosom above her camisole. His urgency grew until he thought he must take her right there. He was mad with wanting her.

"Elisabeth, I love you," he whispered as he moved her lower on the sofa. "Marry me. You must become mine. I can't live without you."

Her own body was responding to the newness of his touch in intimate places, and she could not resist his fire. Her body throbbed in strange ways and she yearned for the release she sensed she could find in him. Her words were powerless before his ardor. Where he was taking her she did not know but suddenly she wanted him with all her might. What were career, reputation, sins of the past compared with the ecstasy of the present moment?

She opened her lips to him just as she arched her body slightly to the movements he was making against her.

"Say yes," he whispered against her ear, even as his hand found her soft thigh above her gartered stockings. "Say yes."

She was beyond reason, guided only by his passion

filling her, and her own needy heart. She murmured his name, murmured she knew not what as he worked his magic. She would never be his, never marry him. She knew that. His fame would overshadow her, swallow her ambition. She could not fall before him. And yet . . .

"Yes, Marco, yes . . . yes . . ." she blotted out tomorrow.

An hour later they sat together on the sofa, their clothing restored, the light still dim. They sat in the shocked intimacy of what had happened between them, few words spoken.

Already embarrassment crept into the fulfillment Elisabeth had felt. Her aching body still celebrated his touch, and his scent still clung to her. But her mind was filled with the fears of what this meant.

"Why will you not marry me?" Marco asked softly. "I have told you I love you."

She wouldn't look at him. "I can't marry you. Surely you can see that I want a career of my own. It is . . . I'm not sure I can explain it to you. It is something I must do."

He pulled his mouth into a grim line. "You must prove something to yourself."

"Perhaps. I only know that marriage is not for me. Surely you realize . . ."

He turned his body toward her but still did not touch her. "Elisabeth, what happened to you in the past is not part of the present. It is not part of us."

She winced.

He saw the struggle she was going through, and he was not about to insist. "Very well, if you won't marry me, we must carry on as we are now."

She opened her eyes wider and looked at him, her face full of emotion. "We could never do that."

"What do you mean, after we just . . ."

She raised a finger and pressed it against his lips. Her heart ached, but she had to say what she felt.

"What happened just now was," she moistened her lips. "Perhaps it was madness, some insatiable need, I don't know."

He grasped her fingers and wrapped his hand around hers. "And you don't think it will happen again? Surely you can see how we are meant for each other." His other hand drifted across her unbound curls.

"If you won't have me for a husband, then I'll be your lover."

"No."

His hand stopped. He peered into her tear-filled eyes. Then his hand resumed its motion and he tipped her chin upward.

"No one would know."

She moved her head from side to side. "Too many secrets," she said sadly. "Secrets from the past added to secrets in the present. I couldn't stand that."

His heart contracted. Surely she didn't mean it. But he saw the pain in her eyes, felt the struggle in her heart. She was courageous, but he couldn't force her to accept either a proposal of marriage or an intimate arrangement. Already he wanted to make love to her again, and he couldn't help the steely resentment that crept over him at the thought of not having her. But he couldn't break her spirit. Perhaps if he gave her time, she would change her mind. But he was not always a patient man.

When there were no more words to say, they both stood, and Elisabeth saw him out down the dimly lit corridor to the main staircase. They walked sadly down it. She knew that once she shut the door on him, it would be the end of their brief affair. Her heart tore with the desire to change her mind, to be able to throw herself into his arms and accept love from him on any terms. But the old determination and the pride that Marco had correctly surmised lay within her helped her keep her back straight. She would carry his love with her, perhaps, but she could do no more. She had her own road to travel.

She didn't expect Marco to wait years for her for a time when perhaps she'd had her success as an artist, however small, and would be ready to accept a mate on equal terms. Such a thing might never happen. She might fail. But if she didn't try, she would never know. And if she lost Marco in the process, which she very well expected she would do, she would have to accept the responsibility. She couldn't make a compromise.

At the doors, he stopped and looked at her one last time, reading much of her thoughts in her eyes. He didn't challenge her. Rather, he lifted her fingers to his lips and kissed them. She saw the love in his dark eyes in the moonlight that shone through the door.

Then he opened the door and was gone.

True to her resolve, Elisabeth didn't see Marco for

the next several weeks. Her practice sessions became longer as she drove herself to learn every note of the roles she was studying. The dramatic interpretation came naturally to her, and Professor Schlut guided her carefully on phrasing and dynamics.

To distract herself when she wasn't working on her music she went on outings with her friends. She was pleased when Alva Vanderbilt invited her to sing at an evening's entertainment for the Duke of Marlboro in the white and gold salon at Marble House in Newport. Every opportunity to perform strengthened her confidence and helped her refine her stage manners, though her socialite acquaintances still didn't know that she intended to have a career. Apparently Consuelo had either forgotten what she had said during their tête-à-tête in the park, or was too enmeshed in her own whirlwind of activity to care.

Alex squired her on the balmy spring evening in Newport after the recital. They stood on the patio overlooking the steep cliffs and the dark ocean below. Inside lights from the crystal chandeliers glimmered on diamonds, satins and jewels as the intimate gathering of a hundred-and-fifty or so greeted the Duke.

Alex was entertaining her with an anecdote about something that had happened at Maxim's, to which Elisabeth was half listening. Every so often Alex broke off his own conversation to raise his glass or otherwise greet one of the other guests. Elisabeth turned to gaze at the barely visible white-tipped waves rolling toward the shore far below.

"You seem distracted my dear," said Alex.

"Oh, sorry. I suppose I was thinking."

"Haven't you done enough of that for one evening? Your head is filled with melodies and words. You should relax now and drink your champagne."

"I suppose."

She tried to enter into the social atmosphere, but found that the large social gathering tired her. What she longed for was a quiet place to rest, enjoy the night air, partake of a few refreshments and if there was no mental stimulation to be had, go to bed and read the biographies of the composers she was studying.

"Come, come, Elisabeth, you work too hard." His tone turned more serious as he closed the gap between them. "I see you are still driven in the direction of a musical career."

She glanced up at him and read the intelligent perception in his eyes. He had dropped his social veneer and spoke in a way that told her he wasn't fooled. His concern surprised her.

"Perhaps I am," she said, meaning, *what business is it of yours?*

Alex sighed, lightening his tone. "Elisabeth, you know how I adore you. I have offered more than friendship, but alas you do not seem to have a heart. What more can I do? I was very proud of you tonight as you sang. Such beauty, such radiance, I told myself. She will surely be a success."

His flattery made her smile in spite of herself. "Do you really think so?"

"Oh yes." He nodded gravely. "But when you're a big success, I shall insist on escorting you about town. I'll be the envy of all my friends."

She laughed at his mixture of humor, self-indulgence

and flirtation. At least Alex didn't disapprove of a woman having a career on stage. It was at least a contrast to her father's constant and overt disapproval. Because she was not in any way tempted by Alex's courting, it was easy to banter with him. At least if he didn't press her any harder than this, they could remain friends.

"We'll see about that," she said. "I don't go out much and shall go out less if I actually have a career."

"Nonsense," insisted Alex. "All great actresses have an active social life. After the thrill of applause, where can you go to relax but to an after-theater supper with the other thrill-seekers."

She blinked at him, and his smile flashed and then transmuted into an attempt at conservatism. But it was too late. She understood the implication. He had hinted at it once before. It was perfectly all right for her to be an actress in Alex's eyes, but her status would change. She would no longer be a prospect for a wife, but for a mistress.

In the moment she and Alex looked at each other, the knowledge was clear. Elisabeth stifled the acid words that began to form on her lips. She turned angrily toward the facade of the mansion where party guests moved between the patio and the reception rooms inside. *Hypocrites!* she wanted to scream at them all.

At that moment a gentleman of medium height with a touch of silver at his temples approached them. He coughed, with his hand folded against his mouth.

"Excuse me," the man said. "I do not mean to interrupt a conversation. Ah, Mr. Rochat, I thought it was you. Perhaps you will be so kind as to introduce me to this young lady."

Alex recovered himself, searching for the man's name. The gentleman helped him.

"You may remember that we met at the Goelet's last week."

"Oh, er yes, of course, Mr. . . . ."

"Prescott. Percy Prescott, at your service."

"Yes, yes of course. Mr. Prescott, may I present Elisabeth Sloane. Elisabeth, this is Mr. Percy Prescott of . . ."

"Boston," the man supplied. He bowed. "Beautiful singing tonight, Miss Sloane. As I was listening to your touching rendition of 'O mio babbino caro,' I had but one thought."

Elisabeth raised her brows. "Oh, and what was that?"

"I have a friend who must hear you sing. You could be the answer to his prayers."

Chapter Eighteen

"What do you mean?" asked Elisabeth.

"My friend is an impresario," Prescott explained. "Of the Boston Lyric Opera Company. He is at the moment in a difficult position. One of his leading sopranos has a contract with the Berlin Opera, and her leave of absence from that company is up. She has asked for an extension, but the negotiations are not going well for my friend. It appears that she must return to Berlin in the coming months.

"Alas this is a tragedy for the opera company. Where can you get a competent singer on such short notice to perform the role of Mimi? And then I heard your rendition of two arias from *La Bohême* this evening, I was entranced, if I may say so."

He paused to bow his acknowledgment, and Elisabeth exchanged glances with Alex, who was listening with interest.

"Thank you," she said.

Prescott continued. "Forgive me for being so presumptuous. I do not know if you are interested in such a proposition. Do you have a manager, my dear, to whom I could speak about such a matter?"

"Why no," she answered. "I'm still studying with Professor Theodore Schlut."

"I could advise Miss Sloane on any financial matters," interrupted Alex.

She gave him a sidelong glance. "Alex!"

"Only until you have proper management, Elisabeth," he said. "Mr. Prescott is right. You must have someone to advise you. I would be happy to step in for the moment."

Prescott seemed satisfied. "It is not a problem. Between Mr. Rochat and your Professor Schlut matters might be arranged. But first, if you are interested, you must sing for my friend, Walter Berry."

Alex cleared his throat and stroked his moustache. "And where may Mr. Berry be contacted?"

"He is in Boston presently. I will wire him tomorrow. He'll be coming to New York on business. Perhaps we can arrange an audition."

Elisabeth was speechless, but tried to find words. "I'd be happy to sing for him, of course."

Prescott smiled in satisfaction. "And where may I reach you?"

She hesitated. "I live with my father in New York. But perhaps it would be better to send a message to Professor Schlut. My father is—shall we say—not prepared for me to have a career."

"I understand. Then if you will give me Professor Schlut's address."

Alex took a gold pen and notebook from his pocket and wrote down the address Elisabeth gave him. He handed the paper to Prescott, and the two men shook hands. Prescott bowed over Elisabeth's hand.

"Then you shall hear from one of us very soon, I hope."

He left them, and they watched him rejoin the party. Elisabeth turned back to the railing.

"An audition," she murmured to the sea. What would Marco think?

She hated the fact that her first thought was of Marco. It seemed he was an integral part of everything to do with music in her life, and therefore indelible from her unconsciousness. She had resisted his amorous advances for the reason that he would overshadow her. She hadn't seen him for weeks, and yet he was still present in her mind as if he were standing beside her and had taken part in the entire conversation.

"Well now," mused Alex beside her. "It seems things are happening rather fast, are they not? I suppose you'll not tell Winston."

"No, I couldn't."

"Hmmmm. Well, you can rely on me for discretion. As to this matter of being your manager...."

"Oh, Alex, you can't be serious. You're not a manager of artists. Besides, we don't even know if the audition will go well. The impresario may not think me ready."

"We shall see about that. You are right, of course. I cannot serve in this capacity indefinitely. It would not be quite the thing for a man of my position. My only thought was to protect you."

"Thank you, Alex," she said in wry understanding of his position. "But I am sure that if Professor Schlut thinks I'm ready for such an audition, he can recommend a manager to look out for my financial interests."

Alex rubbed his chin. "Then I must speak to your professor."

"Very well."

She would not waste time arguing with Alex, though why he thought he had a say in her affairs was beyond her. She had made her relationship clear to him. Her mind was already spinning toward the role Mr. Prescott had said the opera company needed filled. If only she could do it. It would be a dream come true.

The rest of the evening passed in a blur. She spoke to many of the guests, saw Consuelo and the Duke circulating in their glittering dignity. She stood with Madelaine, who gossiped incessantly in her ear, but after her friend left her, Elisabeth did not remember a thing she had said.

She spent the night in a comfortable room with the windows opened to spring sea breezes, but she hardly slept all night. The next day she rode with Alex and Madelaine on the train back to New York, staring out the window for most of the journey.

Madelaine noticed that she seemed distracted and commented on it. Alex, of course, knew what she was thinking about, and she made the effort to contribute to the conversation after that.

At home, she briefly described the party to her father, who hadn't attended due to business engagements with foreign bankers in town. Then she went to her room to compose a message to send to Professor Schlut. She did not want to ring him up on the telephone for fear the rest of the household might overhear her.

"I must see you on an interesting development," she penned. "Have met a Percy Prescott who wants to introduce me to a Mr. Walter Berry, impresario of an opera company in Boston. I would appreciate your advice by return note."

That would do it, she thought as she folded the note and put it into an envelope. If either of the men were disreputable or if the professor thought it madness to audition at so early a stage in her training, he would let her know. She had complete faith in her teacher. If, however, there was a chance that he favored such a move, he would help her prepare.

She did not trust the message to any of the servants. Though they seemed loyal to her, she knew that her father would keep an eye out for any secretive action on her part, and servants gossiped. Nor did she want to wait on the regular post.

Rather she found one of the boys on the street, always ready to earn some money for such an errand. She wrote out the address on the envelope and instructed the boy to wait for a reply. Then she returned to the house. If she didn't hear back in three or four hours she would assume that either the professor was out or the boy had gotten sidetracked, in which case she would go herself.

She spent the intervening time at the piano, going over the role of Mimi, and as she practiced her excitement grew. Such a role was meant for her.

At the sound of the door bell, she jumped off the seat. Gunther would answer of course. She hurried along the corridor, and when she reached the foyer, she saw Gunther turn.

"Ah, Miss Sloane. A letter for you."

"Thank you, Gunther."

She took the note and hurried upstairs to her room, ripping open the envelope as she went.

"Come to the studio tomorrow morning at ten," the professor's scrawl ordered. "We will have much work to do if you are to sing for Berry. I shall cancel all my other morning lessons."

He approves! she thought with joy. It was difficult to think how she would get through the remaining hours of the day and the night until the morning arrived.

When the time did arrive, Elisabeth presented herself and her music scores. Even Governor Worthy seemed agitated by the new development. Berry had wired, saying he would be in New York the following week. He would be happy to hear Miss Sloane sing if she would be willing.

"And what did you reply?" asked Elisabeth as she followed him to the piano where he deposited the music scores.

"That you would be ready to sing for him, of course."

"Oh, Professor Schlut, I can't believe it. My first audition."

"You must try not to work yourself into a state, my dear. Who can tell about these things?"

"Have you ever heard of his company?"

Professor Schlut gave a small shrug. "It is a new opera company, well-supported by its small but loyal public. It seems our Mr. Berry is in dire straits. He cannot hope to book a leading soprano on such short notice. Most contracts are negotiated far in advance, as much as a year. This trouble his prima donna is having with Berlin..." His meaning was clear from his gesture.

In reality Elisabeth could not dare to hope she would be good enough to fulfill the role that Mr. Berry needed to fill. While she felt confident with the music, it seemed so soon. And yet, one gained nothing unless one tried.

"Then let us begin," she said as if she were the professional already running her own career.

Elisabeth sang for the professor that day as she had never sung before. Her voice spun a web of gold to match the morning sun beaming in the windows. She became the Bohemian Mimi in heart and mind. But the professor did not let her simply ride on her own emotions, he stopped her here and there to make her go over a phrase for emphasis. He showed her how to caress the words, to use her vocal instrument to ring delicately and move her listeners.

By the end of the session, Professor Schlut sighed in satisfaction. Then he peered at Elisabeth over his pince-nez glasses.

"If you sing like that next week, Mr. Berry cannot help but be impressed."

Her hand went to her heart. "Thank you, Professor. I do not dare hope."

His hand fluttered in a gesture of speculation. "One can never tell what will be in his mind. But it cannot hurt you to be heard. As to his making an offer. We will face that when it comes."

He folded the music shut. "I had a note from your businessman friend, Alexander Rochat."

"Oh Alex," she said on a breath. "He was present when Mr. Prescott told me of this opportunity. He is insistent that I be represented."

"A wise piece of advice. You will need a manager

if you sing professionally."

"Well, Alex could not possibly be qualified."

Professor Schlut smiled. "But at least he seems to have your best interests at heart."

She gave him a look of exasperation. "He has his own motives."

"Ahhh." The professor seemed to understand. But he waved it away. "No matter. He can be present in case an offer is made. Mr. Berry will be used to such arrangements."

The professor walked her to the door. As he did so he rubbed his hands together.

"Yes, it does sound like a likely arrangement. I shall send word when I hear from Berry as to time and place. He'll want to hear you sing from a stage. This room will be too small for him to tell your capabilities. But do not worry. I shall make those arrangements."

"Oh." She wondered what stage she would be singing on.

As she rode home on the horsecar, she pondered. She would not mention the audition to her father. If she actually got the role, she would have to travel to Boston. She could just imagine the embarrassment it would cause her father, and she felt the old twinge of regret that her parent did not understand her. Why could he not remove the blinders that kept him from seeing that times were bound to change? Someday society's rigid boundaries would become blurred. A class could not feed on itself forever.

As she approached the house, she put her thoughts aside. She let herself in and climbed the stairs to her room.

From the landing, she heard two of the maids singing

as they worked at the end of the hall. She paused by the door in curiosity and then smiled as she recognized a gay rendition of "I'm Called Little Buttercup."

Gwendolyn and Hildie, the other maid, broke off in laughter and applause at their own attempts. Elisabeth backed away, not wanting to ruin their fun or embarrass them. But she held a secret smile on her lips as she took the other stairs to her room. She had sung the song so many times that the two girls must have picked it up. What pleasure to think that her music was being shared by someone, even if it was only the servants.

Professor Schlut arranged for Carnegie Recital Hall to be used for the audition. It was a small hall in the same building as the larger auditorium and the studios, and it would demonstrate Elisabeth's voice in the appropriate setting.

She left the house that morning bursting with nervous excitement. When she entered the door to the east of Carnegie's main entrance, the dim, cool interior only increased her excitement. She heard voices in the recital hall, and then Alex broke off when he saw her.

"Good morning, my dear," he said. "Are you in good voice?"

She smiled at his managerial demeanor. His frock coat was impeccable as usual, his cravat neatly in place, his moustache trimmed and waxed. In his hand was his tall gray hat.

He took her elbow and steered her forward. "I have just been talking to Mr. Walter Berry. Mr. Berry, this is Miss Sloane."

A gentleman of medium height with frizzy brown hair and a receding hairline turned from Professor Schlut and observed her. His moustache drooped like a weeping willow. Like the other men present, he wore a dark three-piece suit, wide cravat, and stiff, white collar. A watch chain dangled from his vest pocket.

"Ah, Miss Sloane, my pleasure. Your colleagues have been telling me about you. If my friend Percy Prescott has ears at all, I'm sure I am in for a treat." He chuckled. "And these two gentlemen are here to make sure I am an honest man and do not sell you into white slavery."

He laughed very loud at his own joke while the other three chuckled politely. Then he gestured toward the front of the auditorium.

"Let us begin. I believe the kind professor will accompany you."

She nodded. As Alex and Mr. Berry took seats in the middle of the small auditorium, Professor Schlut escorted her up the steps at the side of the stage. She thought of Marco, and wondered where he was. She half-wished he were here to share the excitement of her first audition, but she was half-relieved that he was not, in case she did not do well.

Professor Schlut had her stand facing him for a few moments and led her in some warm-up exercises, which also gave her time to adjust to the feel of the stage and the acoustics.

"You do not need to strain, my dear. Relax. That's it," he coached as she sang the pattern he played on the piano. "Now again."

When he felt she was sufficiently warmed up, he nodded. "All right. Let us begin. Just sing the way you sang for me the last time you were in the studio."

She smiled. She remembered the exact emotion and tonality they had achieved at that practice session. And as she heard the notes of the introduction, she let the role overtake her.

She concentrated not on the two men listening to her but on recreating the scene. Soon she was lost in it, remembering at the same time to listen carefully to the pitch, controlling the dynamics of her voice.

By the end of the piece she felt she was fully into the opera and when she dropped her eyes and ended the last note, she wished she were in a real performance so that the scene might go on.

Instead, after a moment of silence, loud clapping came from the audience of two. She broke her pose and bowed, smiling at the two men.

Mr. Berry said nothing, but waited, for he had been informed that she would sing several pieces. She returned to the piano, while Professor Schlut shuffled the music. When they were both ready, he nodded and began the second piece.

She was already in character, and the second piece went even better than the first. She felt that the ice had broken, and she could have sung all day. An exuberance of spirit seized her, and she was swept away by the music. Any nervous tension that had plagued her at the beginning was lost in the creation of the moment. Every fiber of her being was involved in the performance.

Again the applause echoed from the audience, this time accompanied by Alex's shouts of, "brava." She paused to catch her breath and saw Mr. Berry rise from his seat. He approached the stage.

"Very nice, my dear. I understand that you have studied the entire role. Is that true?"

"Yes," she said, looking down at him from the stage.

"Would you be so kind as to sing the duet from Act III? I myself will sing the part of Rudolpho."

"Of course."

He walked to the piano while Professor Schlut turned to the piece that had been requested. When she was ready, she again took her position at the center of the stage.

The music began. Elisabeth heard not a piano, but the instruments of an orchestra. In her mind's eye the stage settings for the Parisian tavern materialized around her.

The vision of Marco in the role of Rudolpho came unbidden, and when she began the poignant melody, her emotions went out to him. She was lost in the music while at the same time remembering the techniques of singing. She experienced the strange combination of one world superimposed over the other, the real world being the dimmer, but present enough to anchor her to her purpose. Stronger than ever was the notion that the performance was not that of an audition for one gentleman who could launch her career, rather she was transported already to the bigger stage with a living, breathing audience listening to her interpretation.

The final notes died as she bid Rudolpho farewell. When she glanced up in time to see Berry approach, she blinked, jarred out of her artistic creation back to the real world. The piano died away, and she slowly relaxed her pose.

Mr. Berry reached out a hand to assist her to her feet. "I do not mind telling you I am impressed, Miss

Sloane. Your voice has much potential. You have been fortunate in having a teacher to coach you in the nuances of the role while not pushing you beyond your limits. If you are serious about wanting to be engaged, I believe we can work something out."

Elisabeth rose to her feet, her head still swimming from the exhilaration of the performance. His words seemed to come from a great distance.

"Thank you," she managed to say.

Footsteps sounded on the steps. Then Alex was on the stage, shaking hands with everyone and kissing her on the cheek.

"Let us retire to my studio," Professor Schlut finally said. "My housekeeper will bring us tea, and we can iron out the details."

The party took a back passage to the lift and went up to the studio. Professor Schlut ordered a tray of tea and sandwiches, and after a great deal of conversation and conviviality, they all got down to business.

By the time she left two hours later, Elisabeth understood the details of her contract. She would travel to Boston for a week of rehearsals with the company and then sing in several performances. The company presented opera in repertory, which meant that on the nights when *La Bohême* was not being performed, she would not sing. Berry would take care of her hotel and transportation arrangements. She would take her own maid to help her dress.

It was only when she came out on the sunny sidewalk that she faced the idea that her life had changed. She would have to tell her father. She glanced down Seventh Avenue as if she could see the seventeen blocks to the Metropolitan Opera House where Marco was probably busy rehearsing. She wanted to share the news.

But she pressed her lips together. She was with effort limiting her contact with Marco, for while he served as an anchor in the world of music, he was dangerous to her heart. She flushed as she remembered what had happened between them the last time they met. Her body tingled with the remembrance, and she turned away from the direction of the opera house and set her face toward the park.

Uncertain of what to do with her womanly desires, she must concentrate on the job before her. At the same time she needed Marco's musical reassurance, she could not again risk her responses in his arms.

As she walked toward the park, she tried to still the rising anxiety in her heart. Her excitement at having gotten a part was dampened only by the knowledge that her father would not approve.

What her society friends would say, she did not know. But what they thought was of little consequence to her. It was her father that she cared about. Their inability to meet in understanding ever since she had had a life of her own plagued her like a heavy weight. She decided to walk all the way home in order to try to frame the words to tell him.

She entered the park and took a path beside the winding road. Trotting horses pranced by, throwing dirt behind their sharp hooves. The day was breezy, but there was a bright sun, and children chased about under the trees. Gentlemen sat on benches reading the paper during their lunch hour. The city prospered. But the pleasing surroundings did little to help her with her problem.

There was no way around it but to tell Winston what had happened. She would have to pack for Boston. If he wouldn't let Gwendolyn go with her, she would have to hire another maid.

Cutting through the park, she came out on Fifth Avenue, walking briskly until the mansion was in view. She felt the exercise of the walk and the exhilaration of having achieved her goal. Unfortunately, what the mansion symbolized for her was not the joy she wanted so badly to share.

After waiting for some traffic to pass, she crossed the street and entered the iron gate. She passed through the cool interior of the entry hall and went up the stairs. When she saw Opal on the second landing, she asked if her father was at home.

"No Miss. Gone out. Said he'd be home by four o'clock. I expect he'll want his tea by then."

"Thank you, Opal. I want to see him when he comes in."

"Yes, Miss."

"Oh, and Opal. Could you ask Gunther to bring up my trunk? I'll be packing for a journey."

"Oh? Of course."

She almost told the housekeeper her news. But it wouldn't do for her father to hear it from the servants before he heard it from her own lips.

Upstairs, she opened her wardrobe and highboy and began to lay out clothing she would take. She called Gwendolyn to take things that needed airing or pressing.

Around four o'clock, she happened to be leaving the music room downstairs and heard her father come in. She waited a few moments in the passage where she could hear him speaking to Gunther in the main entry hall. Then from the sound of his footsteps, she could tell that he had taken the stairs and was probably on the way to his study. She closed the music room door softly and followed.

Outside the study, she faced the door and took a deep breath. Then she knocked.

"Come in," called Winston.

She entered and shut the door behind her.

"Hello, Elisabeth," he said, looking up from the sheaf of papers he had just removed from his portfolio and laid on the mahogany desk.

"Hello, Father." She took a few steps closer.

When he looked up he saw that she had something on her mind.

"Please sit down, my dear. You look as if you have something to say."

"I do."

She sat on the edge of an oval-backed brocade chair.

"Well?"

She swallowed. "I've been invited to perform with a small opera company in Boston. The impresario heard me sing today and offered me a role."

Winston raised and lowered his bushy eyebrows. "A role? In Boston? What does this mean?"

Unable to stay seated, she jumped up. "It means that I have accepted my first professional role."

Winston stared at her and then walked around the desk. He opened his mouth to speak and then closed it again. "I don't suppose you really mean to carry this out," he finally said.

"I do."

He glowered. "Boston? To perform on the stage?"

Then his bluster crumpled and he sank into a chair. He seemed to age visibly before her eyes, sinking down in the chair and crossing his legs.

"Why are you doing this?" he asked in a softer voice.

"I know you don't approve of my wanting to perform," she said. "But it's what I want to do with all my heart."

"But becoming an actress? I tried to help you cover up your previous indiscretion," he said, sitting up a little straighter. "But if you are to expose yourself to the public like this, I can do nothing more."

"I know, Father. It is entirely my own doing. It is just that I feel it is time for the old prejudices to be set aside. I have a life of my own now."

"But Elisabeth, you don't know where this will lead. You may give up all chance of marriage and a home. It's your future I'm worried about." He rubbed his forehead tiredly.

She sat down again. "Please try not to worry about it, Father." She even gave in to a wry smile. "If my behavior is too outrageous for our friends to accept, what will I have lost except invitations to perform at soirées and to attend balls? I don't think there's any harm in that."

He opened his mouth to speak and then seeing her determination, shut it again. She took advantage of his weakening.

"Don't worry, Father. I'll make you proud of me. You'll see."

Then before the moisture overtook her eyes, she rose and walked to the door. She turned and attempted to smile.

"May I take Gwendolyn with me? I'll need a maid."

He fluttered a hand in a preoccupied manner. "If you need her."

"Thank you."

She left the study. Outside, she sighed in relief that at least the exchange was over. Then she hurried toward her room. She saw Opal at the other end of the passage.

"Opal," she said as she lifted her chin and approached the housekeeper. "I have news. I will be performing my first operatic role in Boston. I have been invited to sing Mimi in *La Bohême*."

"*La Boheem?*" She mispronounced it. "Why Miss, is it the truth?"

Elisabeth nodded. "It is. We begin rehearsals next week. The soprano engaged to sing cannot remain in this country, for she's been called back to Berlin. I'm to fill in."

Opal's eyes widened and her expression lit with curiosity.

"My heavens. Wait 'til I tell Gunther." Then she raised a hand to her lips as if to cover her urge to spread the gossip. But Elisabeth didn't mind.

"Indeed."

Seeing that her mistress didn't mind if she spoke of it to the others, Opal went on. "I'm sure you'll do marvelously." The housekeeper flushed. "That is, from time to time I, myself, passed near the music room when you were practicing. I said to myself that you had a voice, I did. All the staff thinks so."

Then she broke off in embarrassment again. But Elisabeth smiled. She knew the staff had been listening to her music, and she didn't mind in the least. They had been her first audience.

Chapter Nineteen

Twenty times Elisabeth picked up the black earpiece to the telephone desk set in her father's study to ring up the Ansonia Hotel where Marco had his rooms. She wanted to share her news with him. But always she hesitated, pondering her words, and ended by replacing the ear piece on the hook.

She had rejected Marco's offers of love and marriage. It would not be fair to bring him into her life again, even to share in her good news. She wanted him as mentor and friend in the world she was about to embark on. But that did not seem possible. The pull between them was too strong. Only by denying contact all together could she concentrate on the tasks at hand, and that with difficulty.

She did telephone Maurice Grau at the Metropolitan and tell him the news. He was overjoyed, of course, wishing he could be in the audience in Boston to hear her debut. But of course his duties at the opera house would regrettably keep him in New York.

When she hung up the ear piece she was satisfied that

from there the news would spread throughout the company. Everyone would know that their former wardrobe mistress was going to step onto the stage. Then she almost wished she hadn't told them. What if she did badly?

She was glad her debut would take place somewhere else. At least the audience would not be full of those she knew who could say, "I told you so," if she were not a success.

Marco would hear of it either from Maurice or someone else. She would have to be satisfied with that. He might be angry that she didn't tell him personally, and at that she felt a tug at her heart. He had encouraged her from the first. Didn't he deserve to be the first to hear the news? And so the debate went on in her mind as she prepared to leave.

When she was not packing she restudied the role. She knew every note by heart, but how would they sound when she was on stage with singers she had never met before, an orchestra and a conductor she would have to follow?

Alex could not get free from business to travel to Boston until the night of the first performance, and Elisabeth was glad. Now that the details of her contract were settled, she really had no need of him, and in his role of pseudo-manager, he would only be in the way. Still, he insisted on driving her to the station the day she departed.

On the fine spring morning she was to leave, Alex arrived and had her trunk loaded on the top of his brougham. She couldn't help the flutter of excitement as Gwendolyn rushed about the room stuffing her portmanteau with the last of the toiletries. Then the excited maid rushed off to her own quarters to get her own bags, which the groom and coachman likewise loaded.

Elisabeth was dressed in a fashionable traveling suit of brown and golden brown striped linen, felt hat with egret plumes, and her maid in a new mauve suit with boater hat.

Alex returned from seeing to the luggage and met her on the landing. "All ready, my dear. You look lovelier than all the flowers blooming in your garden."

"Thank you, Alex," she said distractedly, pulling on her gloves. "I believe we're ready."

He consulted his pocket watch. "Plenty of time, but we'd best get going so we can get you situated properly."

She had told her father good-bye the night before and had regretted the awkwardness between them. He did not forbid her to go, but she could see the disappointment in his eyes as if he were losing his daughter again. It was regrettable, but she could only hope that one day he would see things differently.

Alex handed her into the carriage, followed by Gwendolyn, then took a seat opposite them. The carriage moved out the drive slowly with the weight of the luggage, but once on Fifth Avenue, the horses picked up their pace. They were off.

"Did you remember everything, Elisabeth?" asked Alex.

"I believe so."

"Your music?"

She smiled in amusement. "How could I forget it?"

He gave a look that said he was just trying to do his job.

Grand Central Depot was glutted with hansoms and horse-drawn jitneys, but they found a place to unload. The coachman and groom handled the luggage while the two girls alighted with Alex, who steered them into the station. He found seats for them in the waiting room while he went to buy the tickets. Gwendolyn was wide-eyed with excitement and rambled on about their adventure.

"Wait 'til I tell my sister about this. Is Boston very far?"

"Not far," answered Elisabeth. "We'll be there later today."

"Just imagine, myself as personal maid to an opera star." The maid shifted her hat to a more jaunty position on her head. "Why I've never even been to a fancy theater. Just to the vaudeville shows. But an opera where fine ladies go, it'll be something to talk about for sure."

Elisabeth smiled. "This is a small company, Gwendolyn. Mr. Berry said the dressing rooms are quite tiny."

"But he's putting us up in a fine hotel, isn't he?"

"A modest residential hotel."

"Do other stars stay there?"

"I don't know."

Alex crossed the floor, tickets in hand. "All ready. Track nine."

Elisabeth was still laughing at Gwendolyn as Alex reached for her arm. She smiled up at him, caught up in the excitement.

At that moment across the room and unseen by Elisabeth and Alex, Marco entered the station with his mother and sister. He spoke in Italian to Franco, who followed with the women's luggage piled on a handcart. Marco turned, saw Elisabeth with Alex and stopped in his tracks.

"Ci vuol tutta!" he swore.

"Marco, what's wrong?" Rosa and Lucinda halted to get out of the way of a porter carrying luggage.

"Nothing, Mama. I thought I saw someone I knew," he glowered.

"Hurry up then, Marco. We'll miss the train."

He saw his mother and sister onto the train for Philadelphia, where they were going to visit their cousins. The party raved in Italian and gesticulated until the whistle sounded.

"Get off the train, Marco," admonished Rosa. "We're leaving."

He kissed his mother and sister good-bye and then stepped down to the platform.

His family handled, he turned his attention to Elisabeth. Glancing around, he didn't see her party on this platform, so he made his way out of the train shed, stopping twice to sign autographs. He smiled and charmed those who made the requests and then sent Franco to look for Elisabeth or the tall blond man who'd been with her.

He caught up to his footman in the waiting room.

"Track seven," said Franco. "They got into a first-class compartment."

Marco frowned.

"Grazie. Wait for me in the carriage."

The servant left him, and Marco crossed the waiting room to Track seven, chastising himself for acting like a spy. But it angered him that she was going somewhere with that fellow and hadn't told him. Jealousy steamed

311

in his heart. Could it be possible that they were engaged?

By the time he reached Track seven and was marching down its platform, blackness filled his heart. She had stayed away from him, which was hard enough. He had tried to respect her wishes, but in the end it had turned to resentment of her stubborn pride. She had melted in his arms, they had filled each other with love, and she was too blind to see it. He had given her time. But this betrayal was monstrous. To think that she had rejected Marco Giovinco for that fop! He could not find words for the disgrace.

Marco saw Alex step down from the car just as the steam billowed out from under the wheels. When Alex turned he was face to face with Marco, who had drawn himself up.

Alex would have walked right past him, but recognition dawned at the same time Marco stepped in front of him.

"Excuse me, sir," said Marco. "I believe you were just escorting Miss Sloane?"

Alex blinked. "Why, Mr. Giovinco. You caught me off guard. Excuse my bad manners."

"Caught off guard? I see. And where might I ask, was Miss Sloane going?"

Alex frowned. "I don't believe that is any of your business, sir."

Marco glowered. "I will decide about that."

Alex, who had resented Marco's influence over Elisabeth for some time, seized on the opportunity to tell the great star what he really thought of him.

"If the lady did not see fit to inform you of her engagements and travel plans, then it is my duty to protect her privacy."

"Engagement?"

Alex enjoyed seeing Marco stumped. "Then you don't know, after all."

Marco misunderstood the nature of the engagement and presumed Alex meant that he himself was engaged to Elisabeth.

"Am I to believe that you've taken advantage of the girl and led her down a dangerous path?"

"Dangerous?" Alex laughed. "It is what she wanted after all."

"I cannot believe that until I see her for myself. I demand to know where she is going."

In moments their argument disintegrated into shouted words and accusations. "I will not stand for this insult," Marco finally said. "I demand satisfaction."

"What kind of satisfaction?" Alex inquired, still goading his rival.

Marco folded his arms across his broad chest. "The only kind that befits gentlemen."

It took Alex a moment to realize what Marco was talking about. Finally he looked at him and scoffed.

"My good man, perhaps you forget that this is not the stage. You have reality mixed up with the fantasy world in which you perform. Duels have been out of fashion for eighty years, or haven't you noticed?"

A small crowd had gathered around them, attracted by their raised voices, many passersby recognizing Marco. The crowd whispered to each other, trying to place the other man. Surely he was someone important to be engaged in a public argument with Marco Giovinco.

Marco's temper made him forget the crowd watching them. Alex's insults only fueled his mounting anger. "Surely the method that has withstood tradition for centuries cannot be said to be out of date. Or are you too cowardly to meet me under such circumstances?"

A little gasp ran through the crowd, compounded by a train whistle.

Always easily persuaded, Alex met his rival's black gaze. "Of course I'm not cowardly. If you insist on such dramatics, name your time and place. My second will contact yours."

Another gasp from the crowd as the news rippled toward the station. A duel! A newspaper man happened to be in the waiting room and as soon as he got the tip a group gathered around him to give him the details of what they had heard.

Marco scribbled Franco's name across a card that had his address at the Ansonia. Alex extracted his card from his vest pocket and likewise wrote his servant's name. The two duelists exchanged cards as if they were making a business appointment.

Marco even gave a brief nod of the head as he pocketed Alex's card. "You will hear from me sir," he said.

Then he turned on his heel and strode toward the waiting room. Passersby stared at him, but he was used to that. Only when the newspaper man leapt toward him, keeping pace with him as he continued toward the door did Marco quite realize what a stir he'd created.

"Is it true? Are you going to duel Alexander Rochat?" asked the newspaper man above the din of voices around them.

Finally Marco realized what he'd done. The world would know in seconds. He started to give an answer, then thought of Elisabeth. In one horrifying moment he saw that her name would be dragged into the papers.

"No comment," he finally said, escaping the crowd and making his way through the door.

Giovanni had the carriage waiting and Marco climbed in. Franco shut the door and climbed on while they pulled away, leaving the crowd behind them.

They made their way up town by way of Broadway. When they pulled up to the entrance of the Ansonia, Marco climbed down and turned to his groom.

"You'll be hearing from the second of a Mr. Alexander Rochat," he told Franco. "You're to arrange a duel between Rochat and myself. You'll have to acquire some pistols and find an agreeable place outside the city. Let me know the time and place."

"*Mamma mia*, a duel?" said the stunned servant.

"That's what I said, man. You'll have to serve as my second."

"But you cannot risk a bullet. You have a contract to sing."

"I won't be harmed," said Marco with his typical assurance. "If it makes you feel better we'll practice with the pistols before the arranged date. Get the pistols today, we'll drive upstate tomorrow. That should take care of it."

Giovanni and Franco exchanged glances, but they knew Marco was not to be argued with. A duel it would be.

Franco sat beside Marco in the brougham as they

drove along the isolated country road five miles out of Yonkers, trying to talk his employer out of the foolish thing he was about to do.

"What will the opera do if you cannot sing?" asked Franco.

"The season is over in the states," said Marco. "It is a month before I must leave for Europe."

"You will not go at all if you are dead."

Marco let go a string of Italian. Then more calmly he reasoned, "You are to be my second, do not advise me to turn coward."

"I know you since we are little boys," Franco said. "Even though I work for you, you are my friend. You think I want to lose my friend over the cause of a woman? After the duel at the theater, two actors get up and walk away. This is not a play, my friend. One of you may die."

"We will speak of it no more."

The carriage turned off the road into a grove of trees. Marco looked around at the quiet countryside. They were in an isolated spot, and they had seen no other traffic on the road. The seconds had found a good location.

At the other end of a small field, Marco could see Alex's carriage. He and two other men were pacing off the distances. Marco got down, and then Franco and Giovanni left him to speak to Alex's seconds.

Marco inhaled the fresh spring air. "Ah, a fine morning. Not a morning on which to die." He murmured a prayer in Italian.

While the seconds were examining the weapons in the distance, Marco paced across the soft ground where long grass lay heavily from its own weight. The dew clung to his shoes and trouser cuffs as he walked. In the early morning sun, Marco was not unaware of the sense of drama of what he was about to do. But his hot temper would not let him back down. He would not shoot to kill Rochat, only to wound him, to teach him a lesson. Honor was at stake.

Giovanni returned to say that they were ready and Marco followed him back to the center of the clearing. Alex nodded curtly to Marco, and then his servant explained the rules. Alex's seconds looked as nervous as Franco and Giovanni. Only Alex and Marco glared soberly at the weapons displayed for their use.

"On my count you will take ten steps in opposite directions. Exactly on the count of ten you will turn and fire. Each pistol has only one shot. Do you understand?"

Marco and Alex nodded.

"Gentlemen, take your positions."

The two stepped toward each other and turned their backs. Then Franco handed Marco his pistol. Marco felt the weight of it with both hands. A crow cawed above them in a tree, but Marco focused his attention just as he would at a performance.

"One," began the second. "Two . . ."

At the count of ten Marco turned, raised his arm, aimed and fired. Almost instantly his ears throbbed with the explosions and he felt pain sear his left arm. He dropped the pistol in the other hand, staggered and grasped the wounded arm with his good hand. Then he peered through the smoky haze at the figures gathered around Alex Rochat twenty paces away, who was lying on the ground.

* * *

Rehearsals in the small theater in Boston went well, and Elisabeth was made to feel welcome by the company. It took all her concentration to learn the blocking and how to relate to the other singers. But she learned quickly, and the days passed in a blink.

On opening night, Gwendolyn fluttered around the hotel room trying to see to all the details. Elisabeth was dressed in a simple muslin dress for the role of Mimi, and Gwendolyn had dressed her hair so that it fell about her shoulders in curls.

There was a knock at the door and Gwendolyn went to answer it. A delivery boy stood there with an enormous spray of roses.

Elisabeth's heart missed a beat. Gwendolyn tipped the boy and carried the roses inside, placing them on a low table. Then she pulled off the card.

"For you, Miss," she said with evident curiosity.

Elisabeth ripped open the envelope.

"Good luck tonight," the card read. "A nasty accident has befallen me. Won't be able to attend. Be up and around soon. Nothing serious. Alex."

Her heart fell. Not from Marco after all. And Alex had had an accident. He said it wasn't serious, she hoped not. Probably fell from his horse in the country. Madelaine was coming up for Saturday night's performance, so she would have the news. There was no time now to wonder about it, for they were due at the theater.

"Are you ready, Miss?" asked Gwendolyn.

During the carriage ride to the theater, Elisabeth tried to concentrate on the performance before her. Percy Prescott was at the stage door to greet her.

"You look lovely, my dear," he said. "From what

Berry says, you'll be a success."

She was glad to have someone to encourage her, for the butterflies were starting in her stomach.

In the tiny dressing room, Gwendolyn saw to the final details. But it was not until the stage manager knocked on her door that the full realization hit her that she was making her debut as an opera singer. She stared at herself in the mirror. It was unreal that this was finally happening. She thought of the dressing rooms at the Metropolitan Opera where she had worked with the wardrobe. The Met was a long way from this modest company, and she most likely would never sing there. But at least she was making a start.

As she walked from the dressing room to the wings, careful not to muss her costume, nervousness turned to excitement, and when she took her place to wait for her entrance, the tenor, a good-looking Swede with whom she'd been rehearsing all week, whispered, "Good luck."

There was no time to think. The orchestra played the overture. The curtain rose, and the opera began.

Once on stage all else was forgotten but the performance. At the end of the first act, the audience applauded her. At the end of the third act, they stood and cheered. By the time the opera ended, she was a great success, and as she took her bows an usher handed her a large bouquet of roses from the company.

It was a thrilling moment to stand at the footlights and revel in the wave of love that flowed toward her. The Swedish tenor grasped her hand tightly, and when she left the stage, Walter Berry and Percy Prescott beamed at her. Everyone talked at once.

She had to return again for another curtain call.

Finally it was over, and she felt completely ecstatic. She was walking on a cloud from which she felt she would never return to earth.

"Let us celebrate," suggested Prescott. "We must all go out for oysters on the half-shell."

Elisabeth returned to the dressing room and changed into a satin and velvet gown perfect for a celebratory party. But as she looked at herself once more in the mirror, she felt a twinge in her heart. The audience had loved her. She was going to celebrate with people she hardly knew. The people who meant the most to her were not here.

She began to wish she had told Marco herself instead of leaving it to rumor to reach him. If he did find out he probably would not send any good wishes. He would be angry that she herself had not shared her good news with him first hand. And her father still could not confront the idea of having a daughter who had gone on the stage by choice.

"Do you want your cloak, Miss?" asked Gwendolyn.

"Oh, yes," she answered distractedly. She fought back sudden, irrational tears. Was this what it was going to be like then? One had to force back one's own emotions and wear a smile for the public. But even amidst the pangs of loneliness she knew she'd brought it all on herself. It had been her choice, and she must stand by it.

When Gwendolyn opened the dressing room door to Percy Prescott, who bowed and offered Elisabeth his arm, she couldn't help but wish he were someone else.

Chapter Twenty

Elisabeth groaned and turned over. She thought she heard a knock on the sitting room door to her suite, but she wasn't ready to wake up. In a few moments she heard the knock repeated and then Gwendolyn's voice, mingling with someone else's.

What time was it? Elisabeth wondered turning over and looking at the black hands of the porcelain clock that sat on the little round table in the corner.

The voices in the next room got louder, and then both Gwendolyn and Walter Berry came into the room. Elisabeth reached for her dressing gown, but Walter paid no attention to her state of undress. He was waving the front page of the newspaper at her.

"Incredible, just incredible, and such a coincidence too. Read this," he finally said, thrusting the paper toward her.

Elisabeth blinked and then stared at the paper he lay across her lap. Staring back at her were her own picture, as well as that of Marco and one of Alex. The headline read, TENOR DUELS WITH SOCIETY

SON OVER NEW FACE IN THE MUSIC WORLD.

"Oh no," her own voice came out a rasp. She hastily scanned the story while Walter and Gwendolyn chattered excitedly in the background.

"Thank God," she whispered when she came to the part that said both men were wounded, but neither one seriously. They were recuperating after being patched up by a Yonkers surgeon.

They had actually dueled. She couldn't believe it. Dueling was, of course, illegal, and they'd both been arraigned at court, but it was unlikely the charges would stick. Whoever had acted as seconds were not talking. The two men's servants had mysteriously gone on holidays and could not be found, and no witnesses could be produced. The doctor who saw them was told only that there had been a hunting accident. But the bullet he extracted from Alex's thigh was not from a hunting rifle. A bullet had also passed through Marco's arm. The news of the alleged duel had leaked out to the press.

Elisabeth held her hands to her flushed face. "Good heavens," she muttered. "Those idiots. I can't believe it. They might have killed each other."

She grabbed her dressing gown, slid out of bed and put it on. "This is awful," she said. But Walter and Gwendolyn both spoke excitedly at the same time.

"Gwendolyn, pack my bags. I must return to New York at once. This is intolerable." She walked to the wardrobe and threw it open.

Walter finally saw what she was doing and seized her arm. "And where do you think you're going?"

She glared at him. "To New York. This is all my fault."

He waved a finger in front of her face. "Not so fast, my girl. You have a contract to fulfill. You can't just walk off from it."

She hesitated only a moment. "I shall cancel the contract and return the fee."

Seeing that the legal threat meant nothing to her, he tried to appeal to her senses. "And what good will that do? This is publicity, my dear. The crowds will flock to see the woman who has two men, and both of them well known in their circles, killing each other for you. Don't be foolish. The performance tonight will be sold out, standing room only. You're not going anywhere."

She fumed. "But they've been hurt! I must see them."

He grasped one of her flailing hands and led her to a seat. "Now, sit down Elisabeth."

She did as he said. "That's better." He took a seat on the ottoman opposite her. "Now. Neither one is seriously hurt. They may not even want to see you right now."

Elisabeth put her hand to her face. "I can't face an audience, Walter. You don't seem to see that this is the ultimate embarrassment." She shook her head. "This is exactly what my father warned me about."

Unable to sit still another moment, she got up and went to the window, looking through the lace curtains at the street below.

"I can't face anyone." She turned around and crossed the room in nervous agitation. "Why did they do it? Neither one of them has the sense of a hedgehog. Oh," she wrung her hands in exasperation.

"Now, now, my dear. I understand your agitation. But let's be civilized. Perhaps your maid will send for breakfast. You will feel differently with something in your stomach."

"How can you say that! Yes, very well. Gwendolyn, send down for breakfast. We all need sustenance."

Then she stopped pacing and faced Walter, her hands on her hips. "I suppose I might as well dress."

He bowed gallantly. "Please. I will entertain myself in the sitting room with the newspaper until the coffee arrives."

"Oh," she groaned again at the mention of the newspaper, but shooed him into the sitting room so she could dress.

By the time she joined him, a table with breakfast had been rolled in. Gwendolyn poured hot coffee from a silver urn, and Elisabeth took a seat at the small table where they ate. Her mood had not improved.

Shame washed over her as she stuffed a roll into her mouth and choked it down with coffee. Walter polished off eggs and a rasher of bacon then wiped his mouth with a linen napkin.

"Delicious. This hotel is known for its cuisine." He put the napkin on the table and poured himself another cup of coffee. "Now, my dear. I see it is time to explain some things to you. In the first place, you have done nothing wrong. There is nothing to be ashamed of. All you have done is capture the hearts of two men who adore you. What could be more romantic?"

She said nothing but fumed silently. Marco and Alex had a strange way of vying for her attention.

Walter continued. "You are the object of adoration of two men who are apparently willing to die to prove it. You were a success last night. Soon the world will be at your feet. What more could you want?"

She rolled her eyes and threw her napkin across the table. "This is not love," she replied sarcastically. "This is simply two men caught up in their own egotistic pride. It is nothing less than a scandal." Tears threatened as she thought of the humiliation she would suffer at home.

Walter patted her hand. "Now, now my dear. You're upset. I advise that you go out for a walk. It's a lovely spring day. Your suitors are recovering nicely in New York. You will sing again tonight. The audience will love you. Everybody loves you."

She thought of her father. "Not everybody."

She got up. Walter might be right about taking a walk. She felt stifled in this room, and she needed to do something to use up her nervous energy. A walk would give her time to think. She still had the urge to take the train back to New York, but the weight of the professional responsibility began to dawn on her. Her life was no longer her own.

"Very well," she said. "I shall go out."

Walter smiled as he got up. "That's better. You'll see. It will all come right."

She shook her head. "I don't know. Is this what it's like then?"

He gave a shrug. "Who can say? A performer's life is not a normal one. But surely you didn't expect it to be? If you're a success the world watches you. Privacy does not exist. But there are rewards." He started toward the door. Then he turned back, looking at her and nodding sympathetically. "It is your choice," he said softly and then opened the door.

She watched him go. Choice? What choice had she? She was bound to the Boston Lyric Opera for three more weeks. After that she didn't know. She could return to oblivion except for this fiasco. She picked up the paper and glanced at the three pictures, her stomach knotting up.

"Oh," she muttered, tossing the paper into a wastecan and holding her hand across her waist. She put on a hat, took a parasol and told Gwendolyn she intended to go out.

"Do you wish me to go with you, Miss?" asked the maid.

"No, I think I'd like to be alone. Do what you please until four o'clock. I suppose I'll have to get ready to sing again tonight."

"Thank you, Miss."

Elisabeth descended in the lift to the tasteful carved mahogany and cherrywood lobby, where several guests were seated in velvet upholstered sofas and wing chairs in the waiting area between four pillars. She looked straight ahead as she passed by the desk, wondering if people would turn to stare. But the thick veil drawn over her face helped her keep her anonymity.

The lobby was a little dim with the electric chandeliers turned low, and a man in a bowler hat rushed into the entrance, passing her on the way to the desk. When he got the clerk's attention, she heard him ask, "Tell me, sir, is this the hotel where the singer Elisabeth Sloane is staying?"

Keeping her face averted, she hurried out. On the sidewalk, she kept up a brisk pace until she turned a corner and went down a block. She zig-zagged through the streets until she had the courage to look over her shoulder. The man was not following her. She had escaped.

Boston's Back Bay was a quiet residential area of fine homes, some of them from Colonial and Federal times as well as townhouses built more recently with big bay windows and stained glass fanlights. Elisabeth tried to be cognizant of the blooming plants all around and of the neat lawns enclosed behind wrought iron fences. But the homes and the sounds of children out with nannies only served to remind her of New York, and from there her mind returned to her personal troubles.

She began to grasp the sacrifices demanded of a performer. Was this what she had really wanted? She had thought so. During the last months when she had practiced so hard, even for the two years before that when she had watched the performances so avidly from the wings at the Met and had sung the roles at home in the boardinghouse parlor, she had only one dream and that was to sing on a stage.

Last night she had achieved that goal. And after the elation was over, she had come home to an empty hotel room and sorely felt the lack of anyone to share her victory with. This morning the world was shining, but her heart was torn apart. New York society would make mincemeat of her. And what terrified her most was that some reporter would dig into her past and drag all that up as well.

The embarrassment made her walk faster with her head down. How could she face anyone? Her father had been right. Her dreams of singing were foolish if they had led to this. Not once in her self-recriminations did she stop to blame Marco or Alex. They had been foolish of course, and she would lecture both of them. But she had brought it on. It had been her fault. She should write to her father, but what could she say? She tried to formulate the letter in her mind, but nothing would come. There was no way to explain.

Her walk brought her to the public gardens on Arlington Street, but even the calming sight of the radiant flowers did nothing to ease her anxiety. She turned on Commonwealth Avenue and made her way back. She was breathing hard from the exercise, but slowed down when she saw the facade of the hotel. There was an entrance from the side street, she would take that.

Once in the hallway that led to the main lobby, she slowed her steps, looking out for reporters. There appeared to be none. She decided, however, not to risk the elevator at the side of the lobby, but turned up the red carpeted stairs and swiftly climbed to the second floor. Deciding to walk all the way to the fourth floor, she grasped the polished mahogany balustrade and pulled herself upward.

When she reached her room, panting, she had a surprise. Madelaine was there. When she entered the sitting room, Madelaine got up from the sofa.

"There you are. I cajoled the clerk into letting me in, but I couldn't imagine where you'd gone."

Catching her breath, Elisabeth removed her hat and veil, and Madelaine kissed her cheek.

"Hello, Madelaine. You're here early, aren't you?"

Madelaine stepped back and put her hands on her hips, eyeing Elisabeth as she unbuttoned her jacket. "You don't look glad to see me."

In truth Elisabeth had forgotten all about Madelaine's promise to attend the Saturday night performance, and she felt flustered.

"Of course I'm glad to see you, Madelaine. It's just that . . ." She turned to face her friend. "Surely you've read the newspapers. It's awful."

Madelaine grinned. "You're famous."

"Infamous, is more like it."

"Oh come now, my dear. Your name is on everybody's lips."

"But that's terrible. I don't want everyone talking about me like I'm some—some hussy." She dropped onto the sofa and shook her head. "I just can't believe it."

Madelaine seemed to take the same attitude Walter had. She seated herself beside her friend. "But my dear, it's so romantic. I had no idea that handsome Italian tenor was in love with you!"

Elisabeth sighed. "He's not in love with me. He just thinks he is."

"Oh Elisabeth you're being just like a woman. Did he tell you he loves you? After all he fought a duel to defend your honor."

"He probably fought a duel for publicity. He knew I didn't want to have my name dragged through something like this. How shall I ever live it down?"

"Why, dearie, it's far too delicious to live down. Why, if I were you I'd enjoy it."

"Well, you're not me."

Madelaine's brow creased. "Elisabeth, you are really upset, aren't you?"

"Of course I am. I didn't ask for any of this."

"Didn't you?"

Her question made Elisabeth blush. Hadn't she just been blaming herself for the whole incident. It was none of Madelaine's business however.

"I don't see how I can face anyone," Elisabeth went on.

"Well, you'll have to face your public tonight. And I shall be there to support you."

"I'm glad you've come."

"Now, now, you'll see. Everything will be all right."

"How, how is Alex doing? The article said his wounds weren't serious."

"A slight bullet wound in the thigh. He's doing all right, ordering the nurses about in the hospital where he was when I went to see him, complaining about the food. He's home now. Don't worry on his account."

"I'm sorry he was hurt. He might have been killed. Whatever possessed him?"

Madelaine looked amused. "Why he could not refuse the challenge, the way he tells it."

Elisabeth got up and paced the room again. "So it was Marco's idea. Whatever possessed him? He must have been mad."

"Not mad, just jealous."

She looked questioningly at Madelaine. "I don't understand."

"He approached Alex at Grand Central, took offense at Alex having seen you to the train and challenged him to a duel. That's all I know."

Elisabeth's eyes rounded. "Why that's insane. In the train station?"

"Well, love is often a little insane."

A tremor of emotion passed through Elisabeth as she heard her friend's words. She had been so angry at Marco and Alex for creating such a scandal at her expense that she hadn't stopped to think about them. What had actually led up to the duel? She hadn't been aware that Marco was at the station when Alex had put her on the train. Had he seen them?

Her thoughts and emotions about Marco were so embroiled and complicated by what had happened between them, by her own misshapen past and by what she was trying to do now that she could hardly think straight about him anymore. Perhaps he really did care for her more than she thought. The thought made her shiver. Even if he did, she couldn't allow that in her life. Passion alone was a thing of the flesh and did not mean real love. And she didn't think she could have real love in her life.

But the outlandish way Marco had shown his devotion suddenly touched a streak of humor in her that she hadn't found before. The humor was tinged with hysteria, admittedly, but it made her smile in irony.

"It does all sound a little insane," she finally said in reponse to Madelaine's last comment. "Still, no one can understand how embarrassed I feel."

"Well dearie," said Madelaine. "I suppose you'll just have to live with it. Is this not part of being a great actress?" She gave her friend a coy look.

"I don't know, Madelaine. I honestly don't know." She shook her head. "Walter, he's the impresario, says I must sing tonight. I do have a contract to fulfill."

"Of course you must sing. Why ever not?"

"Because I'm the center of a scandal."

Madelaine waved a hand. "Oh, pooh. Don't worry about that. You know how people are, especially our set. They'll twitter about you tonight and forget you by next week. Don't tell me you're going to give up being on stage because of a little gossip."

"It's the sort of thing my father warned me about."

"So? Our parents warn us about a lot of things. But to tell you the truth, Elisabeth, our parents have led rather stuffy lives, don't you think? Since when have they had any fun?"

Elisabeth blinked. The way Madelaine said it sank into the armor of self-defense that Elisabeth had built around herself. Madelaine came from the same society that had alienated Elisabeth before, and yet here she was brushing it off as unimportant. She hadn't ever thought Madelaine particularly enlightened, but there was truth in her simple words and observations. Elisabeth felt a tiny sense of relief she couldn't explain.

"Perhaps you're right," she said.

"Of course I'm right." Madelaine. "Now stop fidgeting and sit down. You'll be a sensation, you'll see. Soon everyone will be at your feet. And," she lifted one shoulder and dropped it. "Then you can have the man of your choice."

Elisabeth almost laughed. "But I'm an actress. That's not respectable."

"Heavens, you mean that Mrs. Astor will write you off the list of the sacred Four Hundred? Fate worse than death."

Then Elisabeth did laugh and so did Madelaine. Their chuckles relieved the tension. By the time Gwendolyn appeared, it was time to get ready for the evening's performance. Madelaine sat in the bedroom and chatted as Elisabeth dressed and Gwendolyn did her hair.

The moment Elisabeth walked on stage that night,

her personal problems were forgotten as she shed her own life and took on the far worse problems of Mimi in her cold little garret. She once again melded with the role she was playing. Every ounce of her was bound up in concentration and the performance itself. Her emotions, close to the surface as they were, portrayed even more eloquently the drama of the girl doomed with illness.

At the final curtain the audience went wild with ovation. She was forced to return for curtain call after curtain call, bowing deeply to express her thanks.

Walter met her at her dressing room door. "Marvelous, my dear. You were marvelous. Did you hear how they clamored for you? Photographers are waiting outside to take your picture."

She dropped her mouth open. "Photographers?"

"At the stage door." He followed her into the dressing room where she sat on the little stool in front of the mirror. "They want interviews. But," he coughed behind his hand. "You really would not have to say anything. Just smile."

She looked at him in the mirror. "I'd rather not."

"Rather not?" he blustered. "Why, may I ask?"

She turned around to face him directly. "You know why, Walter. I'm sorry, but I simply cannot make a spectacle of myself. I sang tonight, and I will fulfill my contract. But please do not ask me to put in appearances for the newspapers aside from that."

Walter's face reddened. "You are being stubborn, Elisabeth. You have a career before you. You really must decide whether you want it or not. I will leave you to think about it."

He nearly collided with Madelaine, who opened the

door just as he turned to exit.

"Excuse me, Miss," he said to Madelaine, then blustered out.

"Who was that? Your impresario?"

Elisabeth had turned back to the mirror. "The very man."

"Well, wasn't he happy? You were wonderful. Better even than at your soirée and at Marble House."

"Thank you, Madelaine. No, he liked it. He simply wanted me to present myself at the stage door for more photographs for the papers."

Madelaine sighed as Gwendolyn started helping Elisabeth get out of her costume. "And you don't want to?"

"No, I don't. I want to be an artist, it's true. But I don't want to achieve it by cheap publicity."

"Well then," said Madelaine slyly. "You'll just have to achieve it as a mystery woman."

Madelaine remained in Boston visiting friends until the performances of *La Bohême* were over so that she and Elisabeth could travel back to New York together. As it turned out, her comment about Elisabeth becoming a mystery woman proved true. Elisabeth's nonappearance except on stage for the nightly performances created an even greater furor, and all the papers carried stories about the woman two men had fought over. The papers also reported on the conditions of Marco and Alex as they both recuperated. Marco was scheduled to sing a benefit concert, and everyone was waiting to hear if he'd be able to perform.

As Elisabeth rode in the train back to New York with Madelaine she pored over the most recent article as they sat in the parlor car. She sighed, and Madelaine turned from watching the speeding scenery to look at her.

"What is it?"

Elisabeth shook her head and dropped the newspaper on her lap. "I never thought I'd be reading the papers to learn news of my very own friends. Life surely has changed."

Madelaine lifted her blond brows. "Didn't you think it would?"

Elisabeth leaned her head against the plush seat, her body vibrating with the rhythm of the wheels on the track below them. She still worried that reporters might trace her life back to her past. Even if they only went as far as the boarding house, she knew Mrs. Runkewich's greedy heart was not above giving them a story. And a greatly manufactured one it would most likely be. She remembered Mrs. Runkewich's door creaking open the first night Marco saw her home. Would the landlady recognize his picture in the newspapers and call the reporters herself? It was not unlikely.

Chapter Twenty-One

Elisabeth stepped into the lobby of the Ansonia hotel where a number of stellar clients, many from the musical and sporting worlds, kept apartments. The seventeen-story hotel was a baroque mass of scrolls, balconies, cornices, and satyrs leering over doorways with domed towers at each corner. Crystal chandeliers inset with mosaic and lit by electric lightbulbs illuminated the lobby. The scroll work continued here in the baroque painted ceiling, the molding, the lighting fixtures, and the Persian rug into which Elisabeth's shoes sank slightly as she crossed it.

She passed onto the marble floor of the anteroom and waited for the lift. She felt she owed Marco this visit. He had gotten shot on her account, but more than that, she regretted not having told him of her engagement in Boston. And once she got past thinking of the awkwardness of their meeting, she wanted to share with him how well her performance had gone.

All this floated through her mind as she rode up the lift with several other passengers and got off on his floor. Even on the upper floors the grandeur of the design was every bit as elegant as the Waldorf, but the hotel's location on the Upper West Side had put it outside the area so far patronized by the upper crust of society. This was just as well as far as Elisabeth was concerned. She need not worry about anyone seeing her call on one of the men linked to her in the scandal sheets.

Stopping in front of Marco's door, she gathered her courage before raising her hand to knock. Then she lifted the knocker and let it drop twice. The door was opened by a middle-aged female servant in black bombazine, crisp white apron and frilly cap. She had olive skin and salt and pepper hair that was pulled back into a bun. When she spoke Elisabeth recognized her accent as being Italian.

"I am Elisabeth Sloane, a friend of Marco's. I've come to see him. Is he in?"

Recognition flashed in the woman's eyes, otherwise her expression remained neutral.

"Come in, please." She admitted Elisabeth into a hallway and then led the way to a sitting room. "I will tell him you are here."

"Thank you."

Rather than sitting down, Elisabeth wandered to the window. The room was round, and she realized this was part of the corner tower. The window, looking to the southwest, offered a panoramic view of the city and the river. She was busy orienting herself to the view and picking out familiar landmarks when Marco entered the room.

She turned to see him standing there in smoking jacket draped around his shoulders, white shirt and dark trousers, and felt her heart flutter. One arm was in a sling. His expression was aloof, but not without a touch of humor.

"Marco." She started toward him then stopped. "How are you?"

He bowed his head a little stiffly. "I am as well as can be expected, thank you. To what do I owe the honor of this visit?"

She gave a helpless gesture and walked toward a striped sofa.

"May I sit down?" she asked.

"Of course."

As she seated herself on the sofa, Marco sat in a mahogany oval-backed chair with matching striped upholstery, placing his good arm on the chair arm.

"The doctor trussed me up like a chicken, but it is quite a lot better. I thank you for inquiring."

Their eyes met, then she looked away. "Marco, why—?" But she couldn't form the exact words.

He shrugged. "Where we come from . . . Oh, well, it is of no account."

Her spirit revived now that she saw he wasn't bedridden. "Marco, our pictures have been in all the newspapers. This little incident of yours has drawn a great deal of attention to the three of us, in case you didn't know. Did you do it for publicity?"

His face darkened. "No, I did not."

"Oh," she said in exasperation. She got up again and went to the window. The gold tassels on the green velvet drapery jiggling as she pushed it aside in agitation. Marco would have liked to have followed her, but he felt more comfortable in the chair.

"You and Alex behaved like a couple of schoolboys.

Why ever did you challenge him to a duel?"

"My jealousy was unmanageable when I saw Rochat take you to the train."

She turned from the window. "It meant nothing. Alex was acting as manager for me since I don't yet have one. He was simply escorting me to the train. There is nothing between Alex and me."

"He certainly takes a great interest in you for there to be nothing between you. It is not natural."

"Oh Marco, be sensible."

"That is not always possible when it comes to matters of the heart."

"I am not planning to marry Alex, if that's what you're thinking. I have already told you I don't plan to marry anyone. I have a career. Now more than ever I must nurture it."

He lifted a dark brow and eyed her with challenge. "Your career. Another piece of news I had to find out third-hand. I am quite insulted."

"I know I should have told you of my luck. In fact that's why I came here today. I really want to share these things with you, Marco. You of all people can understand how it was for me."

"I see. You came to tell me of your musical victory, not because you cared about my welfare."

"That's not true. Of course, I care." She lifted her chin so as not to sound too sympathetic. She had to fight to maintain her position.

Marco pushed himself up from the chair with his good arm. "Then come away with me upstate where I plan to recuperate in fresh air. You can tell me about it then."

"What do you mean, upstate?"

"There's a lovely old hotel on a lake where it's possible to rest and be rejuvenated by nature. My doctor insists I take a holiday there. Come with me."

Her father's accusations about theater people's loose morals echoed in her mind, and she stiffened.

"I can't."

"Why not?" He moved awkwardly toward her, and she realized he must still be in pain, so unlike his normal graceful movements was this clumsy gait.

"Because . . . it wouldn't be right."

"Ah, of course. We must protect your already endangered reputation. Well, you are right of course. But there are ways to arrange such matters. A concert, perhaps. I have a friend at the Mohonk Mountain House. Perhaps a word in that quarter . . ."

Her eyes widened. He was plotting again, and the thought was disconcerting. Her defenses were also falling before the dark, handsome face that came nearer, the remembered effect of the arms that had surrounded her. She backed against the drapery.

"I, I don't know."

"You need exposure, Elisabeth. Now that you have been launched, we must keep you in front of the public. Audiences are very fickle, you see. They love you only so long as they can hear and see you. It would be a wise move to sing again soon."

"Yes, but—"

He raised his good hand. "I know I am correct. If you advertise a concert, and if I happen to stop at the hotel at the same time, no one can accuse you of anything untoward. Mohonk House is palatial in size. Our rooms can be in opposite wings."

She risked saying, "That would not stop you . . ."

He stood very close to her, gazing down at her flustered face. "Hmmm. It would not. But your refusal would stop me."

Her breathing quickened. For a moment she said nothing. Now that she was with him she recognized her suppressed need for him. Already she reveled in his presence, in his breath fanning her hair. She raised a hand to his chest to push him back a step, but instead he grasped it in his own hand. The contact sent a wave of desire coursing through her.

Recognizing that she was responding to him the way he was to her, he slid his good arm around her and lowered his mouth to kiss her. "Elisabeth," he whispered just before his lips took hers.

She resisted only a trace before giving in to the kiss. She was not quite gone when she pushed Marco away again.

"That's not what I came for," she managed to say.

He looked disappointed but didn't press her. "I see."

Trying to explain her feelings was useless. "I just wanted to see how you were."

"Oh yes." His voice was touched with cynicism, but he wasn't angry. "And to tell me about your great victory in Boston."

"Well, I would hardly call it that. But I was received warmly."

"I know."

She looked surprised. "How do you know?"

He crossed the room. "I am not being a gentleman, am I?" He winked at her. "I mean, I have not offered you refreshments."

He picked up a little bell on a small round table and rang it. When the housekeeper appeared, he said,

"Sophie, please bring us some coffee and sandwiches."

When the woman had disappeared, he asked, "Or would you prefer something stronger, like cognac?"

"No, no, coffee will be fine."

He returned to his seat, and she sat tentatively on the sofa again.

"I'm sorry I didn't tell you about Boston," she said.

He leaned back gingerly, holding the wounded arm to his side, looking suddenly tired. She brushed her skirt nervously.

"I should have told you, but I was afraid . . ."

"Afraid? Of what?"

She shrugged. "I don't know. That I wouldn't do well. That . . ."

The housekeeper brought the tray and sandwiches, and Elisabeth was grateful that she didn't have to go on. She accepted a cup of coffee and then bit into a sandwich. After she had eaten, she sat back on the sofa.

"It was exciting to sing in front of an audience. It was . . ." She searched for the right words.

"All-consuming," he said.

She looked at him. Of course. He knew. "Yes, yes, it was."

He reached for another sandwich. After he had swallowed, he said, "then we must keep you in front of audiences since you love your newfound profession so much."

"I really don't know if it is a profession yet," she said modestly.

"Time will tell," he said. "You will need a manager. A real one, I mean. Did not Prescott volunteer his services when he met you?"

"Why, do you know him?"

343

"I do, slightly. He does manage some artists. I'm surprised he didn't offer to take you under his wing."

She thought back to the conversation at Marble House. "He might have, but when we met I was with Alex. That is, we were conversing after I had sung at Marble House," she went on to explain, so as not to arouse Marco's suspicions. "Percy was representing Walter Berry. When he mentioned the Boston Lyric Opera Company, Alex said I would need someone to represent my interests, and that he would do it."

"And so Percy did not interfere. Very like him. But now that you are serious about this business you need a professional."

"Yes, of course. Alex was being generous, but I told him he knew nothing about the music world." She shook her head and chuckled. "He probably doesn't even listen to half the operas he attends."

Marco smirked. "You're probably right. Well, leave things to me. I'll speak to Percy myself and explain the situation if you're willing to send Rochat on his way."

She colored at the implication. "Of course."

He took a sip of coffee and then leaned over to put the cup back on the silver tray. "I'm glad things went well for you in Boston, Elisabeth. I only wish I'd been there."

Something tugged at her heart and she prepared to leave. "I must go, Marco."

He struggled to his feet. "Thank you for coming." He restrained his other thoughts.

They walked together to the door, and she turned to tell him goodbye. She looked up at him shyly. "I hope you do feel better."

He wanted to kiss her, but he resisted. He was

beginning to see that Elisabeth Sloane must be met on her own terms, and no one else's. He smiled gently.

"I feel better now."

Since the performance at Boston, Elisabeth was careful whenever she went out to make sure there were no reporters hovering about the door. After the first few days of waiting to catch a glimpse of her, they gave up, and the furor died down. Her father had given her a cold reception, just as she expected, and the matter was not discussed. He dined at his club much of the time, and she took her dinner in her room. But after a few days of this, life became extremely boring, and she began to wonder what she would do.

She stood holding Miranda in her arms in the Goldsboro room, where the cat was not supposed to be. But Elisabeth had brought her up from the kitchen and stood, staring out the French doors. She had practiced for several hours, and did not want to strain her voice. She had tried reading, but nothing interested her. She looked across the street at the park, and considered taking a walk, but she wanted someone to talk to. She had decided to put on her hat and call on Consuelo when Opal tapped on the door.

"Yes," she answered, turning around, still holding the cat.

"A Mr. Percy Prescott is on the telephone for you," she said.

"Oh, thank you. I'll come right away."

She followed Opal out and went down the hall to her father's study where the telephone sat on his desk. She was thankful he wasn't there. She dropped the cat and took a seat at the desk, positioning the desk set so that she could speak into the mouth piece. She held the earpiece to her ear.

"Hello," she said.

"Ah, Miss Sloane. Glad I caught you," came the disembodied voice of Percy Prescott.

"Yes, it is fortunate. How are you?"

"I am well," came the voice. "I have a matter of business to discuss with you, and I wondered if I might call on you tomorrow. I'll be in the city then."

She realized he must be calling long distance. "Yes, I can be in. What time?"

They arranged to meet at ten in the morning, and she replaced the earpiece in its holder. Now she had something to look forward to. Miranda jumped up on the desk and rubbed against the telephone.

"That's right, my girl. Mr. Prescott is coming to see me on a matter of business." She said it in a mock English voice. "Very important."

Her sense of humor had been restored and she went to fetch her hat and drag Consuelo out to the park.

Just as she mounted the steps to the elegant mansion on Fifth Avenue, she saw curtains move on the third floor, and she thought she saw Consuelo's face. When she asked to see Consuelo, a starched, prim servant led her into a sitting room.

Instead of Consuelo, she was met by Alva Vanderbilt herself. Alva wasted no time on formalities. Instead, in a cold voice she informed Elisabeth that her daughter did not wish to see her ever again. In fact, Elisabeth was not welcome in this house.

"I'm sorry," said Alva icily. "But Consuelo must be very careful about the company she keeps until her wedding with the Duke of Marlboro."

Elisabeth's face flamed. Evidently the Vanderbilts had read all about the duel and were scandalized. Furthermore, as a singer, Elisabeth evidently did not fit into Alva's idea of genteel society. But she would not be humbled by the witch. She held her head high as she walked past Alva, deliberately turning her back on the woman as she headed for the gilded, paneled doors.

Before she made her exit, she turned and said in a hostile voice, dripping with syrup. "I'm so sorry for Consuelo. Please convey to her my sympathy."

Then before the horrified Alva Vanderbilt could expand her brocade covered bosom to take a breath, Elisabeth was gone.

Percy Prescott greeted Elisabeth warmly, and she took both his hands with enthusiasm. He looked debonair as usual, his silvery hair brushed away from his temples. She ordered tea, and after they were situated in comfortable chairs with a low coffee table between them, Percy got down to business.

"Mr. Giovinco has spoken to me about your, ah, situation. He led me to believe that now you are serious about a career in music you need a competent manager."

She nodded. "That is correct."

He smiled in understanding. "Forgive me, but Mr. Giovinco also explained to me your business arrangement with Mr. Rochat."

"That was temporary." Then she risked a joke. If Percy Prescott managed artists, then he must understand them. "But of course by now you will have read all about it."

He took her meaning. "Quite. And of course, assuming it was no business of mine, I did not interfere. And besides, the newspapers rarely print the truth. I was surprised to receive Mr. Giovinco's call. And pleased of course. I would be honored to have you as a client. I saw the potential the night you sang at Marble House."

Elisabeth could not resist a smile at that, having just been thrown out of Alva Vanderbilt's New York residence.

"Poor Alva. Little did she know that she was launching an opera singer that night. She would be shocked."

Percy brushed his moustache with the side of his finger. "I understand she is rather a snob. I daresay I would not have been invited there myself that night had she known what I do for a living. I happened to be taking a holiday in Newport and was brought to the party by a friend of the Vanderbilt's, publisher."

"I suppose being a literary figure is not quite a scandalous as singing on the stage."

They both chuckled, and she found relief in being able to poke fun at her own situation.

"It's true that the stories about Alex, Marco, and me were grossly exaggerated in the newspapers," she told him.

"Don't worry about that," he said. "Other artists have had similar experiences. No doubt you have infuriated the reporters by refusing to talk to them, but you have maintained your dignity."

"Do you really think so?"

"Of course. You've created enough mystery to make people curious while not agreeing with one word they have said."

"I didn't do it for publicity."

"Of course not. None of that incident was your fault."

Already she felt she was putty in his experienced hands. If he could actually advise her on her career, then she felt she had found the right man.

"If you were to manage me," she said, "what would be your plans?"

"Ah. I'm glad you asked. I would discuss everything with your teacher, of course. But if he feels you're ready, I would arrange a number of concerts to get you before the public. You will have to go to Europe. There is more opportunity for opera there, and I would get you heard by as many impresarios as possible."

Europe. How ironic that she might actually go where all her friends thought she'd already been to study music.

"I see."

"Would you be willing to go abroad?"

She shrugged. "I must tell you that my father approves of none of this. I do not believe he'll support my plans." She looked at her hands. "He thinks more like Alva Vanderbilt's generation. I have embarrassed him beyond belief."

She did not want to think of the breach between her father and herself that she had only succeeded in widening, but if Prescott was to manage her, he needed to know everything—almost everything.

"I see. In that case we would need to arrange it so that your tour there would be at least partially self-supporting. I'll see what I can do."

"I have a little money left to me by my mother. I could afford passage over and have a little pocket money until, er, business arrangements were arranged."

"Fine. Then I'll start looking into the possibilities. In the meantime we'll start on our home turf. I've spoken to the manager of Mohonk House, a lovely and famous hotel upstate, situated on a beautiful lake. He would be most happy to arrange a concert for you. You'd need repertoire for about two hour's singing, with an intermisson of course."

Marco! He had already set things up. She could hardly refuse since she was going to agree to have Percy manage her.

"I see. Well . . ."

"It would be an excellent opportunity for you and so soon after your Boston success. I'd planned to wire them your acceptance directly after we spoke."

She swallowed. "I suppose I must." She was thinking of Marco.

Percy looked at her questioningly, evidently not understanding her reticence. She did not want to appear temperamental.

"Of course I accept. That would be fine."

He rose to go. "Good. I'll have a contract sent." He took her hand and patted it with his other one. "I'm sure we'll have much success together. And on this misunderstanding with your father, perhaps I can intervene there as well."

She frowned doubtfully. "I don't know. But if you think you can reason with him, I have no objection."

Who knew? Percy Prescott acted and dressed every

inch the gentleman. Maybe here was the man who could change her father's mind. She felt hopeful for the first time since the morning she had awakened to the devastating newspapers in Boston. She shook Percy's hand firmly. Hiring him was a sound decision, she just knew it.

Chapter Twenty-Two

The scenery in upstate New York was breathtaking. Approaching Mohonk Mountain House from the train station in New Paltz was like coming upon a castle standing guard over the freshwater lake tucked away on top of the Shawangunk Mountain ridge.

"Would ya' look at that, Miss," said Gwendolyn, whose life had changed since Elisabeth had begun singing. For a maid was always needed to help her mistress appear her best at performances.

Indeed the sprawling resort was the largest Elisabeth had ever seen. She didn't know if Marco had kept his word about recuperating here, but if he had he would have no difficulty securing a room in a wing so far from hers he would have to walk half an hour to reach her.

Towers rose above the chaletlike wings of the hotel, all of which curved around the lake. Lofty cliffs rose at one end of the lake, and she could see another higher ridge above them. Coming onto the grounds, she caught a glimpse of gardens and a greenhouse with gazebo. And paths invited visitors to explore the surroundings. She began to relax and be glad she'd come.

The trap pulled around the hotel to stop in a shady drive where verandahs reached out from the sprawling building. Percy Prescott, who had traveled here yesterday to see to arrangements, stepped off the wide porch to greet her. He was sportily dressed in white trousers, gray vest, jacket and boater hat.

"Welcome, my dear," he said, helping her down. "I hope your trip was satisfactory."

"Quite." She straightened the large bonnet that had started to slide sideways on her head. Bell captains dressed in the hotel's uniform came to unload the luggage.

She couldn't help but feel light at heart in the mellow surroundings. The air was clean. Birds sang in the trees. Visitors ambled along the grounds. She felt at once that the pace was much more relaxed here than in the city.

"What a lovely place," she said to Percy, who led her up the steps and into the lobby.

"It is. And the managers are delighted that you've agreed to give a concert."

"I hope they like me."

He patted her hand as they approached the desk. "How could they not?"

The clerk handed them the key to her room and then they crossed the lobby, which was rustic but genteel. Heavy wooden pillars supported a beamed ceiling, and rattan chairs as well as comfortable rockers were placed in groupings throughout. Sunlight filtered in through filmy white dimity curtains. And in one corner, two elderly gentlemen concentrated on a game of checkers.

Percy showed her the spacious parlor where the concert would be held. After Elisabeth surveyed it, he escorted her to her room on the second floor.

Gwendolyn followed behind, taking in the spectacle of the spacious hotel with such long hallways covered with green and gold striped wallpaper and dark stained oak trim. They pushed Elisabeth's door open, and as they stepped into the room Elisabeth saw the basket of flowers on the marble-topped mahogany dresser.

"Oh, how lovely." Thinking the flowers might be from Percy, she crossed to them and opened the card nestled in the bouquet.

"Welcome to Mohonk House. Marco," it said.

Her heart tripled its beat. He was here then. She hid her expression by smelling the flowers.

"They're from Marco Giovinco," she said when she finally stood.

Percy lifted an eyebrow. "Very nice. Well, you'll want to get settled. The accompanist will be here at three o'clock. The concert is at eight. You'll no doubt want room service to bring you something nourishing at the supper hour." He knew that most artists eschewed a noisy dining scene until after they had performed.

"Yes," she smiled mysteriously. "Until the rehearsal, I believe I'll explore the gardens."

He nodded and left her. Gwendolyn had opened the curtains, and while she was directing the bellmen as to where to put the trunk, Elisabeth looked out at her view. The gardens were directly below, laid out invitingly. She told Gwendolyn where she was going and gave instructions for the maid to lay out the things she would need for the evening. Though not all the rooms came equipped with bathrooms, this one did, so Elisabeth planned to return in plenty of time to rehearse with the accompanist, bathe, get ready and relax by herself as well.

She made her way downstairs and out a door that led down steps to the gardens. Here she stopped to breathe in the sunny, spring air, so fresh and invigorating. Winding paths led between brilliant rows of crocus, tulips, narcissus, hyacinth, and jonquils, and she strolled among them. The small rustic gazebo stood a little distance away, and Elisabeth decided to explore in that direction. She was walking around inside it when she heard footsteps on the gravel path behind and turned to see Marco standing on the path below.

He looked healthier than when she had last seen him, and her first impulse was to move toward him. But she settled for smiling down at him.

He smiled back and gestured grandly at the view off the ridge that was visible from here. "Is the setting acceptable to Madame?" he inquired.

The rolling hills and jagged cliffs were more than acceptable. They gave a sense of space that she had forgotten possible, so wrapped up in her own world had she been these last months and so caught up in the wheels of city life.

"Very fitting," she replied. "What production did you have in mind?"

He climbed the steps to the gazebo and came nearer. *"The Elixir of Love?"* he said, taking her hand and squeezing it.

She gazed into his face and then turned back to look at the view. Why could she not give herself wholeheartedly to this man who desired her? she asked herself. Why was she stopping herself? She knew his passion, was beginning to believe that he loved her, and yet she still wasn't ready to surrender. There were still too many hurdles to cross.

He dropped her hand and turned to business matters. "You are settled then? And you have seen the room where the concert will be?"

"Yes, and I'm to rehearse at three o'clock with an accompanist Mr. Prescott has hired."

"Then all is satisfactory."

"I think so. It's a lovely place for a concert. I hope the guests will enjoy it."

"I believe they will be in the right frame of mind. I have brought my mother and sister here also."

She turned back to him. "Oh really? Where are they?"

"I believe they're by the lake. I took them out in a boat this morning. Lucinda seems well. I believe she thrives in such an outdoor environment."

"That's good. I'd like to see them."

"I'm sure you will."

She walked across the wooden floor of the gazebo. It was truly uplifting to be here. She could almost forget her father's spiteful words and all the troubles of her past. Marco said nothing, but strolled with her as they left the gazebo and walked among the flowers. Shortly, they came upon Rosa, Lucinda, and the nurse, and Elisabeth greeted them delightedly.

"How good to see you, my dear," said Rosa, kissing her on both cheeks. "We look forward to your concert this evening."

"Thank you. I hope I do your expectations justice."

"I'm sure you will if what Marco says is true."

Elisabeth greeted Lucinda, who took her hand and nodded somberly. While the girl didn't seem effusive, one wouldn't know there was anything wrong with her except that she didn't speak much. Marco was probably right about the calming surroundings being good for her troubled mind.

Elisabeth walked and talked with the two women for a short space of time, then remembering her rehearsal, she excused herself. The day was going all too quickly.

She met Percy and the accompanist in the parlor, which had been closed for the rehearsal, and the next two hours sped by. At last she found herself in her room while Gwendolyn scurried around getting everything ready for Elisabeth's appearance.

She found that she was not at all nervous, rather she felt excited and ready to do her best. The audience that had gathered in an assortment of chairs in the parlor greeted her cordially, and it was a pleasure to sing to them. She gave herself wholeheartedly to the performance, which was a complete success. At the end the hotel manager came to hand her a bouquet of roses and then raised his hand for the audience to cease their applause.

"We have another special guest in the audience," he said. "If he can be persuaded and if Miss Sloane will agree, we may be able to persuade these two artists to sing something together for us."

Elisabeth was not surprised, and so nodded her acquiescence as the audience turned and murmured expectantly.

The hotel manager went on. "May I ask Marco Giovinco to come forward?" At which the audience stirred and began applauding.

Marco stood from where he had been seated in the back with his mother and sister and graciously acknowledged the applause. He made his way to the piano and bowed to Elisabeth. "Things Are Seldom What They Seem?" he whispered to her.

She nodded as the accompanist shuffled the music to find it. They hadn't rehearsed the duet together since singing it at her soirée, but she'd practiced it herself recently and knew it well.

As the accompanist began the introduction, Marco took a pose and looked at Elisabeth. The Gilbert and Sullivan music was a joy to sing and the music that commenced between them enlivened everyone present. Not satisfied with one duet, the audience wouldn't let them go until they'd been treated to two more. They finished with the love duet from *Lucia,* which they'd also done at the soirée.

At last the evening came to a close. Rosa and Lucinda waited until the other guests had departed and then came to the piano to congratulate Elisabeth.

"You are everything Marco said you would be," Rosa said.

Elisabeth blushed. "I hope you liked it."

The older woman observed her speculatively. "Of course."

"I believe this calls for a celebration," said Marco. "If you ladies will accompany me to the lounge, surely this establishment can come up with food and drink."

Now Elisabeth could relax, and she felt comfortable with Marco's family. While Lucinda did not speak much and stared at her surroundings openly, she was not unmanageable. Again, Elisabeth admired the fact that they didn't hide Lucinda behind closed doors as many people did with relatives who weren't mentally right. Rather, putting her welfare first, they took her where they felt she'd benefit.

Being with the warm-hearted Giovinco's made Elisabeth's heart swell. She found herself gazing at Marco with the old affection, always touched by the sensuality he aroused in her. And in her celebratory mood, she began to wonder if she'd been wrong in resisting him so hard. She'd made it clear that she would not marry him. But if he asked again, she just might change her answer.

Marco saw her to her room, kissing her circumspectly on the cheek. She felt herself wanting to pull him to her, but he had left his family on the landing. This was no time for passion.

"I'll see you in the morning," he said, giving her a long, romantic look.

"Yes," she whispered breathlessly. "Good night."

That night, she dreamt of roses, starlight, and moonbeams and awoke refreshed.

She was finishing her toilet when a knock sounded on the door. A moment later, Gwendolyn came into the bedroom to announce that Alex Rochat was here.

"Alex? Here?" She rose and walked to the sitting room, her good mood reflected on her face.

"Why, Alex, what a surprise."

But the glower on his face surprised her. "I'm sure it is surprise."

"Are you completely healed then?" she asked, her concern genuine. "Healed enough to make one last effort to save you from ruin, Mrs. Kendall." He paused for effect.

Elisabeth drew in a breath, and her eyes widened. She stared at him for a long moment. Hearing her married name was a shock that she did not expect. Her knees weakened and she walked as gracefully as she could to the nearest chair and sat down. Then she summoned Gwendolyn and told her to take the morning off. As soon as Gwendolyn put on her bonnet and left, Elisabeth spoke again.

"Sit down, Alex, and tell me what you're up to."

He lowered himself stiffly. "Only that I know about your former alliance."

In a single moment all the idyllic feelings Elisabeth had experienced were shattered. Just when she'd thought she might at last be able to put her past behind her, Alex's words dredged up everything.

There was no use pretending. "How do you know?"

"Mrs. Runkewich."

"I see. And how did you come to meet my former landlady?"

"You're fortunate that I did. A reporter did some digging. Luckily he came to me with the evidence, asking for a statement. It took some powerful persuasion, but he agreed not to print what he'd discovered."

Elisabeth felt herself go rigid. She swallowed then said, "I see. Then I owe you a debt of thanks."

"So it is true then?" His pitiful look betrayed the fact that even with the evidence presented to him as it had been, he was still hoping there was some explanation. But her defensive look told him his information was correct.

"What if it is true?" Elisabeth said.

Alex straightened. "I am hurt and crushed that you

lied to me," he said. "But I would still marry you, Elisabeth. If you will give up the stage, I'll keep the secret of your widowhood and your time working at the opera house."

Anger at the way he said it flashed through her.

"In other words you're offering me common blackmail. Alex, what do you think I'm made of?" She shook her head. "No, I'm sorry. I can't return to what you consider 'normal' life. Music is in my soul, and I must share it with the world. The drawing room isn't big enough for the spirit within me that's taken flight. If it means that I must face scandal and lose the love of my father and the respect of our so-called friends, then so be it."

"Do you not want a home and family?" he asked one last time.

"I want it all," she said. "And I know I can't have it."

She stood up and crossed to the window. For a moment last night, she thought she could have it all. But Alex brought with him the reminder of harsh reality, and her dreams were crushed.

Alex bestirred himself, getting off the sofa. When he spoke, his voice was weary. "I remember a time when I too wanted it all. I wanted to spend my nights drinking and gambling and my days building my wealth so I could bring it home to a wife and family in a grand house on Fifth Avenue."

She smiled ironically through her tears. "You wanted to put me in a fine house on Fifth Avenue, like a bird in a gilded cage. Come, Alex, let's go outside. The air in here is oppressive. I wish to be in the sunlight."

He accompanied her silently, and they made their

362

way downstairs to the garden.

"So what will you do with this new knowledge about my regrettable past?" she asked, afraid of his answer since she had not given in to his terms.

He shook his head wearily. "Nothing. I will live on, disillusioned, but I will not sully your reputation. You need not worry."

She felt slightly relieved. "And what about common gossip? Need I expect our friends to know?"

He shook his head. "My lips are sealed."

She studied him. She was not fooled into thinking that Alex Rochat would ever truly change his ways. But perhaps for the moment her fate was not in danger. If some night over too much drink, he let her secrets slip, then she would have to live with it.

Strangely, thinking that was not as difficult as it once had been. She was committed to a musical career. Whatever news and gossip followed her she would have to find ways to rise above it. Imbued with the sun and the blooming, peaceful garden, she felt her courage return. She would be able to face whatever publicity came. She would have to be.

From his window Marco saw Elisabeth and Alex walking in the garden and he murmured a string of oaths. His mother, who was in the sitting room, responded in Italian.

"What is it, Marco?"

He attempted to gather his temper together. He had already shot the man once. He could hardly do so again. He paced across the room, telling his mother who was in the garden with Elisabeth. When he took a breath, Rosa interrupted.

"Marco, I do not think you have to worry."

"What do you mean not worry? I am not worried."

Rosa knew how to speak to her son without offending his pride. She got up and looked out the window at Elisabeth bidding Marco's rival good-bye. Even from here Rosa could see there was no passion in it. Rosa had been impressed with Elisabeth the two times the girl had been with their family. She had a feeling about this that Marco would not understand. Call it woman's intuition.

"She is worth waiting for, is she not?" said Rosa.

"I do not wait for anything," he said stubbornly.

Rosa smiled wisely, but said nothing. The way Alexander Rochat bowed stiffly in the garden, and the way Marco moved unevenly, still favoring his arm, she did not think the two rivals seemed so ferocious anymore.

"Let us not think of it then," said Rosa. "Will you be taking Lucinda boating?"

"Of course. I'll meet you at the boathouse in half an hour."

He flung a jacket over his shirtsleeves and went downstairs, seeking an outlet for his pent up energy. He was not necessarily intending to speak to Elisabeth, but he ran into her on the back verandah.

"Good morning," she said cheerfully.

"Is it?" he grunted. "I hadn't noticed."

Seeing his agitated temper, she smiled. "It is as fine a day as one could ever hope for," she said.

"Oh, and is that because you've just been with that imbecile from New York society?" He at once forgot that he'd been determined not to show his jealousy, considering that it was beneath him.

At that Elisabeth laughed, her voice tinkling with humor like the musical notes she sang.

Marco didn't see what was so funny, and waited for explanation. "Why are you laughing, if I may ask?"

She took his arm and walked down the steps with him. "I just turned down the gilded cage."

Elisabeth returned to New York that day, while Marco stayed with his family so that they could enjoy the surroundings for another two days. But she felt so refreshed that when she arrived in the city she responded to the invigorating rhythm of the hustle and bustle in Grand Central Station.

Her father was out when she and Gwendolyn went home, and so leaving the maid to unpack, she decided to go out. She was in a contemplative mood and set out for a walk with no particular destination in mind. A few blocks down Fifth Avenue, she decided she wanted to visit the opera house, and hailed a passing hansom.

The cab let her off in front of the opera house, and she went in by the stage door. The guard greeted her, remembering her from when she had worked there.

"Theater's dark now, Miss. Not many people here today. Mr. Abbey and Mr. Grau, they already went home."

"Thank you, Henry, I'll just look around."

She didn't mind that there was no one to visit, it was the opera house itself that she'd come to see. She walked through the backstage area, smiling in memory at some of the familiar props and scenery. A single electric bulb lit the stage from above, leaving the hall in darkness. She walked out onto the stage, feeling the boards beneath her feet. At center stage, she turned and faced the audience. She wondered if she might someday sing here. A year ago that dream would have seemed like a fantasy. Now, because of some luck and a great deal of perseverance, there was the tiniest chance that it might happen.

She conjured a scene in her imagination and bowed to an adoring audience, hearing the applause in her mind. When she arose, she imagined Marco as her leading man, holding her hand. She felt the ecstasy of the shared love the audience could give them. Then she opened her eyes and came back to the present. The same doubt that had crept into her mind before now assailed her. She loved the theater, but would that be enough?

She walked slowly back across the stage, turning once more to look at the darkened audience and the boxes that would glitter with satin and jewels tomorrow night for a benefit concert. Pulling herself once more back to the present she left, bidding Henry goodbye.

"You come back, now, Miss Elisabeth, anytime."

Leaving the theater, she walked up Broadway, finding herself thinking of Professor Schlut. When she reached Fifty-sixth Street, she decided to call and see if he were in. He was, and he was delighted to see her.

"I was just about to have some tea. Will you join me?" he asked, ushering her into the sitting room.

"That would be lovely. I just had a long walk."

"And you must tell me everything about Mohonk House."

"The concert went well." She smiled. "The audience demanded three duets, which Marco sang with me."

"Ah, very good."

He rang for tea to be brought up, and then he and Governor Worthy sat down to listen to her account of the affair upstate. After filling herself up with several cups of tea and sandwiches, Elisabeth gazed at her mentor.

"Professor, there is something I am curious about."

"Yes?"

"I have never understood how my music lessons came to be paid for."

He nodded, replacing his teacup in the saucer thoughtfully. Inspiration struck him. "I have sworn never to reveal that information," he said. "However, if someone were to break into my private papers and find out for themselves . . ." He gestured helplessly. "What could I do?"

She began to follow his train of thought. "And where would I look if I were to be so bold as to disturb your personal things?"

He vaguely gestured toward a locked writing desk. "That desk is locked, But, alas, I have been careless with the key. Let me see now, where did I last put it?"

He rose and rummaged about the room, dipping his hand into nooks and crannies, at last knocking his hand against a small blue vase. The vase tipped, and he caught it, but not before a number of keys spilled out of it. Elisabeth opened her eyes wider.

"Oh, how clumsy of me. But, my goodness how time has flown. I must take Governor Worthy for a walk or he will be quite perturbed with me. You will excuse me if I leave you here alone for half an hour?"

"Yes, of course," she said, glancing curiously at the vase beside the keys.

"Make yourself at home then. I'll be back before long. Finish your tea, my dear, finish your tea."

He went to fetch Governor Worthy's leash from the other room.

Chapter Twenty-Three

The door closed, and Elisabeth was left alone. Curious and excited, she rummaged through the keys in the little vase and tried several before finding the one that unlatched the desk lid. Then she lowered it.

Confronted with cubbyholes and drawers, she didn't know where to look first. She didn't want to go through all of the professor's personal papers. Indeed, he must trust her a great deal to allow her access to his desk. She picked up a few envelopes, discerned they were personal letters or other business papers, and replaced them.

Then her eye fell on a large cardboard portfolio, tied by a string and resting in one of the vertical slots. She extracted it. Her fingers nearly burned as she untied the string, somehow knowing this was what she was looking for. When she had it open, she extracted several sheets of good quality paper, stamped and signed by notaries. Her eyes widened as she read the top of one sheet. Her late husband's last will and testament.

Her heart pounding, she sat in the wooden swivel chair and started to read the document. Her own late husband, the man who now seemed like a figment of her imagination, spoke through the formal words of the document. Skimming the legal language as much as she could, she got to the paragraph where her name jumped out at her. She had to read it twice to understand. Then she gasped and dropped the paper.

He had arranged for money to go into a trust fund for her educational pursuits. She stared at the paper unbelievingly. She picked it up and read it again. There was no doubt. It was dated just after they had been married.

She felt dizzy and leaned her elbows on the desk for support. He must have had this drawn up while he still had some freedom from the prison. She shook her head.

Then her eye fell on another paper. This was a personal letter signed by her husband. It was addressed to Whom it May Concern. Her eyes flew over it. He stated in the letter that the money he was leaving for his wife came from a trust fund his uncle had set up for him. It was honest money, none of it came from his illegal pursuits. He felt death closing in on him and he did not want to leave his wife penniless. However, she must never know. Should he not be able to save himself, he wanted her to forget him and begin her life anew. He did not intend to lauguish in prison. He intended to find a way to end his life. If Providence accepted his repentance, perhaps he would meet his wife again in the next life.

Tears dropped from her eyes onto the letter as she reread it. He must have jumped from the ship that transported the prisoners, welcoming the storm that made the ship founder. In her mind's eye, she conjured the scene, her heart filling with sadness, regret and pity. She realized at last that the document must have found its way here by way of her lawyer, Lindsay Whitehurst. She remembered telling him that she was going to study music. Having the trust money to hand, he must have made the arrangements. And she had thought it had been Marco paying for the lessons.

She did not know how long she sat there. But finally, she pulled herself up, tucked the papers back into the portfolio and replaced it in the desk. After locking the desk and replacing the key, she gathered her things. The studio was just as the professor had left it, but he would know that she had found out what she wanted.

She left Carnegie Hall and walked along Seventh Avenue in a daze, hardly aware of passing pedestrians and vehicles. After some time she awoke from her reverie, and finding that she had walked downtown instead of uptown, she hailed a cab and had it take her home.

Elisabeth moved through the next weeks with a renewed dedication to her music and a new awakening toward life. She thought of Marco often, and felt disappointed that he didn't try to see her. She began to wonder if she'd offended him. Then she decided that he'd finally taken all her refusals at their word and was going to court her no more. She could hardly blame him. It was what she had wanted. Only now she was no longer sure.

However, she had little time to dwell on her domestic

situation for Percy Prescott brought word that he'd arranged a tour in Europe for her. They were to sail almost immediately. Once there he would take her to a number of auditions with various opera companies. He felt confident that something would happen.

Before she left, she would present one more concert at Carnegie Recital Hall. He thought it best for her to do that so the New York public would remember her name when she came back. The concert would be comprised of most of the music she'd been singing the last few months.

The night of the final appearance came quickly, and Elisabeth, dressed in her blue tulle and gauze was ready. When she arrived at the concert hall, she found a dozen roses from Marco, which lifted her heart. But the note was very formal.

"Best wishes for a successful performance. Marco." A thoughtful note from a fellow performer. Nothing more.

She swallowed, turned her concentration to the job at hand and faced the stage. As she bowed to the audience in the intimate hall, she saw that Madelaine, Alex, and Consuelo were seated in the front row. She threw them a smile. As always, she radiated as the music poured forth from her soul. The evening flew by, and after the concert, Madelaine and the others came backstage to congratulate her.

She was just accepting their kisses and congratulations when she looked over Madelaine's shoulder to see Marco standing in the shadows. She drew in a breath. The others' babbling subsided as they all turned. Madelaine walked toward him and extended her hand.

"Mr. Giovinco, how nice to see you. Did you hear the concert?"

He bowed formally over Madelaine's hand, but his eyes drifted to the rest of the little group still gathered by the curtains.

"Only the very last part. Very lovely as usual."

"Yes," said Madelaine, glancing at the others. "I believe you remember Elisabeth's friends."

Alex and Marco nodded curtly to each other as the three women tried to cover the embarrassing fact that the one-time duelists were trying to be polite. But it was Marco who eased the situation.

"I do not mean to interrupt," he told them all. "I simply came to wish Miss Sloane *bon voyage.*"

"Yes," said Madelaine. "We're losing her. But if she is to become famous in Europe, surely we'll have her back here before long. Isn't it exciting?"

"Quite," agreed Marco.

Elisabeth faced the others. "If you all will excuse me for a moment, I won't be long."

"Please don't be," said Alex, not looking at Marco. "I have a great craving for oysters at the Waldorf. We'll be waiting."

The group moved off to speak to other acquaintances who were mingling after the concert, and Elisabeth turned back to Marco. He smiled at her with a touch of melancholy.

"So, your career is beginning," he said, taking her hand.

Her heart turned over at his touch. She was so glad to see him she didn't know what to do. She half-wished he would tell her not to sail tomorrow. But he did not.

"You will do very well," he said, his eyes caressing

her face, but his expression formal. "And then you'll return to New York and take the town by storm."

She sighed. "It will be a long while before that happens," she said. "You of all people ought to know it won't happen overnight."

"No," he said, looking away from her and then back deliberately. "It does not. But you have a good start."

She swallowed. Is this all he had come to say? To wish her well on her career? Suddenly she wished more than anything that she could roll back the calendar, but she felt instinctively that it was too late for that. So she gazed up at him longingly and tongue-tied.

"I cannot keep your friends waiting," he said.

"Oh, why don't you join us? We're going to the Waldorf. They would be delighted if you came." And I would be much less miserable, she thought.

But he shook his head gently. "No. This is your night. I do not want to stop you."

She swallowed. This was not what she wanted to happen, but she was powerless to stop it. Before she could find words, he was kissing her hand.

"Good luck, my beautiful dove. The world awaits you." Then he dropped her hand and bowed low.

When he rose she took a breath and reached out to stop him, but he walked away too swiftly.

"Are you coming, Elisabeth?" Madelaine called. "The carriage is waiting."

She turned. "Yes, yes, I'm coming."

Marco left the concert hall as quickly as he could and climbed into the carriage. Franco shut the door and they pulled out. Marco leaned into the corner, shutting his eyes. He had seen a marvel of talent sing tonight on the small stage of the recital hall and he had seen the audience adore her. He had no right to snatch her away from that.

He willed the ache in his heart to cease, but it would not. He had tried to make her his own, and she'd refused. Now he could understand the reason. She had much talent, and it didn't deserve to be lost. He had seen it in her eyes tonight. He might have been able to take her with him. For a moment, he had wavered. But he knew what he must do. Elisabeth Sloane belonged to the world of the music now, not to him.

He shut his eyes against the pain in his heart as the carriage rolled uptown to take him home.

Gwendolyn had everything packed by the next evening, and at last Elisabeth was ready to leave. She went to tell her father goodbye and found him waiting in the study. He turned from looking out the window. Outlines of the trees and shrubbery were still visible in the pale June evening outside.

"Hello, Father." She was dressed in a new traveling suit, and the self-confidence that she emanated was apparent to Winston when he looked at her.

"I see you're ready, my dear."

She gave a jerky little nod. "Yes."

Winston sighed and came forward. "You look very confident, Elisabeth. I'm sure you'll acquit yourself quite well."

She was surprised at his words and moreso by his honest, appraising expression.

"I will do my best."

"I know you will." He smiled almost with a touch of

nostalgia. "I have had a long conversation with your chaperone, Mr. Prescott." He refrained from calling him a manager. "I believe him to be an honest man. I feel I can entrust you to his discretion."

"Thank you, Father. I feel so too."

She sat down, sensing there was more he wanted to say. There was. He paced toward the mantel and looked at a photograph of Elisabeth's mother in an oval frame. Then he turned to his daughter.

"I do not want there to be bad blood between us at the outset of this voyage, Elisabeth. I have had difficulty understanding your decisions, but," he hesitated in his pacing and straightened up. "There's been enough heartbreak in this house. Your mother would not want us to part with animosity."

The lump in her throat prevented her from speaking. But he turned in time to see the tears form at the corners of her eyes. He continued, his own voice hoarse. "You are going to sea. Things might happen. I would not wish the sea to claim the only flesh and blood I have left without . . . without . . ."

He lost control, but Elisabeth jumped up and flew into his arms. "Oh, Father," she mumbled, her tears spilling on his shoulder as she buried her face in his neck. "In spite of what you may think, I love you, Father. I never meant to displease you, not even when . . ."

She sobbed against him, and he stroked her back. "Shhh, shhh," he said, his own heart swelling tenderly.

They embraced for some moments, and then she stepped back, smiling through her tears. "Does this mean you forgive me?" she asked.

He looked at her with the love she'd been missing

these many months, and she felt it reflected in her own heart.

"I suppose it is I who must ask your forgiveness for not trying to understand you. I always thought I was acting for your best interests. But," he shook his head sadly. "Times are changing. My own fears for your future have blinded me."

She hugged him once again. "Don't worry, Father. I know you cared for me. It was just that I somehow could not fit the mold that most other young women do. I never wanted to disappoint you. I wanted more than anything for you to be proud of me."

He held her away so he could gaze at her face. "And so I shall be," he said, wiping a tear off her cheek. "If what Percy Prescott has told me is true, I believe that I shall be."

A knock came at the study door, and they stood apart. Gunther opened the door slowly. "Pardon me, Miss. But your ship sails at midnight. You must go."

Elisabeth wiped her nose with a handkerchief her father handed her. "I'm ready."

"We shall go together," said Winston. "I shall see you off."

She pressed her lips together, afraid she would cry again. "I would like nothing better," she said.

Once in the carriage, she asked the driver to go by way of the opera house. She wanted to tell Maurice Grau goodbye. They had enough time for her to spend a few minutes there and still get to the dock comfortably.

Leaving her father in the carriage, she entered by way of the stage door. A spring benefit concert was in progress on stage and the backstage was dark. She inquired of the stage manager if Maurice were in the theater and learned that he was in his office upstairs. She listened for a few moments to the glorious notes and the tempestuous orchestra thundering out the fourth act of *Rigoletto,* which they were presenting in concert version without scenery and costumes, for the benefit of a worthy cause.

In the spring and early summer, with no opera to attend, Society loved to pay exorbitant prices for benefit tickets and thereby have a reason to go out in the evening.

Maurice was delighted to see her and got up to come around the desk where he was working by the light of a single lamp. "Why my dear, how wonderful you look. I understand you're leaving for Europe. I'm sure you will have them at your feet."

She laughed. "And when I come back?"

He smiled. "One never can tell, can one?"

She was really only teasing. Singing at the Met was a big dream indeed, but one that would be a long time coming if it came at all. He saw her to the door and pressed her hands wistfully. "Safe voyage. And do let us hear from you. I expect you to bring back copies of all your reviews."

"I will," she promised. "And thank you for everything."

She left him to his paperwork and made her way downstairs. The music of the final quartet in *Rigoletto* drifted upward and she stopped, her hand on the railing and one foot extended to take her next step. Marco's voice. He was singing in the concert tonight. Her heart took flight excitedly, and then with caution she moved down the steps. Reaching the stage level, she walked quietly to the wings.

Shutting her eyes as she listened to the magnificent quartet full of tension between the four singers as the lecherous Duke sang of lust; the innkeeper's daughter flirted cunningly; the poor heroine sang of lost love, and her father of the vengeance he planned to extract for the Duke having ruined his daughter.

Tears came to Elisabeth's eyes at the passion ringing in Marco's sensual voice. And she imagined the helpless heroine before him on stage. Marco. When would she ever see him again? She had been loved by him, but had feared to love him back, fearing she would one day lose him to adoring audiences while at the same time existing only in his famous shadow. Then when she had been ready to give in to the love she could not deny for him, he had withdrawn, perhaps to allow her to spread her wings in the way she so coveted. She loved him the more for that. The music grew and swelled, filling the house and taking her soul with it. If she stayed one more moment, her heart would break.

"Goodbye, Marco," she whispered into the darkened wings as the thunderous chords of the orchestra crashed loudly, signifying the storm outside the inn where the tragic heroine of the opera would meet her fate. Elisabeth hurried out into the night.

The pier was crowded where the elegant passenger liner was at berth. The luggage was unloaded and checked, and Winston escorted Elisabeth up the gangplank followed by Percy and Gwendolyn. They were met by the captain, then a steward showed them to their staterooms.

Elisabeth's was quite comfortable, and Percy's was next door. For her father's sake she tried to appear cheerful during the remainder of the hour before guests were asked to depart. After opening a bottle of champagne in her stateroom, they strolled about the deck, looking at the New York skyline at night and the crowd gathered on the pier to wish friends and family *bon voyage,* or there simply to witness the excitement of an ocean liner setting sail.

Elisabeth could hardly enjoy the beauty of the glittering lights of the city before them, nor the half moon that dusted the harbor with moonglow. All she could think of was the music she had just heard and Marco's emotion-filled, ringing voice soaring above the thunderous chords of the orchestra.

Nostalgia had her in its grasp, and she wondered if she would be able to root herself to the deck as the ship set sail. Maybe this voyage was all wrong. Maybe Percy was wrong. Europe might not even like her, and then she would have lost it all.

The foghorn gave a blast and Winston turned to tell his daughter goodbye. She closed her eyes and embraced him.

"Thank you for coming to see me off," she told him. "And for everything else." Her words were cut off by her tears.

He kissed her cheek then held her away. "You be a good girl," he admonished. "And don't forget to write home."

"No, I'll never do that. And I'll be back as soon as I can."

He shook hands with Prescott, who was standing nearby. "Take care of my girl," he told the manager, whose silver hair was being ruffled by the breeze.

"I don't think she needs much taking care of," said Prescott, clapping Winston on the back. "But I'll do my best."

Another blast on the foghorn and Winston lifted his hand and then made his way toward the gangplank.

She leaned over the railing watching him go, but as her eyes scanned the pier, it was no longer her father she was watching for. Hope against hope, she wondered if Marco might not come at the last moment to see her off. But as the ship was secured for departure, the gangplank raised, there was no sign.

She grasped the railing as the big ship pulled away from its berth. Slowly, slowly, the pier receded. The lights of the city blurred into a fairy land as the water began to rush beside them.

"You mustn't get chilled," said Percy, stepping up to her elbow. "We must take care of your voice, you know." He gently pried her hand from the railing and then guided her back toward her stateroom.

"Would you like anything?" he asked as he held open the little door.

"No, thank you. I'll see you in the morning."

She sent Gwendolyn along to her own small cabin on a lower deck. "I'll manage myself," she told the maid. "Get some rest."

Indeed Gwendolyn was too wide-eyed to rest, but she left her mistress as she was bid. In truth Elisabeth knew she could not sleep either. She lay back on the small bed, but even the gentle movement of the ship did not comfort her. Grief still welled up in her heart when she should have been excited about what was happening.

Suddenly the stateroom seemed too small, and she stood up, fetched her cloak and put it around her shoulders. She would rather have bracing sea air than a small cabin where she was alone.

There were still a few couples strolling about the deck, and she walked toward the stern to watch the lights of New Jersey as the ship approached the narrows. The moon was low on the horizon and she imagined that they might run into it as they sailed off the edge of the earth.

Then she turned, the fantasy doing no good for her brooding feelings. The waves sent spray to her face and she grasped the railing. Then softly the words came to her, *"Verranno a te sull'aura."*

They were sung sotto voce, and she was sure she had imagined them. Marco, Marco, I must forget you, she said to herself. But then the words came nearer and this time she whirled at the footstep on the deck.

She blinked, afraid she was truly dreaming as she breathed his name. But he stopped singing and murmured the words to the love duet in his natural voice.

She started to cry as his hands gripped her arms. "Marco? Is it really you?"

He pressed her to his chest. "I love you, Elisabeth, I could not let you go."

She sobbed tears of joy. "I thought it was too late," she said as he rained kisses on her face and temples. "I was wrong, Marco. My life would be hollow without love. I thought I couldn't love anyone, but I love you, dearest Marco, I love you."

Her heart thundered against her chest as he kissed her. Then he murmured into her ear. "If you won't marry me now, I'll have to jump overboard."

Then she looked up at him. "But how did you get here? You sang tonight. I heard you."

"You were at the opera house?"

She nodded. "I suppose I just had to say goodbye."

He understood her meaning. The opera house had a life of its own aside from the people who ran it.

"I thought I could let you go," he murmured against her hair as he held her in the gentle mist that sprayed upward. "I didn't want to stand in the way of your dreams any longer."

"They would be hollow dreams if I had them alone. I was foolish to think otherwise. Oh, how foolish I've been."

He gazed lovingly at her face. "Then we are made for each other?"

Joy and happiness mingled with relief as she smiled through her tears. "Yes, Marco. You're right."

He embraced her again. "Your dreams will come true, my turtle dove," he murmured softly. "And you will dream them in my arms."

LET ARCHER AND CLEARY
AWAKEN AND CAPTURE YOUR HEART!

CAPTIVE DESIRE (2612, $3.75)
by Jane Archer

Victoria Malone fancied herself a great adventuress and student of life, but being kidnapped by handsome Cord Cordova was too much excitement for even her! Convincing her kidnapper that she had been an innocent bystander when the stagecoach was robbed was futile when he was kissing her until she was senseless!

REBEL SEDUCTION (3249, $4.25)
by Jane Archer

"Stop that train!" came Lacey Whitmore's terrified warning as she rushed toward the locomotive that carried wounded Confederates and her own beloved father. But no one paid heed, least of all the Union spy Clint McCullough, who pinned her to the ground as the train suddenly exploded into flames.

DREAM'S DESIRE (3093, $4.50)
by Gwen Cleary

Desperate to escape an arranged marriage, Antonia Winston y Ortega fled her father's hacienda to the arms of the arrogant Captain Domino. She would spend the night with him and would be free for no gentleman wants a ruined bride. And ruined she would be, for Tonia would never forget his searing kisses!

VICTORIA'S ECSTASY (2906, $4.25)
by Gwen Cleary

Proud Victoria Torrington was short of cash to run her shipping empire, so she traveled to America to meet her partner for the first time. Expecting a withered, ancient cowhand, Victoria didn't know what to do when she met virile, muscular Judge Colston and her body budded with desire.

Available wherever paperbacks are sold, or order direct from the Publisher. Send cover price plus 50¢ per copy for mailing and handling to Zebra Books, Dept. 4077, 475 Park Avenue South, New York, N.Y. 10016. Residents of New York and Tennessee must include sales tax. DO NOT SEND CASH. For a free Zebra/Pinnacle catalog please write to the above address.